THE QUIET BOY

ALSO BY BEN H. WINTERS

Underground Airlines

Golden State

THE LAST POLICEMAN TRILOGY

The Last Policeman

Countdown City

World of Trouble

Bedbugs

Android Karenina

Sense and Sensibility and Sea Monsters

THE QUIET BOY

BEN H. WINTERS

MULHOLLAND BOOKS

Little, Brown and Company

New York   Boston   London

Mulholland Books / Little, Brown and Company
Hachette Book Group
1290 Avenue of the Americas, New York, NY 10104
mulhollandbooks.com

First Edition: May 2021

Mulholland Books is an imprint of Little, Brown and Company, a division of Hachette Book Group, Inc. The Mulholland Books name and logo are trademarks of Hachette Book Group, Inc.

The publisher is not responsible for websites (or their content) that are not owned by the publisher.

The Hachette Speakers Bureau provides a wide range of authors for speaking events. To find out more, go to hachettespeakersbureau.com or call (866) 376-6591.

ISBN 978-0-316-50544-4
LCCN 2020942643

Printing 1, 2021

LSC-C

Printed in the United States of America

For Diana Winters,
Andrew Winters,
Sherman Winters,
and Milton Winters, of blessed memory

All my life's beautiful lawyers

I'm gonna get myself in fighting trim
Scope out every angle of unfair advantage.
I'm gonna bribe the officials,
I'm gonna kill all the judges.
It's gonna take you people years to recover from all of the damage.

—The Mountain Goats, "Up the Wolves"

PART ONE

THE KEENER BOY

The phone was ringing at the Killer Greens, but what business was that of the Rabbi's? His job was straight chopping. He didn't cover front of house, never worked the cash register, had no involvement with the taking of orders. His business was what came across his cutting board and under his knife: transforming waxy, bulbous sweet potatoes into neat golden cubes; removing the bulky brain stems of broccoli and butchering the bushes down into bite-size hunks; dicing slender stalks of spring onion into the thin tokens that could be sprinkled into a soup or a salad.

Two or three times hourly the Rabbi might venture from behind his station to bus detritus from one of the steel tables, clearing bamboo bowls and brown biodegradable napkins. On occasion, need arising, he'd take out the wet mop and dance it across a spill of juice or smoothie. Once a shift he was on the hook to swab out the gender-neutral restroom.

But no, under the Rabbi's mandate fell nothing forward facing. No customer service, no conversation. And no—thank you very much—no phone.

It kept ringing, though.

The Rabbi was vexed. He laid down his Santoku knife and looked around. Where was Sunny? Lawrence was working the register for the shift, so he should have been the one taking phone orders, but he'd left on one of his epic cigarette breaks, which meant answering the phone fell to the manager on duty.

"Sunny?" the Rabbi called out, lining up the fat ends of four carrots. "Phone."

"Yeah, dude." Sunny appeared from nowhere, slid in next to him with her elbows on the edge of his station. "I can *hear*."

The phone rang again, and she gave it the finger.

"It's 11:30. It's gonna be a writers' room with some big complicated order." Sunny rolled her eyes, annoyed at the gall of it, bunch of jerks wanting to spend money at their location.

The Rabbi frowned and bent to his chop as Sunny sidled away.

This kind of casual disavowal of responsibility made him deeply uncomfortable. He liked it when people were appropriately committed. He liked regular order. The Rabbi was punctilious about his duties. He arrived on time and stayed until the store was closed, and he had finished tomorrow's prep, and the last of the boards was cleaned and hung gleaming to dry. Never did he poach food from the edges of his cutting board—unlike, say, Lawrence, who was known to slip the occasional piece of ham into his mouth, so you'd find him smiling with cheeks puffed like a chipmunk.

And, again, contra-Lawrence, the Rabbi took exactly the amount of off-clock time allotted to him, although his preference was to cluster his three fifteen-minute short breaks into a single long one, take it all in a forty-five-minute chunk at the end of his shift. Then he would leave work and run home, three and a half miles from Park La Brea to Koreatown: the Rabbi on the run, head down, no earbuds. The soles of his tennis shoes slapping the cracked LA sidewalks. Heart thumping, sweat breathing down his back. On his days off, he ran twice: six miles in the morning, four and a half in the afternoon.

OK, this was—what the hell? The phone had started again.

He set down his knife and stared at the store's cheap plastic landline, where it sat like a fat black frog beside the cash register. It rang again.

The Rabbi felt a low, quivery dread, which was something that happened sometimes.

Sometimes at work; sometimes just, like, on the street. As if he had accidentally brushed through a curtain of shadow, or as if it had brushed through him.

"Sunny? Are you getting the phone?"

"Just ignore it, Rabbi," she called. "*Ignore* it."

She wandered back over to him now, a white table-wiping rag slung over her shoulder. "How *are* you, by the way? You *look* super-hot. Did I tell you that, when you came in?"

She had. Sunny, despite or because of the advent of #MeToo, was a frequent and enthusiastic sexual harasser, although only, it seemed to the Rabbi, of him specifically. She would sigh with cartoon amorousness when he walked in at the beginning of his shift; she would sneak up behind him and squeeze his arms, a risky proposition when a person was engaged in careful slicing. His biceps (which along with his broad scrabbler's chest and fucked-up right ear were a souvenir of his long-ago time as a middle and high school wrestler) were, per Sunny, "a national treasure." She called him a piece of ass. She urged him to wear tighter pants. She insisted that it was why she had hired him.

The phone had stopped again. The Rabbi looked at it. Maybe that was it. Maybe it was done.

"Oh, hey, I meant to say—in re: our conversation yesterday, about the two of us potentially getting it on at some point?"

Sunny tried to affect a serious whisper but couldn't keep the laughter out of her voice. It had not been a conversation; more of a monologue. The Rabbi had listened, shaking his head and chopping, as he did now. "You should know that my dad's a gun nut. A former Marine. He was—what's it called? A SEAL."

"OK, Sunny."

"So I'm not saying *no,* I'm just saying: buyer beware."

The Rabbi happened to know, and did not think it was a particularly obscure piece of information, that the SEALs were Navy, not Marines. He also knew it wouldn't matter: called out on her bullshit, Sunny would wink and shrug. The Rabbi wiped down his board with a paper towel, opened a plastic bag full of lumpy beets, and got to business.

The Rabbi actually liked Sunny quite a lot, which was remarkable given how few people he liked at all. All of the *you look hot* business was just teasing, of course—he knew exactly what he looked like—as was the nickname, which she had bequeathed to him in October of 2016, five months after he started working there. He had requested a particular Wednesday as a personal day, and Sunny, grilling him relentlessly over what *kind* of personal day ("A *chick* personal day? A *dude*? One of each?"), had at last elicited the information that he would be fasting for Yom Kippur.

"What?" Sunny had yawped, bringing her hands up to her mouth, gasping, astonished. "You're fucking shitting me!"

The combined facts of his being both Jewish and Asian had struck Sunny as somehow fascinating and hilarious. This despite the fact that she herself, like most of the people who worked with him at Killer Greens, and like seemingly everybody in Fairfax–La Brea, was mixed in some complicated way. Sunny's dad was half-Black and half-Latin, her mom half-white and half-Laotian. "Which makes me"—she liked to say, laughing, pretending to do the math—"fucking *gorgeous.*"

Now the door made its cheerful little chime, and Sunny said, "Look alive, Rabbi. She's here."

"Who?" he said, but he knew. He looked up, too quick, and Sunny snorted and shook her head with pursed lips.

"Damn, son, you're making me jealous. I swear to God."

"Shut up, Sunny."

He made a final, decisive chop and flipped his board, now dyed murder-scene red by the beets, into the sudsy water of the wash sink. The girl Sunny had pointed out was one of the many young and good-looking women who frequented the half a dozen exercise studios that lined the surrounding blocks. Pilates, Spinning, various kinds of bespoke "boot camps." All the customers and instructors equally stunning and fit. The girl now airily examining the specials board was a waiflike woman with hair so blond it was nearly transparent; today she wore brightly pinkish orange athleisure pants, her small breasts in a red sports bra under some sort of flimsy breathable top.

She sighed at the specials and brushed her hair back with a thin finger, let her gaze move past the unmanned register to the prep area behind the row of salads, and you could almost imagine, if you really wanted to work at it, that she was, indeed, looking at the Rabbi with some sort of interest.

"Dude." Sunny, who should have been at the front, leaned in to the Rabbi's ear, murmuring solemnly. "She wants in. To your pants, I mean. Or into your *robes,* I guess. Not pants. Wait—what do Rabbis wear, actually?"

"Sunny. Stop."

"Go take her order." She said it dirty, like a command: "*Take* it."

"No." The Rabbi pulled down a fresh cutting board, wiped his Santoku with a rag. "No."

His job was straight chopping. He did not cover front of house.

He lined up a row of celery stalks. He cut them furiously.

"Rabbi. Dude." Sunny pointed. The woman was waiting. "I'm serious. Take her *order*."

"No. Sunny. Stop."

The phone rang again, and the Rabbi jumped and the Santoku slipped and cut off the finest tip of the index finger of his left hand.

"Fuck," he shouted.

The exercise girl took a frightened half step backward from the cash register, and Sunny clapped one hand to her mouth and her eyes went wide at the blood, and then Lawrence, finally returned from his smoke break, got the phone—"Killer Greens?"—and then said "Hold on" and called over, his voice rich with incredulity.

"Hey, Rabbi. It's for *you*."

"What?"

He walked to the front and took the receiver. He hadn't wrapped anything around his finger. Blood ran freely in a steady drip from the cut.

A man's voice on the other end: "Ruben? Honey?"

The Rabbi had to close his eyes.

That voice, sweet and cunning. That old trickster's wheedle.

It was him, it was his father, the old god of his youth.

November 12, 2008

1.

The cherry-red flip phone was not his normal phone, it was a *special* phone, and so the very instant it rang, Jay Shenk answered it, snapping it open and holding it to his lips and singing out, high and hopeful.

"Helloooooo?" he called. "Hello?"

"You're gonna love me so much today, Brother Shenk," said the gruff voice of the only man who had this number.

At the sound of Malloy the Boy on the line, Shenk's whole body brightened. His skin prickled and sparked. His spirit beamed and reached up toward heaven.

He pumped his fist and ran faster.

Jay Albert Shenk, attorney-at-law, was running on the treadmill in his office, doing a nice steady six miles an hour, looking out onto the intersection of Overland and Palms, and he had his cell phone connected up so he could talk via the little speaker built into the dashboard of the treadmill. Shenk was jogging in an undershirt and track shorts, and there was sweat on his temples and his ponytail was bobbing pleasingly against the nape of his neck, and he was working his five-pound arm weights too, up and down, up and down, and through the office window he was catching the sweet breeze wafting up from Gloria's Glorious Donuts just downstairs, and he was watching a foxy young mom navigate her stroller around a hobo who'd colonized the patch of sidewalk right up to the curb line, and he was just generally reveling in the scruffy workaday glamour of West Los Angeles while he listened to Malloy the Boy's basso rumbling out good news.

"You're just gonna love me to fucking bits," said the Boy, and Shenk laughed.

He already did—there was no denying it—Shenk had loved his man Malloy forever. His affection for Malloy the Boy, the most reliable of his various intelligence agents, was like a wide blue rush, borne before the tides, river-wide and river-strong. Jay turned one of his arm weights sideways and used the fat end to hit STOP on the treadmill, and then he rolled off backward and surfed the momentum over to his desk.

"Ready, brother," he said, and leaned forward, dripping sweat on a fresh legal pad, clicking open a ballpoint, *clickity-click-click.* "What've we got?"

"Wounded bird," rumbled Bobby, and Shenk's body tightened with anticipation. His eyes glowed.

"Sad," he said.

"Always," said Bobby. "But unless I'm way off, Jay, this one's a real humdinger."

Bobby's voice was low and conspiratorial, like a sexy midnight disc jockey. Jay could picture the man, a goateed male nurse, a burly white guy somewhere north of six foot seven, crouched in a storage closet at the Pasadena hospital where he worked. All 300-plus pounds of Bobby, in his pale green scrubs, with his gleaming bald head and pirate earrings, big Bobby crowded in with the folded sheets and the blood pressure cuffs, the ID bracelets and syringes and gowns.

Bobby sat at the center of a statewide web of nurses and nurse's assistants and orderlies, many or most of them small, efficient Filipino ladies who paid keen attention to their bustling wards, who were simultaneously supremely competent at the work itself and smart enough to read between the lines of the charts, to see with a single sidelong glance the invisible dollar signs imprinted thereupon, and who knew right away when to slip into a stairwell and fire off a text to their friend and patron, Bobby the Boy Malloy—who would in turn call it in to Shenk & Partners, the little law office that could.

Jay took copious notes on this new humdinger, filling page after page of the legal pad with his florid hand. Bobby didn't have a lot by way of details. It was all piecemeal, all coming through filtered, from Bobby's nurse to Bobby to Shenk, but the nitty-gritty wasn't Bobby's part of the job. All the careful collection of facts, the arrangement of those scattered stars into a constellation of meaning, which could then be translated into the threat or the reality of legal action—all of that would come later. All of that was Shenk's job.

Sweat was drying on Jay's chest and at the small of his back. Out the window, a guy in a Dodgers cap hustled out of Gloria's Glorious, clutching the top of a paper bag, lust in his heart.

"OK, Bobby! OK! That's wild." Shenk studied the notes. Wild. "And we're pretty confident of the sourcing on this?"

"Damn right we are," said Malloy, his tone slightly affronted. "This is from Rosa. Rosa knows her stuff."

"Of course, of course," Shenk said. "Just making sure. You know me. I've met Rosa, haven't I? From the fractured pelvis? In Dana Point?"

"No, Jay. That was Marina."

"Yes, right, of course. Marina." Shenk could not keep these

women straight, but he didn't need to. He had but one nurse. He had Malloy the Boy.

"All right, then, so where does Rosa work? Providence? In Burbank?"

"Naw, man. Valley Village."

Shenk nodded, jotting away. At some point he had planted himself in his office chair, and his restless right foot bobbled while he wrote. Valley Village Methodist was a midsize not-for-profit, located in North Hollywood despite the name. It had a bustling ER, a regionally regarded practice in ortho and peds, and a total operating revenue northward of $665 million per annum. Valley Village was covered for both general liability and medical malpractice by the Wellbridge Insurance Group, Shenk was pretty sure, but he could look that up. He made a note to look it up.

Shenk had been doing this for nineteen years, since he came out from under the wing of the cantankerous sharpshooter J. J. Barnes, and he could give you the lowdown on every sawbones, on every hospital and clinic and urgent care in Southern California. Which doctors dispensed opioids like they were Peanut M&Ms? Which doctors couldn't resist trying out their charms on the nurses, opening themselves up to harassment claims and distracting themselves from their life-or-death work? Who among the preening cohort of Beverly Hills cosmetic surgeons had a heavy hand with the Botox, and whose breast implants burst most frequently? Which ERs, though so alluringly busy, were naught but a constant churn of immigrant laborers with ladder falls or gardening accidents, none of whom had so much as a Medi-Cal card in their pocket?

Malloy the Boy's knowledge was similarly encyclopedic, and he shared Shenk's appreciation for all the variety and nuance of their distinct but overlapping trades, which was part of what had made their partnership so efficient and remunerative lo these many years.

In their time together, Malloy had directed Shenk's keen attention toward the wounded, toward the grieving next of kin, in every corner of the Golden State.

Most recently had been one Marvin Thomas III, a handyman whose pelvis had been shattered by a three-story fall he took, through no fault of his own—the fault lying entirely, or so Jay successfully argued, with the wobbly stepladder produced by a deep-pocketed Canadian steel-machining company. When all was said and done, Newfoundland Tools had been good for $250,000, negotiated out in a pretrial settlement, meaning without any trial costs, meaning a cool eighty grand and change for Shenk & Partners. A few weeks after he deposited that check, during a wholly unrelated social call to Malloy the Boy's surprisingly tasteful gay-bachelor pad off Sunset Boulevard, Shenk had absent-mindedly left behind a doughnut box containing a half dozen of Gloria's most glorious, along with four grand in tightly rolled hundred-dollar bills.

Not that all the Boy's phone calls ended in clover—not even close. Medical malpractice claims in particular are trickier than they look, as Shenk liked to tell his son, Ruben, when he was reading him the specs on a case, testing its soundness out loud for the boy's edification: you gotta show a specific doctor was responsible for care, *and* that the doctor failed to deliver that care up to the standards of the field, *and* that the failure caused an injury, *and* that actual damages resulted from the injury.

"And that, my love," Shenk would say, spreading the file out over the kitchen table, "is a lot of ands."

Meaning a lot of solid-looking med-mal cases melted under the heat of close scrutiny. The potential payout would be too low to make it worthwhile, or the victim or victim's kin would lack the stomach for a fight. Or, worst of all, one of his shark-suit scumbag competitors would snake in first and snatch the prospect before Shenk could make his pitch.

This one, though—this call—there was something special here.

Gleaming up from among the Boy's handful of details, there was an undeniable sense of potential. Elusive but brightly present, like the fairy glow from a forest floor.

Shenk, with two fingers of his right hand on his carotid, feeling his pulse begin its post-run descent toward normal levels, ran his left hand very gently over his notes, tenderly touching the individual pieces of information like children.

"All right, man," said Bobby into Shenk's thoughtful silence. "Lemme know how it turns out."

"You know I will. Thanks a ton, my brother."

"I live to serve."

Shenk closed the flip phone and stood gazing out at Palms, just giving the moment its moment, tilting his chin up slightly so the sunlight could catch him on both cheeks. Maybe he'd cut Malloy a little something extra on this one. Yeah—probably he would. Shenk lived with a constant low fear of Bobby's getting restless, finding himself some other lawyer to whisper to, in some other second-floor office.

Shenk peeled off his undershirt and mopped sweat out of his chest hair, which had lately begun a midlife transformation from pure black to a pleasing manly color, like dark slate. He looked at his watch, calculating how long it would take to run home, grab a shower, and get on the 405, and was disappointed to find it was before two o'clock.

Ah, well. Without letting the thought take conscious root, he had been hoping it was after three fifteen, when he would have been able to scoop up his son, Ruben, from school and bring him along for the ride out to the Valley. Let the kid play wingman while he ran this thing down.

Should he wait the hour and a half? Maybe even go over to the school and pull him early? Rubie was a freshman at a small and mildly shmancy private high school in Playa Vista called Morningstar, where the administration was always touting the importance of teaching "the whole child"—a dictum Shenk was often tempted to interpret as a mandate to educate his son on the workings of the law.

No, he thought. *Don't do that. Leave him be.*

The wisest voice in his head still spoke after all these years in the raspy-sweet tones of his Marilyn, of blessed memory. The voice reminded him that school came first, and that after school Monday/Wednesday/Friday Ruben had his poetry-club thing, and he shouldn't miss.

Jay smiled, tightening his little ponytail. He was so proud of that boy. Tonight they would have dinner together, just the two of them, and Ruben would fill him in on his busy little life, and Jay would tell his son about the new case.

The humdinger, Shenk thought. Hoped. Believed.

Trotting down the metal staircase outside his office, waving to Gloria behind the counter of her eponymous doughnut shop. *A real humdinger.*

2.

Shenk in a hospital lobby was Shenk in full: chin angled up, chest thrust forward, ponytail dancing at his nape, marching forward like a man at the head of a parade.

Shenk was an aficionado of hospital lobbies, of their informational kiosks and layered odors and vast, soaring atriums. How many times had he passed through the whoosh of automatic doors, strode along the speckled linoleum tiles and down the beige hallways, past the seascapes and the still lifes and the soft-light portraits of elderly philanthropists?

He loved all the lobbies, without prejudice or discrimination. He loved the slick modern lobbies with their ergonomic furniture and meditation gardens and minimalist sculptures; but just as fervently did he love the humble old-school lobbies, like this one at Valley Village — with its dribbling water fountain and analog signage, with its dreary little gift shop, offering generic teddy bears and individual Mylar balloons, each balloon tethered limply to its cardboard stick.

And the people! As Shenk bounded through the Valley Village lobby, his heart swelled with love for the hospital people. Here, a clutch of prideful doctors in sneakers and scrubs, speaking softly to one another by an elevator hallway; here, a small, cheerful legion of nurses in six shades of hospital green; and here, a bulky orderly in repose, fists wrapped around the handles of an empty wheelchair, awaiting his next charge.

But whom did Shenk love the most? Most of all, Shenk loved the clientele — the consumers — the *customers*. The sick and the families of the sick, murmuring and muttering, worried and weary, leaning on the walls or wandering confused in search of a vending machine or a bathroom. Or just slumped in those lumpy over-stuffed lobby sofas, under the too-bright lights, hungry but unable to eat, weepy but unable to cry. They were alone or stood in groups of two and three, clutching at scraps of tissue and sipping lukewarm coffee and staring wanly out the tinted glass, in baffled contemplation of a loved one's mortality and, inevitably, their own. They sat grimly, waiting for news; they made exhausted phone calls, keeping someone out there in the loop or keeping themselves tethered to the rush of life that continued while they were in here, in the tedious no-time of hospital waiting.

"No," a woman was saying—shouting—at some pinhead administrator she'd buttonholed, backed up against a door to a NO ACCESS hallway. "That is unacceptable. That's not gonna cut it." He tried to answer, but the woman wouldn't let him. She jammed her finger into the man's chest, her pocketbook bouncing angrily on her shoulder, her voice rising and rising. The administrator raised his hands in the air, placating or protesting or just protecting himself from being hit.

Shenk loved this lady. He loved the terrified administrator too. He loved them all. As he made his way to the massive semicircular Volunteer Desk, Shenk's spirit flew out to all of them—all the hospital people gathered in the purgatorial half-light of the lobby—his own heart a corona of empathy expanding outward through the damaged world.

"Good morning," said a very old woman as Shenk laid his hands flat upon the shining surface of her information desk, as he tilted himself forward toward her. "Do you need some help today?"

"I do, yeah, thank you." Shenk offered a concerned, anxious smile to the white-haired Samaritaness, who peered back at him stoically through tinted bifocals. A small gold badge declared her name to be MRS. DESMOND.

"I'm looking for a patient."

"All righty." Mrs. Desmond arranged her fingers on her keyboard. "What name?"

"Now, that's the funny part," said Shenk, and dialed the smile down from nervous to sheepish. "I don't *know*."

Mrs. Desmond's squint deepened suspiciously.

"He's a boy," Shenk continued. "Or a teenager, actually, I guess. He's in ninth grade—that's a teenager, right? And he had some kind of accident at school and they brought him over here."

Mrs. Desmond sucked at her teeth, which were slightly loose

in her mouth, and before she could ask the obvious question he asked it for her.

"How do I not know his name, right? Well, it's a funny story." He grinned. Mrs. Desmond did not. "I've got this friend at work, Daryl, and *he's* got a golfing buddy, and *that* guy's on a three-day business trip, and apparently he—not Daryl, the golfing buddy—apparently he got a call about his kid, but the message was garbled somehow? All I know for sure is, he was at school, one of the big high schools out here, and he had some kind of bad fall."

Shenk was tossing out the few bread crumbs Malloy had provided, waiting to see some kind of recognition light up in Mrs. Desmond.

"But yeah, so, I don't know much more than that. That's kind of the sticking point."

Mrs. Desmond remained silent, examined him with her pinched expression, presumably deciding among the many very obvious holes in this story to poke at.

Shenk had, over the years, curated a private typology of Old Dames Who Volunteer in Hospitals. You had your basic cookie-cutter grandmas, with the dimpled cheeks and the baby-powder smell, the blue hair rinse, little old ladies from picture books. Shenk called these the Permanent Widows, who had suffered the loss of dear Harvey or Stan, who after months of hanging around at the hospital had just sort of decided to make a career of it.

Then by contrast you had the Semi-Pros, retired church secretaries or executive assistants, who brought the brisk efficiency of their professional life into the new milieu. More rare were the Grief Vampires, who took an odd and quasi-perverted pleasure in wading all day through other people's pain.

Everything about Mrs. Desmond, though, seemed to place her in Shenk's least-favored class of hospital-lobby matron: Disapproving

Headmistress. She studied him with pursed lips, her red-tinted glasses making her eyes look gigantic. Her head was craned forward on her thin neck, avian and wary, and her clean white eyebrows were so sparse you could count the hairs individually.

"And your business friend, he didn't tell you the child's name? Not even the last name?"

"No, I know, it's crazy," Shenk said, shaking his head at how crazy it was. "But, seriously, all I really need to know is if the kid's been admitted, and if so, then what room, so I can tell Daryl, so he can tell the dad. If that"——he smiled, one more time, let his voice rise into a question——"if that makes sense?"

Shenk waited, his fingertips sweaty on the desk. He needed to get that room number; that's all he needed. He needed to get it before some scumbag ambulance chaser caught a whiff of this thing. There were some bottom-feeding monsters out there, there really were, who would just sail up and down hospital hallways, peeking into windows.

But Mrs. Desmond wasn't playing ball. "This is a large facility, sir. We see many, many patients here."

"Oh, I can see that," said Shenk, breaking in. "I can see that."

The truth was, Valley Village Methodist was large by national standards but decidedly midsize, as far as Southern California was concerned, especially for a Trauma 1. But there wasn't really any need to get into all that with the Lady Desmond. He had his methods to get around obdurate old sweethearts like this one, of course, these petty martinets with their CVS reading glasses and blockish white sneakers. Shenk was the sweetest of sweet talkers, an endlessly inventive fabricator, and, all else failing, a dexterous hand with a palmed twenty. Many people would be surprised, Shenk knew, that your average dowager in lipstick was as open to simple street bribery as a crooked cop or maître d'.

But there were different faces for different conversations. Different tones of voice. Different tilts of the head.

There have to be. Being a lawyer, like being a person in general, comes down to a series of performances: improvisatory or scripted, linear or non-, experimental or traditional, high-flying or grounded in the pedestrian rhythms of the everyday.

"Listen. Ma'am. I'm just trying to be a good guy here. You know what I mean? I'm a"—he sighed, opened his hands as if revealing a gemstone he'd been hiding in his palms—"I'm a father myself, and I just hate the idea of this guy, my buddy's buddy, not knowing what's going on, you know what I mean? That's the part that kills me. The not knowing."

Shenk paused to move a tear, a real one, from the corner of one eye. He *was* a father. He really *did* feel bad for this friend of Daryl's, even though he himself had invented Daryl and Daryl's friend just a few minutes ago. "I'm sure the guy's just going crazy, you know?"

Mrs. Desmond huffed a little, shaking her head, but then— wonder of wonders, miracle of miracles—she softened. Just enough to ask, "What about the injury? Can you provide any information about the injury?"

"Yes!" Shenk practically shouted. "I can!"

Mrs. Desmond, taken aback by the enthusiasm, chirped a little "oh" and even smiled, a tiny and nervous smile. They were getting closer, the two of them. Something was happening here. Soon they would marry, he and Mrs. Desmond, and start a life together, find a place down in Laguna, maybe, a one-bedroom with ocean views, with gentle seaside breezes to soothe their old bones.

"Kid fell down. Knocked his head. Here." Shenk tapped his forehead, right between the eyes. "And I guess the nature of it was, they had to operate on him, straightaway. Right when he came in."

"Huh," said Mrs. Desmond, still with no light in her eyes, but then—then—then came a sharp hissing—*hiss*—from the farther arm of the big horseshoe desk. A second volunteer, who had seemed not to be listening, who had been tapping with rigorous care at her own keyboard, had looked up sharply. Now she came over and stood just behind Mrs. Desmond.

"Are you talkin' about the Keener boy?"

"I—" Shenk's heartbeat burst into a gallop. *The Keener Boy.* He didn't know. And yet, he did know. That was it. The Keener Boy.

"Yes," he said. "That sounds right. Keener."

"Beverly?" Mrs. Desmond said to her colleague, turning her head, plainly irritated at the interruption. Shenk could see, in that one sharp look, a whole rivalrous history between these two volunteer deskmates, some passive-aggressive struggle over scheduling, or appropriate attire, or God knows what else.

Beverly was short and squat, with a round face covered brightly in pink makeup, and a shiny pile of elaborately salon-treated hair, stiff and glassine as ribbon candy. She would have looked ridiculous, another paragon of hall-lobby biddy, if not for the grave way she was staring at Jay Shenk.

"The patient he's looking for is named Keener," Beverly informed Mrs. Desmond. "Wesley Keener."

Wesley Keener. The name glowed to life. It burned like a little sun.

Beverly bent and whispered to Mrs. Desmond, who became wide-eyed and solemn in her turn.

Shenk strained to hear the whisper, across the width of the desk, but could get nothing.

Mrs. Desmond's authoritarian sternness melted off her face. She looked at him straight on, pity filling her eyes.

"Ninth floor," she said, and Beverly nodded and confirmed: "Nine."

"Oh gosh, thank you so much," said Shenk. "Really. And is there a, uh, a room number?"

Beverly shook her head. She reached out and, very softly, touched her fingers to the back of Shenk's hand.

"Just go up. Just go on up to nine."

The elevator rose, the bell binged, and the doors rattled open onto dead quiet.

Shenk stepped off the elevator. He looked around.

He thought, and may even have said: "Where is everybody?"

Normally, of course, you come off a hospital elevator in the middle of an afternoon and there are people everywhere: it's a blur of motion, it's masks and sneakers and hollering, *How is she holding up?* and *How ya feeling this morning, Mr. Jones?* and *How many milliliters?* and everybody is hustling this way and that.

Here, instead, was perfect stillness. No activity at all. The only sound the anxious sizzle of a fluorescent light, just overhead.

Shenk took a step and cocked his head. To the right there was a duty desk, abandoned as if for fire alarm or active shooter. A magazine was open on a countertop; a half-eaten apple lolled on a napkin.

Dimly now Jay heard the squeak of a rubber wheel on linoleum, somewhere on the other side of the world. The hushed inhale-exhale of a respirator from behind one of the patient room doors.

"Hello?" he called out, walking slowly down the hall. "Hello?"

It was like the end of time. He was Rip Van Winkle, waking to find that the world he knew was gone.

A couple of doors stood ajar, and he peeked through one but the room beyond was empty, the bed neatly made, the TV switched off, sunlight flickering over the scuffed floor.

He continued slowly down the hallway, looking for signs of life, like an explorer on a distant planetary surface. Until, rounding a corner, he saw a thick cluster of people crowded into a doorway.

Shenk walked a little faster. He scanned the room numbers as he got closer. Nine oh two. Nine oh four.

Then he stopped.

There was *something* to see in room 906, and everybody was trying to see it. Doctors and nurses and orderlies, a sea of white coats and pale green scrubs, everybody angling for a view into the room, like the crowd along a parade route, jockeying for position.

Whatever was going on with the Keener boy, it seemed like every doctor on the floor—Jesus, maybe every doctor in this hospital—was trying to get a look.

Shenk got closer, and as he did his bright anticipatory tingling (new work! a new case! a *humdinger*!) was shadowed by another feeling: a dark, uneasy stirring way deeper down. And maybe this was one of those moments where he should have just stopped. Should have just turned around.

Instead, Shenk took up a position at the back of the crowd, turned sideways to try to slip through the crush of people and get to the door.

"Excuse me," he murmured, but no one gave ground; no one moved, no one turned.

Shenk couldn't rise enough onto his tiptoes to see over anyone, and neither could he shoulder through. While he craned his neck to try to see, the sounds of the world seemed to return one by one, each as if through a filter: the hush of a doctor's sneaker shifting on the tile; the nervous murmur of a single nurse, speaking sotto voce to another: "What the fuck..."

And then, there, at last, the boy.

A young teenager, walking slowly in a circle around the room.

The boy's face held no expression. His mouth was slightly open and his eyes stared straight ahead. His arms hung at his sides.

He walked slowly, one step after the other. Each step was stiff and automatic. His back was straight. He walked like something that was not human but had learned to replicate the way that humans walk.

The doctors were all watching, from the distance of the doorway. Staying back. Giving him room.

Shenk stared at the boy. Everybody was staring at the boy. Who was just walking, after all, only walking—but what was it in his face, in the stiff posture of his upper body, in the uncanny deliberateness of each step?

When he reached the window, Wesley Keener turned and walked back toward the bed.

"What's going on?" Shenk asked quietly, generally. "What's the deal?"

"They don't know." Shenk looked at the woman, a young African American doctor with her hair hidden under a paper covering, wearing black leggings under her scrubs. "They're trying to figure it out."

Shenk had seen doctors in every attitude. He had seen them cocky and argumentative in the witness box, defending their professional acumen from his lawyerly assaults. He had seen them kindly and sympathetic, when he had been in a hospital like this one, over all those months, pleading for reassurance or hope from the parade of oncologists and specialists who had tried and failed to keep Marilyn on this side of the good gate.

But this doctor, now? There was nothing in this young woman's eyes that he had seen before, this mixture of puzzlement and fear.

Shenk looked back at Wesley Keener.

His mouth, his eyes, his hanging arms. The boy's slow progress had by now taken him all the way to the rear of the room, where he turned again and started back toward the door.

One step after another, just walking. From the door to the window, from the window to the door.

Hollow.

The word came forcefully into Shenk's mind and he felt that it was absolutely right.

They hollowed him out.

"Hey," he whispered to the doctor. "Where are his parents?"

Shenk had walked right past the mother on his way in, and she was still down there in the lobby. Beth Keener, in her stupid itchy work clothes, white blouse and black skirt and sensible shoes, laying pure hellfire on this bullshit pencil-pusher prick.

"No," she told him, for the hundredth time. The thousandth. "Fucking *no*. Try again."

Unbelievably, he did. This prick had one sad little thing he said, and he just said it over and over, like a parrot. "If you would leave me your name and the patient's name and room number, I will look into the situation and make sure——"

"Jesus Christ. Dude." She threw up her hands. She shouted. "*No.*"

The prick winced. He was thin, bland, blond. He had a neat buzz cut and a laminated badge that dangled limply from a lanyard around his boneless neck. The badge said that he was ASSISTANT DIRECTOR OF PATIENT SERVICES, the same thing it said on the office door against which she had backed him up. The badge also said that his name was Brad, because of fucking *course* it was. After a half hour of banging her head against a wall, of people not telling her jack up there on the ninth floor, Beth had stormed down here and demanded an actual human being come and talk to her, but apparently no human beings were available because they had sent her this dumb lump of crap, who could only say that he understood her concerns and that he and his team were committed to the highest standards of patient care and blah fucking blah.

Nope. No. No, thank you.

"I was waiting an hour up there, and I'm not gonna sit and wait anymore. OK? I'm not gonna wait around for you to pretend to call someone so you can pretend to tell me that no one answered, or—"

"Mrs. Keener?"

"—or that someone is on the way to talk to me. No—"

"Mrs. Keener—it's Keener, right?—I assure you, that is not how we do things here. I will look into the situation, personally, and get you some answers as soon as possible."

"Sorry, Brad," she sneered, "but *as soon as possible* isn't fucking soon enough."

Brad blanched. "It would be best if you could keep your voice down."

Beth snarled. She was small, but she had been small her whole life and she knew how to make herself bigger. She rose to the tips of her toes, her feet straining inside of the cheap shoes.

"Sorry, Brad," she shouted in his face. *"I can't keep my voice down."*

Her son, Wesley—her *son*—had come out of surgery an hour and a half ago and *something* was not right, *something* was fucked up, but none of these dipshits in their white coats, with their clipboards, seemed willing to take two seconds to tell her what it was. Just tell me, she kept saying. Whatever it is, fucking *tell* me. And instead all of them, even the main guy, whatever his fucking name was, the fat neurosurgeon with the big beard, kept saying they'd let her know as soon as they were able to.

No. *Unacceptable.*

There was nothing about this situation that Beth could control, but she could control this. She could control the pale-faced, mush-mouthed Brads of the universe.

"Look. My son—my *son* is—"

It all collided with her then, in the middle of the sentence, everything she had not allowed herself to actually experience thus far, what it all looked like and how it all felt. Wes on that stretcher, his unconscious body bundled and jostled and strapped; Wes hyper-illuminated by the surgical lights, surrounded by strangers, his body just a shape under a sheet. His scalp, his skin, the ugly hum of a drill as it burred into his skull.

Goddamn it, no. No one is crying. No. Not here in the lobby. Not in the presence of *Brad*.

"I know how it works, all right?" she said. "Different people are treated differently, and I am not going to let you fucking do that to me. You understand?"

"Yes, no, I understand. All of this must be very upsetting."

"Yeah. Upsetting." Beth was burning hot. She was shaking. "I'm not upset because he's hurt. OK? I'm not upset because he had to have surgery. He fucking hit his head. The doctors said he needed an operation, OK, fine. I know what surgery is. I've had stitches. I had my appendix out. I've pushed two human beings out of my vagina, *Brad*."

He smiled nervously, glancing over her shoulder, down the hallway, in search of rescue.

"I am *upset* because I want information and you fucking pricks won't give it to me." As Beth advanced, Brad backed up yet further, flattening himself against the doorway.

"I wish there was more that I could do." His eyes were round with pleading. Beth thought she might grab the lanyard and choke him to death.

"Hi. Sorry."

Someone was coming up the little carpeted Patient Services hallway, hands raised, like a hostage negotiator showing he had no weapon. Beth whipped around, and the man smiled gently at her, turned an affable gaze on Brad.

"I wonder, Mr. —"

"Willoughby," said Brad. Brad Willoughby, Beth thought. Jesus Fucking Christ.

"Mr. Willoughby, I wonder if you've tried putting a call in to the HOA?"

"What?"

"Is there an admin who handles all surgical?"

"Uh—yeah. Yes."

"OK, perfect. Perfect! So maybe the move here is, skip the attending, because he or she might be still trying to get all the ducks in a row, and just page the operations admin, see if you can get just a temporary *here's what's happening*. You know?"

"Yes." Brad was nodding. "Sure. That totally makes sense."

The new arrival turned toward Beth, gave her a wink. "The attending surgeons, you know, God bless them, sometimes they're hesitant to tell you anything until they can tell you *everything*. But you don't need every detail, right? You just want a status update."

Beth had unlocked her angry gaze from Brad and trained it on this guy. Did he work for the hospital or what? A silver suit. Tan shoes. Hair pulled back into a ponytail.

"Am I right?" he asked.

"Yeah," said Beth. She nodded. The pulse of adrenaline began to ease. She nodded again. "Yeah, exactly."

3.

Shenk waved away any thanks. What had he done? Nothing. He hadn't done anything.

"Please," he said. "Don't mention it."

"It's just these people drive you crazy, you know? *Crazy.*"

They were outside the hospital now, he and the mother, Beth Keener, he leaning back against the concrete exterior wall, she digging through the massive canvas pocketbook she had dropped between her feet. Shenk glimpsed a lipstick, a broken ballpoint pen, a scatter of tampons like bullets.

"They act like it's their job *not* to help you. To tell you nothing, for as long as possible."

"Oh, but that *is* their job," said Shenk. "Not all of them, but some of them. Trust me. I've seen it before."

Brad Willoughby was in there now, making the call that Shenk had gently persuaded him to make, and Beth was going to check back in after fifteen minutes. They stood together here, just beyond the glass doors—the diesel stink of the parking lot, the muted midday sunlight, the garage-entrance gate arm going up and down, up and down, like a mini-golf hazard—and Shenk was in repose, waiting for his moment, which would come, as his moments always did.

"Are you uh—" he said, to the top of her head, as she rummaged into the depths of the canvas tote. "Are you by chance trying to find a cigarette?"

"Yeah, I, uh—I can't—" She looked up and exhaled. "Oh, thank you, man. Fucking lifesaver."

"I had a feeling."

Jay Shenk did not smoke, and was actually pretty firmly anti-smoking on general principle, but was always prepared. He carried cigarettes like he carried twenty-dollar bills and breath mints and a notepad and pens, like he carried business cards by the boxful, and clean shirts in dry-cleaning bags in his trunk. He held out the single Camel Light, pinched between two fingers at the end of his arm, extended all the way out to create maximum distance between himself and the stranger, to avoid any whiff of wolfishness. He was no sex fiend, just a nice guy, that's all, who had arrived in the nick of time and seemed to have everything she needed.

Wesley Keener's mother took the Camel, and Jay smiled.

And look, *of course* he was an opportunist, or if you want to go that far, then OK, he was a predator. He had followed her and found her, he had waited for his moment to strike, and even now, as he crept into her confidence, his heart was fluttering like a schoolboy's. Not because this was an attractive woman, but because it was an attractive situation—and because, yes, he believed that he was the very best at what he did, and what he had to offer was at least as valuable as what he was wanting to take—and why, after all, couldn't both things be true? In the end, his interest in Wesley Keener's mother would redound to her benefit as well as his. She would emerge from their association as much a winner as he, if not more.

Winner/loser, giver/taker, hunter/prey. What good was it, really, to divide the world into those kinds of artificial binaries?

Beth Keener was a short and tough-looking white woman with frank dark eyes. She had cheap plastic sunglasses, pushed back high on her forehead so the stems disappeared into the thickness of her hair. She was dressed for some kind of low-stakes office gig, in a plain black skirt and a white blouse, but she had a little cluster of tattoos high on her forearm, a pair of tumbling dice, it looked like, and some sort of little gnome or devil. This woman had something about her of the biker chick, the savvy hardheaded working-man's wife—this was Shenk, now, analyzing, sorting people into categories for later use—but also something of the harried mom, packing lunches and putting out fires. Furiously dedicated to those she loved.

She dragged on the cigarette, letting her eyes flutter closed for the pleasurable instant of inhale. Then, when the moment had passed and another had begun, Shenk broke the silence.

"I'm Jay, by the way." He stuck out his hand, awkwardly, for her to shake, and she said "Beth" and shook it. Her thin lips twisted to blow smoke out against the wall of the hospital.

"So what—do you work here?" she asked him, and he said "Sort of" and was about to say more, to pivot into business, when she made a sudden, sharp tsking noise, scowling at the parking lot. "I don't know where the hell my husband is. He ought to be here by now." She jerked up her arm to look at a watch that wasn't there. "Do you know what time it is?"

He did, and he told her, and Beth said thanks and then "For God's sake."

Richard was a carpenter, she said, a set builder currently working at a studio complex on Sunset, and he had to turn his phone off when they were shooting, so he didn't even know for the first hour what had happened, and now he was stuck in traffic on the 110. This even though she had *told* him to stay off the fucking 110— she had texted him, *stay off the freeway*—but now here she was by herself trying to figure out what the hell was going on.

"I just—"

She stopped talking. Her lips went tight and white and Shenk could see the energy sparking behind her eyes, all the confusion and horror.

The unholy silence of that hospital room. Her child, moving in silent circles, head locked in place, staring straight ahead. Lord God, thought Shenk, what this lady must be feeling.

"Ten times I told him," she said bitterly, flicking ash against the wall. "Take Mulholland. Stay off the fucking freeway."

She was going to finish the cigarette soon. She would go back inside to hunt for Brad, to go back up to nine. Her son was inside; she wouldn't stay out here for long.

"So your boy," said Shenk carefully. "He's had an accident of some kind?"

"Yeah," said Beth. "Of some kind."

Walking. Door to window, window to door. Round and round. Eyes open.

Hollow.

And now, again, way down low — below the mild exterior Shenk had assumed for his approach, below the panting eagerness of his lawyer's heart — he felt a slow tremor of unease. He looked at Beth Keener while she took a last long drag and flicked the cigarette away, and Shenk knew he was still within the time frame where he could just *leave.* Wish a stranger well and slip out of her life as he'd slipped in.

But instead:

"I'm really sorry," he said. "What happened to him?"

And she told him. She launched, as people in extremis sometimes launch, as they sometimes *need to,* and Shenk simply listened.

He was kind, and his kindness was versatile. He could widen it like a searchlight beam, expanding empathy parabolically, or he could do what he did now, narrowed it to a candle's breadth, made of himself a glowing steady kindness, to which this suffering woman could gather herself and find the warmth she needed.

She told him about the accident that Wesley had at school, and what had happened at the hospital: the whirlwind of the ER, the confusing bustle of doctors and nurses, and then, suddenly, the surgery. They drilled into him. His head. His *brain.*

While Beth talked, two ambulance drivers emerged from the

rear of their rig and stood in the driveway, chatting in Spanish and laughing, their calm workaday chatter an agitating backdrop to Beth Keener's pain, her bombed-out expression. One person's baffling nightmare is another's day at the office.

"I am so sorry," said Shenk when she was done talking, and he held out his two hands and she took them and squeezed. "I cannot imagine."

And he couldn't: Shenk could not imagine.

We can allow for skepticism, but if Jay's small, alert face looked like the face of a man whose heart was breaking, it is because his heart was breaking. He was simply devastated for this woman, who within the last few hours had received the worst possible phone call, who had watched as holes were bored into her child's skull, and who found herself trapped in the confusing complicated horror of whatever was happening now. Sincerely did Shenk partake of her grief, and yet he was pretending.

Pretending not to have come here specifically to find her, pretending to have only a stranger's empathetic interest in her sad situation. Shenk's tears were real, his love for her was real, just as real as his need to land this case, to sue this hospital, to turn this tragedy into something tangible. For her, for the boy, for himself. It was all true at once.

They stood together with hands clasped, trembling, like cousins at a funeral, and for Shenk everything was true.

"I'll tell you, Beth," he said. "One thing my wife used to say, don't invent reasons to suffer. Things may turn out just fine in the end, so don't torture yourself needlessly. Right?"

"Sure," she said, looking down, nodding. "Yeah. It's just..."

"I know. I know."

He looked at her and she held his eyes, and he felt in his body the sharp snap of connection.

This would happen. That was the fact of the moment, absolutely clear and absolutely true.

Jay Shenk had married very young and had become a widower way too soon after that, and in the years since had only dabbled, never plunged, into the anxiety-provoking and time-consuming universe of romance. He had taken a pass on all of it, the matchmaking and the speed dating and the new websites promising connection and chemistry for a monthly fee. There had been dinner dates, there had been occasional partners for the relief of the base urges, but this right here, the forging of lawyer-client bonds, was the form of relationship at which he was most practiced, and by which he felt the most rewarded. Client development was not the same as sexual pursuit, of course, but for Shenk it fell into the same category. Two human beings, strangers at first, enter into a negotiation with unspoken rules, each evaluating the other and evaluating themselves, making a thousand small calculations, and then after due consideration entering into contract. Both of them aware of what this thing is — that it is transitional, impermanent — but who nevertheless develop strong feelings toward the other that ultimately transcend the transactional origins of the relationship.

"Jesus Christ," said Beth, pushing tears from the corners of her eyes with her knuckles, making a wry face. "What a baby."

"It's OK."

"I'm not a crier," she said. "I don't cry."

"It's really OK."

"You're a doll," she said. "Tell me your name again?"

"Jay. Jay Shenk." He took a breath and looked at her with composure and confidence. "I'm a lawyer."

He held up his card by one corner. It was a brand-new card, freshly printed, and at the angle he held it, it was made so white by the sunlight that it looked like there was no writing on it. Blank and gleaming, like the business card an angel would carry. Beth took it from him and turned it end over end, felt the matte weight in her hands.

"Personal injury," he told her. "Slip-and-falls. Vehicle accidents. And malpractice, of course."

He said the magic word, *malpractice,* with tremendous care, as if he were delicately hanging it upon a hook in the air between them.

There were many people who would have tossed the card on the ground, torn it in half maybe, a lot of people who no matter how thoroughly Shenk had cast his spell would be disgusted with him now, on discovering that the whole thing was a pickup scene.

But Beth Keener said, "No shit?" She said, "A lawyer."

He had her, and then he lost her. There was a screech of tires, and Beth looked up, distracted. A truck had slammed to a stop in the hospital driveway, and a man was lurching out. He was a big man, sturdy and broad. Heavy boots on the asphalt, and Beth immediately calling for him: "Richie! Baby!

"Rich!"

November 19, 2008

1.

Young Ruben Shenk had a thing he did, when he was very excited, which was that he kept his narrow body as still as he possibly could. He pretended there was something fragile inside him, balanced between the bones of his rib cage, and if he moved too quickly it would fall and break. The more anticipation he had about something, the more *feelings,* the less he wanted anyone to see those feelings or know he was having them. He didn't know why this was. He had always been this way, and though he was older now, a teenager, he still felt it. He felt it even more intensely, actually. *Be still. Don't move.* When he was most worked up inside, he tried hardest to keep his exterior even and calm.

Right now was definitely such a time. *Definitely.*

His father's excitement had gotten *him* excited. He was churned up, agitated by his curiosity about this new case.

Not a new case. A *potential* new case. *Do not jinx it. Do not, do not jinx it.*

They were out on the metal catwalk that overlooked the strip mall parking lot, Ruben and Jay Shenk like two sailors abreast at the rigging. Ruben took his glasses off with a precise movement and cleaned them on the sleeve of his shirt, and then slid them carefully back onto his nose. He was wearing khaki pants and his checked button-down shirt. His father hadn't told him to dress nice. He hadn't needed to be told.

He looked at his dad now, and his dad smiled down at him, a big, beaming grin, and clapped him on the shoulder.

"So glad you're here, pal. Seriously."

Ruben nodded, just a tiny bit, let a smile flick on and off his face. "Me too."

There were only nine spaces in the parking lot, which served not only Shenk & Partners, but also Gloria's Glorious Donuts, the ramen restaurant, the nail salon, and the massage place, which was called Happy-Go-Lucky. Seven of the nine spots were taken, and Ruben was concerned. What would happen if the new clients couldn't park? Would they just drive away?

Potential clients, Ruben reminded himself. Come on. Come *on*.

He and his father had spent the morning together, preparing to welcome the Keeners, arranging the conference room chairs in a neat semicircle. Ruben had run down to Gloria's for an assorted dozen and one of those temperature-stable boxes of coffee, and now everything was ready and they were just waiting, shoulder to shoulder, four hands on the railing, squinting out at Palms Boulevard, Ruben now feeling his anticipation like a small star, bright behind his heart. This was a big case, his dad had told him, *potentially,* a *potential* humdinger, so he had kept him home from school even though it was a Monday and his work-study at Shenk & Partners was supposed to be just on alternate Tuesdays between one and four o'clock.

Ruben's progressive private high school allowed motivated students to make arrangements for a quote-unquote "offsite work experience." Generally speaking, this work experience wasn't supposed to be at a family business, but Ruben's father had paid a visit to the school to request an exception. He had planted himself in the office of the dean of students, Mr. Cabrera, and argued the point with fervency, as he argued everything: "Listen, what if *all this kid wants* is to be a lawyer? What if it's *all he's ever wanted?*"

"And what if"—pausing here to laugh, to give Mr. Cabrera permission to laugh—"what if the boy's old man just happens to be the best personal injury lawyer in LA County? What are we supposed to do—*punish* him?"

Shenk had winked at Ruben on the way out to the car after that meeting, a dishy acknowledgment, just between us, that they'd gotten one over on the Man.

But all of it was true. It was bullshit *and* it was true, because Jay (Ruben knew to a certainty) believed in his heart that there was no better place for his son than at his side.

"Shenk & Partners," just for the record, was a legal fiction. Jay Shenk had no partner and no interest in acquiring one, which he had explained to Ruben more than once. The name had a nice ring to it and it looked sharp on the website and the business cards, but Shenk & Partners was just Shenk. It was Shenk and Darla the bookkeeper, who only worked three half days a week; Shenk and Angela the cleaning lady; Shenk and Gloria Jiménez of Gloria's Glorious Donuts, who gave them a standing 40 percent discount in exchange for occasional review of their health-department and ADA compliance.

Most of all, Shenk & Partners was Shenk and his only child, who'd be a partner in full one day, but for now, for today, stood beside him, home from school to do some new-business development. The law was in Ruben's blood like it was in Shenk's, for though he was not of Shenk's blood he was of his spirit, and Shenk's spirit was the spirit of the law—not the law of regulation and statute book, but the law of justice and love, the law of setting wrongs to right. Ruben had a lot to learn and he would learn it.

Shenk's own and only boy, the good quiet child of his heart.

"You know, they might not even show up," Jay said—suddenly, offhandedly, cricking his neck and yawning.

"I know," said Ruben.

"OK. Just so you're not too disappointed." Shenk smoothed his tie with exaggerated casualness, working at a spot where the fabric had gotten bunched. "People change their minds. They get cold feet. Maybe Kennerly poached them. You never know."

Ruben wrinkled his face at the mention of the other lawyer. Darius Kennerly was the Haman of their household. He was a blindingly white-toothed shyster whose oversize moon head adorned bus-station benches all over West LA and one gigantic billboard at Sepulveda and Pico. Shenk considered Kennerly a mercenary, a charlatan, and his archenemy.

"Dad," said Ruben. "They'll be here."

Ruben could tell his father was nervous. His life was spent carefully tuned to the calibrations of Shenk's voice, its pitches and pauses, its rises and falls; he could hear the distinct timbres of nervousness, excitement, aggression, and, rarest, fear. He loved especially to listen to Jay's voice in conversation with a client, maybe a reluctant or uncertain one—to hear him talk his way around a legal matter in a way that made others feel comfortable, that drew them in and gave them courage. That's why Ruben was so excited about today; the idea that his father wanted him here for a new-client meeting made him feel lightheaded. He would do his best. He would be ready with anything Shenk needed.

And, depending how long the meeting stretched, he would probably miss Classical Poetry Confab, a fact that filled him with a combination of giddiness and unease. Ms. Hutchins, the World

Languages teacher who ran the program, had been very clear that missing the weekly after-school meetings would mean forfeiting one's spot on the Tournament of Poets team, and, eventually, having to withdraw from the confab altogether. Which Ruben would not have minded, because he actually preferred coming home after school, and because he didn't even really like poetry. Ms. Hutchins was always saying how much the poems made one *feel,* and Ruben would read them, and read them again, and then just sit there wondering what was wrong with him, feeling nothing, staring at the dead wooden words.

But dropping out of the club would mean letting down Ms. Hutchins—and, worse, letting down his father, because it had been on Jay's insistence that he had signed up in the first place. This after a group of Morningstar parents, with sepia-tinged memories of their own boarding-school childhoods, had inaugurated the thrice-weekly poetry-themed after-school program, and Shenk—who on occasion would scan the weekly "Around Campus" email—said it sounded like a blast. Memorizing and declaiming from classic texts is a great way to build confidence, he'd said, that's first of all, and also, Rubie, this is how you *meet* people, this is how you make new friends, which now that you're in high school would not be the worst thing. Right?

The truth is, Ruben had met people. He had, for example, met a sophomore girl named Annelise McTier, who had shocking red hair and shiny black boots. Ruben almost even thought there was a friendship developing between them, as when (for example) they silently rolled their eyes together at Willy Dorian's comical stumbles through Yeats. But if today's meeting went long—if he had to stay and help his dad—Ms. Hutchins might pull him from the tournament and maybe even eject him from the confab, which would be a shame but, also, secretly sort of a reprieve. Ruben held himself still, feeling this jumble of feelings roll over in his gut, clutching the railing till his knuckles glowed white.

Oh God. Another car had pulled in and was parking, one of those terrible Range Rovers that took up its own space and a prohibitive slice of the next one over.

Ruben looked at his watch. The clients—*potential* clients—would be here any minute. Now what? Now the lot was *full*.

"The place looks really good," said Shenk, glancing into the windows of the office, then back out on the street, back and forth. "We did a great job. It's just a little hokey, right, the doughnuts and the paper plates, but not too hokey. Not too hokey, not too professional."

"Totally," said Ruben. He had heard this speech before, this riff. He could have given it back to his father; he could have said it a half step ahead, like a parishioner singing along to the hymn.

Oh good. There. Two ladies had emerged from the nail salon and were hugging goodbye, meaning leaving separately, meaning— yes—two new spaces were opening up.

"But see, that's what people want. They don't want to walk into an office with all the tinted glass, the mahogany tables, and all the—you know."

"The fancy furniture," murmured Ruben.

"Exactly!" said Shenk, as if Ruben weren't just saying what he'd heard Shenk say a million times. "All the fancy furniture and that stuff. What people need is a fighter. An underdog."

Ruben nodded solemnly. "I know, Dad."

"You're the best, my boy." And he bent down now, and clasped his son by the cheeks. Ruben blushed but did not pull away. "You're the absolute best."

Ruben grinned. "Thanks, Dad." He rubbed his cheeks where his father had squeezed them and turned away, smiling.

"So," said Shenk again, absolutely offhand, out of nowhere. "OK. So when they get here..."

"Yes?"

"We say hello, we introduce ourselves."

"Yes."

"We offer them coffee, doughnuts, et cetera."

"Obviously."

"Obviously." A Shenk grin. A Shenk wink. "Then I will usher the Keeners into my office. You stay outside."

"Oh." Ruben blinked. "OK."

"Because I need you, Kemosabe—this is key—I need you to keep an eye on the kid."

"The kid?" Ruben was confused. The kid was surely still at the hospital. If the kid was well enough to come to the meeting, then this case wasn't nearly as serious as he had understood.

"The sister, I mean. Not *the* kid. The little sister. You hang out with the little sister while me and Mom and Dad get into it."

"Oh," said Ruben. "I see."

And he did. He saw. This was how it was with Jay: the truth sometimes came in late, and unannounced. He hadn't wanted Ruben here to participate in the meeting, but to *allow* for it. Of course. The Keeners could hardly discuss a complex civil litigation, relating to the debilitating condition of their elder child, in the presence of their younger. So Ruben's role was not to sit in on the client meeting, but to occupy the kid in the meantime. To babysit, in other words.

"I told you, buddy," said Shenk. "I need you on this."

"Of course, Dad."

Ruben looked out at the parking lot. He bit his lower lip with his upper teeth, thinking sadly of Poetry Confab, thinking for one longing instant of Annelise McTier, of the red hair and black boots.

But this was fine. It was good. He could do this. In a law office, everybody had their role to play.

"Hey, hey," said Jay. "Here they come!" He squeezed his son's hand, just a bit too hard. Ruben smiled, tilted his face toward his father's happiness.

The vehicle navigating into the parking lot was a white pickup truck: enormous tires, mud spattered around the wheel wells. In the driver's seat, a big man with a thick beard and aviator shades; riding shotgun, a short woman with round sunglasses; a little girl sandwiched between them.

"You ready?"

Ruben nodded. "Ready."

This was mid-November. California in the autumn, seventy degrees and bright and blue, right at the beginning of it all. Ruben Shenk was fourteen years old. A freshman in high school—the same as Wesley Keener.

2.

"All right, man," said Richard. Before sitting down, he emptied his pockets—thick black wallet and chunky flip phone and the keys to his truck—and tossed it all onto Jay's conference table. "Let's hear it."

"Jesus, Rich," said Beth. She was still over at the side table, where Shenk had set up the doughnuts and coffee, pouring a cup for herself and one for him. "Maybe wait a second?"

"What for?"

Richard sat back and crossed his heavy arms over his chest and looked coolly at Jay, as closed off and unyielding as a sealed tomb. His aviators were pushed up over his brow. His hair was thick and dark, and he wore a longish and unkempt beard. "We're here. Let's do it."

"Well," said Shenk, and took a breath. How does one start? One starts with gentle words of welcome, with expressions of condolence and sensitive inquiries about the current condition of the afflicted family member. Delicately asking if there had been any change.

You moved from there to the outlines of a plan, a process, but only in general—*hey, here's how these things usually work*—until slowly but surely you downshifted into the particulars of this case. But Wesley's father was not going to sit still for all that. He sat there glaring, nostrils flaring slightly, waiting to be impressed.

"You should hire me because I'm very good at what I do," said Shenk, keeping his face solemn, thrusting out his chin. "And because when you hire me you *get* me, not some associate, twenty years old, still learning how to write a brief. *Me.* You need me, I'm available. You call me, I call back."

Shenk moved his gaze back and forth between Rich and Beth, who was now placing a powdered doughnut on a paper plate in front of her husband, setting down the coffees.

"Number two is, you'll pardon the expression, I don't fuck around. I work hard, I move fast, and I win. Once I have the details I need from you folks, we can have our notice to file in on the hospital by the end of the week. Not next week. This week."

That was enough for starters. Shenk left it there.

He spared them, for now, all the gory details of a multiparty medical malpractice lawsuit. How they would be suing to recover three different forms of damages: for pain and suffering, for medical costs, and for future medical care. How the suit would target not just the hospital, but the neurosurgeon who performed the surgery to relieve Wesley's subdural hematoma, a big shot named Dr. Thomas Angelo Catanzaro, as well as anyone else from the hospital staff who was implicated as discovery got underway, potentially including surgical nurses, ER staff, radiologists, and so on. How ultimately, when an appropriate settlement was reached, they would be recovering damages not from the doctors and nurses nor even from the hospital, but from the insurance company that stood behind them.

There would be plenty of time to explain everything, Shenk figured. If they got that far.

Rich was looking sourly at Jay. "Honestly, man?" he said. "That's all well and good. But it's a question of trust. Why should we trust you?"

"Fuck's sake. Rich. Come on." Beth reached over and flicked him with the side of her hand, an irritated swat on his hairy forearm. "Eat your doughnut." Then, to Jay, she said, "I'm sorry. My husband is not in a great place."

"Of course not," said Shenk. "Of course. Although. Having said that . . . it's a fair question. Why *should* you trust me?"

This, Shenk understood, was the question of the day. This was not a meeting about legal tactics or money or medical details. Beth Keener he'd had from go, from the moment they laid eyes on each other in the lobby of Valley Village, two souls thrown together by fate. Beth was his. But Rich's trust would have to be earned. Rich the set builder, the union carpenter: this was a man of *materials,* of wood and metal and beams, a man accustomed to relying only on things he made with his own hands.

"How can you know who to trust, or what to do, in this awful situation?" Shenk said. "What I'm wondering, Mr. Keener, is if you can suspend that decision for the moment. Accept me, for today, for this hour, as your—your—" What was the word he was seeking? What was the word Rich would respond to? "Your *champion.* OK? Let me walk you through my process; let me tell you about some of my other cases. Let me tell you about my firm, my family. I think you met my son on the way in?"

"Yeah." Beth smiled. "Nice-looking kid."

But Rich was shaking his head. He was standing up. "Yeah, no. You know what? I've heard enough."

"Rich," said Beth.

"Thanks anyway, man."

"*Rich*. Sit."

With the woolly beard and the thick neck and wide shoulders, Rich had an imposing, bearlike quality, but he looked down at his wife with a touching helplessness.

"Baby, come on." His voice had that gruff-and-tough thing, but he wasn't telling her, he wasn't insisting. He was making a case. "You said I had to come and meet the new guy. I did it. I met him." He bent down a little, swept his keys, phone, and wallet off the table and dumped them in his jacket pocket. "So now let's go."

But Beth didn't get up. She looked at Jay, shaking her head and exhaling in a controlled fashion, like the mother of a toddler, working to stay patient. "Nobody ever taught him to express his emotions, so when he's sad he acts like a freakin' gorilla." Shenk flicked a glance up at Rich, fearful of his reaction...and saw, by how he was gazing at his wife, his mouth set tight but his eyes lit with tenderness, that Beth could say anything she wanted about him, anything in the world.

Even in their anger and irritation with each other, as they navigated this unaccountable nightmare world of doctors and lawyers they had been pitched into, their love for each other was vividly present in the room.

"I'm not a gorilla," muttered Rich.

"I didn't say you were a gorilla, babe. I said you were *acting* like one."

Then she turned back to Shenk, still shaking her head, marveling at her husband's obdurateness. "He thinks, well, this is just what happened, that's all, and we have to just go along and it is what it is."

"That's not what I think."

"Yes, it is."

"Elizabeth," said Rich. "I have to get back to *work*."

"He doesn't understand that sometimes you have to fight for what you deserve."

"This guy," said Rich, very suddenly, and very loud, pointing a thick finger at Shenk, "doesn't give a *shit* about what we deserve." He smacked his hand down on the table, knocking over all three coffee cups at once. "Guy like this cares about money. That's what he cares about."

He stood there unspeaking, heaving breath, and Jay understood that he had about a half a second here to answer this charge in a way that would keep Richard from storming out, with or without his wife. Jay had speeches he could deliver about truth and justice and decency; speeches about his dear dead wife and her last days in the hospital; he could conjure something quickly comparing the dignity of his work to that of Rich's own, how there was nothing so different about building sets for TV shows and building legal arguments.

But there was an old line Shenk liked—was it David Mamet?—*always tell the truth, because it's the easiest thing to remember.*

"Of *course* it's about the money," Jay pronounced. "Of *course* it is." He gave the table a little smack of his own, and one of the fallen coffee cups rolled off the table onto the carpet.

"*And* I do it for you. For my clients. It's *both* things. Both reasons. It has to be."

And this sounded sincere because it was sincere. It sounded like he meant it because he did mean it, and this was the great secret of Shenk's heart: he loved the money and he loved the people and his loves were in alignment.

Richard squinted and furrowed his brow, and for that moment he did look like a gorilla, just a little bit. Beth looked down at her hands and smiled, very slightly, and then Richard sighed and said, "Am I allowed to smoke in here?"

"Alas," said Jay, "Los Angeles County says no. But...you know what..."

He ducked beneath the table to recover the cup that had fallen, thinking *I did it,* and then passed the cup over to Rich and Beth's end of the table. Richard dug himself out a cigarette and used the coffee cup to ash in while Shenk—very slowly, very carefully, like an anthropologist tiptoeing through a forest—took out a legal pad and set it down. Took out a pen. Took out his mini recorder and set that down, too.

"Now," he said. "Mrs. Keener. Let's start at the beginning."

Beth told the whole story, an expanded version of what she had told Jay in the parking lot on the day of the accident. Everything to which she had borne witness in the hospital, the scraps and pieces of information she'd gotten from the doctors during and after the surgery, supplemented by what she'd since heard from Wes's friends who had been there when the accident happened—when he fell, when he was briefly unconscious, when he had been loaded onto the stretcher and taken away.

Rich said nothing, just sat smoking. When he was done with his first cigarette he lit another. Shenk took notes in his eccentric shorthand, getting down as much as he could, trusting the mini recorder to capture the rest. And of course all of these details— the accident and the ambulance ride, the triage room and the ER floor, the radiology room and the surgery—would be repeated a hundred times, repeated and recorded and transcribed.

Sometimes, though, he did put in a small question, not so much for the answer but to gently jostle Beth out of the agitated silence into which she occasionally lapsed.

"Do you happen to know," said Shenk at one such moment, "how long the ride to the hospital lasted?"

"In the ambulance?"

"Yes."

"Um—I don't know." She winced, picked at a thumbnail, agitated. "Can we find that out?"

"Of course," offered Shenk, "absolutely. When we file suit, those records will come in through the discovery process."

Beth nodded earnestly, taking this small piece of procedural information as a tonic. So it was that Shenk—slowly, ever so slowly, as careful as a lover—began to ease the Keeners into the zone where this was already a done deal, where he was already their guy—slipping the word *we* midway into the sentence—*when* we *file suit*—quietly and unofficially yoking their interests to his ability.

"And do you remember how long he spent in the ER, before being moved to surgery?"

"Um, no," Beth said. "A while. I think."

"A long while?"

"I don't remember."

Beth's chin trembled for a startling instant, and Shenk saw the flash in her eyes he recognized as anger: not at him. At *herself.*

"Goddamn it," she said. Rich passed her a bright-pink Gloria's Glorious napkin and she furiously blew her nose. "Motherfucker."

"It's OK, Mrs. Keener," Jay said, murmuring, reassuring. "There is no rush. We have all the time in the world."

He smiled at her, and then at Rich, who did not smile back.

"Once Wesley was examined," Shenk continued, "did the doctors tell you they had to operate immediately?"

"Yeah," said Beth. "Yes."

"And did they say exactly what they were going to do?"

"Yeah. I guess. I didn't really—they said they had taken these scans—"

"*Scan,* singular, or *scans?*"

"I don't—"

"A CT scan?"

"I think so."

"OK. Go on, I'm sorry. What else did they say?"

"They said it appeared there was a buildup of blood in his brain—"

"They used that word?"

"Which?"

"*Appeared.* They said it appeared there was a brain bleed, or that there *was* one?"

"I . . ." She held up her hands. Her nails were bitten nearly down to the flesh. It looked like it hurt.

"It's OK if you don't remember."

"I don't remember. I'm sorry."

"Don't be sorry. Mrs. Keener, did you consent to the operation?"

"Um—yes. Yeah." She bit her lip. "Shit. I did."

"Consented just by saying so? Orally? Or were you presented with papers to sign?"

"Yeah. I mean—not orally. I signed something. They gave me a copy . . ."

She opened her pocketbook, realized this wasn't the bag she'd been holding, and snapped it closed. "Damn it."

"It's OK. Mrs. Keener, listen. This is OK. This is all just for my information. How much time did they give you to sign those papers?"

"What?"

"Was it like"—Shenk mimed a big rush, turning his hands in windmill circles: *Here, here, sign this, fast, please*—"time is of the essence?"

"Yes," Richard said.

Shenk jerked his head, stunned, toward the husband, who had arrived in the conversation like a bowling ball dropped from a height—*bang*—answering for his wife in a single firm syllable. He rubbed his jaw and went on:

"She told me that. That they rushed her." He pantomimed a sniveling egghead doctor, face grotesquely contorted. "Sign it. Sign it. Come on."

"Thank you," said Shenk.

Rich held his gaze for a moment and then nodded curtly, *you're welcome,* and Shenk nodded back.

"Assholes," Rich added, his voice still holding weight. "These doctors. They're a bunch of *assholes.*"

Rich's hands were clenched, the knuckles white, and Shenk saw how right Beth had been about her husband's mental state, how unmoored he was by this slowly unfolding catastrophe. His neck had strong muscles in it that tightened when he pursed his lips, as he pursed them now, his jaw set in perplexed fury. Beth was sad and afraid and frantic, scrambling to find solutions to a thousand different problems; her husband was a fist that did not yet know what to smash into.

"Well, they sure can be assholes," said Shenk. "They sure can be. But we are not suing them for being assholes." The word again: we. We, we, we. "We're suing them because they screwed up."

―――――

Slightly later, as Shenk with great delicacy took out the two-page contingency agreement that Darla had prepared, he made a solemn pronouncement, a version of what he always said at this moment in the process:

"Now, look, you signing this paper, this isn't like you're hiring a plumber or something, OK? This isn't just a contract. You sign this, and I'm *your guy*. I'm your man. A lawyer is a promise."

"What?" said Beth. "What does that mean?"

"It means once I am your lawyer, I am your lawyer forever."

Shenk bent slightly forward, emphasizing his point, palms flat on the table and fingers extended. Beth gripped the pen tightly while she signed, Richard standing beside her with another pen that Shenk had handed to him, his expression elusive and ungiving. That moment got frozen there. Just as if a flashbulb went off. Like someone clicked a button.

3.

The waiting room at Shenk & Partners wasn't really a room. It was a windowless alcove, crammed tightly with two brown armchairs, off the short hallway that ran from the door past Darla's desk and the photocopier/fax machine to Jay's office. Ruben sat in the larger of the armchairs, his hands resting on its upholstered arms, smiling politely at Wesley Keener's little sister.

She sat on her hands, staring back at him.

Her skin was so white it was almost translucent. She wore a jean skirt and a sleeveless T-shirt with a picture of a unicorn on it. Her hair was straight and brown, with a single barrette set precisely above each ear and the bangs trimmed neatly across the front. Every time Ruben made eye contact with her she made a twisty little half smile, and sometimes she bugged her eyes out, like she was still learning how to make facial expressions.

"Your name is Evelyn?" Ruben asked, when it seemed like he ought to say something. She nodded. She squirmed a little, rocking back and forth on her hands.

Ruben made a mental note to tell his father they ought to keep some magazines out here. *National Geographic Kids,* something like that. There was one called *Cobblestone* they'd had at his elementary school, about history.

He was desperately curious, of course, about how things were proceeding inside his father's office, but Ruben was determined in the meantime to fulfill his mandate as best he could. The problem was, although the assignment made a certain logical sense, since they were both kids, he really had no idea what to say to this girl. Ruben was the kind of child who was for the most part uncomfortable in the company of other children.

"Hey, do you want some water?" he asked Evelyn.

"No," she said quickly, and made a face.

Did she not like *water*? Do kids think water is stupid? He thought about the other students at Morningstar, in the cafeteria, and tried to remember if they drank water.

"I could also get you a soda. Are you allowed to drink soda?"

The girl shrugged. Did that mean yes or no? She probably wasn't allowed to drink soda. Ruben shifted in the big chair, trying to sit up straight.

"Would you like to have a doughnut?" he asked, and she shrugged again.

"We have blueberry crumb, maple frosted, chocolate . . . a lot of different kinds."

"Strawberry? Are there strawberry doughnuts?"

"I think so, actually. Yeah."

"Oh."

"So—should I get you one?"

"Actually—no. No. That's OK."

"You sure?"

She shrugged a third time, and then it was quiet. Ruben wondered if maybe she was thinking that accepting the doughnut would have been like taking candy from a stranger. Then he felt bad for having put her in an awkward position.

Ruben glanced at the closed door of the inner office and hoped his father was handling the conversation carefully. He knew his dad had a tendency to overdo it. Push too hard. He hoped he'd play it cool this time, if he could. Ruben wished he was in there.

The girl spoke suddenly.

"So are you Chinese?"

"What?"

"Sorry." She shifted her butt, freeing one hand, and twisted her hair. "I'm sorry."

"It's OK."

"That was so rude."

"It's totally OK. Actually, I'm Vietnamese."

"Oh. Huh."

Ruben smiled. In general this was not a favorite subject. His sixth-grade English teacher, Ms. Klein, had assigned them all to give a presentation about their cultural heritage, and Ruben had literally been so anxious at the prospect that on the day of the presentations he vomited in the hallway outside the classroom. But he was glad to have something to talk about with Evelyn Keener.

"I mean, I was born in the country of Vietnam? But I came to America when my parents adopted me, and I was still really little. I'm basically just American. And I'm Jewish. Like my dad."

"Oh." Her smile broadened a little with interest, transforming her face. "Huh."

"And actually, Judaism is not just a religion," Ruben went on. "It's like a—a people? It *is* a religion, but it's also a web of cultural feeling." This was a direct quote, something his dad said often. Evelyn looked back at him curiously.

"So I'm Asian in appearance, but, you know—" He didn't like to say *I'm not really Asian,* because he was, obviously, and it would probably seem crazy to claim otherwise. "We're Jewish."

"Oh," said Evie. "Cool."

Ruben smiled uneasily. He feared they had run their conversation to its end and now would sit in silence until the grown-ups returned. But no—Evelyn Keener had opened up somehow. Now she wanted to talk.

"I have this stupid report I'm supposed to do," she said. "On birds. For science. I had to pick a bird and for some random reason I picked emus. It's like—what? Why did I do that?"

"I don't know." Ruben scoured his mind. "Aren't they, like—big?"

"Yeah. I guess. I just started." Evelyn yawned and moved restlessly in her seat, like she was bored of talking about emus and was wondering who had brought them up in the first place. "So wait," she said. "Do you have a mom?"

"Uh..." Another delightful topic. "Well, I have a *biological* mother somewhere. My *adoptive* mother died when I was little. She had cancer."

"That's too bad."

"It's fine. I mean, it's not fine, obviously, but..." He scratched his nose where his glasses sat. "*I'm* fine." He shrugged, trying to show Evelyn she didn't need to pity him. The last thing she needed right now was a dose of *his* tragedy. "You too. I mean—your situation too." Ruben cleared his throat. "I'm really sorry for what you and your family are going through."

"Yeah," said Evelyn and nodded decisively. "It sucks."

Ruben was doing a fine job, he decided, out here in the waiting room. The little sister was content and entertained, and maybe this was even a good sign for how things were going in Jay's office, with the Keeners. Ruben glanced at his watch, and it was after three o'clock. The Classical Poetry Confab had begun. Ms. Hutchins would be asking if we were expecting Ruben today. He wondered whether Annelise McTier had noticed that he wasn't there.

Evelyn had covered her eyes with her hands.

"I haven't gotten to see him."

"What?" Ruben returned his attention to the girl, feeling bad that his mind had wandered.

"My brother. Wes." She uncovered her eyes. "They say he's not feeling well enough to see people yet. But, like, what it sounds like is that he's not even really sick. What my mom was saying was that he was just, like, *different*, somehow."

The word *different* leaped out of the sentence. Ruben, a medium-to-intense devotee of the Fantastic Four and the X-Men, flashed on a comic-book word: *doppelgänger*.

What if the boy's condition was not medical at all? He recalled his father's brief and hesitant description of what he had witnessed in room 906. The boy walking, eyes unseeing, expression fixed. What if Wesley had been replaced, or—or *transformed* somehow?

And then he thought, shut up, Ruben.

Through the thin door of his father's office he heard Shenk's voice, bold and reassuring, saying something about how a lawyer was a promise, a promise forever, and he felt a rush of satisfaction. It was working. He had them.

But Evelyn Keener had started crying. Her cheeks were pink, and her chin was all scrunched up. She raised her hands to her face.

"Hey," said Ruben. "Hey." He got out of his chair and kneeled before her. "Are you OK?"

"*No.*"

She was trembling. Her whole body was shivering. "My brother plays in a band. Did you know that?"

"No, I didn't," said Ruben. "The school band?"

"No," she said adamantly, almost angrily. "A *rock* band. With his friends. He plays *guitar*. He's going to teach me to play guitar. Plus he does wrestling. He's—I don't know. He's my *brother*."

And then she really was crying, no question big-tears crying, her whole body shaking, and Ruben without thinking put his arms around her, and she leaned forward into him, weeping into the stiff cotton of his dress shirt. She smushed her nose into his chest. Ruben wasn't sure if he had ever hugged a girl before. Maybe, like, in kindergarten. And he'd hugged his *mom,* of course, when his mom was alive.

"It's my fault," she told him, and he immediately said "No" and patted her on the back, very delicately. He felt the bones of her spine, a range of small, fragile knobs.

"Yes, it is my fault. When he got hurt, I was just, like, at school." She looked at Ruben helplessly, her face a mess of tears. "I wasn't even *thinking* about him."

"But—I mean—why would you have been?" Ruben said.

"I was drawing horses. With my friend Carmen."

"It's OK," Ruben told her, and he held her. The clients' kid was upset, and she needed someone to hold her, so he held her. He *did* have a purpose in this. There *was* a reason that his father had kept him out of school today and stationed him here. Jay had been right.

"Listen, Evelyn. Hey. My dad is the *best*." He was not authorized to talk this way to clients, but Evelyn wasn't the client, exactly, and anyway this kid was obviously in serious distress. She was shuddering, all bunched up against his chest. "He'll find a way to fix it."

She pulled out of the hug and looked away, embarrassed.

"Sorry," she said, and then "God," and then, noting the slick of snot she had left on his chest, "Yuck."

The door to the inner office opened and the girl's parents came out, with Shenk behind them. Ruben stood up hurriedly and stepped away from the daughter, hot with embarrassment.

"You all right, honey?" said her mom, and Evelyn Keener nodded rapidly. "I'm fine."

She adjusted her hair and stood up. She glanced back at Ruben on the way out, and he realized he'd been wrong. He had thought she was ten or eleven, but actually she was closer to his age. More like twelve or thirteen.

January 15, 2019

1.

There is a version of the story where the events of Jay Shenk's life, in the years following *Keener v. Valley Village Hospital Corporation,* were unavailable to his conscious memory.

A version where he passes through the intervening ten years in a fog of half-life, each day indistinguishable from the one before. In which Shenk in the wake of his career's defining case disappeared into a kind of twilight, walking automatically through his own existence in a manner pointedly analogous to that of Wesley Keener.

But no, no.

Shenk in the aftermath was diminished but not destroyed. He continued to work, and continued to live, and though he ruminated sometimes on the past, sometimes bitterly and sometimes sadly, he never allowed himself to be subsumed in it. He kept on living and working and forming memories, moving as we all do through the long row of days. Taking new cases, hiring and firing assistants, waiting for Malloy to call with his dispatches, each one a pencil-line map leading to treasure from the interior of someone else's calamity. Ruben finished high school and turned eighteen, and then the room where the boy had been was empty.

Slowly Shenk plowed through his midforties and early fifties.

He got older, which could have been predicted, even for Shenk, and by now, by the early months of the futuristic-sounding year of 2019, he felt drafty and creaky, like a barn poorly constructed, wind and rain slipping through the ill-fitting joints. He was the same, except worn and weary; the same, except lost inside a gray haze like low cloud cover; the same, except grief sometimes would come shambling in on its heavy feet and clutch him and hold him down awhile.

At some point Jay gave up on the treadmill. He hung a suit jacket over its handles. At some point the whiskey he favored started to make him feel too bleary in the mornings, and he discovered the more ruminative, less hangover-inducing effects of marijuana, which, as if for his convenience, became not only legal but ubiquitous, for sale in a thousand different forms in brightly lit storefronts.

Physical decrepitude of course could be safely blamed on the passage of time. But what about all the joy? What about the joy that had gone from him, like the water that swirls from the drain when the plug is pulled?

It was out there. Joy, the possibility of joy, an ancient version of himself perfectly preserved, awaiting rescue. A fossil in amber, frozen in time.

The cafeteria of the Superior Court of California was visible from the lobby, and the Rabbi could see the old man waiting.

Ruben Shenk moved slowly through the metal-detector line, emptying his pockets as ordered, submitting to the uncomfortable intimacy of the wand passing over his thighs. His father was in there, tired and gray-headed, one hand on a coffee cup, the other on the table, gently patting it. Looking like he was trying to remember something somebody told him, a long time ago.

As soon as Ruben came over, he gasped: "Oh God, honey, your finger. What happened?"

"Nothing." The Rabbi settled into his seat and made himself absolutely still. "I cut it. That's all."

"It looks pretty bad. Did you need a stitch?"

"No."

"Sweetheart."

"It's fine."

Sweetheart. *Honey.* For God's sake.

The Rabbi, stone-faced, stared down his past.

Give him nothing, he thought. Your face is a wooden face. He looked down at the tip of his index finger, thickly wound in gauze. It probably *had* needed a stitch. Actually. It had been pulsing, as of yesterday morning, a dull intermittent pulse of pain. It was pulsing now. Fuck.

The cafeteria was lit by two long fixtures, which cast a queasy pale yellow light over the scuffed floors. Their table, like all the other tables, was decorated with a chintzy little vase with a couple of bent fake flowers.

"All right, so," said Shenk, pushing a lank lock of hair off his ear. "Can I get you a snack?"

He craned awkwardly around in the plastic chair to gesture at what was on offer behind him: a row of uninspiring pastries, a bunch of fruit cups on ice, a mini-fridge filled with no-brand cartons of milk and juice. There was a hot station, a couple of griddles behind a line of steel warming trays, but the place was pretty deserted, for lunchtime. There were only a couple of workers, both heavily muscled dudes in hairnets and aprons, and they were both over by the cash registers, dicking with their phones.

"No," said the Rabbi to the snack offer—and then, with rigorous formality, added, "Thank you."

"No coffee?"

"*No,*" he said, firm and final, though actually, he could have used a coffee. What he wanted most of all, however, was to accept nothing from his father. Shenk was peering at him with frank affection, his eyes watery and fond. It made Ruben cringe. He shouldn't have come.

But what was he going to do—*not* come?

Yes. What he could have done was say no. He could have known what was best for himself and done that thing.

There was a burst of noise from the other end of the room, and Ruben jerked his head toward it: a sheriff's deputy in regulation LA County khaki had climbed up on a chair to reach the TV, which was bolted to the wall by a metal arm, to turn up the volume or change the channel. The deputy wobbled and the chair's legs danced perilously, scraping on the floor, and the deputy's partner was hollering laughter, not helping. The volume came up, suddenly, a Clippers-Spurs game blasting into the room.

"So," said Ruben suddenly. Here we go. Unto the breach. "You said on the phone that Richard Keener had been arrested."

"Yeah." Shenk nodded. "Yes."

"For what?"

"Uh—" Shenk brought one hand up to his mouth, very quickly, then took it away again, before finishing the tiny, fractured sentence. "Murder."

The Rabbi closed his eyes. He felt things moving inside him. Lord God, just that name—the name *Richard Keener* and the word *murder* with its own ancient shock. *Keener* and *murder,* two words like two stones, banging together.

It was hot in the cafeteria. Too hot. The year had started off a little cold, and Ruben guessed the city had turned on the heat in the courthouse last week, when it dipped below sixty, and now it was like an oven. Jay had sweat at the collar of his shirt, turning his fleshy neck an unhealthy pink. His father, Ruben thought, looked like total shit, his face pale and his long hair now old-man thin. He found the thought satisfying and then, in the next instant, hated himself for the feeling.

Get out of here, Ruben instructed himself. Get up and go.

He pictured himself running. Out there and running. Head down, breathing evenly, not thinking. Wide downtown streets; dirty public parks; the blocks around city hall. Uphill and down. Footfall and footfall and footfall.

"Richard was arraigned last week," said Jay. "But he's being arraigned again this afternoon. In, uh . . ." He looked at his watch. "In twenty minutes."

"Why?"

"Why what?"

"Why are they arraigning him again?"

"Well . . . OK, so . . ."

Shenk trailed off. Forget the way he looked: it was startling to see how slow the famously nimble mind of Jay Shenk had become. Ruben smelled marijuana, sweet and decrepit, and realized with horror that the smell was coming from his father. From his coat? His breath?

"Well, see, Beth—you remember Beth?"

Of course. He remembered them all. He remembered fierce Beth and poor Wesley and—a sliver-gleam of feeling, as clear as birdsong, slicing crossways through his heart—he remembered Evelyn.

"So Beth came to my office. Last week. And she, uh—"

The deputies booed loudly at the TV, and Shenk, startled, stopped talking. Ruben became aware of another table, just next to theirs: a family was settling in with their trays, a man and a woman and two kids, all of them staring sullenly at their ugly plastic-wrapped sandwiches and meager bags of chips.

"Well, OK," said Shenk. "So basically Beth came to my office. Ten days ago. And she told me Rich had been arrested. First-degree murder. Meaning, you know: premeditated."

"I know what it means," said the Rabbi irritably, though he knew what it meant from TV shows and books. "Who did he murder?"

Shenk scratched his head, gliding past the question, and Ruben watched a small dusting of dandruff tumble out of his hair.

"Apparently Richard fired his public defender. In court. Like, *during* the arraignment."

"Why would he do that?"

"Because he wanted to plead guilty. He did it, he confessed, and he doesn't want to put his family through a—you know. A long trial." Shenk massaged his temples, smiling grimly at the part that went without saying: *another* long trial. "But so the public defender told him, you know, *no,* you never plead guilty. On a capital charge, you don't do that. It's craziness. Other kinds of charges, armed robbery or something, you plead out and it maybe gets you a lesser sentence. Save the taxpayer the cost of the trial, all of that. But with murder one? You're getting executed either way, so you might as well force them to prove it." Shenk paused and shook his head, sighed again. "But Richard keeps telling the lady, 'But I did it, I did it.' You know? Basically standing there in court, saying, you know, hey, 'I killed her.'" He stopped, sighed heavily. "And the public defender is like, maybe you want to stop saying that? But this is Richard we're talking about, you know? You remember him. He's, uh . . ."

Ruben's memory supplied a tumble of adjectives. Difficult. Obstinate. Unbending. He remembered how the man's arms had always been crossed, his face always set in some shape of anger or distrust or maligned righteousness.

"Anyway. So he fired this lady, and Beth came in to see if I would take over. The case. Finish it up."

The Rabbi did not respond. He kept his focus on his own body. On his breath, on the individual hammer hits of his heart. This was an old coping mechanism of his, in moments of stress or anxiety, his lasting takeaway from four years of wrestling, wrestling practice, wrestling meets: you can always focus on your body, because it is always there. Listen to it doing its work. The hushed crackle of nerves. The invisible plumbing of circulation. The riverine motion of blood.

It was too hard, though, right now. Here in the sauna heat of this ugly room, windowless and beige, its speckled floors the color of vomit. The basketball game was blaring, unbearable. An argument was brewing at the next table, the man and the woman with their plastic sandwiches starting to get into it. Ruben heard the hiss of the word *bitch,* the sharp smack of a palm on the table.

"You don't practice criminal law, Jay."

Ruben saw Shenk wince at the sound of his first name coming from his son. "Of course I don't."

He'd begun calling his father "Jay" his sophomore year of high school. This was after the private universe of their lives had been exploded. They'd stopped being able to afford Morningstar and Ruben moved to the public school, and buried himself in wrestling, and stopped hanging around at Shenk & Partners, pretending to be a little lawyer.

Then he'd moved out, started his own life, such as it was.

"Did you tell Beth Keener that? That you're not that kind of lawyer?"

"Of *course.* I tried. I said, 'Listen, Beth, this is not what I do. I do civil.' I mean, I always get people calling, for DUI and such, you know, but I tell them, it's like a department store. Shirts and pants are on this floor, housewares are up here. It's a whole different department. But, uh . . ."

Shenk trailed off. Moved his shoulders up and down: *What could I do?*

"I guess she feels that I, uh—I promised."

"Yeah." Ruben sighed. "I remember."

"You do?" Shenk straightened a little. He grinned, and his face became his old face, radiant with the light of the world. "You remember?"

"A lawyer is a promise" is what Shenk had said, a grave and nonsensical commitment, made in the heat of the hunt. Trying to land a sale. "Once I am your lawyer, I will be your lawyer forever."

Shenk looked at his watch, so Ruben looked at his. He twitched at the sound of the sheriff's deputies, hollering again at their game, battering their hands rapidly on the table like drum rolls. Ruben wondered with a flash of irritation where they were supposed to be right now, these guys.

Ruben tried again to take solace in his body, but his body betrayed him. It sent out only signals of pain, the soft agony of his finger, the ancient pain of his right ear, mangled from years of being mashed into the mat.

Shenk started pulling papers from his bag, sliding them onto the table, looking for something. "Richard wants to plead guilty, skip the trial, OK, that's his business. So my job is, I gotta push the sentencing date as far down the road as I can, and then use that time to put together a brief on mitigation. That's a legal term for you. Mitigation. Just meaning, anything we can say to get the judge to lessen Richard's sentence. Get him thirty years, fifty years. Instead of death." Shenk sighed once more, a long, last sigh. "That's the best-case scenario."

He handed over what he'd been looking for, a single sheet of paper, and Ruben ran his eyes along the words at the top. *A mitigating circumstance or factor is any fact or condition that reduces the defendant's blameworthiness or otherwise supports a less severe punishment.*

Ruben ran his bandaged finger down the bulleted list. The circumstances of the crime . . . lack of violent criminal activity in the past . . . was the defendant intoxicated or otherwise impaired . . .

"What did you do, Jay? Did you just print this from the internet?"

"Yes! I did!" Jay barked out a laugh, something a little crazed in it that caused the deputies to look over.

Ruben had noticed what his dad had done. The telltale syllable, the Shenkian devil he'd released into the slipstream of the conversation, disguised as just another fish.

We.

Shenk presuming that Ruben had already agreed to do what Shenk hadn't even asked yet.

Anything we *can say to get the judge to lessen Richard's sentence* . . .

"All right, Jay, let's have it," he said flatly. "What do you want from me?"

"Oh." Jay's smile flickered nervously, like it was plugged in and the cord was slightly loose in the wall. "Well, it's perfect, isn't it? I need some investigation done, on this mitigation stuff. And you know, *I* don't know how to do it, and here my own son is a . . ." He trailed off, opened his palms. "You know."

"No. I don't know." Ruben squinted at his father. What the hell was going on here? "Your own son is a what?"

"A—a private detective."

"No, he's not."

"What?"

"*What?*"

Ruben gaped at his father, and his father gaped back.

"I'm sorry," said Jay. "I don't—you're *not* a private detective?"

"No. Of course I'm not. Where would you..."

Oh Lord. Even as he formed the question, he knew the answer. Ruben was not a social media person and had only been on Twitter for maybe a minute, maybe a year ago, after Sunny heckled him relentlessly for weeks, demanding he join the rest of the fucking human race already. But he hadn't gotten much further than uploading a profile picture (it was Commerce Secretary Wilbur Ross, dozing in a meeting—ironic, get it?, that's not *me*) and it had taken Ruben forty-five relentlessly self-critical minutes to write one of the jokey sentence fragments people use to describe themselves in the text box below their handle.

He had been, at the time, down a rabbit hole of mystery fiction, reading and rereading a handful of crime authors—Ruth Rendell, George Pelecanos, Ross MacDonald—which for whatever reason had suggested to him the halfhearted, self-deprecating pun, which seemed to fit the bill: self-descriptive, brief, and almost-but-not-quite clever.

Private. Defective.

His father had seen it. His father, who of course had been keeping tabs on him over the years. Jay Shenk at the keyboard, at twilight or dawn, his tongue poking from the corner of his mouth, Google searching, tapping one letter at a time. He had seen his son's dumb Twitter account, seen the dumb joke and dumbly taken it for true.

For one hot instant, the Rabbi was alive with love. His father, blinded by feeling, had unquestioningly accepted that he—Ruben Shenk—had actually become a private investigator, that not only had he gotten his shit together and found a career, but one that required guts and smarts and will. A private detective! But of course, as in all things with Shenk, this misplaced faith in his son was driven by ego: Jay believing that Ruben had transformed into Sam Spade was Jay telling Jay a story, allowing himself to think that everything had turned out all right.

Behind them, at the next table, one of the kids was crying. The man shouted, "Shut up," and the woman pleaded with him to keep his voice down. Ruben's eyes sought out the deputies but they were gone, their two trays abandoned like a dereliction of duty. They'd left the TV on.

"I'm not a private detective, Jay. I work at a salad restaurant."

"What is a . . ." Shenk's face wrinkled with confusion. "What is a *salad* restaurant?"

"One of the places where you get a bowl, you pick a protein, and then you—you pick your different toppings and everything. You get a dressing?" He kneaded his temples with his fingers. Now he had to explain fast-casual dining? "It's called Killer Greens."

"Oh. And, what? You own it?"

"No, I don't *own* it. I'm on the line. I do prep."

The Rabbi watched in silence as a gust of disappointment passed across the old man's face. His only son. Fruit of his failure.

"Do you like it?" he asked quietly.

"Sure," Ruben said. "I like it."

This was a lie. He had never thought about it before because no one had ever asked, but no, he did not *like* working at Killer Greens. He had accommodated himself to it. He had over time discovered its satisfying aspects. He liked Sunny. He liked the immersive nature of the work. He liked the neatness, the start and stop, the specificity of the world and the fact that it did not require him to care about anything beyond doing his one job to the best of his ability. Straight chopping. Clear mandate. That was enough.

"OK, Jay. Well. Sorry I can't help you. I'm not a detective."

He pushed his chair back to leave, and Shenk reached across the table and clutched his arm. Ruben jerked it away, scowling.

"Wait, wait, wait. Just a second, son."

"You know what, Jay—"

"You fucking cunt," said the man behind them, and Ruben stopped talking and looked over his shoulder. "You shut your fucking mouth."

The man talking was a wiry dude with a collar of dark tattoos at the base of his neck. Something itchy in his eyes. The woman, pale and tearful, sat nodding meekly, as if in agreement: *Yes, I'm a fucking cunt.* The two kids had turned away from the argument and they faced each other, playing a game of meshed hands, tugging grimly on each other's fingers.

"Please," said Jay, as Ruben turned back—*not my business. Not my story.* "I really need you, son."

"For what? To wash lettuce?"

"Come on," said Jay. "Don't do that, don't run yourself down."

"Stop it."

"What? Stop what?"

Ruben winced. It was too much. The blare of the TV; the heat; the cafeteria stink; his finger, pulsing in its mummy of gauze. It was all too much.

"What?" said Shenk again, and Ruben threw up his hands.

"Flattering me, being sweet—" *Loving me. Being my dad. Stop it.* "Stop."

"*Please,* Rubie." Shenk unceasing, unabating, impossible. "*Please.* It's really, it's just—I need someone smart. Someone who doesn't scare easy. That's you, Ruben. That's *you.*"

Ruben laughed darkly at how far removed his father's version of him was from reality. Someone who doesn't *scare* easy?

But that wasn't the point, of course. None of this was real. Jay

Shenk wasn't looking for a private detective; he was looking for a chance to make everything OK. So he could once again look in the mirror and see a good person. Ruben saw all of this and it was so galling. The presumptuousness of Jay Shenk. Small as he had become, lost inside his suit, it was still him in there. Shenk after all this time doing what Shenk always did: seizing upon a terrible situation and turning it to his own purpose. Yes, he could do a good turn by the Keeners, whom once upon a time he had wronged. *And* he could bend their old resentment of him into a shape resembling forgiveness. *And,* just for bonus points, he could recruit his son to the cause, redeem himself in a whole other arena, bury all their old enmity in new business.

And — and — and —

Ruben felt his dad's charm working on him, the tractor beam of it, the magnetic sweep. Even with the diminishment of years, Jay Shenk was a gravitational force, a dark planet pulling him in. Pulling and pulling.

He had come, hadn't he? Here he was.

There was a sharp snap of sound from behind them, and Ruben wheeled around. He'd hit her: the asshole with the tattoos had smacked the woman, an open-hand shot across the face. He pulled his hand back, quick, like a snake, and stormed out. The woman's face trembled, fear mixed with anger in her eyes. The kids stared at her, scrawny and forlorn.

"Hey," said the Rabbi haltingly to the woman, while his father sat there, slumped and blinking. "You OK?"

"Fuck you, asshole," she said and grabbed her two kids, one with each hand, jerked them up of out their chairs, and left. Ruben watched them go.

His finger had stopped hurting. Maybe, he thought, the nerves had all died.

"Hey. Jay." He spoke quietly. "Who did he kill?"

Shenk looked at his watch, transparently dodging the question. "Geez. I really gotta get up there."

"Jay?"

"What?"

"*Who?*"

Shenk grimaced. Ruben's chest tightened.

"You remember Theresa Pileggi?"

Of course, thought Ruben, and then, immediately, again: Of course.

"Why did he kill her?"

Jay exhaled. "Because he blames her, I guess. He hates her. I guess he's always hated her. I don't know. But, so—can you—Ruben?"

"What?"

"Are you going to help me?"

In Jay's mind, Ruben was sure, it had never even been a question. Of *course* he was going to help. Of course he would say yes.

"No, Jay," he said as he rose to leave. "I'm not."

2.

Judge Elsie Scanlon, of the Los Angeles County Superior Court, appeared from her chambers and moved very quickly to the bench. She sat down, huffed her robes out around her, and rapped her gavel quickly: *pop-pop-pop.*

"All right, then," she said to her clerk, rolling the words together— *allrightthen*—"what do we got?"

"People versus Richard Keener, charge is first-degree murder." The clerk was a prim woman who sat at a low desk just beneath the judge's high one, half-hidden behind a mountain of manila folders.

She seized the top folder and passed it up to Scanlon, who snatched it and snapped it open.

"Right," said the judge. "Keener. Déjà vu all over again."

"Your Honor?" Shenk rose, tentatively holding up one hand. "Respectfully, Your Honor, my name is Jay Shenk, for the defense."

"Hello." Judge Scanlon's head tilted down as she skimmed the complaint, her tiny reading glasses precarious at the end of her nose.

"If it pleases the court, I have limited experience in criminal matters, so I may need on occasion to, uh, to—"

"Shh."

"What?"

Judge Scanlon had a finger over her lips. She was in her seventies, fiery-eyed and skeleton skinny. "Shhh."

"Sorry, I just..." Shenk looked around. The prosecutor was at the other table, stifling laughter. "I was gonna say—"

"Nope."

"What?"

"Stop." Scanlon eyed him evenly over the little glasses. "You're new here, you said?"

"Uh—yes, yes, ma'am. Generally I practice on the civil side. Personal injury, mostly. But I, uh, I have a connection to the family here, and—"

"*Stop.*" The judge waved her hands in Shenk's direction, as if trying to put him on mute. She had some kind of unreconstructed ladies' hairdo, dyed jet-black and swept defiantly upward.

"We're busy here. Busy, busy. You came in through the hallway? You maybe noticed there's a lot going on?"

"Yes, Your Honor."

It was true. Shenk had felt, emerging from the elevator onto the seventh floor, trying to find the right courtroom, like he had stumbled into some sort of chaotic corridor of the damned. Families like the one in the cafeteria, in various states of catastrophe, arguing with one another or huddling with clutched hands, carping at their breathless and overworked defense attorneys.

"We like to keep things moving," Scanlon said. "Chop-chop."

"OK, sure. So—"

"*Sit,* Mr. Shenk."

"I—"

"Sit!" She barked it, like you do for a puppy. "Sit! Sit!"

Shenk sat. He scratched his forehead and looked around the courtroom. He saw Beth Keener, in the same shapeless tan coat and housedress she'd been wearing when she showed up in his office a week ago, resurrected from his distant past, asking him and then beseeching him and finally insisting he come to her aid. Her face had been reshaped by sadness. Sadness and weariness and work. The Keeners had had to sell their place in Studio City and move to a smaller house—not that the Studio City house had been such a palace to begin with, that Shenk could remember. Apparently Beth was cleaning houses, six days a week, except for the weeks when she lived out in the desert, with Wesley. They had him in a cabin or something out there. The details weren't clear.

Shenk steadied his hands on the sides of the rickety lectern thing they gave you in here, to put your papers on. The courtrooms he usually practiced in, the civil courts, they had more windows; sturdier furniture. Just a more high-class experience, all the way around.

Rich was standing just a few feet away, in bright prisoner's orange, hands shackled before him. He did not look at Shenk, or at the judge, or even at Beth. He seemed not to be looking at anything. God, what a reunion, the whole gang of them gathered to witness Shenk's first-ever turn in a criminal court. A command performance for a gathering of ghosts.

"Mr. Thomas?" Scanlon turned her attention to the prosecutor. "Refresh us?"

The lawyer for the State of California hopped up. He was a young and handsome African American man in a cheap blue suit he'd gussied up nicely, with a shiny tie and pocket square. He nodded at Scanlon once quick and said, "It's our understanding the accused is ready to enter a plea of guilty, and the State is prepared therefore to proceed to sentencing." He nodded again, sharp as a razor, and sat.

"OK. Mr. Shank?"

"Shenk."

"Fine."

Scanlon scowled, waved her hands again, generously granting him the pronunciation of his own name. "I seem to recall that Mr. Keener intended to enter this guilty plea against the advice of appointed counsel. Now he's got private counsel. Is it still his intention to so plead?"

"As far as I know."

"As far as you *know*?"

"Yes, ma'am. Yes, Your Honor. Sorry. My client has not, thus far, been open to uh—to communicating. With me. In any way."

"No kidding?"

"No, Your Honor. No kidding."

Shenk tried and failed to make eye contact with his stubborn client. Richard Keener in his jumpsuit wore an expression of stoic dignity, like a captured king. But Shenk was beginning to hope that this efficient, peremptory judge would set the impossible situation to rights: order Richard to act in his own best interests, or maybe bind him over for psychiatric evaluation or something. Could she do that?

"Mr. Keener? Hello?" Scanlon snapped her fingers at the defendant. "You still want to plead guilty?"

Rich nodded, the first indication that he was even paying attention.

"I need it on the record, please. Mr. Keener, do you wish to plead guilty to the murder of"—a glance at the file—"Theresa Pileggi?"

"Yes," said Rich.

"Wait," said Shenk. "If I could just have a moment here."

"Nope."

"But—"

"Sit," the judge said to Shenk, and then, to everyone, "A guilty plea having been entered, we're ready to schedule for sentencing, which by statute occurs twenty days from today, not counting weekends and holidays. Ms. Nguyen? Where does that take us?"

The clerk shuffled rapidly through calendar pages. Shenk, who had just sat down, stood up again. "Uh, excuse me. Your Honor?" He had done his research on this score, put in a call to Herb Schuster, a criminal guy down in Santa Barbara with whom he used to play a little golf.

"The defense respectfully requests a continuance of six months, in order for us to prepare our arguments on capital mitigation."

"Mr. Thomas?"

The prosecutor was up—"Your Honor, the State of California has no objection"—and then down again.

Shenk exhaled. The timeline is pro forma, is what Herb had told him. Everybody pushes it. No one expects anyone to be ready in twenty days for a life-and-death hearing.

"No," said Richard Keener. He was still staring straight ahead. He didn't turn his head to look at the judge, or at Shenk, or anyone else.

"Wait," said Shenk, "hold on," and Judge Scanlon scowled at the defendant and said, "What do you mean, *no?*"

"Twenty days is all right," he said. "We can do it in twenty days."

"Now—hold on—" said Jay. "Wait." He looked pleadingly at Beth where she sat in the benches, and she looked back at him, confused, no help. Shenk pivoted toward the judge, hands in the air. "Your Honor, I object."

"You can't object to your own client, Mr. Shenk."

"Right, but I need *time.* The—sorry, Your Honor. The defense requires more time to prepare. Don't we get more time? If we ask?"

"No," said Rich again. "No more time," and Shenk wheeled back around to him, saying "Richard, come on, *stop,*" and Judge Scanlon smacked her gavel a couple times quick.

Mr. Thomas for the State of California watched all of this with a sly glint. Beth was shaking her head, baffled, twisting the chain of a locket through the intersecting lines of her fingers. She was maybe twenty pounds thinner than on the day Shenk had first seen her, in the lobby of Valley Village Methodist in the autumn of 2008, tearing the head off the dumb-shit apparatchik who'd gotten in her way.

"Your Honor . . ." Shenk began, and Scanlon told him to *hush* again, but at least now she was on his side.

"Mr. Keener, the court strongly recommends you heed your lawyer on this matter."

Rich shook his head, implacable.

"Words, please, Mr. Keener," said the judge. "We need words."

"No. No, thank you."

He was exactly the same. Beth Keener was a tattered copy of her old spitfire self, and God knows what Shenk himself would look like, stood up next to the Shenk of a decade ago. But Richard Keener was the same, solid as old rock. The same.

Shenk was on his feet again. He felt his age in his knees.

"Your Honor, I can't be ready to argue this properly in twenty days. I really can't. Is there anything we can do here?"

"You and I? No, sir," she said, and then stayed ahead of him, not letting him talk. "The right to a speedy trial attaches not to the State, nor even to defendant's counsel, but to the defendant him- or herself."

"Right," said Shenk. "It's just—"

"If the man wants to be sentenced in twenty days, that's what happens."

"But . . . it's like he *wants* to go to prison. To death row." Shenk opened both hands, imploring. "The law can't allow him to do that."

"In point of fact," said the judge, "the law gives me no other choice."

"But . . ."

Shenk stopped. He had nothing to say after *but,* and it didn't matter. Judge Scanlon was done. The gavel came down. She said, "Welcome to criminal court, Mr. Shenk. Ms. Nguyen? What's next?"

The clerk held up a new file and Scanlon snatched it, and Jay watched helplessly as Richard Keener was led out by his elbows.

January 20, 2009

"Uh-oh!" cried Shenk. "Oh boy! Here comes trouble!"

Trouble was coming in the short, squat form of Jackie Benson, chief clerk to Judge Andrew Cates, and it was coming out of the Starbucks on Sixth Street, holding a venti mocha latte, extra whip.

"Don't start with me, Counselor. Don't start."

Ms. Benson scowled playfully and wagged a chubby finger at Jay Shenk.

"I start nothing," he said. "I come in peace. How you doin', gorgeous?"

There were court clerks who scrupulously observed the traditional ethical lines separating them from lawyers who practiced before their judge, but Jackie Benson—whom Shenk had now taken arm in arm, as if on promenade, as they approached the courthouse—was not among them.

"Oh, you know. Got a new cat."

"I saw her on Facebook. Sneakers, right?"

"*Squeakers.*" Jackie guffawed as Jay the gentleman held open the big glass lobby door. "Who names a cat *Sneakers?*"

They waited together for the elevator up to the fifth floor and

Judge Cates's courtroom. Jackie took a careful sip of her latte, and Shenk, daubing a spot of whipped cream off her nose, took advantage of the moment's small, sweet intimacy to make a whispered inquiry. "How's the weather today?"

"Oh, you know," said Jackie. "Mrs. Cates took him sailing, for his birthday."

"Nice. Down at the marina?"

Jackie shook her head. The elevator opened and they got on together. "Catalina."

"*Very* nice. And are the grandchildren in town?"

"All but the oldest."

Shenk grinned up at the tiled ceiling of the elevator. Today was merely the case management conference, the first gathering of all parties in a civil litigation, at which the calendar for the case is established and any small motions can be ruled on, before discovery is opened and the fun and games begin. But it was Jay's long-held belief that the whole tone and tenor of the case are set at the CMC, and thus a relaxed and recharged Judge Cates, fresh from a weekend at sea in the bosom of his nearest and dearest, boded very well indeed.

"Jackie, I must say," said Shenk, one hand upon his heart as they stepped off the elevator. "I've always loved you very much."

"Oh, right. You don't even wear the socks I got you for Christmas."

Shenk gasped, offended. On the threshold of courtroom 5, he tugged up his pants to reveal the very socks in question: lime-green Scottish lisle cotton, patterns of kittens at play.

Thus buoyed, Shenk strode between the aisles of benches and took his place at the plaintiff's table like a man coming home. He set his briefcase at his feet and arranged his folders on the desk, just so, spared a moment to give a warm *how's tricks* wave to Sammy

Beaudreau, the bailiff, and another to toss a salute to the Stars and Stripes that hung between the two banks of high windows, above the great seal of the State of California. He had been in this court-room a hundred times and still always felt a little shiver at the trappings of justice: the vaulted ceilings, the jury box waiting to be filled, Sammy with his badge and gun, the streams of daylight through the great windows. Jay was not naive enough to think of a courtroom as a cathedral, but on days like today — at the dawn of a new case, all parties assembling to seek justice together — it filled him with tremors of awe.

Shenk was in a favorite court-day suit, a well-tailored two-piece of imperial blue, with a pinstripe of such exceeding nuance that it could only be seen when he stood in just the right shaft of window light.

"Mr. Riggs, I presume?" Shenk turned to the heavyset man set-ting down his own briefcase at the defense table and leaned across to stick out his hand. "Jay Shenk."

"Yes." The man looked at Jay's hand for a lingering moment and then took it grudgingly. "John Riggs. Telemacher."

"Oh, I know. Your reputation precedes you."

Riggs raised both eyebrows in justified skepticism. Indeed, though Shenk by this point had seen the man's name atop the various reply briefs in *Keener,* all he really knew of this particular law monkey was that he toiled in overpaid obscurity at Telemacher, Goldenstein, the fat-cat Beverly Hills firm that handled Wellbridge, the general and malpractice insurer of Valley Village Hospital.

"I look forward to working with you," said Shenk with a wink — this being another of his favorite opening lines for opposing counsel, a sly acknowledgment that, though they were not colleagues per se, their working lives would be yoked for the months and even years over which a complex civil litigation like this might play out.

But Riggs's expression—eyebrows up, mouth slightly tightened—did not change. "Really?" he said, and before Shenk could find a way to parry this uninspiring reply, Sammy told everybody to rise.

"Good morning, good morning, everyone," said Judge Andrew Cates, striding up the stairs to the bench, his mane of hair shock white against the black of his robes, his vigorous old-man features looking indeed very slightly tanned. "Have a seat."

Cates settled with a significant exhale into his own high-backed chair and then said nothing—for one long moment that dragged into another and then another—while the courtroom waited. He trained his eyes on the short stack of paperwork in front of him and read through it, page after page, with one long finger moving slowly down the lines of text. Presumably he was reading Shenk's suit and the defense's answer, although for all anyone knew out in the courtroom, silently watching him read, it could have been some other case, or a Ray Bradbury story, or a recipe for chicken à la king. He read slowly, with furrowed brow, tapping his chin and quietly humming something from *La Traviata*. Occasionally he stopped, selected a number-two pencil from the little cord of them on his desk, licked its tip, and added an underline or annotation.

It would have made more sense to review these documents *prior* to the hearing, of course, but that would have deprived Cates of the opportunity to hold a room full of people in respectful abeyance, waiting for him to finish. Midway through this performance, Shenk looked over at opposing counsel in search of a moment of lawyerly solidarity: *Good ol' Cates, huh?* But Riggs was having none of it; he returned Shenk's conspiratorial wink with a small pucker of distaste and kept his own eyes focused straight ahead.

"Interesting," said Cates at last, looking up at some ruminative spot over the head of the litigants. "*Very* interesting."

Shenk smiled. Classic. Andrew Cates saw himself as a great scholar, an eminent professor of constitutional law who by some twist of fickle fate had ended up on the state superior court, entertaining motions on slip-and-falls and med-mals.

"Mr. Shenk," he said at last, tilting his chair down and looking over the edge of his glasses at Jay, who jumped up.

"Yes, Your Honor."

"How does the court find you, Mr. Shenk?"

"Very well, sir. And how is the court?"

"Oh, fine," said Judge Cates, puffing out his cheeks, giving the matter due consideration. "Just fine. Before we begin in earnest, Counselor, I wonder if you have brought with you today any soup?"

Jay laughed out loud, and so did Sammy the bailiff and Ms. Benson the clerk. Even Judge Cates, trying to remain deadpan, cracked his old granite face into a puckish grin.

Oh, this is good, thought Jay. Very good.

"Inside joke," he murmured to Riggs, who blinked back at him, bemused.

When last Jay Shenk stood in courtroom 5, it had been on behalf of a union carpenter named Jerry Mulcahy, who'd lost the use of his right hand after a disastrous reconstructive surgery. In his direct examination of his expert witness, a stiff-necked but highly articulate professor of medical ethics from Stanford, Shenk had elucidated the theory of multiple culpability by drawing a metaphor to a bouillabaisse: there may be a variety of ingredients (to a soup, that is, or to an unsuspecting carpenter's carpal neuropathology), but there are always *certain* ingredients (medical errors) that *must* be present in order for the soup to be delicious (or for the accident to be debilitating and therefore deserving of compensatory damages).

His opposing counsel, Nick Harden of Wildman, Casher, Teller,

Bauman, had risen repeatedly to object; objections as to relevance, as to vagueness, as to the line of questioning's generally florid and digressive quality. Judge Cates had sustained all of these objections—his gnarled hands whanging the gavel down repeatedly in Harden's favor—and finally ordered Shenk, in his exaggeratedly slow warning voice, to "give it a rest with the damn soup." But the *Mulcahy* jury had eaten it up, so to speak. They had sparked to the soup analogy and had rooted for him every time he brought it up, even in the face of Cates's admonitions. They were smiling away over there, chuckling and glancing at one another and nodding those tiny nods of agreement where a juryman doesn't even know he's nodding, but which Shenk, as echo-responsive as any bat, could feel on the atmosphere between him and the box. All of which is to say that even after Harden's umpteenth objection, even after Cates's umpteenth "sustained," Shenk had risen solemnly for the redirect of the Stanford guy, walked slowly over to the witness box, and said, "Some tough questions there, huh? You were really in the soup."

Mulcahy the carpenter, by the way, came home with the maximum allowable $250,000 for pain and suffering, plus another $150,000 on lost wages, and somewhere north of $225,000 on a life-care plan, exactly the terms Shenk's expert had proposed.

Mulcahy had been a grand little victory, and the fact that now, today, Cates was making soup jokes from the bench seemed to indicate that all was forgiven. His annoyance at Shenk's performance during *Mulcahy* would not be taken out on him and his new clients. For the *Keener* matter, a tabula rasa.

"Now." Cates placed one hand on the papers in front of him. "As to today's business. Mr. Shenk. Mr.—" Checking the file, tapping his chin, taking his time. "*Riggs*. Before we ask Ms. Benson to work her usual magic and find us a court date, I offer you both my customary entreaty. As you proceed with discovery, stay in contact with each other. *Communicate.* If there is any way to come to an accommodation, I hope that you will do so. In other words..." He leaned forward in his chair, stern and solemn as a Civil War general. "For God's sake, *settle.*"

If there was one thing trial judges hated, it was going to trial. Andrew Cates, like many judges, saw the long period of discovery and depositions as a chance for the parties to come together, compare their respective desires, and—with or without the help of a mediator—find a way to save the State of California the considerable time and expense of summoning a jury and hosting an actual trial. Shenk could not agree more. There was fun to be had in the dog and pony show, of course, but a jury trial was an expensive proposition and the satisfaction of a courtroom victory could not compare to that of settling. Strike the deal, cash the check, and move on to the next adventure.

"Very well," said Cates, his point made. "Ms. Benson, it is calendar time."

"Your Honor?" said John Riggs, lumbering to his feet. "If I may?"

"What is it, Counselor?" said Cates, and Shenk in his seat felt a cool wash of unease. If he may *what*?

"Your Honor, the defense moves for summary judgment."

Shenk leaped up, both arms raised, astonished. "What?" He turned to Riggs. "What is this?"

"Mr. Shenk," said Cates, and found his gavel and gave it a tap. "If you please."

"Sorry," said Shenk. He turned to Riggs, astonished, and then back at the judge. "Sorry, Your Honor. But I, uh—" He reached up and adjusted his ponytail, pulled it taut, gathering himself together. "Your Honor, we are at conference here. This case is just getting going. No depositions have been taken. We reserve our right, unless I'm missing something, to add additional defendants, if and when new evidence is discovered. So, I mean, Your Honor, surely a request for dismissal is premature." He looked at Riggs pointedly. "Surely it is *vastly* premature."

Shenk opened his hands and ducked his head to await vindication.

"Well..." said Cates, and then paused. He turned his eyes up toward the high ceiling of courtroom 5 and tilted his head back and forth slowly a couple of times. Shenk, his astonishment deepening, looked at Jackie Benson, who looked back at him and shrugged.

Judge Cates should be *laughing* at Riggs. He should be sternly upbraiding him for his presumptuousness. The idea of dismissing a case like this one, where grievous harm had been done to a minor child—dismissing it prior to any substantive briefing—dismissing it before a single deposition was taken—well, it was absolutely bonkers, and this Riggs clown had to know that it was bonkers.

And yet, Cates seemed very much to be considering it.

"Mr. Riggs," he inquired finally. "On what grounds?"

"Respectfully, Your Honor, plaintiff has not proven any allegations of misconduct. And—"

"Your Honor!" Shenk shot out of his chair. Of *course* he hadn't proved anything! It was day fucking one! Cates shook his head and pointed Shenk back to his chair. "Your adversary has the floor, sir."

"Yes, but—Judge."

"*Hey.* Counsel has the floor."

Shenk sat, fuming.

"Moreover," said Riggs, and if he was pleased with his victory, his pleasure did not alter his tone. "As briefing indicates, and as Your Honor may have gathered from press coverage of this case, Wesley Keener's condition is both tragic and entirely unprecedented."

The news coverage had been extensive, to say the least. In the three months since Wesley's accident and subsequent surgery—

three months during which Shenk & Partners had been absorbed with drafting the notice of complaint, with writing preliminary briefs and doing background research, with filing the lawsuit proper—the wider world, inevitably, had discovered the story. There had been newspaper articles; magazine pieces; all manner of clickbait website features. Here was this handsome high school student, in the heart of sunny Southern California, who had suffered an accident and been plunged along with his family into a waking nightmare. His condition utterly bizarre and utterly impossible to explain.

Every news item found space for breathless descriptions of the boy in room 906, walking in his endless circle, never sleeping, never eating. Never slowing down or speeding up, never stopping, never growing tired. And the questions—so many questions: urgent, prurient, provocative. What was happening inside his head? What about his metabolism? Was he growing? What about the bathroom? One monstrous photojournalist, working on assignment for some scumbag British tabloid, had managed with a telephoto lens to get a shot of Wesley through the hospital room window, captured him in his endless slow-motion circuit, face frozen, eyes dead. The picture had been viewed millions of times, tweeted and retweeted, posted and shared.

"Which is to say," Riggs continued in his disinterested drone, "that the plaintiff's contention, that it was medical malpractice which led to the child's condition, is not only unproven. It is *unprovable*. If, as I believe we can stipulate, this condition has never been seen before, then it was impossible for Wesley's doctors to predict or prevent it. Ipso facto."

Shenk was dying. He was seething in his seat. "Your Honor, may I *please*."

Cates allowed it with a deep nod of his head, and Shenk sprang up.

"Due respect to Mr. Riggs," Jay started, looking sideways at his opponent in his ugly brown suit. "But that argument comes from backwards town. It is *precisely* the unusual nature of Wesley's condition that demands the cause be discovered and proper recompense be made."

Shenk stood for another moment, thinking whether he had more to say, hot with his own righteousness. *Ipso facto? Fuck you with your ipso facto!*

Cates tilted way back again in his chair, taking a long moment to weigh the matter, murmuring a snatch of *Tosca* just loud enough for the whole courtroom to hear, the low *bum bum bum* taking on a foreboding air as Shenk waited for him to pass judgment. Flabbergasted that this motion was even being *considered,* Shenk looked again at Jackie Benson, who over the lip of her Starbucks cup mouthed a *wow* of solidarity.

"The motion . . ." said the judge slowly, building tension into the moment of decision, " . . . is denied."

Shenk exhaled, feeling how tense he had become only now that the tension had been relieved. He had been thinking, he realized, of Beth Keener, and of her husband, of having to tell them it was over before it began.

"However," Judge Cates continued. "Defense counsel's point is well taken. I do struggle at this moment to see how tortious cause can be definitively proved for a condition that is, by all appearances . . ."

Cates trailed off and sighed, and then picked up the thought, his voice gruff with uncertainty. "By all appearances impossible to explain."

What wild winds were blowing inside Jay Shenk as he took breath to respond? What intermingling hurricanes of humiliation, irritation, excitement, and fear? Whatever was happening within, he only rose again, very calmly this time, and smiled as wide as ever, and said:

"Yes, Your Honor." The smile growing broader: "*Thank you, Your Honor.*"

On the way out, he placed a hand on Riggs's thick shoulder and left it there, even as the other man stared at him, baffled by this affability. "Hey, listen," he said. "*Good luck.*"

Here again, perhaps, was a moment Shenk might have taken as a sign. The close call of Cates's decision, the hard road the judge predicted. Shenk could have folded up his tents then and there and slinked away, at the sacrifice of merely a few months and a few thousand dollars.

Instead Shenk read Cates's ruling on the motion for summary judgment by the light of his undimmable crusader's optimism. He took this rote procedural victory as a signal that the world was lining up his way, that he was at the starting line of a race he would win.

He misread the portents. He dove in blind. The judge swung the gavel and away he went.

February 18, 2009

Just for himself personally, Shenk could not fathom why anyone was still going to the mall. Amazon and eBay and all these other places had made it so one didn't have to go to an actual physical place, stand in lines with other people, buy clothes after other people had pawed at them and flung them back in crumpled piles.

But here he was today, riding a series of switchback escalators up into the massive dull-stone cathedral of the Westfield Fashion Square. A man on a mission, fully cognizant of how ridiculous he was, like a satirical character from a movie comedy: the middle-aged dude trying to slyly sidle his way into the lives of today's youth. One did what one needed to do, so here he was at 3:20 on a Wednesday afternoon, searching for four particular teenage boys, known widely — or so Shenk's sources had informed him — to hang out here after school.

"Gentlemen," he said, when his sources had been proven out. "Can I talk to you for just a moment or two?"

The teenagers were gathered in a ragged circle around a clump of plastic tables, each with his own tray of fast-food garbage: chicken fingers on red plastic trays, taquitos piled up in a paper bucket like too many passengers stuffed into a fishing boat, sodas as big as washtubs. These were Wesley's friends, the other members of his fledgling rock band, and, crucially, these were those who had been hanging out with him at the time of his accident, way back at the beginning of the school year.

One of them, a bony white kid with a mop of dark hair and smudged round glasses, cleared his throat and said, "Um," and then—"You're the lawyer?"

"I am, yeah. Jay Shenk." The boy put down his pizza slice and shook Shenk's hand with a greasy palm. "I'm working with the Keeners."

"Sure, sure," said another of the boys, an Asian kid with a silver stud earring in one ear. He leaned back in his chair, slid a French fry into his mouth. "I saw you in the paper."

"Ah," said Jay. "Of course."

Jay Shenk was no spotlight hog, not drawn like a certain class of attorney to the fickle flash of media attention, but he had, inevitably, been a sideline presence in more than one media story about the weird case of Wes Keener. That's how they knew him, these fellas, and they eyed him up and down. Obviously they had been told not to engage with strangers asking questions about Wesley. But a lawyer was different, right? A lawyer working for their friend's family.

"All right—so—how can we help you?" said the first kid, the skinny one with the glasses.

"Do you mind if I sit?"

Shenk, in point of fact, was already sitting. He had draped his suit jacket over a chair beside him, just one of the gang. Just a dude with a ponytail, a generation older, hanging out at the mall. "What I want is information. That's it. To do my job properly, I need all the relevant information, and I'm hoping you guys can help me out with that."

The clutch of dudes stared back at him.

They were a motley crew, thought Jay fondly, but show me the group of fourteen-year-old boys who are not. Sparse patches of facial hair, scuffed shoes, jeans with holes. Their bodies still figuring out what shape they would one day take, when they were done with growth spurts, when they had figured out to some extent the relationship between diet and appearance, when the acne had cleared up, when they'd learned the transformative value of a decent haircut.

His own son, Jay reflected modestly, was better turned out. Ruben tucked his shirts in; Ruben combed his hair. If anything, Ruben could do with a little roughing around the edges, a little bit of wandering to the mall after school to eat nonsense food and crack jokes with other awkward teenagers. Jesus—what *did* his son do after school? Was there even a mall near them? He thought with a quick grievous rush of panic that he didn't *know* what his son did after school, but then he remembered: He hangs out with me! He works at the law firm!

Oh, and poems! He does that poetry thing. He loves that. Jay smiled, shaking his head. His fucking kid. Beautiful ridiculous boy.

"Listen, man," said one of the boys who had not spoken yet. He was a green-eyed blond kid, thickset and sturdy, with the faintest outline of a mustache above what were still a baby's fat red lips. "We already *said* what happened." The way the other boys angled toward him as he spoke, Jay wondered if this kid was the leader, the alpha, to the extent that these mild-mannered music nerds operated in any kind of traditional male pack.

"We told Wes's mom the whole story. And the doctors. Like— months ago."

"Yeah, I know. I know. I've read your statements! I read everything."

Shenk winked, and then, pulling a mischievous face, snagged a ketchup-soaked chicken finger. "Sorry, what's your name?"

They introduced themselves, one by one, each mumblier than the last. The blond was Noah; the gangly four-eyes was Bernie; the Asian kid was Cal; the last one, Marco, wore a sleeveless T-shirt and had a pen-drawn tattoo of an octopus high up on his arm.

"All right. Nice to meet you guys officially. I'm Jay. And you're going to be hearing from a bunch of lawyers, believe me. But just so you know: My whole job is to help Wesley. Wesley and his family."

"Meaning, get them a bunch of money," said Noah brazenly— testing the boundaries, seeing what exactly the lines of authority were in this situation.

Shenk nodded evenly, looking back at the kid, just as brazenly. "Yes, sir. *And* get them a bunch of money. A *shitload* of money, if I do my job right."

He grinned. Cal laughed. Marco and Bernie looked at Noah to see if they were supposed to laugh, but Noah had twisted his mouth sourly to the side and crossed his arms, so they did not.

"But really, I just want to make sure I understand everything that happened that day."

Noah kept his arms folded. But Marco shrugged and started talking, and the others chimed in as he went, tossing in details. It had happened during the lunch period, after everyone had eaten. They were in the courtyard outside the cafeteria, near the Cans—the color-coded garbage area, one can for regular trash, one for plastic and glass, one for paper and cardboard—and they were rough-housing, just "dicking around," as Marco said. They were arguing, as they had been doing since the summer, over what to name their garage-punk five-piece, and Wesley had rated Cal's latest suggestion,

Baby Genius, as "idiotic," insisting once again on the name he'd been stuck on for weeks, which was the Reverse Psychologists.

But Cal said that sounded gay—that's what everyone remembered Cal saying except for Cal, who now in the presence of the strange adult protested that he wouldn't have used the word *gay* like that, as a slur or whatever—but the point is, this argument degenerated into a fight—

"But not a *real* fight," Marco clarified. "Just like—dicking around. Like I said."

"Just playing, basically," Bernie agreed emphatically, and Cal said, "You know?"

You know was more than a rhetorical hiccup, Shenk understood. *Did* he know? They *needed* him to know that they hadn't been fighting, not for real. This wasn't that sort of friend group, bullet-headed and belligerent, play-violence pawing on the edges of the real thing.

No. These boys, Wesley included, these were not those boys—these were the boys who hung out after school drinking soda and arguing about how overrated, exactly, Green Day is. Who wrote shitty poems in the margins of their science homework, and later set them to four-chord progressions in Cal's basement. Who maybe every once in a while stole cigarettes from Cal's dad, but they didn't even like them really and can you please not tell anyone?

"Of course," said Shenk. "I get it. You were goofing around, and Wes got hurt."

"*Yes,*" said Cal, and even wary Noah said, "Yeah," and Bernie nodded mournfully at his tray.

Wesley Keener had been chasing after Bernie, charging after him with his head down, like a bull, and Bernie had ducked out of the way, right at the last minute. Wes slammed his head on the corner of the bench and fell to the ground.

All the boys went silent at the memory of the decisive moment. The instant that will not change, that will never change, that will live forever every time they thought about school, about childhood, about being a freshman and being fourteen. The terrible thing that happened, the thing that will never not have happened.

Their friend since first grade, friend and guitarist and lyricist, cracked his head into the corner of a bench and fell down hard. Mouth open, eyes open, flat on the ground. He wasn't dead— God, for a second they thought he was, but then Cal put his head to Wes's chest to make sure—but he was unconscious, breathing shallow, with a froth of spit at the corners of his lips.

"And we were all like—" Cal began, and Noah said, "Shut up," and Cal turned to him and said, with bitter force, "*Fuck you.*"

"It's OK, guys." Shenk the mediator. Father to them all. "It's OK. I *know* this is hard."

Noah tightened his crossed arms and rolled his eyes. Shenk stayed with Cal: "You were all like, what?"

"We were all really scared. OK?" Cal dared a look at Noah, who took a bite of his cheeseburger, ignoring him. "It was just really scary."

"I'll bet it was."

The one called Bernie, Shenk noticed, had gone quiet.

Shenk didn't remark on it, didn't turn to the lad and ask him, *Why so quiet? What are you not saying?* Bernie had receded from the conversation and Shenk let him recede. Let him process whatever he was processing.

He pressed on, meanwhile, with the other boys. Did the school call 911 right away, or did they take Wesley to the nurse or something first? (Right away.) How long did it take for emergency services to arrive? ("Like, maybe five minutes? Four minutes? It was really fast.")

Shenk didn't know what he was looking for. Shenk was looking for everything. You scratched every surface, never knowing what might bubble up. For example:

"Had Wesley ever experienced anything like this before?" he asked, for no particular reason, going down his list, but then Marco gasped, literally *gasped*.

Shenk's eyebrows jumped. "Is that a yes?"

Marco nodded. He pushed his hands into his hair. "In gym. Playing soccer."

"When?"

"Three weeks ago. He ran into Glenn Volpe and they banged heads. *Hard.* But, like—he didn't black out or anything, I don't think. Remember?" Marco said, turning to Cal for backup, but Cal shrugged, kept eating his fries. Shenk kept his eyes on Marco.

"Did you tell the paramedics about this incident, when they arrived?"

"No." He shook his head, worried. "But, I mean—they didn't ask."

Shenk smiled at him tenderly. "It's OK. It's probably nothing."

And it *was* probably nothing, but it was the kind of nothing that could be dressed up as something. If the paramedics had failed to do a comprehensive intake—comprehensive enough to include other recent head injuries—then what else might they have missed? What other crucial information might never have reached the doctors at Valley Village?

Almost certainly, Wesley having bonked noggins with some other dude in PE wasn't relevant; just as likely, Shenk in settlement talks could make it seem like it was.

He patted Marco gratefully on the hand, filing the nugget away, and moved on. What was Wesley like until the ambulance came?

"He wasn't like anything," answered Noah, suddenly, fiercely, with bright, angry tears in his eyes, and then he said it again. "He wasn't like *anything*."

Shenk was reminded how young fourteen was. A fourteen-year-old is a baffled monster, cursed by the gods, the heart of a child in the body of a man. "He was just lying there, OK? Like Cal said." He distorted his voice into that of a moony idiot, a brutally sarcastic dismissal of all sentimentality. "And we were all just so scared. I peed. Actually. OK? Satisfied?"

"Yup," said Shenk, rising, tapping the table, graciously submitting to his dismissal, knowing well what was next. "Of course."

Shenk didn't warn the boys that they were all going to be deposed. He would have to contact their parents to make those arrangements. He said goodbye and left them to their junk-food bonanza and began the long journey across the mall back to his car.

He took his time. He inhaled deeply of the scent of Cinnabon. He lingered at storefront windows, captivated by the wares on display at Old Navy and at Kay Jewelers. He carefully examined the cell-phone cases and screen protectors at the various kiosks. Glancing occasionally over his shoulder, seeking the pursuer he felt sure was coming.

"Uh — Mr. Shenk?"

Jay smiled. Bingo. He was just getting on the escalator that fed down to the parking garage, and here came a voice behind him. "Mr. Shenk, sorry, I . . ."

The boy caught the lip of the escalator and almost crashed into his back.

"Oh," said Shenk, as surprised as he could be, "Bernie."

"Do you have another second?"

"I do. Here. Roll off with me."

The escalator delivered them to a mezzanine level, between the lowest level of the mall and the first of the garage, where it was just them and a smudged glass window looking out into nothing, just them and the parking-ticket-payment machine making its shrill periodic beep.

Shenk looked at Bernie with kindness: "What is it?"

"Yeah, no, it's just..."

Shenk waited. Bernie exhaled heavily, blowing a feathery forelock up out of his eyes. He was a gangle of arms and legs, the kind of string-bean adolescent who would grow up to be either unattractively thin or ropily muscled and athletic. Shenk wished for him the latter and feared the former.

"He, uh." Bernie squeezed his eyes shut tight behind his glasses before he went on. "He was glowing."

Shenk, who was never taken aback, was taken aback.

"What?"

Bernie opened his eyes again. "So he hit his head, right, on the bench, like Marco said. And then before he went down he, like..." Bernie looked pleadingly at Shenk: *Believe me. Please.* "He was glowing." He looked down. "It's hard to explain."

"It's OK. Can you try?"

"I don't—I'm sorry... it was like—OK, have you ever seen one of those fish, or a picture of one, where it's like they are lit from the inside? Like a—what do you call it. It starts with *p*."

"Phosphorescence," Jay hazarded. Bernie nodded.

"Yeah. I swear it was like..." The boy trailed off, miserable.

"Like what?"

"Like there was something inside of him, like some kind of something, a spirit or something, and it was trying to come out."

"Hey," said Jay. "Hey. It's OK. How long did it last?"

"Like—a second? An instant. I don't know. And then it was gone."

"The other boys see it?"

"I don't know. I bet——" He looked off to one side, pretended to study the ticket machine, shook his head. "They'll say they didn't. Whether thcy did or not."

"Huh."

"Yeah."

"Did you tell anyone? Did you tell the EMTs when they came?"

He shook his head. "I mean . . ." he started, and hardly needed to finish. What would they have said? What was Jay even going to say now?

"And——are you——I'm sorry to ask you this, Bernie, but are you *sure*?"

"Yeah." The child looked right at him and stuck out his lower lip a little bit, daring himself to be courageous. "I am totally sure."

"OK. Bernie." Jay put out his hand. "Young man. Thank you."

Bernie shook his hand.

Now, sadly, of course, this was not going to be information that he could use. It was of questionable relevance, from a legal standpoint, and also what the fuck was this kid talking about——he *glowed*?

But still. He let go of the handshake and opened up his arms—— a father's arms as much as a lawyer's——and clasped Bernie very briefly to his chest.

January 16, 2019

1.

Evie — Evie the Haunted — Evie the Sublime — murmured, "Thank you," in a cool whisper and then "Thank you all for coming," and then played a single chord and let it ring.

It rang distorted and loud, and because of the sustain pedal the chord did not fade or threaten to fade, but hung there slowly growing, getting louder and more opulent, while stray whoops and shouts sprouted in the packed darkness of the Echo, someone shouting her name and someone shouting "I love you," someone giggling and someone else telling the giggler to shut up, and all the while the chord was swelling above them, a D played in drop-D tuning, a chord of rich and echoing majesty, and because Evie — Evie of Kindness, Evie of Love — had sounded the chord not only through the sustain but also through a fuzz pedal that had roughed it up, muddied the chord around its edges, there was something ugly in it, something probing and hard to withstand, an unsettled and mysterious chord expanding in slow motion, moving over the crowded Echo like dark weather, rolling out above the heads of the audience and then coming down into the lungs, reverberating in the rib cage, echoing in the skull until it became almost unbear-able, everybody growing silent now and just waiting for the chord to resolve, for a drum to be played, for something or anything to happen.

Then Evie sang. Just one syllable, the first syllable of a lyric line that was only seven syllables long but which she had dreamed up as a kind of endurance test, a marathon, an event—

"No..."

—she sang, and it was a D, not a harmony or even an octave up, but the exact same low D that anchored the chord that was still ringing out unceasing, a spell begging to be broken—

"...body..."

And lo she had made a word, that one word *nobody* a three-note melody lolling upon a spectral pillow of drop D, and her band at last began to come in behind her: drums first, that longed-for single snare hit and then a second, putting in a waltz time but slow, so slow, with such intervals between snare hits that it was not a rhythm at all yet, just a hint, an invisible time signature, a reminder that such a thing as rhythm existed—and then another guitar, Aimee's Strat slashing in another D chord to join Evie's—and then Evie sang the next word,

"feels"

And the chord *resolved,* gloriously, from D to G, shifting from the five to the one like everyone had been dying in their bones for it to do, whether they knew it or not, and the song had been joined in earnest, and it moved in a slow and stately roll, the drums still all snare, the waltz time a guaranteed fact now as Bernie's bass came in, a loop, a circle of notes climbing up and down a six-note lattice connecting D and G, and Evie finished the line,

"any pain..."

And the world exploded at the release, the *arrival,* and Evie sang it again, finding the real full golden melody, the ancient Bob Dylan melody she'd stolen and made her own.

"Nobody feels any pain..."

And the band was speeding up now, falling into time, and once more she sang it:

"Nobody feels any pain..."

This was the song, this was all of it, again and again forever. She would never move to the second line of the Dylan song, she would sing *nobody feels any pain* forever. The crowd caught on and began to sing it along with her, all her invisible lovers out in the darkness, everyone chanting the melody together while the band churned along on the rails it had built.

"Nobody! Feels! Any pain!"

"Nobody! Feels! Any pain!"

And now Evie stopped singing and turned away, for she had given it unto the crowd and they gave it back to her:

"Nobody! Feels! Any pain!"

After which Evie—Evie the Elusive—Evie the Good—Evie in her wings gritted her teeth and tilted her head up toward the lights and felt the heat in all of her bones.

It was a new song for her, only a couple of weeks old, a cover but not really a cover. The Dylan song was long a favorite, it was a ray of light, a slow forest fire, but neither could Evie in good conscience embrace it, not as canon, this story of a strong woman who is built up and built up only to be melted down on every chorus. So Evie the Sly—Evie the Conjurer—had, at a show a few weeks ago, found a way to do it, to swipe it and swap it out, strip it down and rebuild it. She made the opening line a song in and of itself, she just sank into the cool beauty of the four words, of her own voice singing them low and clear, and now her loves came with her, singing, chanting:

"Nobody feels any pain!"

The crowd was in motion as they sang, surging back and forth, leaping up and down, moving as a unit, a wave.

"Nobody feels any pain!"

The guitars and the bass and organ rising together like high water, the drums like the rattling of a hundred doors, the four-word melody transformed into an incantation, the incantation into an exhortation, a battle cry, a howl—and though she was at the center of it, the swelling in Evie's heart was the same as felt all over the room, the swelling of love and the unbearable ache—

—and you might have thought that in this crash and wash of noise, Evie Keener with her back to the crowd, she would never have heard, amid the massed voices of that room, one particular voice saying two words—and not only hear the voice but make out the words and know exactly who it was.

"Holy shit," said the quiet, calm voice, and Evie stopped playing. She turned slowly around to face the crowd again.

The band fell away: the drums first fell out of rhythm and then disappeared after firing a few final shots; and then Aimee laid her hand flat against the strings of her guitar to silence it; and then the organ, too, and only the bass was left: Bernie playing a half measure alone before he noticed that everyone else had stopped.

Evie scanned the crowd, holding her breath, searching.

Later, people who'd been in the crowd that night remembered being scared that it had happened to her now, too, what had happened to her brother all those years ago. Because that was part of Evie's story, of her persona: her burgeoning celebrity flecked with the grit of tragedy, whispered from fan to fan, elaborated on Twitter and the websites: *It's fucking* crazy, *when she was a kid . . . have you heard, her brother . . .*

And now here she was, frozen with her pick hand in the air, her eyes moving as if automatically over the audience, her mouth half-open, mute.

But then the spell broke. Evie gave a small, quick cantering laugh of surprise and said, "*Ruben?*"

2.

"What I flat-out fucking refuse to do is be one of these people who is like, why me? Like—my life is so hard, I can't believe this is happening to *me*. I seriously refuse to be that person."

Evie Keener, in the dim dressing-room light, shook her head with angry annoyance at this self-pitying version of herself she had conjured. Ruben just gazed at her, nodding quietly. He hadn't said much, not yet, dizzy and dazzled as he was to be in her presence after the long passage of years. He'd hardly taken a breath since coming into the dressing room, since sitting down on the wobbly stool Evie had pointed to, across from herself at the big hot-light vanity table with mirror attached.

"You gotta know how lucky you are. Right?" As she spoke, Evie peeled off the wings of lace and wire she'd been wearing to perform, tugging them off her shoulders one strap at a time. "A lot of people have suffered a lot worse."

"I suppose that's true." Ruben's voice came out as a murmur.

"It is, dude. It is a hundred percent true." Under the wings, Evie wore a camisole, sheer and tight as a stocking. "The universe does not revolve around *me*. Oh my God, Ruben—your *finger*. What happened?"

"Oh. What? Nothing."

He looked down at his hand. His circumcised forefinger, the tip still bundled in its cap of white gauze. "It's fine. I cut it with a knife." And then, hurriedly, lest she think—well, who knows?— "It was an accident. At work. I'm fine."

It was probably long past time for Ruben to take off the bandage. See what was going on. But he was frankly afraid of whatever horror show was happening underneath. So he had been showering with one hand held out of the stream of the water, changing clothes carefully so as to not disturb the bulge of casing.

Ruben said he was fine again and glanced at Evie, then looked away, awestruck. It wasn't just the stage lights, the tight jeans and the camisole and the costume wings. She was hot. This was a fact. She had grown up to be very hot.

Reading his mind, Evie intercepted the compliment and reversed it. "It's good to see you," she said. "You look really good."

Ruben winced. He was not interested in pretending that he looked good, even to the extent of acknowledging the kind words. He reached up, brushed a knuckle against his stupid, messed-up ear. He looked down at his wounded hand. There were flecks of carrot skin under his thumbnails. His palms were stained the melancholy purple of beet juice.

"Thanks," he murmured at last.

Other people filtered into the room, fussing with their phones or talking in soft voices, as if, after the loudness of the stage, the balance of the universe required a library hush in the dressing room. Evie's lanky bass player settled down on a couch, still wearing his instrument, and arranged a beer bottle between his feet. There was a pair of other friends, in the dim corner by the rear door, both of them fashionably gender fluid, short hair and flat chests, delicate eyes and cheekbones.

Ruben of course had never been anywhere like this, not even close. Evie Keener was not quite a rock star, not exactly, but she was a certified indie darling, her star ascendant. Her first album had been released in the fall, self-titled and with an enigmatic side-long portrait on the cover, and he had started to see her picture around. Online, mostly, but also in a short *Los Angeles* magazine profile and once, to his astonishment, on a row of posters along a Western Avenue construction site, a series of Evies plastered on the street-level scaffolding. The posters reproduced the art from the album cover: Evie Keener in profile, her hair dyed platinum white and slicked to her scalp, wearing the diaphanous angel wings that were one of her trademarks. Her eyes tilted upward, as if looking for solace or praying for rain. Ruben as he drove past had felt a distant swell of pride at Evie's rise. Like one might feel for the astronauts, looking into the darkness of space, knowing they're up there somewhere.

Now here he was, right next to her in the backstage dressing room, a room lined with scuffed and stickered mirrors, with posters from old shows, with pen-scratch graffiti and the smudged remnants of cigarettes stubbed out on the walls. The room was close and dark, lit by multicolored coils of Christmas lights and a single humming overhead bulb. The air had the salty-sweet tang of BO and beer and marijuana smoke.

"I was onstage when it happened. I checked the time later, when I found out." Evie had turned to herself in the mirror and was scouring the caked layers of stage makeup from her cheeks, clouds of glittered mascara from her eyelids. "There I was, the very moment he's—he's in this crisis. He's doing this horrible thing. I get offstage and I've got a call from my dad's friend, that this had—that he'd done this."

"You couldn't have known," said Ruben, and Evie hissed at herself in the mirror. She scrubbed brutally at her face with a balled-up cloth, watching the pink of her flesh glowing where it emerged, grimacing at the pain.

"Still. Big shot. Fucking Evie the Magnificent. Oblivious."

"That was an amazing show," murmured the bass player, from the sofa, entirely missing her point. "It was wild. Remember?"

"Jesus, Bernie," she said to the bassist, giving him a quick look.

"What? No. It was. You forgot your wings, and you were wearing that cape thing and it was like, swirling, kind of? The crowd was bananas. It was like—yeah. It was awesome."

"Literally the opposite of what I'm saying, Bernie. But thank you."

Bernie went silent and looked down, filled the embarrassed silence with a series of Chili Peppers–style slap-pop fills, watching his hands do their thing.

He's in love with her, thought Ruben. Well, of course he is.

"It was the same thing, with Wesley. When Wesley happened. Me in my own world. Did I ever tell you that?"

"You did, yeah." He remembered. He had been thinking about it. "You were drawing a horse."

"I was drawing a stupid horse."

She squeezed her eyes shut, and tears slipped out, one from each eye. Ruben reached out, very carefully, to touch her leg reassuringly, but just as he was about to, her eyes opened, and he withdrew his hand.

"Fucking Ruben," she said fondly. "Ruben Shenk."

He smiled. "I really just wanted to see if you were OK."

Evie's smile was stark and sad. Her makeup was streaked around her eyes where she had wiped it away.

"Oh sure," she said. "I'm great. Why do you ask?"

Then she laughed, and he laughed too, and they were kids again, just for a moment. Time punched through, past to present. An old circuit lit back up.

"You heard about this mess from your dad, I'm guessing?" Evie said.

"Yeah," said Ruben stiffly. "He actually wanted me to help—he thought I could, but..."

Ruben couldn't bear to get into it, not with Evie. How Jay had thought he was a detective. How he was, in fact, a line cook at what wasn't even a real restaurant. The awkwardness of rehashing it all would be too much to bear. Ruben took his glasses off, squinted at the floor. He was aware of the others in the room, studying him in silence. The bass player and the supercool friends and Evie herself. And who the fuck was he? An outsider. In a rock club, backstage, the glamorous squalor of it, the low cloud of pot smoke in the middle of the night.

He felt a lurching need to change the subject.

"And how is Wesley? He's the same?"

Evie shrugged. "The same. Absolutely the same."

She held out one palm and walked two fingers of the other hand along it. Ruben looked away and saw Bernie staring at them now, experiencing some kind of sadness of his own.

"And what about your mom?"

Evie made a quick, sour face, as if unhappy even to be reminded of her mom's existence. "She's OK, I guess. She's— I mean, she's nuts, frankly. Still. She'll call doctors, new doctors. She still has it in her head that some kind of miracle cure will come through. Lately it's some crazy French dude, some electro-magnetic thing."

"Yeah, I saw that."

"What? Where?"

"In an article about you. In the—I forget where it was."

Ruben blushed, bright red. He hadn't told her he'd been reading her press. Evie had mentioned it to an interviewer, about her mother, about Wes, on some rock-and-roll website.

"Right. Basically, she read this study, in some European medical journal, and cold-called the author and tried to get him to come and do this electric exorcism or whatever it is. The problem is, her

French is pretty shaky, plus when she's manic like that she forgets about how time works. So my dad will find her at 2 a.m., having these, like, insane conversations . . ."

"Oy," said Ruben.

"Exactly." Evie's laugh again, a short little joyful sparkle. "But then most of the time, she's the other way."

"What's that mean?"

"Well." Evie smiled bitterly. "They don't call it manic-depression because you're manic all the time."

"Ah," said Ruben. "Got it."

"Anyway," said Evie. "It's amazing to see you. Under any circumstance."

She stood up, yawned, and stretched, and the gesture rippled through the room like an unspoken announcement: time to go. The hip friends moved toward the door. Bernie slid out from under the bass strap, laid the instrument into the velvet coffin of its case.

But Ruben just sat there. Something had struck him, and he blinked slowly in the dimness of the Christmas lights.

"Hey, Evie?"

"Yeah?"

"What about your father?"

Evie had been gathering herself, tossing her makeup bag and the folded-up lace wings into a slouchy backpack. Now she stopped. "What about him?"

"Is he also—like you said about your mom, about Beth. Is he—like—*crazy*? At all?"

Evie set the backpack down on the vanity table. Ruben slipped his glasses back onto his nose.

"No." She paused. "Although—I mean, no, he's not."

"You kind of hesitated, though."

"Yeah."

She hesitated again. Ruben hunched forward on the stool, his head tilted, feeling curiously alert. "Evie?"

"Well, you know it was ten years in November. November twelfth of last year. Did you know that?"

"No, I guess I didn't. Right." He did the math in his head, 2008 to 2018. Ten years since Wesley. Since the accident, the surgery. Ten years of Wesley walking.

"My mom wanted to do something, with the four of us. I met them out in the desert and we had a—I don't know. A commemoration, I guess. We talked about Wesley. I played a song. He walked around. It wasn't a party. We didn't like tie balloons to him or anything."

Bernie, still hanging around, feet up on his bass case, scowled at this joke.

"But anyway, my dad got super upset."

"Upset?"

"Yeah. It was weird, man. He would just not stop crying. Like—inconsolable. *My boy, my son, oh God oh God.* I remember it because it was pretty frightening. I've never really heard him cry like that before."

Ruben pictured the scene. Massive Richard on his knees like a felled tree. Poor cracked Beth trying to comfort him. Evie, guitar still strapped on, standing uncertainly. Wesley walking. Wearing balloons.

"But that was it," Evie concluded. "By morning he was fine."

"As far as you know."

"What?"

Ruben found that he had stood up. He stood all day, at work, and he was most comfortable standing. He clenched his hands behind his back, bowed his head slightly forward.

"You don't know for certain that that was the extent of it. This breakdown he had."

"No, I——" Evie considered Ruben carefully. "I do not."

"It could have been only the beginning. Of a more serious event, a——a——" He raised one hand, like an actor, conjuring words. "A mental and emotional upheaval. A decade of suppressed grief and anger exploding out of him."

"Sure," said Evie. "Sure."

One side of Evie's mouth had curled up, very slightly, and Ruben could see that she saw where he was going. He sat back down, and so did she. She pushed forward on her stool so their knees were nearly touching.

"It totally might have been, by the way," she said. "The beginning of some sort of——what did you say?——some sort of upheaval. I wouldn't know. I was on the road the rest of November, and most of December too. I didn't see him again."

She was right there with him, they were in it together, conspiring, and her eyes were gleaming like diamonds catching light.

Ruben wasn't sure this was something, but he wasn't sure it was nothing, either. Even though he had rejected Shenk's entreaties today, he had walked out of the courthouse cafeteria holding the papers his dad had thrust at him, including the sad little internet printout of research on death penalty mitigation. Listed among the mitigating factors was whether the defendant was "under the influence of extreme mental or emotional disturbance" when he committed the crime.

"Do you think this could help?" said Evie, peering into his thoughts. "Lessen his sentence? Like, keep him from getting the actual death penalty?"

"I think it is possible," said Ruben.

And then Evie——Evie the Ragged——Evie the Doomed——Evie

threw her arms around his neck and pressed her cheek into his. For a long moment Ruben let himself be held, warm and confused and strangely sad, until Evie let him go.

"You should talk to my mom."

The Rabbi thought it through.

"I think I probably need to talk to someone from outside the family. You said someone called you that night, to tell you what happened. A friend of your dad's?"

"Yeah. Bart Ebbers. He used to help us out with some of the Wesley stuff. Protecting him from the freakazoids, back in the day."

"OK." Ruben wished again he'd brought a notebook, or at least a pen. "Got it."

"You OK?" she asked him as he got up, and he knew it was because his face had changed. He knew what it meant, this little breakthrough—what he was going to have to do next, before he did anything.

"Yeah. It's just—I guess I have to call my father."

March 10, 2009

1.

"Doctor, my name is Jay Shenk, and I am the counsel for Wesley Keener and his family in this matter."

"Yes. Good morning." The neurosurgeon was richly bearded and plumply built and magnificently serene. "I know who you are."

"Good! And so you know what we're doing here today?"

"Yes, I do." Dr. Catanzaro smiled indulgently and repeated himself. "Yes, I do."

The white beard was even more impressive in person than it was on the "Meet Our Team" page of the Valley Village Hospital website. Shenk already knew all about Catanzaro's life and career, the several previous times he had been named in malpractice suits. Everything had been appropriately submitted by opposing counsel for his review. But Shenk had spent several minutes last night examining Catanzaro's picture on the website, skimming his bio, preparing himself to encounter the actual man, like an eager theatergoer flipping through the *Playbill* before curtain.

Shenk had prepared himself for a self-important blowhard, but Catanzaro in the flesh was more Greek philosopher than God-complex asshole. So Shenk recalibrated, adjusting his tactics to suit the battlefield as he found it. This was the whole job. For every deposition you find the right way to play it, the right method to ferret out the details you need to build the story. Already on *Keener* he had butted heads with Dr. Amandpour, the flinty and defiant ER doc; bantered playfully with Maureen Jacobson, the charmingly sarcastic EMT; and zipped rapid-fire through Q's and A's with Judd Smith, her *just the facts, ma'am* partner.

Catanzaro was going to be a tough one, but Shenk liked tough ones. It was the tough ones, he used to tell Marilyn, that kept you young.

"Just so we're all on the same page, Dr. Catanzaro, I'll remind you that this morning's proceeding is a deposition. Though we are not in a court of law, this testimony is being recorded by our very able stenographer."

He tipped a wink to Ms. Clarisa, clattering away at her sleek little portable keyboard. She, as always, ignored him resolutely and completely, as of course did John Riggs, the insurance-company lawyer, who sat heavily to Catanzaro's left behind a short stack of virgin legal pads.

"You are under oath, and obligated to respond truthfully, as you would before a judge and jury."

"Yes, sir." Catanzaro was drinking herbal tea. He took a sip and set it down gently on the blond-wood table. "I am aware."

"Oh, good. So let's begin with your official job title."

"I am the chief of neurosurgery at Valley Village Hospital, in North Hollywood, California."

"OK. And how long have you held that position?"

Catanzaro answered the initial rounds of questioning unhesitatingly, between smiling sips of tea, with a thoroughness Shenk might even have admired, if he wasn't finding Catanzaro's whole gestalt here totally nauseating. The revered physician, saintly in his beard, deferential as a country lad with his pleases and thank-yous. So calm that Shenk knew it was an act, a *performance* of calm.

For good measure Catanzaro had worn his scrubs and white coat, as if even here, in the offices of Telemacher, Goldenstein, he might have to heed his profession's sacred call, rise to his feet, and perform surgery on someone's brain. It had been Shenk's suggestion to allow the deposition process to unfold in the lushly appointed headquarters of his rivals. He didn't mind competing on the other team's turf, as it were, being not the sort to allow himself to feel disadvantaged by circumstance.

He flicked a glance at Riggs, blinking in his pressed suit. How could someone who was such a snake be at the same time such a cow? If you were to close your eyes and imagine *insurance-company lawyer,* you would be imagining John Riggs: the receding hairline and the fleshy contours of the face and neck; the suit of superior quality, sadly degraded by the beefy frame upon which it was draped. Shenk knew Riggs; deep down, he felt he knew the man to a tee. They had not exchanged more than a few perfunctory words over the course of these depositions, Shenk having decided to offer aloof courtesy after that summary judgment stunt, but in his career he had sat across from dozens if not hundreds who carried the same banner. They were cold-eyed calculators of advantage, these insurance-company lawyers, careful readers of charts and weighers of odds. They did what Shenk did; they just did it in pricier suits; they did it without allowing themselves to enjoy it.

Men like Riggs, lacking Shenk's gift for narrative and his pleasure in combat, had powerful weapons in their place: a total lack of compassion for suffering, a will to victory sufficient to quash any stirrings of empathy. Plus, of course, bags and bags of money—resources that the penny-ante, strict-contingency Shenks of the world could never hope to match.

It never ceased to amaze Shenk that it was *his* brand of lawyering that was considered banditry, scorned as "ambulance chasing," when men like Riggs could blamelessly hitch their wagons to multibillion-dollar companies like Wellbridge, whose business model was highly sophisticated bloodsucking: collect and collect and collect, and only pay when forced; when squeezed; when pushed to the wall by the heroic likes of Jay Shenk.

Riggs spoke very rarely as the surgeon presented his version of the events of November 12, 2008, because he didn't need to. The doctor told the story, careful and clean, contradicting nothing that was already on the record. Dr. Thomas Angelo Catanzaro, attending neurosurgeon, had been summoned at 12:42 by the emergency room physicians to find Wesley Keener, Caucasian male, age fourteen, nonresponsive post head trauma. He had examined the child, ordered a CT scan and blood tests, and then consulted with his colleagues on a course of treatment.

Dr. Catanzaro referred to no notes, and throughout he remained remarkably, annoyingly composed. All Shenk's attempts to throw him off his game, to raise small objections to his memories, to slyly question his decision-making...if anything, all these efforts only made the doctor seem more impressive. Angry people say stupid things and then regret them. Catanzaro was as even-keeled as a battleship, steaming slowly through the day of Wesley's surgery.

Well, shit, is what Shenk kept thinking, every time the doctor punctuated yet another precise and highly articulate answer with yet another sip of tea. This man would make a very good witness for the defense.

Shenk paused the narrative, leaving Wesley for the moment on the surgical table, and tapped his chin with his finger, fussed with his ponytail. He had tricks up his sleeve, of course. Sleeves bulging with tricks.

"OK. So. Sir. Just doubling back a second. The radiologist."

"Dr. Allyn."

"Yes. You had her do a CT scan?"

"That's right. Once Wesley was intubated and hemodynamically stable. Which just means——"

"I know what that means, believe it or not," said Shenk sweetly. "OK. So he's stable, and you bring him to radiology?"

"Not me personally, no."

"A nurse brings him?"

"Yes, that's right."

"OK. Excuse me. *Somebody* brings him to radiology, and they give him a CT scan?"

Catanzaro nodded. "Yes."

"And you review it?"

"Together with the radiologist and the ER doctor."

"That's Dr. Amandpour?"

"Correct."

"And you determine that Wesley needs to be operated upon."

Catanzaro nodded, and Shenk said, apologetically, "For the record, please."

"Yes. We do."

"The group of you decide, or you do?"

"Well. I'm the surgeon. Ultimately the decision falls to me."

Shenk tried not to roll his eyes. This magnanimous motherfucker.

"And the diagnosis?"

"Subdural hematoma. The patient's injury had caused a bleed inside his brain, and the resulting buildup of pressure had to be relieved."

"It had to."

"Yes, sir."

"Immediately?"

"Oh yes."

"Did you consider any less invasive treatment options?"

"I did. But—"

"Did you consider, for example, implanting an EVD to keep track of the pressure?"

Catanzaro smiled indulgently—*oh, these mortals.* "An external ventricular drain," he said, "can be a useful tool, in certain cases. As you suggested, the EVD acts as a kind of barometer, monitoring the fluid buildup and related risk."

"So?"

"In Wesley's case, unfortunately, too much blood was already present, and a more urgent intervention was indicated."

"You could see that on the CT?"

"Yes, sir."

"And you made that determination in . . . " Shenk pretending not to remember; Shenk flustering through the papers to find the record; Shenk running a finger down a row of text, muttering, "Let's see, let's see, aha!" and, looking up: " . . . twenty-four seconds."

Catanzaro had his tea bag by the string. He bobbed it up and down into the water. "Is that what is indicated by the record?"

"Yes, sir." Shenk held up a piece of paper. "That is what is indicated by the record. I'm looking at the ER nurse's notes here. Scans come in. Scans are reviewed. Prep patient for surgery. Twenty-four seconds."

"If that's what it says."

"But you don't remember yourself?"

"The exact number of seconds? I do not. But as I say—"

"Would you like to see the chart?"

"No, thank you."

"It's no problem. Here. Have a peek." Shenk mounted a quick one-act play, entitled *The Passing of the Relevant Page:* a single piece of paper lifted from the file, laid down flat on the smooth wood, sailed gently as a whisper across the surface to Catanzaro. Who with a forbearing sigh picked it up.

"Let the record reflect," said Shenk to the stenographer, "that Dr. Catanzaro is reviewing the transcript of the deposition provided by Nurse Emily Bautista-Ocampo, who was working in the emergency room alongside the doctor on call, Dr. Jamati Amandpour." Shenk took pride in his precise articulation of the names. "Dr. Catanzaro, would you mind reading that out loud?"

"He has read it and reviewed, Mr. Shenk," said Riggs from behind his stack of notepads. "Also, I was present at Ms. Bautista-Ocampo's deposition, and at Dr. Amandpour's, as were you. We will stipulate to the contents of the record."

"Okeydoke." Shenk raised his hands in surrender. "But would you mind, Dr. Catanzaro, just *confirming* the amount of lapsed time that Nurse Bautista-Ocampo notes there, between when the consulting radiologist, Dr. Barbara Allyn, comes in with the CT scan, and the moment that *you* take Wesley up for surgery."

"Twenty-four seconds," said Catanzaro, and still Shenk could not detect even the slight shiver of agitation, or anger, below the doctor's placid mien. Shenk took out another stapled stack of papers and sailed it across the table.

"I have here also," said Shenk, "the deposition from Dr. Amandpour. If you would like to——"

"Stipulated," said Riggs, and Shenk shrugged.

"OK. Wow. So. Everybody agrees. You apply your wisdom to these scans for twenty-four seconds—less than half a minute—and he is dispatched to surgery."

Catanzaro tilted his head very gently to one side, ran one hand all the way down the carpet of beard, while Riggs said, "Is there a question, Mr. Shenk?"

"There is." Shenk leaned forward and braced himself on the table with two hands, and all his off-the-cuff affable playfulness was gone in a sharp instant. He aimed across the table like a bayonet. "You examine this kid, if we can even call it an examination, right, it's a quick once-over. Then you order up the CT scan, the CT comes back and you look at it for the famous twenty-four seconds. Basically the time it takes me to take a leak—excuse my French—but geez, twenty-four seconds and then it's go time, we're firing up the electric drill. Can that really be enough time? To make such a difficult decision?"

"No." Catanzaro said this softly but firmly, holding up one finger. "It was not a difficult decision."

"What?" Shenk yelped, a show of stunned surprise mingling freely with genuine stunned surprise. "*Brain surgery* is not a difficult decision?"

"No. It's not." And before Shenk could cry out in surprise again, he continued. "The patient had suffered a trauma here—at the center of his forehead." With one finger Catanzaro tapped the relevant spot, between and just above his eyes.

"This is a particularly well-defended bit of anatomy, to be sure. Well-defended because its contents are precious, and fragile. This young man had taken a hard fall, and the trauma appeared to be severe. He was nonresponsive. Blood tests weren't giving us any information, but physical examination suggested a severe brain bleed. So yes, I reviewed the CT scan quickly, because I could tell immediately that it confirmed what I already knew."

Riggs nodding while he jotted away on his pad.

"I understand that these cases may seem momentous to you,

Mr. Shenk, and of course they are momentous. To the family, to the patient. But this is what I do, Mr. Shenk. Every day."

Catanzaro smiled. Not arrogant, not smug. Just a smile. Confident and calm.

"Now," said Shenk. "Let's talk quickly about your divorce."

A moment passed—a startled instant. Riggs looking up sharply, Catanzaro's whole face transforming.

"I'm sorry," he said slowly. "What did you say?"

Shenk felt the distinct pleasure of a thrill pass along his spine. Now—*now*—Dr. Catanzaro was rattled. Not a lot, but you could see it. A flicker of his lips. A tremor of distaste along one rounded, bearded cheek. He lifted the teacup, found it empty, and glared at it.

Shenk leaned in.

"Your wife—sorry, your *then* wife—testified during a series of custody hearings that you did, on some occasions—"

"No," said Riggs. "No. Stop."

"—enjoy a glass of wine with lunch, even when on call at Valley Village Hospital."

"Where—where— where . . ." Catanzaro repeated the word helplessly, then took a steadying inhale. "Where did you get this information? These are sealed records you are referring to."

"So you concede their accuracy?"

"I object," said Riggs.

The stenographer's eyebrows rose very slightly as her fingers continued to rattle.

"Noted," said Shenk, and kept his eyes on Catanzaro, waiting for his answer.

"I object strenuously."

"Strenuously noted. Judge Cates will weigh the issue."

Catanzaro had become very still. His hands flat on the table, his breathing steady, marshaling all emotional reserves to keep from wringing the neck of this shyster prick still waiting, all ears, for his answer.

"Sharon," said Catanzaro at last, "was mistaken. About that." And then, unable to resist: "As about many, many other things."

"Oh," said Shenk, and nodded understandingly. "That's good to hear."

"We're done," said Riggs. "That's the end."

He stood up sharply and motioned to Catanzaro to do likewise.

"So just to be totally clear," said Shenk. "You hadn't had anything to drink on the afternoon of November twelfth?"

"No."

"Not a drop?"

"I *object*."

"We know, Mr. Riggs."

"Listen to me now. You listen to me." At last, at *last,* Catanzaro's voice had risen, though not to a shout, only to a dark accusatory rumble. "Absolutely not," he said, his eyes flashing. "Absolutely not. I was stone sober, and I did my job to the best of my ability, as I always do. The boy came in with a problem, and I made a determination as to how best to fix it."

"Oh." Shenk caught those last few words. He latched onto them like a handle. "Great. Good. And would you say, Dr. Catanzaro, that Wesley Keener has been *fixed*?"

2.

Beth was astonished. How could this have happened?

She kept asking and kept getting nothing, getting answers that were not answers, getting absolute mush-mouthed gee-whiz-ma'am *bullshit*.

"How could this have *happened?*"

"Mrs. Keener, we are going to find out. We are absolutely going to find out."

"Oh, terrific. I can't wait."

The man in the stupid blue tie nodded earnestly, absolutely no idea that she was being sarcastic. He was the head of security services at Valley Village Methodist Hospital, this asshole, and he seemed to think that they had met before, but if they had Beth had no memory of it. He was a pasty and mild-looking man in his late fifties with a gray comb-over and brown shoes and this absolutely awful blue tie, and he looked no more qualified to be running security at a hospital than she was.

His name was Brad, of course. Brad Corman. Somehow all these hospital idiots were named Brad.

Beth turned away from him, turned to look at the girl who had been caught sneaking into room 906, dressed as a nurse. The girl—being held now by two burly security guys, part of the same elite Brad-led squad who had let her get in here in the first place—was still staring adoringly at Wesley.

"I'm sorry," said this crazy fucking bitch, who was dressed as a nurse but was not a nurse. The police had been called and were on the way. "I'm really, really sorry."

"How did she get *in* here," said Beth, "is what I'm trying to figure out. What *we* are trying to figure out."

She turned to Richard, who stood beside her with his arms heavily crossed, staring at Brad the security schmuck, who—plainly terrified—would not meet his gaze. It was pretty crowded in 906: the crazy girl and the hospital guards, Beth and Rich and Brad.

And Wes himself, of course. Wending his way between them, back and forth, from the door to the window. Step by step, his arms at his sides. Staring straight ahead.

Beth looked at her boy and then away, back to Brad. It was easier to be angry. So much fucking easier.

"I thought you had him under some kind of special protection."

"Well, he is, of course," said Brad. "He absolutely is. And we are committed to the safety of all our patients."

"Sorry, but—can I just say one thing?" said the girl in the nurse's uniform. She had blond hair, streaked with brown, gathered into two loose, disheveled ponytails. "I would *never* hurt Wesley. *Never*. I *love* Wesley. I *love* him."

"You shut up," Beth told the girl, who smiled sweetly and mouthed the word "Sorry" while Beth jabbed a finger at the security Brad, poked at his chest behind the blue tie.

"I don't care about all your patients. OK? Most of your patients aren't getting the fucking *National Enquirer* coming to take pictures of them, right? Are they? Most of your patients don't have fucking lunatics trying to break in, so they can see him or touch him or—" She looked at the fake nurse again. "God knows what."

"Marry him," said the girl serenely.

"What?" said Beth.

"Shut up, sister," said one of the hospital guards, but she ignored him.

"We are to be married," she explained to the Keeners. "We're to be wed. Not in this life, though. In the next."

Beth shuddered. In the girl's purse they had found a syringe loaded with a clear liquid that Brad said he thought was sugar water but which had yet to be tested. Beth was glaring at the girl in the nurse's costume, clenching and unclenching her fists, thinking she might have to leap at this lunatic and strangle her with her bare hands. Rich, sensing this possibility, put a hand on her shoulder and squeezed it hard. Beth exhaled.

Brad, meanwhile, had put his hands on his hips. He addressed

Beth and Rich together in a tone that was probably meant to be firm. "Unfortunately, our resources *are* limited. It will never be possible for us to protect a patient like Wesley from *every* person determined to do him harm."

"Oh, OK. OK. Well. As long as you protect him from *most* people determined to do him harm. To kill him, or marry him, or"—she looked at the girl, who was gazing openmouthed at Wesley again, at Wesley as he plodded dead-eyed from the window to the door—"or both."

"Ma'am," said Brad. "I understand your frustration. We at Valley Village Methodist are committed to—"

"Jesus Christ," shouted Beth, as loud as she could, because here they were, back at the beginning, the conversation circling and circling and circling.

Brad Corman, as maddening as he was, had a point about the difficulty of providing around-the-clock protection to a single patient in a busy hospital and soon enough the Keeners and Valley Village would arrive at a special accommodation. At the end of that week, Wesley would be discharged from room 906; he would be moved down to the basement of the hospital, where he actually *could* be put under a permanent armed guard. The cost of this service would be billed to the Keeners, who of course could not pay it, and the invoices would be added to the growing ledger of permanent-care costs for which Shenk was suing.

In the meantime, the cops did come, and the fake nurse was taken away. She was arrested and charged and subsequently remanded for psychiatric evaluation. The liquid in the syringe when tested was found to contain not sugar water but a solution of bleach, Windex, and various other over-the-counter cleaning products.

When the room had emptied out—when the intruder had been taken away by the police, when Brad's guys had gone back to their rounds and he to his office—Beth walked beside Wesley for a few minutes, petting his back as she did sometimes, reassuring him, as if he could hear her words, that everything was going to be OK and that they would protect him forever.

Richard through all of this kept his peace. Totally silent. Watching. Locked up inside himself. He looked angry, of course, but he often did. In public? In situations? That was the default. He always looked pissed. Something about his size, the way he held his head, the scowl that seemed etched in his features. People always thought, and especially during the dark period inaugurated by Wesley's accident, that Rich's silence was a seething silence, that his arms were crossed over his chest to restrain the furies boiling in his heart.

He wasn't angry, though. Not at that moment, and not in many of the moments when people read his silence for anger. If you could see through his eyes into his brain, if you could find a radiologist to perform the appropriate scans, what you'd find was that he was praying.

3.

"It would be so funny if you were faking," said Evelyn.

This was a few nights later; the same week as the fake nurse, the unsettling near miss; the week that would end with Wesley being transferred to the basement, where he would stay until that arrangement, too, proved unsatisfactory.

It was dinnertime. Beth had gone down to the lobby cafeteria to get them two of those rubbery bagels and squeezable packets of cream cheese. Evelyn had asked if she could have a ginger ale too, and Beth said maybe.

Evelyn sat in the big armchair, waiting, her legs folded under her, peering at Wesley as he walked.

"I was just thinking, if you just like suddenly blinked your eyes and were like, I'm OK."

She waited.

Wesley walked. His eyes still looked like his eyes. They had the same kind of eyes, she and her brother, dark and wide. People were always saying that. *God, your eyes.*

She knew her mom thought he was gonna get better. She didn't know what her dad thought, but she saw how Beth looked at Wesley, when she was fussing around in here, dusting the night table, walking next to him, neatening his hair. She thought it would get better.

Evelyn didn't think so. She spent a lot of her time in the hospital listening to the nurses murmur. Whispering to one another, tilting their heads toward room 906.

"No growth," they would say. Stuff like that. "Zero."

"None."

"Five months. No change."

"One hundred twenty-seven pounds."

"To the *pound*."

Evelyn heard it all. How he never stopped walking, unless you physically held him in place, how even then his legs would keep moving, until you moved out of the way. Like a windup toy. How he never pooped, never peed. Never slept, never grew, never stopped walking.

They had tried to give her brother solid food, but he didn't chew it. It just fell out, like food you put in a doll's mouth. They had given him an IV, even, hung a plastic bag of fluids on a mobile cart for an orderly to wheel along at Wesley's side, trying to pump in nutrients. But nothing happened. He didn't absorb anything. He didn't—what was the word?—metabolize it.

"Everything disappears," a nurse said, not knowing Evelyn was just beyond their station, sitting cross-legged with a book of word searches, listening.

"He's like a black hole," said another nurse, and made the sign of the cross over her chest. Evelyn saw her do it. Evelyn didn't think her brother was like a black hole. But she didn't think he was going to just suddenly wake up, either.

Or—not *wake up*. That was wrong. He *was* up. He was always up. He was walking.

She knew how dumb it was to think he might be, like, putting everybody on. But it couldn't hurt to ask.

"I heard Mom say to Dad that when you come home we're going to get a dog."

Evelyn had heard no such thing. Beth was badly allergic. It was a nonstarter. Evelyn used to ask, when she was little, but hadn't in years. Not like it mattered. Wesley kept walking.

Evelyn looked up at the squeak of a cart's wheel on the tile.

"Oh," she said. "Sorry."

The woman who had come in, carefully piloting the cart, had high cheekbones and hair in sculpted waves and sturdy plump arms. She wore scrubs with Tweety Bird on them and electric-blue high-top sneakers.

"You're so pretty, sweetheart," said this woman.

Evelyn said "Thank you" very quietly. She didn't think she was pretty. The prettiest girl in her grade was named Daphne Voss, and Evelyn basically paled in comparison.

"How old are you? Are you ten?"

"Twelve," said Evelyn.

"Twelve!" said the woman, and wagged a finger at her. "You're gonna break some hearts, honey." She had not so much as looked at Wesley, who was walking. Who just now reached the window and turned. "You're gonna break some real hearts."

"OK," said Evelyn. "Thank you."

"Now, you listen to me," said the nurse, or orderly, whatever she was. She was suddenly very serious. Suddenly it seemed as if she had actually come into 906 just to talk to Evelyn.

The whole rest of her life, Evelyn would wonder what her name had been. She'd be in the studio, or listening to her tour manager talk about festival invitations, and she'd have a sudden vivid memory of this stranger, this moment, the wobble of the fat of the woman's upper arms, as she crouched before Evelyn like a penitent and laid her hands on her bony knees.

"Don't you walk forever in a shadow, OK?"

"What?"

"Do you hear me? Everybody gets a life."

Wesley walked past, so close to the kind stranger that his hand brushed her back, but she didn't turn. She squeezed Evelyn's knees, both knees, until it actually hurt a little. She smelled like some kind of lavender bath rinse. "Even you. Especially you. OK?"

What do you say to that?

"OK," said Evelyn.

"OK."

The woman rose and took hold of her cart and was gone.

January 17, 2019

The Rabbi had a shift in the morning.

A nine-hour shift, starting at 7:30 a.m., which was now just five hours away.

But he had never been good at going to sleep, and he knew that tonight—after seeing Jay, after seeing Evie—sleep would be a lost cause. He would lie still. He would stare at the ceiling, his mind buzzing and burning.

His T-shirt smelled like the musty beer-stink of the club.

He paced around his small apartment, not looking at the file.

The file was on one of his two Ikea chairs, the pair of them among the very few pieces of furniture he owned. It was a manila file, a few pages thick. What Jay had thrust at him in the cafeteria: *People v. Richard Keener.*

As he flipped open the file he could hear his father's sickly-sweet voice, cheering with triumph—*He's in! He's gonna do it! My boy!*— and he shut the file again.

Instead he gazed out the window of his apartment, at the Koreatown streets six stories below. Ruben lived in a studio apartment in a medium-size building on Oxford Avenue, in one of the dense sub-neighborhoods of vast Koreatown. Ruben had no roommates and had made no friends in the building. It was mostly Korean families; a handful of working guys who kept themselves to themselves and looked Salvadoran or Guatemalan; a young white boyfriend-girlfriend couple, gentrifiers with Whole Foods bags, their nervous apologetic smiles in the hallway a constant unspoken acknowledgment of privilege.

Ruben had ended up here because the realtor had mentioned that K-Town was one of the most densely populated areas in the whole country. He liked to think about the crowdedness of his neighborhood when he was heading home after work, and when he was sitting alone in his apartment: one among a hundred thousand strangers, sliding anonymously past one another in a hundred overpopulated blocks.

But it was quiet out there now, late enough that even Western Avenue was mostly deserted. A few straggling drunks and night owls. The occasional pair of headlights cruising past in the darkness. In the morning he'd be back at his cutting board, flicking his knife up and down, parrying Sunny's pretended advances.

OK, here we go, thought the Rabbi.

He opened the file.

Richard Keener had murdered Theresa Pileggi with malice aforethought on the night of December 20, 2018, in room 109 of Cosmo's, one among a stretch of budget motels along Sepulveda, just south of Venice Boulevard.

Mr. Keener had planned this murder for months, according to the signed confession provided to police detectives in the early hours of the following day. He had contacted Dr. Pileggi at her home in Indiana, on a pretext having to do with his ailing son, with the sole purpose of luring her to Los Angeles so he could kill her.

Intending to take his victim by surprise, Mr. Keener had arranged to meet her at a local restaurant but then went instead to her motel room, where he forced the lock and waited for her to return. When she did, she found Mr. Keener standing in the center of the room, brandishing a handgun; something called a Donner P-90, an 8mm semiautomatic pistol that had briefly been manufactured in Austria in the 1970s. He had purchased this weapon at a gun show many years ago and always kept it in a safe in the basement for emergencies. He told the police he had never told his wife about the handgun, not wanting to scare her, knowing she would make him give it away.

He had told the police everything.

He'd told them how, when Dr. Pileggi entered the room, he immediately opened fire, missed, fired again, and missed a second time. The victim then attempted to flee the room, but Mr. Keener prevented her from doing so by grabbing her and pushing her up against the wall. After a brief struggle, Keener seized a lamp from the bedside table and struck Dr. Pileggi on the back of the head with its heavy base, causing her death.

Then he called the cops and waited for them to come.

When they arrived at 9:22 p.m.—this was all according to the police report and Mr. Keener's subsequent confession—they found the door to 109 open and Mr. Keener sitting on the bed with the gun on his knees. He was covered in blood, which proved, when tested, to be a mingling of the victim's and his own. More blood was found elsewhere in the room: blood splattered onto the wall against which Pileggi had fallen when struck; blood in the fibers of the carpet where it had seeped from her shattered skull.

"I did it," Richard told the cops when they entered, guns drawn. As they forced him down on his knees, as they handcuffed him and read him his rights. "I killed her."

When Ruben was done reading, he placed the file back on the chair.

None of what it said was important, really. The events were not in dispute. Richard had done these things—he had never tried to deny it. He had confessed in detail.

What mattered was what Jay had found out about mitigation, the various factors a California judge was allowed to consider in reducing a sentence. If Richard really had been unbalanced, if the anniversary of his son's catastrophic accident had sent him into some sort of psychological tailspin, it could be presented to the judge as a mitigating factor, and it might spare Evie's father the death penalty.

Or—more likely—nothing would happen.

More likely he would try, and fail, and let her down.

Ruben sighed, pushed his fingertips into his eyes. I don't have to do this, he told himself. Then he said it out loud, to his distended reflection in the window. "I don't have to do this."

Meaning, get involved. Be pulled back into the slipstream.

We think of our lives as being composed of thousands of small stories, different chapters and sections, but really it's just one story. One long story, looping and overlapping, and so naturally Rich Keener had killed Theresa Pileggi and inevitably here was Ruben Shenk, age twenty-four, in his studio apartment, reading his father's notes on the case, trapped inside an endless spiral, the same as the Keeners, the same as everyone.

Ruben had thought many times how he could permanently disengage himself from Shenk, disclaim this relationship by referring back to its origins. He held no blood of this man in him, after all. They shared no genetic code. Their bond was of the laws of man and not of nature, and the laws of man—as Jay Shenk of all people was well aware—were not as permanently wrought as people liked to pretend. Ruben could sign papers, pay money, and permanently undo the connection. Renounce any claim of Shenk upon him.

But if he was going to do that, why hadn't he done it years ago? He didn't feel that he could. If he was not Shenk's child, then whose?

On the other hand, if Ruben *did* get involved...

Evie in the dressing room, leaning so close her knees brushed his knees. The two of them thrown back together, speaking softly as they used to, contemplating possibilities.

Ruben saw himself reflected in the window glass and saw that he was smiling. His body relaxing into the pleasure of that possibility.

Then he screamed—sat upright and lurched around, screaming. Reflected beside him in the window, sitting in his other chair, was a man in a tank top and flip-flops, with long tangled hair bleached by the sun, smiling the serene smile of a maniac. The face of this man was injured, cut and bleeding profusely, but still he was smiling—

"Hey, man," said the stranger, who was not a stranger, whom Ruben had known for all his life, "long time no see," and Ruben flung himself toward him, his muscles tense for the kill, and slammed into the empty chair, which wobbled and crashed.

Ruben lay in silence, panting and bruised, his arms tangled with the chair's cheap metal legs, thinking helplessly, *again*—

...again again again...

1.

"Consciousness is not a 'mystery.' We need to be careful about the words we use, and what they mean. There is no 'mystery of consciousness.'"

The slight and disheveled woman at the front of the lecture hall looked down at her notecards and paused, as if she had found, written on one of the cards, the word *[pause]*.

"The word carries mystery, an association with the supernatural, with the spiritualist, or even with the religious or theistic. As we turn from specific pathologies of the brain and toward questions of its unified functioning, it is imperative that you eliminate the word *mystery* from your vocabulary."

The woman squinted at her cards and then looked up at her audience.

Was it over? Shenk shifted hopefully in his seat.

She flipped to the next card. No. Not over.

"Especially pernicious, and especially to be avoided," the lecturer continued, "are certain simple *solutions* one hears suggested, regarding this quote-unquote mystery. Such as what is called the 'theater of consciousness,' or 'Cartesian theater.'"

The woman carefully pressed a single button on her laptop, and the PowerPoint projected behind her advanced to its next slide, showing a cartoon: a man in his kitchen, looking at an apple, while—inside the man's head—a tiny version of the same man sat in an armchair, gazing at an apple projected on a television screen. The cartoon was satisfying and clear: everything we look at, it suggested, is projected inside our minds, on a kind of screen.

The lecturer glared at the cartoon, her mouth a twist of dissatisfaction.

"This is wrong," she said to it, and then again, to her audience. "Wrong. There is no little person inside of your head, synthesizing external stimuli."

She clicked to the next slide and continued. Her voice was flat and uninflected, her speech spiked with academic jargon that was making little impression on the bored undergrads who sat in clumps and clusters, spaced out through the raked tiers of the half-filled auditorium.

But the real question was, how would it go over with the pair of middle-aged Jews who sat in the very last row, a set-off pair within the larger group, like the two codgers in the *Muppet Show* balcony.

"So?" said Ira Liptack to Jay Shenk. "What do you think?"

"Well, she sure is something," murmured Shenk. "She's something all right."

Liptack winced. He knew a Shenkian dodge when he heard one. A lapsed cardiologist who had been Shenk's medical-expert scout since dinosaur times, Lippy was on the hunt for an expert in rare brain conditions, someone who could provide the definitive analysis of the Keener boy.

Shenk knew that if he was going to fix blame for Wesley's condition on the hospital, he had to explain it, and he hadn't yet found a doctor who could do that—and not for lack of trying.

Dozens of them, neurologists and psychologists and virologists and specialists of all stripes, by now had made the pilgrimage to Valley Village Methodist to watch the boy walk his endless circles. Some on Shenk's invitation; some on the hospital's; some on the steam of their own curiosity. They came from other parts of LA; they came from the rest of California; they came from all over the world.

Beth Keener would stand beside each new doctor, down in the basement room where Wesley was now kept, biting her nails, trembling with hope, and Shenk would stand beside her, shifting from foot to foot, her nervousness his as well. She wanted the child healed; he wanted someone who could make a convincing case that he had been the victim of malpractice. The doctors came and stared into Wesley's empty eyes, writing in their pads, murmuring dictation. They took notes, they took blood, they took Shenk's number, but they never called. No one was prepared to make a diagnosis, to stake their reputation on announcing definitively what the hell was going on with this kid.

But if Lippy thought *this* lady, clicking her way through her little PowerPoint here, was gonna be the golden ticket on this thing, then Lippy—bless his heart—had lost his frikkin' mind.

First of all, this professor—wait, no, not a professor, a *lecturer*—this Theresa Pileggi, she looked to be maybe seventeen years old. Which obviously she could not be, not if she was professing to a couple hundred undergrads on the mysteries of the brain—sorry, can't say mystery—at UC Riverside. But in black flats and a limp ponytail and a beige pantsuit a half size too big, she looked like a high school junior up there, giving a poster-board presentation about climate change.

More to the point, she couldn't hold the room. This fact Shenk could confirm with a quick glance down the rows of seats—

those of Pileggi's students who weren't nodding off were engaged on their laptops, playing video games, chatting in text bubbles, tooling idly through auction sites. If *Keener v. Valley Village Hospital Corporation* went to trial—again, worst-case scenario, God forbid Shenk couldn't settle this puppy—he'd need an expert who could ensorcell twelve honorable citizens. In big cases like this, jurors tend to pay too much heed to the Thomas Angelo Catanzaros of the world, with their white coats and wise faces. *Who are we, mere mortals, to play Monday morning quarterback to this noble doctor, this healer of men?*

What was needed as corrective, then, was a plaintiff's witness smart and charismatic enough to present a credible counternarrative to the medical history, but also to rewrite the myth of the case. This is not a tale of a heroic doctor, striving mightily but unable to turn the tide of fate, but of a tragically afflicted family, laid low in the aftermath. A family deserving not only of empathy but of recompense, a financial reward that will never replace their loss, but should still be pretty darn big.

So what you needed, if for whatever reason you *couldn't* settle, was to find precisely the right expert.

But this lady? This lady was not that.

"Which brings us to the central question," said Pileggi, her voice stuck in its monotonic drone. "Once we have ejected this homunculus from the seat of consciousness, what, if anything, is in its place? Which is to say: is there such a thing as a person?"

She waited, but none of these undergrads hazarded a guess.

As far as Shenk was concerned, the answer was yes, there was such a thing as a person, and furthermore this person had to pee and then get back on the road for his ninety-minute drive back to West LA.

"All right, Lippy?" he whispered. "Shall we?"

"Yup," said Liptack. "Sorry about this one."

"Excuse me? Gentlemen?"

Theresa Pileggi had found them back there. She was squinting, shading her eyes with her non–index card hand, peering to see them from all the way in the front.

"Oh, sorry." Shenk waved to the teacher and then, merrily, to the rows of students who had craned their necks around, mildly roused from their stupor by the random interruption. "Sorry, ma'am. We're going."

"Doctor," Pileggi corrected flatly. "Not ma'am." She kept her gaze locked on him. "And I might have guessed, Mr. Shenk, that having come all this way you would at least wait until we can speak directly."

"Oh. I, uh—" He looked at Ira, who had not told Shenk that Pileggi knew they were coming. Ira looked at his thumbs. "Listen. I hear ya."

"We break in twenty minutes," continued the professor, her tone forceful. "Let's talk then. In the hallway outside."

Shenk gave her a thumbs-up, feeling on his neck the heat of some ancient residual high school capacity for public embarrassment. Pileggi clicked to her next slide, a brain like a pink and wrinkled planet against a field of dark, as her students returned to their respective internets and Liptack pursed his face to keep from laughing.

"Listen, no hurt feelings and all, and I thank you for your time, but it's not going to be a good fit," Shenk told Dr. Pileggi when he and Liptack met her as commanded outside in the hallway at the break. "For what I need."

"I understood you needed an expert witness."

"Well. First of all, hopefully not. Hopefully, we're going to settle it. No witnesses required. Secondly, uh—frankly . . ."

Shenk didn't want to offend. He had to admire her moxie, he really did. And her voice in conversation was not nearly so monotone. She had, in fact, a certain fire in her, a certain firmness, out here in the hallway that was entirely absent at the lectern.

Still, though: No chance. In no universe would he be putting this assistant or adjunct or whatever she was in front of a jury, this frizzy-haired young woman with the nubby pantsuit and the ill-matching flats, with a comically large messenger bag hanging from her shoulder like a sack of fruit.

He wanted to say it without hurting her feelings, but then she said it herself.

"You think I am too young, and that I look younger."

"Yes. Well, that is part of it. That is all part of it."

"I understand your concerns, Mr. Shenk, and I would only counter them by saying that I know what is wrong with that child."

Shenk tilted his head. "You do?"

"Yes, Mr. Shenk."

"You've never seen him, though."

"No. But I've examined the materials I was provided by your associate."

Neither of them looked at Lippy, who was leaning against the wall, under the NEUROSCIENCE DEPARTMENT billboard with its VOLUNTEERS NEEDED fliers and yellowing *Far Side* cartoons, waiting for them to wrap up.

"And from that you have diagnosed him."

"Yes."

"Very impressive."

She nodded. Of course she was impressive. It went without saying. She was persistent. She was smart. Her self-confidence was a marvel.

"Enlighten me on something," said Shenk, smiling softly. "What is a lecturer? Exactly? Not quite the same as a professor, is it?"

"No."

"So, like, an assistant professor?"

"Not quite."

"Right. And—just so I'm clear—as far as the actual practice of medicine goes..."

Pileggi clicked sharply, like an insect. "I'm not an MD, no. But I don't need to be."

"What do you mean?"

"For your case. For this."

"The thing is," Shenk said, "and I don't want to be an asshole, pardon my French, but for my cases it's actually important."

"Not this one," she said immediately, and he said, "Yes, this one," and then he felt like a little kid, doing *are-not-am-too* on the schoolyard.

"You were going to tell me how, in *this kind of case,* you require the testimony of a practicing doctor, to point out the medical errors that were made in the course of treatment." She straightened abruptly, swiveled toward him. "In this particular case, however, what you need is someone to testify not on the *mechanics* of the brain, but on its *chemistry* and *neurophysiology.*"

Pileggi pronounced each of these terms with clinical over-articulation. And because she was so young, or young-looking, there was something charming about her precision. It was like she was a child, condescending to explain something complicated to her parents.

Shenk tried to figure out how old Dr. Pileggi actually was. Maybe she was thirty, but a young-looking thirty, an uncoordinated and girlish thirty. Hair uncombed, pale face blotchy in spots with acne. Eyes wide set and staring.

"I know what is wrong with this child, and how it happened. I can explain that to a jury. I would, of course, need to examine the patient in person in order to do so properly."

Aha, thought Shenk, and said, "There it is."

"There's what?"

"Your angle. No offense. But there's your angle."

Pileggi pursed her lips and narrowed her eyes, making her small face even smaller, like it was condensing into a suspicious point.

"You wanna get a peek at the weird workings of this kid's noggin, maybe write him up in a medical journal. Elephant Man kinda thing."

Shenk kept his tone pretty light, making sure she knew he was just joshing and all, but Pileggi did not smile.

"I did not become a neurologist in order to satisfy petty curiosity, Mr. Shenk, and my ego does not require it."

"So why, then?" said Shenk. "Why so eager for the gig, if not for the—you know. The weirdness. Why dragoon me and keep me waiting out here while you finished thrilling the masses with today's lecture?"

"Money."

Shenk's eyebrows shot up. Liptack looked over from the wall, and the two shared a frank, amused glance. This, now, thought Shenk, this I like.

"Expert witness work, I have been led to understand, is highly remunerative. I am, as I said, an absolute expert in my field. The fact of my being a young woman, or a lecturer rather than a full professor, should not disqualify me from participating in this work and being rewarded for it. Obviously, yes, I am drawn to the complexities of this young man's condition, and I would welcome the opportunity to examine him firsthand. But the two motives are not exclusive, Mr. Shenk. For me, they are entwined."

Shenk almost laughed out loud. This confession of mixed motivations, this reframing of contradiction as nuance, even as multiplicity of spirit, was a line he gave to clients or prospective clients all the time. Including, most recently, to the Keeners themselves.

I want to make a living, *and* I want to help your son.

Both.

"All right," said Shenk, with a quick glance at his Rolex. "So what is it?"

"What is what?"

"You said you know what he's got. So? What's the diagnosis?"

If Shenk thought he was going to take Pileggi off-balance with the abruptness of his transition, his certainty was misplaced.

"Hire me," she said flatly. "Write me a check. And I'll be happy to explain."

Shenk smiled. He told her he would think about it. He and Liptack started out, and then he turned back.

"So you're the one, huh?" he said.

"Excuse me?" said Theresa Pileggi.

"You're the one who can heal him."

"I said I had diagnosed him, Mr. Shenk. I didn't say I could heal him." Pileggi frowned minutely. "He cannot be healed."

2.

The Shenks, father and son, lived in a three-bedroom one-story house in Mar Vista, on Tabor Street, off Palms, a four-lane connector running west from Shenk & Partners all the way over into Venice.

The house on Tabor had been discovered by Marilyn, appointed by Marilyn, decorated by Marilyn, and left largely as she left it, lo these many years since her death. In the years of his widowerhood Shenk had done nothing with the place, not so much as moved a chair from over there to over here. Not necessarily out of nostalgia, Ruben knew, but more because he was just as busy now as he was when Ruben was little, when Marilyn was alive, when their days were Shenk at work and Marilyn schlepping her infant son from the appliance store to the furniture store to the wallpaper display room, making all the small decisions, making it perfect.

And though there were pictures of his late mother everywhere— notably the famous snapshot of her at an LAX baggage carousel, beaming at the camera while infant Ruben gawks wide-eyed at his new native land, reaching out his hand toward his mother's tiny Starbucks espresso cup—it was in the spaces of the house that Ruben found her every day, in the spaces and the colors: his mom in the bathroom tiles and his mom in the springtime green of the drapes. He'd gotten such a short time with Marilyn Shenk, but he carried his memories of her like we all do of our mothers from our childhood: snatches of feeling, elusive and overwhelming, frustratingly small and impossibly large.

Right now, waiting for his father to come home, Ruben was playing with one of Marilyn's many tchotchkes, a little handcrafted turtle, too precious to be a toy, too chintzy to be of real worth. The turtle's cartilaginous back was formed of two symmetrical ceramic planes, each individual hexagonal panel studded with a green-hued semicircle of glass. The little mouth opened and closed with a tiny lever seated just behind the head, and that's what Ruben was doing now, opening and closing the turtle's tiny mouth, toying with it as he had been toying with it through various anxieties for as long as he could remember.

He ran his thumb over the satisfyingly textured dome of the turtle and made it talk while rehearsing the conversation with his father, now imminent, which he had been dreading since he got today's mail and read the letter that he had folded and jammed into his pocket, and which was still there, one sharp corner jabbing his thigh.

The letter would emerge from his pocket soon and be unfolded. As soon as Shenk came through the door, if Ruben had the courage. But it would be OK. His father would understand.

"Of course he will," said Ruben to Ruben. "It'll be OK."

He looked to the turtle, and the turtle looked back, incapable of offering a consoling word or look, eyeless and speechless.

The letter was from the school, and though it had been addressed to Mr. Shenk, Ruben had opened it, maybe because a self-preserving instinct had sensed the danger within. It was dry and informational, simply to inform the Morningstar parent community that beginning in the fall all students would be *required* to participate in at least one extracurricular or after-school activity. *As our records indicate that your child*—the name *[Ruben]* inserted in brackets—*is not currently involved in any such programming, we invite you to attend...* and then a list of the various fairs and other top-of-the-semester opportunities for kids to find their passions.

Jay was meant to sign the letter and send it back. The school had a fetish for paper signatures, for open and clear and recorded communication. Which just meant Ruben would have to finally explain how, after repeated absences, Ms. Hutchins had expelled him from Classical Poetry Confab. This had happened months ago, and he had never mentioned it. He didn't know exactly how his dad would react, but all options were bad. Jay might blame himself for Ruben's repeated absences, which had all occurred when Jay had needed his help with *Keener;* or Jay might deliver a series of speeches about how much he was spending on tuition, and the least Ruben could do was take full advantage of the opportunity; or (worst of all) Jay could become indignant and charge over to that school and demand this Ms. Hutchins tell him who she thought she was.

So for months now, all through the end of first semester and into spring, whenever Shenk remembered to ask him how the poetry club was going, Ruben had just said great. Going great. Super-fun. He had gone so far, once at dinner, as to mumble through a half-remembered sonnet, making up most of it as he went. Whereas in reality, he'd just been spending that time after school hanging around campus, haunting the school library, reading his way through the Dragonlance books and watching other kids goof around. It was from the library windows that he had watched the fitful courtship of his erstwhile Poetry Confab clubmates Annelise McTier and Willy Dorian, the two of them meeting up at 2:55 to walk into the World Languages building together, in time for club; he bore witness to what was either their first or one of their first kisses, feeling a burning mixture of jealousy and shame before sticking his head back into his book and reading—scowling, furious—until Confab ended and he could go home.

All to avoid the conversation with his father that now was being forced by the stupid letter.

Ruben threw his head back and smushed it into the scratchy back of the sofa. He ran his thumb repeatedly over the turtle's ridged back, trying to pull apart this clot of distressing feeling. What he hated most of all was the idea of giving his dad a *task,* pulling him into the small dumb drama of Ruben's world, handing him this piece of small-ball parenting bullshit to deal with now, of all times, when they were hip-deep in *Keener v. Valley Village Hospital Corporation.*

The door clicked open. Ruben rested his hand on the roof of the turtle and sat up straight in Marilyn's gold-trimmed sofa.

"Ruben! Boychild! Rubie, where are you, buddy?"

Jay Shenk entered the room like a change of season, bringing his own wild, enthusiastic weather in with him, pushing the door open with the sole of one brown Oxford, tossing his gym bag in one direction and his briefcase in another, letting his coat drop on the floor behind him, tugging the rubber band out to let the ponytail fall from his hair, grasping his only child by the cheeks and planting a firm kiss on the top of his head.

"I have returned from the distant land of Riverside. This lady, man. You're never gonna believe this lady."

"What do you mean?"

And Ruben, who had been ready to spill his guts, whose non-turtle hand had already reached for the letter folded tightly in his pocket, instead settled back in the sofa.

The senior partner of Shenk & Partners had been keeping Ruben well abreast of all developments. Shenk had debriefed Ruben on the various depositions, had replayed for him his interviews with Wesley's pals, shared the details of the accident, the trip to the hospital, the chaos of surgery. Each night he brought these reports from the front for them to dissect together over dinner, two generals huddled over maps inside the tent.

And now, tonight, he laughingly recounted his trip with Lippy out to Riverside and his impressions of Dr. Pileggi. In the small kitchen, above the sink, there was one window that looked out onto three lemon trees: Marilyn had had them planted just there, in that arrangement, for her husband, who loved lemons, and for herself, who loved the Mediterranean symmetry of lemon trees framed in a kitchen window.

Shenk cracked open a San Pellegrino and poured the whole thing out over ice, cut himself a fat wedge of lemon, and dropped it in with a magician's unthinking handiwork. Meanwhile Ruben could feel the crinkle of the paper in his pocket, the sharp corner of letterhead stationery.

"Dad?" he said at last. "There's, uh—something I need to tell you."

"I think we've got it, buddy," pronounced Shenk happily. "I think it's fine."

He hadn't heard Ruben; either the son had spoken too softly, nervous as he was, or the father was entirely inside his own head.

"Did you figure out what happened?" asked Ruben softly.

"No, I did not," said Jay. "But I'm close enough." He wheeled around, his grin as wide now as a sunrise, and counted on his fingers. "I got maybe some bad calls from the EMTs. I got maybe a drinking problem with the surgeon. I got maybe a diagnosis from a brain expert—truly the world's worst expert witness, to be honest, but nobody has to know that. I don't even have to put her on the record. Just wave at her existence. *I got a lady that's got a theory.*"

Ruben listened, mesmerized as always by his father, by the endless magic of his father's words.

"Now maybe, maybe we keep working on this, I follow one of these threads and it takes us to the end of the rainbow. On the other hand, when the iron is hot, you don't miss your chance to strike it. You know who said that?"

"Mom?"

"Goddamn right."

Shenk set down his drink. He stretched, pulling his hands up over his head, bending one way and then the other. Ruben, half automatically, made the same gesture.

"So you think we're gonna win?"

"Oh, no. No, son." Shenk, triumphant. Shenk, all smiles. "We're going to *settle*."

By the time his dad gave him a final smackeroo on the top of his noggin and wandered off to change, and to place the call to John Riggs, Ruben and the ceramic turtle, his confessor, had a plan of their own. Among his occasional duties at Shenk & Partners, after all, was in helping to tame the constantly accumulating correspondence, and if there was one thing he knew how to do, it was forge his father's signature.

When Ruben actually committed the deed it was later, much later. He set his bedside Casio alarm clock for 2:30 a.m. and accomplished the act properly, furtively, in the dead of night. He never forgot it: the motion of the pen, the feeling in his gut as he did the wicked deed.

Of course none of it would matter.

All this ticky-tacky childhood business? His schoolboy crush on Annelise, his fitful participation in the social life of Morningstar School, his expulsion from the Classical Poetry Confab and his cowardly dodge of the consequences . . . all were soon to be subsumed. All would serve in retrospect only as a signpost of how simple his life had once been, and how complicated and inexplicable and violent the world could turn out to be.

Soon Ruben's small boyhood streams of anxiety would be overrun by larger, wilder rushes of adult worry. Soon Ruben would walk into the conference room at Shenk & Partners and find a man waiting for him there, a man with sun-bleached hair and a vacant surfer's smile, with a sly and challenging gaze, radiating menace and sin.

But somehow, to young Ruben and to Ruben as he grew, it

would always feel, all evidence to the contrary, that *this* was the moment that did it, *this* decision, to sign his father's name on a piece of paper, that changed everything—this the ruining moment that toppled the universe.

Probably it wasn't so, but who can say for sure?

April 11, 2009

The restaurant was nice. You had to give that much to John Riggs, Esq.: the restaurant was really very nice.

Shenk crunched a breadstick. He sipped his sparkling water. He smiled. Shenk was not a classy person, he knew that, but he did consider himself a connoisseur of classiness, and the Beverly Hills lunch spot Riggs had chosen for their chat was classy all day long.

Shenk spread his napkin on his lap and opened the menu, which was only two pages, and not on any kind of embossed or laminated paper, just regular old typewritten paper, because they changed the dishes frequently to reflect seasonal vegetables, and they wanted you to know it. Shenk respected that kind of showmanship; he absolutely did. He also loved seasonal vegetables.

It was Shenk who'd reached out and suggested the get-together, but he'd allowed John Riggs to choose the venue. Tomasso's for Fish, located a few blocks from the gold-and-glass office building in which Telemacher, Goldenstein plied their sorcerous arts, was a seafood mecca with fifty-dollar swordfish and high-back chairs and very bright lights so you could see how good-looking and expensively dressed were your fellow diners. White-clad waiters hustled from table to table, bending low with their pepper grinders and gracious smiles and endless iced-tea refills. From their back-corner banquette, Shenk had a clear sightline on a young TV star with five-day stubble and a carefully curated trucker hat. The hat, paired with an artfully distressed sleeveless T-shirt, was a bid for attention disguised as a bid for anonymity.

It was definitely Riggs's turf, but Shenk considered the whole world to be his turf. There was no restaurant or club or corner of the city where he could not find a way to feel at home. Seated across from Riggs, eating on Riggs's dime, he nevertheless wore the relaxed expression of host: "Well, listen," he said, around a mouthful of delicious complimentary breadsticks, "thanks so much for coming."

Riggs sipped his water. Their waiter, an older man with an undertaker's fine attention to detail, took their orders and collected the menus and rushed away. Shenk, always a fan of people who were good at their jobs, watched him go admiringly.

"Swordfish, huh?" said Shenk to Riggs when the waiter was gone. "I don't do bones, myself, with fish. Tiny bones."

Riggs murmured something noncommittal and sipped his water. Shenk opened his mouth to make another comment about swordfish and Riggs said, "What is it you wanted to discuss?"

Shenk sighed. He would have done small talk forever. For years. Shenk loved small talk. But what the hell.

"Well. Here is the nub of it." He tossed his tie over his shoulder with a jaunty pirate swoop, billowed his napkin out across his lap. "I think we can both agree that this case is not going to make it all the way to trial."

"Oh?" Riggs's pudding face shifted into a moue of surprise. "Can we?"

"I think we can, yes. For one thing, Cates will knock our heads together like Moe and Curly if we don't find a way to settle.

Right? So—hey, don't look now, but I think Jay-Z is here. I said don't look."

Riggs hadn't looked. He kept his eyes steady on Shenk, his face a poker player's ungiving mask.

"Number two is the matter of cost. As you were so eager to inform the judge, whatever this kid's got is one of a kind. I believe the Latin term is sui generis?" Shenk gave a provocative shrug. "And whatever else that means, it means that once we start calling experts to sort it out, it's gonna get expensive fast for your friends over at Wellbridge Insurance Group. Yes? No?" He studied Riggs's face for reaction, and, getting none, he sighed. "Anyhow."

Shenk held up a finger, took a sip of his seltzer. The truth, of course, was that it was his own finances that concerned him. He would never share this anxiety with John Riggs, any more than he would have shared it with Ruben, but the sooner he could get this thing in the rearview mirror the better, given the steadily increasing toll *Keener* was taking on his pocketbook. He was paying extra hours to Darla in the office; he had paid a small fortune to Ira Liptack in the fruitless effort to find a decent expert; he was paying a soulless forensic CPA named Joanie Capra to draw up a lifetime care plan; he was filling up the tank of the Prius three times a week schlepping to depositions. His document costs alone, all that photocopying, was gonna run him into the tens of thousands. This was all before the lost-opportunity cost, all the cases he wasn't taking in the meantime.

And if they nosed closer to trial? If he had to fork out for an expert like Theresa Pileggi—or, even better, an expert who could actually do the job? Forget about it.

He crunched another breadstick and wagged the stump end at opposing counsel.

"The other thing, about my victim, with this sui generis condition of his, is that a jury is going to find him rather compelling. Can we stipulate that?" Shenk waited, but Riggs said nothing. "I'm in the jury, and I hear about this kid? I see video of this kid—which, by the way, I've got plenty of video—well, look, I don't want to give money to this kid's family. I want to throw it at them. I want to dump it on their heads from a bucket. Right?"

Riggs adjusted his napkin in his lap.

"And listen, I like your doctor—Catanzaro, right?—he seems like a stand-up fella, maybe he likes his wine, but anyway, I showed the CT scan to seven different hotshot neurosurgeons, and they all agreed that your guy was crazy to cut the kid open. They say the prudent course was to put in the EVD, let the hematoma resolve itself."

Riggs furrowed his brow, made something approximating a facial expression. "I have experts who will say otherwise."

"I don't doubt it." Shenk's grin widened. "But I also got a professor at Riverside says it's a dead cinch Catanzaro crossed two wires in Wesley's cerebral cortex." Shenk was bluffing his way through Pileggi's theory here, but what the hell? He'd also invented six of the seven hotshot neurosurgeons.

Riggs frowned. "I don't see how that can be proven."

"Listen, this is my point!" said Shenk cheerfully. "You put your guys up, I put my guys up, the jury doesn't know what to think! The safe move for both of us, I would think, is to find a nice middle ground together. Today. Ah! Good! Our food!"

Shenk rubbed his hands together at the sight of his massive crab salad. Riggs, for a long moment, and with solemn dignity, palpated his swordfish in search of bones. "You have, I presume, a number in mind."

Shenk grinned. "As it happens, I do."

Jay had, once or twice in his career, actually done the whole movie-lawyer business of writing a figure on a napkin, sliding it facedown across the table. He did not peg Riggs for the kind of lawyer to participate in that tradition.

"Four point five," he said, and Riggs said "No."

Just like that. Riggs batted away the offer like a Wiffle ball. Then he set to slicing his fish into morsels, as if to make his food so small he wouldn't have to taste it.

"I don't know how this works in Beverly Hills," said Shenk, "but where I come from, the song is played—offer, counteroffer, offer, counteroffer—till everyone sings together in the chorus."

"My clients are blameless in this matter."

"Oh!" said Shenk. "They are? Why didn't you *say* so?"

Shenk held up a finger again, and then pulled a small bit of shell from the tip of his tongue, deposited it primly on the rim of his plate.

"I understand how outraged the hospital must feel to be dealing with all this, with them being entirely blameless. But see, *my* clients, they have a boy who's been turned into a lump of clay."

Riggs's hands moved, conceding the sad reality, as Shenk went further. "*But* who, at the same time, and this is the interesting part, is not dead. Who shows every sign of living a long life, as they say, although obviously not a long and *full* life. We're talking about a young man who had tremendous potential. His test scores were tremendous. His grades were off the charts. All signs pointing to college, probably to grad school, and on from there to a richly rewarding career. Maybe a lawyer? Or then again maybe something respectable." Shenk paused, smiled, plunged forward. "And he was an athlete too, apparently a heck of an athlete. A wrestler, I think? *And* he played guitar. Just a lot going on. A lot that was lost."

Riggs stopped chewing and stared dyspeptically at Shenk. He was beginning to sense the argument Shenk was marshaling here.

One of the problems with doing malpractice law in the great State of California was that the most one could recover for pain and suffering was $250,000, which was—in the grand scheme of things—not a whole heck of a lot, especially after your lawyer takes his (well-deserved!) cut. But what you can add to that, what indeed you *have* to add, if you're going to make the numbers work, is a claim for medical costs: pain and suffering plus whatever it's gonna cost to keep him stable in the precarious state to which your client's malfeasance has consigned him. That's what Shenk was paying Joanie Capra to figure out. But he was *also* paying a clever devil named Smithy Greene—God, what a payroll he had going on this thing—to work up a lost-earnings memo, to put all of Wesley Keener's possible futures into a handsome binder full of charts, determine what each might earn him, take the average of all those hypotheticals, and add it to the balance due from Valley Village for having cut short all the potential paths. Of course, a claim for economic damages was pretty ballsy, when you're talking about a fourteen-year-old child. But that was Shenk for you. That was Shenk in a nutshell.

Riggs took a bite of his fish.

"So," said Shenk, "having said all of that, I think you'll agree, and I think your clients will too, if you ask them, that if we were to go down to four point one million dollars, that would be a very generous concession."

"No."

"No. No what?"

"No. We will not be settling."

"Why not?"

"I already told you. You can dance around your lack of a case, if you'd like, and you can even claim economic damages for a minor child, but it is our intention to put this matter before a jury."

"Mr. Riggs——"

Riggs held up a finger. "This was a tragic event. Granted. We will not, however, allow you to compound that tragedy by assigning blame where there is none."

Lord God, thought Shenk. This sandbag isn't kidding. He's not making a play, he's not holding out for more. He's for real.

"You're not going to counter."

"I am not authorized to settle, no. And I wouldn't, even if I was."

Shenk looked around. The TV star had finished and left, and a small team of busboys was cleaning off the table, scraping crumbs and clearing cutlery like a NASCAR pit crew. The guy Shenk had thought was Jay-Z had not turned out to be Jay-Z.

Shenk set down his fork. "If you're a flat no on settlement, what the hell are we doing here?"

"I don't know, Mr. Shenk. You called *me*."

Shenk gaped at the other man.

He had built his life, his practice, on a steady, sure sense of knowing what was going to happen next. Maybe he wouldn't have all the details—he wasn't a fortune-teller—but he knew the outlines. The big picture. He figured he'd be walking out of here with 4.1, OK, even down as far as 3.5—or even walking out of here with *we'll pick this up next week,* with *let me have a discussion with my clients.*

But this. A flat refusal. A slammed door. This!

"My clients intend to take this to trial," Riggs said. "Where they will win."

"I think you're making a mistake," said Shenk.

Riggs took a final bite of fish. His plate was scrupulously clean. "I guess we're going to find out."

June 19, 2009

On Wesley's birthday, which was also the day after the last day of the school year, his friend Bernie came to visit. He brought a cake, which was ridiculous, but he did it anyway. Carried the heavy box from underneath, balanced on his two flat hands. Said "Hey" and "Thanks" to the armed guard who was watching the door.

There had been various rumors about the "incident" that got Wes moved from room 906 down to a restricted wing in the hospital basement. It was a nurse, everyone had said at first, but then Bernie heard his parents whispering that, no, some kind of violent lunatic had *attacked* a nurse in room 906 and tried to drag Wesley away. A senior named Ed Nestor, whose dad worked at an office building near the hospital, said someone pretending to be a doctor was caught in Wesley's room, trying to smother him with a pillow. Marco had it from a tenth grader who hung out in Venice that it was some crazy skateboard chick from the beach, who had snuck in in the middle of the night and tried to give Wes a blow job.

Point is, *something* fucking happened. People were still freaking out about Wesley Keener, eight months after it started—whatever it was. Since Wesley started walking. Coming in today with his cake,

Bernie had seen a news truck idling outside, and he'd had to duck around a cluster of Jesus freaks walking in a circle in the lobby.

Wes was down here in the basement now, at the end of a secure corridor, and you had to have a laminated badge to come and see him. But Bernie was on the list. He had asked Mrs. Keener. He came a lot, the only one of the guys who still did so.

Bernie set down the cake and watched Wesley walk past it. They'd been friends since first grade. There were no windows down here in the basement room, which was a fucking bummer. At least the lights were on. Wesley was in pajama pants and what Bernie knew to be his favorite T-shirt, from the Who concert they'd all gone to at the Hollywood Bowl last summer; his mom and dad must have put it on him for his birthday or something. He imagined them holding Wesley still long enough to put it on, lifting his arms up, tugging them through the sleeves.

Jesus, Wes, he thought. Jesus fucking Christ.

"So what's going on in there, dude?" said Bernie, who sometimes talked to Wesley and sometimes didn't. He flicked open the cake box and ran his finger through the frosting at one corner.

By *what's going on in there* he meant *in your head.* Wesley didn't answer. Wesley went on walking.

It was awful. It was always awful. The stale smell of hospital air and bleach. And his bright, hilarious, obnoxious friend with his big, sharp, outraged laugh and his goofy duck walk, now moving in his endless slow circuit around the room, his arms hanging down, his hands like stones at the ends of his arms. Eyes open. Looking at nothing. Just fucking *looking.*

Their band, the Reverse Psychologists, was pretty much a done deal by now. After Wesley, it had never been the same. They fucked up their first actual gig, at some lame after-school activities place called Club Soda, because Noah broke a string and hadn't brought any backups. Then around Christmas, Cal and Marco got into a dumb-ass fight about a junior girl named Karina Trotter, who they both liked but who neither of them ended up going out with anyway. After that it was just a matter of time.

Bernie kept practicing on his bass, though, all by himself. Crouched in the corner of his room, walking through scales and teaching himself Rush songs, playing along. "I've actually gotten— not good, but, like, not *bad,*" he told Wes. Went back for another dip of the frosting. "To be honest."

By the end of junior year, Bernie wouldn't be friends with any of those guys, except to say "What's up?" in the hallway. Marco, unexpectedly, decided to try out for cross-country, and it quickly consumed his life. Noah's family moved to Arizona or someplace. Bernie played in his room, every night, alone, and his ear in time would find the bass line in every song on the radio, the subterranean motion prowling beneath the surface of the melody. Pads of calluses sprouted on his fingertips.

Eventually, it would only be Bernie who kept up with Wesley, even after the Keeners pulled him from the hospital entirely.

That was after a couple more scary incidents, when Beth got really crazy about it, and insisted that not only Wes but the whole family become impossible to find, at least until the publicity died down; at least until the trial ended. So they found some tough guy that Richard knew from work, a former detective who worked as some kind of security consultant, and this guy set up a whole system of moving them from location to location, staying ahead of the gawkers and the dangerous freaks.

But wherever they went, Bernie would visit. He would text Evie, Wes's sister, to find out the latest, or he'd call Mrs. Keener, who was always pretty nice about it, and then he'd drive to wherever it was and just hang out. He'd set up his phone and open Spotify and play songs by bands he'd discovered that he knew Wes would dig: the Mountain Goats and the Hold Steady and OK GO. He would bring flowers. He would bring stories about their friends and their teachers, about who had turned out to be crazy and who a slut, who was named homecoming king and who ended up in rehab and who was confirmed to be gay. He would tell him the whole crazy saga, at the end of junior year, when Mr. Delahunt got arrested for jerking off in the girls' locker room.

Bernie visiting Wesley, following him around metro LA, bringing him the world.

Bernie would get older, like everybody gets older. His body changed shape, he got better and better at the bass guitar, he fell in and out of love, he experimented with smoking cigarettes and thought they were dumb, he lost his virginity to Becky Carrol in Jane Essman's basement, he took the SAT, he grew a mustache for a while and then shaved it, and Wesley stayed exactly the same.

"All right," he said now. He got up and stood in Wesley's path so he'd stop walking, and kissed his buddy roughly on the cheek. "Great to see you."

He left the cake, and Wesley walked around it in a circle. Six hours later, when Beth took the hospital's back stairs down to the basement to spend the night, there were ants crawling over it and she threw it away.

PART TWO

NOBODY FEELS ANY PAIN

November 8, 2009

1.

A stubborn winter mist had seeped in from off the ocean and spread itself out across the Westside, clammy and cold, and it was like they came with it, these people, like they materialized out of the weather, a small tribe of strangers, born of the rain and fog, creaking up the metal stairway of Shenk & Partners.

They were goons. They were kooks. Shenk was in no mood for it.

"All right, people," he told them after ten irritating minutes. "You can go ahead and see yourselves out."

"No, no, Mr. Shenk. Please."

This one seemed to be the spokesman. He was very calm, very sincere and plainspoken. He had introduced himself as Samir, plus a last name that Shenk didn't quite catch, because he hadn't been listening and didn't care. Samir Whatever It Was was thin and polite and dressed neatly in a button-down shirt and pressed pants.

"It really is important that we talk to you. It'll really be just a moment."

"I have given you too many moments already, folks." Shenk hopped up, walked past his treadmill, and flung open the door. "Out you go."

"No, wait. Can we just . . ." Samir's friend, or maybe girlfriend, was named Katy. She peered at Samir anxiously, clutching one of his narrow biceps.

"Look," Samir said, ducking his head. "I am sorry we lied. That wasn't right."

"Yeah," said Katy. She wore a white blouse and had blond hair, and she carried a black pocketbook no bigger than a paperback book, suspended from her shoulder by a thin strap. "That was lame."

"Yes. Lame," said Shenk. "And, actually, illegal, because you're trespassing. Did you know that you were trespassing?"

Samir grimaced, and Katy looked horrified. Shenk, who did not practice criminal law, didn't think making an appointment under false pretenses would actually count as trespassing, but if the invocation of a criminal-trespass charge helped hasten the departure of these clowns, terrific. It had been Shenk's part-time bookkeeper, Darla, who had fielded the incoming new-client call, and Shenk—who had for the most part stopped taking new work, pending resolution of *Keener*—wouldn't have met with them at all except they told Darla their case had to do with asbestos. That bastard Darius Kennerly had the market more or less cornered on asbestos-related mesothelioma, and so Shenk hadn't been able to resist the chance to snatch a potential class action out from under that grinning peacock.

But none of these dingbats had mesothelioma. It had been a pretense to get into his office. Samir and Katy and the other one, the one still sitting silently in the corner, they wanted the same thing that everybody wanted: a piece of the Keener boy.

"All we want, honestly, is if you could help us have a word with Mr. and Mrs. Keener," said Samir.

"Oh," said Shenk, "is that all?"

"Or just tell us where the boy is," said Katy. And then added, like a little kid, "Or maybe just, like, give us a *hint*?"

"I'm pretty sure I asked you people to get out of my office."

The truth was, Shenk had no idea where Wesley was, right at that particular moment. First the hospital had moved him from the recovery floor down to some kind of special room in the basement, but even that had proved not sufficiently secure. The boy wasn't in the hospital anymore. He was somewhere else. That was all Shenk had been told; Rich had made it very clear that the details were on a need-to-know basis.

"Geez," Jay had said. "It's like you've got the kid in witness protection."

Beth had managed a dry smile, but Rich didn't laugh. "If you've gotta see him," Rich had said, "we can take you to see him."

So no, Shenk was not surprised that these jokers had turned up at Shenk & Partners with their bullshit asbestos claim, trying to find the Keener boy. Samir and Katy were both thin and neat-looking, with short, conservative haircuts and energetic, expressive eyes. There was something disconcertingly well-mannered and articulate in their manner, especially for people in their twenties—something very Mormon, something very Jehovah's Witness–like about their whole deal.

The third person, over in the corner, was a different story. He was lanky and disheveled, wearing board shorts and a tank top and sandals despite the winter chill outside—as if he had come here from surfing, or was going surfing after. While Samir and Katy gave their whole rap—about the asbestos in the ceiling at some middle school where they'd all supposedly worked—the third man didn't say anything, and instead of joining them at Jay's desk he'd dragged the one chair over to the window and planted himself there, looking out into the parking lot. He had a patchy blond beard and a growth of uneven stubble on his neck. He made no sense with these other two, Shenk thought, looking back and forth: they were polite, chirpy, plucky as ducklings, and he looked like some kind of drifter, blown in off the water.

"Mr. Shenk, please don't get upset," said Samir. "We just really need to see him."

"I think when you hear the whole story," added Katy, "you will change your mind."

"I'm, A, not going to hear the full story, and B, not going to change my mind," said Shenk. He stood by the door, glaring at the man-child in his chair by the window, who looked back at him vaguely, eyebrows raised. "Now, are we done here, or do I need to call the police?"

"Oh no. Please don't do that," said Katy. She looked alarmed, and her fair cheeks blushed pink.

"Let me ask you something," said Samir hurriedly. "Has the boy, as far as you know, become—illuminated?"

"What?" Shenk said it softly. He raised one hand and steadied himself on the doorframe. "What did you say?"

Katy picked up the thread, glancing excitedly at Samir. "Has he, like, *glowed*? From the inside?"

Shenk stood for a moment, his grip frozen on the doorframe, and he felt as if he needed to be holding it tightly or he would fall down. He tried to remember who if anyone he had told that little detail. What poor rattled Bernie had told him, about the moment just after Wesley's accident, before the paramedics arrived. That business about the light. The phosphorescence.

He had told no one, was the answer, no one but sweet Ruben— which wasn't to say that Bernie couldn't have told people other than him, or that one of the other kids hadn't seen it also and told someone else.

And yet. But still. Fuck's sake!

Samir got up from Shenk's desk, seizing the moment, so eager now he tripped over the edge of the running machine and nearly collided with Shenk by the door.

"It's yes, isn't it? Is it yes?" He grasped Shenk by the shoulders, and Shenk shook himself loose.

"Who the fuck have you people been talking to? Where did you hear that?"

Samir and Katy shared a look. "Oh my God," said Katy. "Oh my *God*."

"What *is* this?" said Shenk.

Samir had him sort of cornered now, by the door. He leaned into Shenk, and Shenk leaned away. The young man was practically panting with urgency.

"There is another world beneath this one, Mr. Shenk."

"Not beneath, exactly, but behind," said Katy. *"Below."*

"A better world."

"In all ways better."

They talked quickly, back and forth, breathlessly finishing each other's sentences. One long sentence.

"And it is with us, but invisible."

"It is here, but out of reach."

"Like a memory, or a feeling. A — a — "

" — a version of our world, but without — " Samir stopped. Took a breath. "Without pain."

Shenk finally spoke. "What the *hell* are you talking about?"

"Without pain, Mr. Shenk. Without pain, or grief, or guilt. Without all of these burdens we carry around." Katy was crying. Suddenly and completely, her voice choked, her blue eyes glistening with emotion. "Without *hatred*. Without *sadness*."

"Think of your life's suffering, Mr. Shenk. Think of all of its pain."

For Jay this meant Marilyn, and he was dropped back into all of it, as if through a trapdoor: the agony of watching her die, of watching her body corrupted and watching her courage fail, of watching little Ruben, baffled by anger and sadness.

"This better world is with us, even now, below us and beneath us and all around. A good and golden world, Mr. Shenk, and it's *here*." Samir brought up his hands in the empty air, as if he could feel it, this other place, as if he could see it and touch it and bring it to his lips. Katy raised her hands, too, open palmed, shoulder level, and she swayed with her eyes half-shut, transported.

"And this other world," Jay said, forcing his lips to sneer, pushing sarcasm into his voice. "It's what? It's trying to—to break through, somehow?"

Samir and Katy cried out "Yes!" in unison, and Shenk threw up his hands, suddenly outraged. Why was he still standing here, listening to this messianic crap?

But he had to ask. What was he going to do—*not* ask?

"And how do you *know* all of this?"

Katy and Samir looked at each other, smiling, two lovers sharing their ecstatic secret.

"OK, so you want to hear something...crazy?" said Samir.

"I think that horse is out of the barn, pal," said Shenk. Somehow they had migrated back to his desk. He was sitting down again, behind it, and Katy and Samir were standing, hovering on the other side, clutching each other.

"It was a dream," said Katy.

"A *vision*," said Samir, and brought his voice down to an awed hush. "A *revelation*."

"I mean, can you *imagine*," said Katy, "just lying on the beach and looking up at the sky and suddenly it is *revealed* to you, this good and golden world, the better world that this one could be, if we could only learn how to welcome it in."

"No," said Shenk.

"What?"

"I can't imagine."

This actually made it easier. A dream? A revelation? These people couldn't come up with a sturdier backstory? No tablets in a cave? Nothing tangible to support their tin-pot mythology? The truth of the whole goddamn universe just breezed in on a summer wind? Katy was shivering on the other side of the desk, and Samir put his arm around her, holding her tight as if to keep her from shaking to pieces, so overcome was she—so overcome were they both—with emotion.

"And this happened to you when?" said Shenk. "This vision?"

"Oh, not to *me*," said Katy, aghast. "To Dennis."

Jay had almost forgotten there was someone else in the room. But now they all turned their heads toward him, the sun-bleached dude at the window. He raised one hand slowly, almost sheepish, and grinned.

"Yeah," said Dennis. "It was fucking crazy, man."

He yawned for a long moment, mouth uncovered, revealing perfectly white teeth on top and bottom.

"The thing is, though, is that it matched up." His voice was slow, cool, SoCal casual. "With other dreams that people've had. Other visions. I'm talking about over the centuries. A whole lot of people, it turns out. Books have been written and all that. It's all over the internet, if you know where to look."

"I'm kind of the research department," Samir added modestly, but Dennis didn't even look at him. His dreamy, smiling eyes stayed on Shenk as he rose slowly and stretched. He was tall, rangy and muscular, with a long wingspan. Shenk was reminded of some of the tattooed skateboarders he'd seen on the Venice boardwalk— just young guys, hanging out and having fun, but with something menacing just under the skin. Hazy and relaxed, but with steel at the core.

"I'm not the first person to have this revelation," said Dennis. "This thing goes back. It goes *way* back. As far back as anything."

"As old as man," said Samir.

"As old as sorrow," said Katy.

After these ritualistic interjections, Dennis tilted his head toward his companions and rolled his eyes; separating himself from the others, attaching himself to Shenk, the other real adult in the room.

"The revelation was a dream, man, a vision of how beautiful this world could be. Our world, made new. All people stripped of all their pain."

"Right," said Shenk. "I heard that part."

"And then . . . I was presented with a riddle."

"Oh yeah?" said Shenk. He almost laughed. Come *on*. "And what was the riddle?"

"I can't tell you." Dennis smiled, benevolent and smug. "I mean it. I can't."

"Let me guess," said Shenk. "It's a secret."

"No," said Dennis. He let his eyes meet Jay's and held them there. "Because it would blow your fucking mind. This is not like, if a tree falls in the woods, OK? I'm talking about a mindfuck of the highest order. I'm saying, if I gave you this to think about, you'd never think about anything else again."

Shenk didn't know what to say. "But *you* heard it. Why are you OK?"

"Oh, I'm not, man." Dennis's face twitched, a quick agitated spasm, and he laughed darkly. "I'm not OK."

There was a pause then. Dennis stared evenly at Shenk, and

Shenk stared back. Katy and Samir were holding hands, their arms trembling. The room was cold.

Shenk still wanted these people out, but he had stopped trying to get them out.

"Here's what I knew when I woke," Dennis said, and by now his cheap California boardwalk cadence was gone; now he sounded like a preacher, a snake-charmer, a saint. "If I contemplated the riddle that had been presented to me, if I concentrated my mind upon it, then I would be . . ." He trailed off, gazed up at the ceiling of Shenk & Partners as if at the whole unfolding wonder of the universe. "Then eventually I'd be *emptied out*. So that the other world could use me as its vessel. The good and golden world would flow into me. Like a gas. Like a spirit, a merciful spirit. And it will fill me up, and I will be its conduit, and then—and then—"

Samir was murmuring to himself, eyes shut, and Katy had begun crying again, doleful little hitches of breath. And Shenk, for all the work he had to do, for all that this was self-evidently nonsense, he kept listening too, to this boardwalk Rasputin, with his cheap sunglasses and his scraggly beard, weaving his spell.

He couldn't stop listening.

"—and then we will all of us be healed. All of the pain and all of the sadness and all of the unending worry—jealousy, anger, anxiety, fear. *Gone from our lives forever.* And all we gotta do is let the other world into this one." Dennis paused, coughed, breaking his own spell. He shook his head. "It just needs a way in. It just needs the vessel."

Hollow, thought Shenk suddenly, remembering how the word had dropped into his mind, when he first laid eyes on Wesley in room 906.

Hollow.

"So let me get this straight." Shenk made his voice grandiose and mocking, spread his hands wide, but still he was thinking

Hollow...hollow. "Some lucky SOB serves as the vessel, so the better world, the—what did you call it?"

"The good and golden world," whispered Katy in a marveling quaver, while Dennis only smiled.

"So the good and golden world can come through, and everybody's problems are solved. Everybody is happy forever."

"Well, you're being kind of sarcastic there, but *yeah*. That's it, man." Dennis shrugged, sighed. "Funny thing is, I been working on it for a long, long time. While my friends here tend to my earthly concerns."

Shenk glanced at Samir and Katy; Samir stood up straight and Katy flushed.

"I been working on the riddle that was revealed to me. Tryna get empty." Dennis paused, sighing at the injustice of it all. "I've been trying for ten years to get to where that kid got by banging his head on a fucking bench."

For a second the mild and peaceable face hardened, before the anger rolled away like cloud cover and he was all sunshine again.

"I gotta talk to that family," he said. "I gotta get to that kid."

Shenk noticed that Samir and Katy had said *we*. Over and over. Not Dennis. Dennis said *I*.

"Well, that's not happening."

There was no way. Of that, at least, Shenk felt certain. No way would he put these people in touch with the Keeners; no way would he add to the nightmare of their grief and confusion with some cultic cock-and-bull story. "You're not going anywhere near that boy."

"He's not a boy," said Dennis. "He used to be a boy. Now he's a vessel. He's got the future inside of him. It's gotta come out."

Shenk was trying to figure out how to respond to this when Dennis's gaze shifted toward the door.

"Oh, hey." He smiled, an immediate thousand-watt smile. Shenk hadn't heard the door open, but it had.

"Is this your son?"

2.

Ruben had been at his mother's bedside, in the ICU, ten years ago, on the night she died. He was four and a half years old, a toddler, really, a baby. They were in his mother's hospital room on the intensive care floor, he and Jay together, and he had fallen asleep in his dad's lap in this big overstuffed armchair they had in the hospice rooms for families to sit quietly and be with their loved one, hour after hour. There were two chairs but they were together in one. He was sitting on his dad's lap while Marilyn slept. She was bald and bone thin. Only her eyes were the same as they were supposed to be. Big and blue and warm.

They didn't know it was the night that she would die. They were just there; they came every evening. Marilyn sometimes would be awake, or she could come awake, and she would always be so happy to see him there; she would read him a few pages of a story, or just stroke the back of his hand and tell him how handsome he was getting.

This time she was asleep and she stayed asleep. She was going. She was almost gone.

Ruben was sleeping too, lying on his father's lap in the big armchair, and Jay, Ruben was sure, would never have left him alone in the room except that he was fast asleep, and Jay's phone rang—Ruben pieced this all together later—so he just kind of slid Ruben off his lap and laid him gently in the chair while he went outside to take the call.

But then Ruben woke up and it was just him in the room with his dying mother, the dark of her eyelids and her bald head and the heavy respirating whoosh of the machines, until he realized then there was someone else in the room. In the other armchair. A lean man with lank blond hair and a scruff of beard, gazing lazily at Ruben and then at Marilyn and then back at Ruben.

"Who are you?" said Ruben, and the man said "I'm a nurse," but Ruben had met all the nurses and he hadn't seen this man before. "I know," the man said, and winked, a lingering, lurid wink, and said "I'm the night man."

And yes, he was dressed as a nurse, in pale blue scrubs, but he didn't look like a nurse; his hair was too long and his beard was ragged and he was wearing *sandals*—Ruben remembered it vividly—sandals or flip-flops or something, his strange craggy toes like crooked branches coming out from under the cuffs of the pastel pants. Ruben said "Why are you here?" and the night man rose and reached out and took the wires that connected Marilyn to the machines. "Taking care of your mom, buddy." He seized hold of the wires and the tubes, like a rampaging giant gathering up a handful of telephone lines, and he began to *twist* them between his fingers, still looking at Ruben, Ruben calling out "No" and "Stop" but not getting up, not *doing* anything. And then the machines cried out in protest, long shrill *beep*s while Marilyn jerked and spasmed in the bed and the night man laughed, no, not laughed but giggled, as he yanked and tugged on the wires, until they popped out of the machines and their free ends danced in the darkness, and Marilyn thrashed and gasped and then Ruben woke up and it was morning.

The bed was empty and stripped. The room was cold and the daylight was flat in the window. Jay was sitting on the edge of the bed, where Marilyn had been. His eyes were raw and red. His hair was down.

"She's gone, my love," said Ruben's dad, his voice a tired ache. "She's gone."

Ruben didn't tell his father about the dream of the night man. Why would he? He hadn't been able to stop the night man from doing what he did. But he hadn't tried. Why hadn't he *tried*? So he hadn't told Jay about the man in the hospital room, he had *never* told him, because it was only a dream, and he hadn't *done* anything about it.

And now the man was back.

He sat at his desk, trying to do his homework, eight hours after he'd walked into his dad's office and seen the terrifying and familiar smile. How could he be *back*?

Even before the nutbars came in that day, Shenk had been in an ugly and unsettled mood. Coming up now on the one-year anniversary of *Keener,* he was slowly coming to terms with the fact that what had begun with such extraordinary promise had turned into a plaintiff lawyer's worst nightmare. Far from being a humdinger, it had evolved into the kind of sandpit his mentor J. J. Barnes had always warned him about: a big, expensive suit with no payday on the horizon, and no way out.

Three times over the summer he had called Riggs with sequentially lower offers than the one he had tendered at Tomasso's for Fish, and three times he had been cursorily rebuffed. Indeed, Shenk was embarrassed to recall, the third call had been returned not by Riggs but by someone named Billy Gershon, a first-year associate whose uncertain voice and uneasy grasp on the fundamentals of the case were probably intended as a deliberate insult to Shenk and his increasingly desperate proffers.

With five months left until trial, Shenk was out of ideas, and facing the brutal possibility that Beth and Richard Keener would end up with nothing; leaving Shenk himself, after all the money and time he had poured into this case, with forty percent of nothing.

He had taken *Keener* home with him today, schlepped three document boxes full of discovery back to the house on Tabor Street and spread the whole case out on the kitchen table, thinking all he needed was to take it from the top: go over all the charts again, re-read the depos, see what he had missed.

What was he failing to see?

A little after midnight, Shenk got up from the kitchen table, grasped the table's edge, and tilted it, slowly at first and then at a dramatic angle, until the case slid off and landed in a messy heap on the linoleum.

Then he poured himself a double whiskey Coke, no ice.

He was not, in general, a big drinker, but at this particular moment he didn't know what else there was to do. His best hope, at this point, was that the small tribe of lunatics was right, and some sort of portal was going to open, and our world would turn into a better one, and everything would be OK.

He finished the whiskey and stood, already a little drunk, to pour himself another.

It was times like this, he thought, catching a bulging funhouse reflection of himself in the steel of the refrigerator, that he wished he had a pinball machine. If he had to be a drunk loser lawyer he could at least be one like Paul Newman in the opening scene of *The Verdict,* the patron saint of drunk loser lawyers, getting increasingly smashed while sending out ball after ball to clang around awhile and make lights flash and then disappear into the gutter. Each wasted ball a reminder of how dumb it is to be a personal injury lawyer in the first place.

Shenk raised a toast to himself in the quiet of the midnight kitchen. "You, sir," he said, "are no Paul Newman."

He sipped the whiskey and then set it down.

He was no Paul Newman, unless he *was*. He dropped to his knees and started to sift through the pile of *Keener* papers he had dumped on the kitchen floor.

Digging faster, thinking, Those fuckers — those motherfuckers!

He had just put his hands on the interrogatory he was looking for, a sheaf of six papers stapled along the left-side margin, when he heard Ruben.

"Hey, Dad?"

Shenk pulled himself up from the floor and saw Ruben looking down at him from the top of the steps with a troubled expression. He was seized as he often was at such moments by a love for his child that was so strong it was almost like fear, or grief. A strong clutch of feeling that made him rise shakily to his feet, reach to steady himself on the kitchen table, and put his other hand over his heart.

"What is it, my love?"

"It's, um . . ." Ruben trailed off and Shenk knew what he would say next. "Are you OK? What are you working on?"

"Nothing. Nothing. Rubie. Come on. Come here."

Ruben was worried about something. With Ruben it was always something. That dual nature of his only child pierced him as it always did. Ruben, good-natured and considerate, but always with the dark flush of worry on his cheeks. Jay wished as he had wished many times that the kid would find more to love in the world and less to be anxious about. Jay had always thought that his son was too serious a soul. He *liked* that the kid took things seriously; he was proud of it, and he encouraged it. But there was a tentativeness and a cautiousness to Ruben that Shenk had devoted some not insignificant portion of his own boundless energy to correcting: teasing him, needling him, grabbing at him and pulling him forward, toward life's endless churn. If only he could give the kid some portion of the joy with which he naturally overflowed. If only that was how parenting worked: that you could slice off some portion of yourself, some quality, and simply graft it onto the child. Build him out of your own spare parts.

Instead you could only lead and hope they came along after you. Give and hope they take. Stand there holding your sign, like a livery driver at the airport, and hope they follow.

Ruben sat down reluctantly across from his dad at the kitchen table and got to work on the loose corner thread of a place mat. "I seriously don't want to bother you."

"I'm seriously not bothered." Shenk squeezed Ruben on the shoulder. "I live to serve."

Ruben paused. The clock ticked loudly above the sink. Shenk had his hand laid flat on the sheaf of stapled documents he'd found, keeping them warm until he could dive back in.

"It's, uh—" Ruben looked away and then back. "It's that girl."

And Shenk, wise and perceptive as he was, probably should have known, or guessed, that Ruben was lying. He'd actually been lying for a good long time now about Annelise McTier. One day when Jay had asked him, in a casual moment, if there was "anything cooking in that department," meaning the love-life department, Ruben had decided to invent a budding romance with Annelise from Poetry Confab, although he hadn't been involved with the after-school for almost a year, and his friendship with Annelise had faded by now, to the point where they didn't even really acknowledge each other if they crossed paths at lunch.

But we see what we want to see, even or maybe especially those of us who are like Shenk. "Uh-oh," he said, and tilted back on the feet of his chair and smiled. "Trouble in paradise."

And so they got into it: Ruben, having decided he didn't want to burden or confuse his father with the real source of his anxiety—the whole weird business with the night man, the dark memory, the boogeyman in flip-flops—instead offered the details of a teenage lovers' quarrel gleaned from books and TV shows. Shenk offering nuggets of kind but rote parental advice, his mind mostly consumed with the new *Keener* strategy he was suddenly sure would salvage the case.

"Hey, Romeo," said Shenk in conclusion. "I love you."

And then Ruben, from the stairs, faintly and maybe not even heard by Jay, who was already reading the papers, back to work, "I love you too, Dad."

When his son had gone back to bed, Shenk read the document carefully, and then he read it again, pencil in hand, jotting chicken-scratch notes along the left-hand margin.

He considered it was possible that he had been more distracted than he realized all along, just by the sheer fucked-upped-ness of *Keener v. Valley Village Hospital Corporation.* By his client's unique and disquieting condition, by all the dangerous eccentrics who'd come circling around the central oddity like moths. For whatever reason, Shenk had made what was essentially a beginner's error: sifting again and again through what was *here,* looking for the answer, when the answer was to be found in what was *missing.*

Not *what* was missing, but *who.*

"Oh, you ding-dong," whispered Shenk to Shenk in the shadows of the kitchen, scrawling his notes and laying new plans. "Oh, you fool!"

But he forgave himself the error. There was still time. Discovery didn't close until sixty days out from trial. There was time to find what his instincts now told him he was missing. What had been hidden from him.

He stood up like a soldier and stared out the little kitchen window and dialed the number of a man whom he knew to keep late hours. While the phone rang he admired the quiet poise of the lemon trees in the moonlight.

"My brother," he said, when Malloy the Boy picked up. "Let's say, hypothetically, I had a human resources question for you. How wired are you on the human resources side?"

Upstairs, Ruben lay in his bed, perfectly still, his hands flat, palms down, on his sheets. He took shallow and terrified breaths, as if even the movement of his own respiration would rattle him to pieces.

He couldn't sleep. How could he sleep? How would he ever sleep again?

Instead he lay in silence, staring at the ceiling, frozen, eyes wide as two moons. For hours he lay awake, thinking of the night man.

November 20, 2009

Shenk the Shark cut through the water, working a choppy but steady Australian crawl, up and down the lanes. He wore a baggy yellow swimsuit and big round goggles and he had his long hair baggily gathered under a swim cap. A middle-aged man, getting his laps in, too young to give up on exercise, too old to care how he looked doing it.

Splashing away now: cresting and falling, cresting and falling; the ungainly flip turn at the wall. He made a half-decent speed, if he did say so, although it was nothing compared to the athletic young man in the next lane, who moved through the water slippery and swift as an eel. The young gentleman's name was Paolo Garza, and he was twenty-four years old, and he did not yet know he was the man that Shenk had come to see.

Malloy the Boy had gotten him close, but not all the way. But that was OK. Jay had taken the baton, taken the scraps of info Malloy had put together, and decided it was time for some emergency measures—time, almost literally, for a fishing expedition.

Try to hide a secret from Shenk, you white-shoe bastards, and Shenk will root it out every time.

Paolo Garza, when not doing his job as a radiological technician at Valley Village Hospital, was quite the avid swimmer, a fact that Shenk had divined by some light stakeout work. He had also divined that, stroke of luck, Garza did his swimming at a modest Thousand Oaks country club—modest enough that two twenties and a five, slipped to the right valet, had bought Shenk admittance for the evening.

And so here he was, floating to a stop as young Garza pulled himself dripping out of the water and into the night.

"Showing some good form out there, young man," said Shenk, coming out of the water one lane over and a moment behind. Garza, who had begun toweling himself off, raised a hand and dismissed the compliment with an airy wave.

"You shoulda seen me in high school."

"Come on, now," said Jay, grabbing a towel of his own. "If you're old enough to feel old, then where does that leave me?"

Garza laughed, towel wrapped around his waist, and cocked a hand on his waist. "You look like you're doing all right, sir."

"*Sir*," Shenk said, aghast. "Now you're just being cruel."

Garza laughed. "My apologies. I'm Paolo, by the way."

"Jay."

"Pleasure."

"Likewise."

Paolo Garza had a sleek tan complexion and a very slight trace of an accent—Brazilian or Chilean or something—that gave him a hauteur, like a displaced Latin aristocrat. Gay or not gay, his voice had a kind of offhand sparkling effeminacy, which lately had become not only acceptable, in certain quarters anyway, but well-nigh fashionable. Jay liked him, right away and completely; there was a self-confident savviness about the lad. He wore earrings in both ears, tiny gold studs that caught the early moonlight.

"I'm gonna hit the hot tub," said Shenk, very casually. "You in a rush?"

Five minutes later, each holding a beer from the bar, they slid together into the boiling roll, both of them leaning back with eyes shut, letting the water do its relaxing work.

The reputation men have, for being bad at making friends, is only true in certain circumstances. Try getting their heart rates up, try getting them more or less naked, try making it a Friday night and bringing the temperature down to an early-evening cool. Sprinkle a handful of stars across the velvet of the sky. Set them down in a small bubbling pool, with the temperature hot enough to bring beads of sweat to the temple, to slow down conversation so there is room for long, contented sighs.

Men will get to talking, as did Paolo Garza and Jay Shenk, about their own lives or the busy life of the world. Garza had strong opinions about Republicans in Congress (pricks) and *Breaking Bad* on AMC (fantastic). And then Jay took hold of the conversation and turned it, like a thing on wheels, toward its destination.

"Were you working today?"

"Every day but Sunday," said Garza. "Nine to five. What about you?"

"Oh yes." Shenk raised his beer, and so did Garza. "I work pretty much all the time, since my wife died."

"Ah," said Garza. "I am so sorry."

"Oh, it's all right. She had cancer. It was—you know. Nothing we could do." Shenk sipped; Shenk sighed, sadly. He took a moment, gazed over Paolo's shoulder at the water of the club pool behind the jacuzzi, the blue water accented by ripples of moonlight. He had brought up Marilyn as a transition, as a bridge to the conversation's next promontory; he had brought her up in character, but now she was here and momentarily he was lost in remembrance—in character and not; fake Jay grieving the death of fake Marilyn; real grief forever alive in the real man. Marilyn had gone quick, thank you, all-forgiving God, his loving Marilyn transformed in a handful of weeks from the amused and amusing pillar of his every day to a frail shell, turned sideways in her hospital bed because it hurt to sit upright. He went in with little Rubie every day: he held the boy up where she could see him, and reach to smooth his hair where it stuck up.

Now Shenk told this kind stranger about her illness. About how hard the doctors had worked. All of them: the doctors and the nurses and even the radiology department. And of course Garza, brimming with sympathy, proud of his tribe, took the compliment. Took the bait.

"That's nice to hear," he said. "That's what I do, actually."

"No kidding?" said Jay, all innocence. "You're a doctor?"

"No, no. I'm a radiology tech."

"Oh," said Shenk, and then: "I know." His eyes had been closed, and now he cracked one open, just enough to see Garza peering confusedly at him, not getting the joke.

"What?"

"I said I know who you are, Paolo."

"What does that mean, you know?"

"Again, my name is Jay Shenk. I'm a lawyer." He paused to let this much sink in. "I represent the family of Wesley Keener."

"Oh my God," Garza said, too loud. Aghast. A pair of bikini-clad young mothers, each with a wineglass, glanced over from a cabana. "You're a *snake*." He jerked away, as if Shenk was a real snake that had slithered out of one of the bubble jets. "Oh my *God*."

"The problem I'm having," Shenk went on, calm as he could be, "is that the HR department over there refuses to tell me where I can find Dr. Barbara Allyn. She was your boss, right?"

"This is insane." Garza flipped out of the hot tub and stood at the edge, one hand on his hip, water streaming down his chest and legs.

"She was your boss until she abruptly retired. Right?"

Garza pointed at him. "How *dare* you!"

"How dare *I*?" Now *Shenk* became indignant, pointed back up at the radiology tech. "This lady was party to a surgery that had disastrous results, and then she retired. *Three days later.* When we sue, she submits a written response, hopes no one will follow up."

Shenk was worked up now; his spine stiffened with righteousness. He slapped a flat hand on the water, and it jumped. "But no one will tell me where she's retired *to,* so I can ask her some more questions. She's, like, incognito. But you—you, my friend, you worked with the lady for six years. You were colleagues. Friends. You know where she is, don't you? Paolo? Don't you?"

Garza said "Oh my God" again. But he was still standing there. Arms crossed. Dripping. Looking up at the moon.

"Look." Shenk spoke slowly. Shenk stayed in the water. "You feel affection for Dr. Allyn. You feel loyalty. You don't want to see her get in any trouble. I commend you."

"That woman," said Paolo Garza, "is a saint."

"I do not doubt it."

"She did nothing wrong. With the Keener boy. *Nothing.*"

"Right!" said Jay. "Exactly. Doctors are good people. They tried their best to help my wife, and I am sure they tried their best to help Wesley Keener. But mistakes happen. Accidents occur. And if Dr. Allyn did nothing wrong, I just need her to tell me that. Isn't that fair? Shouldn't everyone who was part of this thing be on the record telling exactly what happened?"

"I mean—" Garza made a noise in his throat, something like *uch* or *ugh*. Then he put up his hands. "She's a good woman. A saint."

"You already said that."

Shenk held Garza's gaze for a long moment. Whatever the truth was about Dr. Allyn, this kid had a good heart in him—he could see that pretty clear. "Look, Mr. Garza. Something happened. The family deserves to know. Right?"

He waited, and he had him—he knew he had him.

"Paolo? Right?"

"Are we joking here?" the movie star said. "Is this a fucking *joke*?"

The movie star was wearing a metallic coat. He peered out into the darkness that surrounded him, squinting and scowling, demanding an answer. He was holding a prop up over his head, furious. A crowd of people stared back at him, the incandescent center of the universe, a movie star under hot lights. Technicians, set decorators, boom ops, assistants with clipboards and walkie-talkies, everybody frozen in the force field of the star's displeasure.

"Is this seriously what this thing looks like?" he said, wielding the slender black prop he'd grabbed angrily from the other actor, a far lesser star who was smiling nervously, like a hostage hoping for rescue. The offending item was a thin black tube with a red light glowing at one end. The movie star shook it like a cheap toy. "This is what it looks like?"

"No." A voice spoke from the darkness, a placating voice over a public address system; the director, wherever she was in the darkness of the soundstage. "We're gonna sexy it up in post."

"Uh-uh," said the movie star, shaking his head. "Fuck that. I don't work cheap. I won't do it. I told Barry I wouldn't, and I won't."

The set the movie star was standing on was some kind of futuristic library. Behind him were rows and rows of book-lined shelves, disappearing up into darkness to give the trompe l'oeil effect of continuing forever, infinite knowledge. The movie star, the hero, some sort of sci-fi detective, had been stopped at the entrance to this archive by a guard cutely referred to as a "Librarian," who was reading his mind with a gadget that was supposed to look sleek and futuristic, but which the movie star thought looked like a bunch of fucking bullshit.

It looked pretty impressive to the Rabbi, who was just inside the threshold, peering inside. Looking at the set, just three high wooden walls and a painted floor, Ruben felt a kind of pull from it—a welcoming sense of a new reality being made available to him. Despite the smell of sawdust, despite the extension cords that snaked below his feet, taped at junction points to the ground, he felt like he could walk ten yards, step over an invisible line, and begin a new life in whatever alternate reality this was supposed to represent.

"The only reason I'm doing a fucking TV series," the movie star fumed, gesticulating with the unsatisfactory prop, "is because I was told it was gonna look right. If it's gonna look like bullshit, I'm not interested."

"It's gonna look great," said the voice on the PA.

"Don't baby me, Jackie. I won't be babied. Barry promised I would not be babied."

The movie star scowled and peeled off the metallic trench coat. Ruben recognized the man from a dozen different movies but couldn't summon his name. He was wide-bodied and pug-nosed and brutishly handsome, and for a second Ruben thought it was James Gandolfini, from *The Sopranos,* until he recalled with a disappointing jolt that that man was dead.

"You know what?" said the star. "Forget it."

"No, please," said the voice on the PA, starting to sound pleading. "Let's get one take."

"No."

"One take, Bobby. Please."

"Honestly, man?" said someone at Ruben's ear. "This could go on all day."

Standing at Ruben's side, offering a lopsided smile, was a bald-headed Black man with broad shoulders and a wide smile, sharply dressed in khakis and a blazer. "Bart Ebbers." He stuck out a friendly hand. "How you doing, young man?"

"I'm OK." Ruben's hand felt tiny in Ebbers's. "Is now still a good time?"

"No time like the present." Ebbers pointed to the movie star, now trying to make his point by snapping the offending prop over his knee but struggling even to bend it. "We're gonna get three rounds now of this guy calling UTA, UTA calling the producer, everybody working each other up, then chilling each other out. We got ten minutes at least, Mr. Shenk. That's it, right, Shenk?"

"Yeah. But—Ruben is fine."

"Well, it's good to meet you, Ruben. Only a shame about the circumstances. Rich Keener, you know?" He shook his head, exhaled noisily. "You hate to see it."

"I know," said Ruben. "I know what you mean."

"Come on." Ebbers sighed again, tilted his head toward the massive door behind him. "We'll talk outside."

Ruben followed, hurrying to keep up with Ebbers's confident strides, watching him point and smile at a cameraman; at a thin guy in a headset and a black T-shirt; at another guy, sitting behind a bank of small-screen computers, who rose for a fist bump and a hug. Ebbers's name badge ID'd him as the deputy chief of security for the Warner Bros. lot, and at his waist was the unmistakable bulge of a firearm.

Outside, Ebbers explained that he didn't normally sit in on shoots. He was just doing it today because of Mr. Fancy Pants in there, bitching about props and everything else.

"None of these dudes want to admit there's no such thing as a movie star anymore, so they all gotta be divas, make sure everybody knows that they're slumming it, doing the small-screen stuff, even though there won't *be* a theatrical business, five, ten years from now. Know what I'm saying?"

Ruben nodded. "Sure."

Ebbers waved to a pair of young women in cafeteria whites, strolling the broad avenue between soundstages, holding cups of coffee. "How you ladies doing?" he said, and they waved, called out "Hey, baby," as Ebbers turned back to Ruben: "Anyway, I like to come hang out when we got this kinda, uh, personality on set, make sure him or his goons don't get too worked up. And yeah, he's got goons. They all travel with goons."

Ruben nodded and nodded, swept up by Ebbers's cheerful volubility. The man had a big, toothy smile that flashed out between sentences. Ruben toyed with the lanyard around his neck, as if to prove to himself he was really OK to be here. He felt dwarfed by the soundstage behind him, dwarfed by Ebbers's sturdy body and wide grin and big personality.

"I won't keep you long, Mr. Ebbers," he said finally. "I appreciate your willingness to help."

"Sure, sure. Of course. God, yeah, Richard Keener, you know? I saw Beth, you know, *Mrs.* Keener, over at the jail," Ebbers said. "She was with that lawyer, and she asked me to help any way I could, and of course I said OK. The lawyer's name is Shenk too, right?"

"Yeah. Yup. He's my dad."

"That right?"

Ruben didn't look like his father's son, and there were some people who dwelled on that fact and some who didn't. Ebbers just smiled his bright confident smile and stood waiting, ready to get to business. Ruben took out the fat little Moleskine notebook he'd bought at a CVS on Reseda on the way over here and realized that he had neglected to unwrap it. Or bring a pen. He put the notebook back in his pocket. Over Ebbers's shoulder, a red light buzzed to life, indicating that they had started shooting the scene again.

"OK, so—you and Richard have been friends a long time, I understand?"

"Well," said Ebbers, and tilted his head at the sun.

"Wait—you haven't?"

"Friends?" Ebbers spread his hands out, shrugged. Who could define such a thing as friendship? "Rich is not like a—a *friends* guy, you know what I mean?"

Ruben nodded. He thought he did know.

"But me and Rich, you know, we've known each other on and off over a lot of years. I used to bump into him, in different work contexts. And we'd talk, talk about basketball, that kind of thing. But the main way I know Rich Keener is when it all started with his son, me and a guy I was partners with, guy named Jordan—partners then, not anymore, though—ex-cop like me—anyway, we helped them figure out how to keep the family safe."

The door opened and there was a burst of noise from inside, which muted again as the door swung closed. Ebbers glanced over his shoulder, then kept right on talking.

"For a time there, it was pretty scary. Not only the kid's condition..." He stopped a moment, pursed his lips. "But also, you know, strangers tryna get to him. All kinds of strangers."

"Yeah, no, I remember. I was, um—I knew the family at that time, also."

Ebbers jutted out a lip and furrowed his brow, like that didn't add up, somehow, but then he just said, "OK, so you remember."

A caravan of golf carts chugged by: tourists taking the tour. Families packed in like they were on a coal train, gawking at the phony streets, at the bungalows, at the lots, which were nothing more than oversize warehouses with green roofs and big garage doors. But movies had been shot here, movies they had probably seen. One chunky tourist mom raised her phone to snap a picture, and Ebbers raised one hand slowly and waved, gave a magnanimous thumbs-up, as if he were a movie star. The people on the caravan looked closer, trying to figure out who he was.

"What would be helpful"—Ruben cleared his throat—"is if you have particular recollections of Richard in recent months. I'm trying to piece together if he was acting unusually, or—or seeming to be, I guess—odd."

"Odd?"

"Yeah. Odd."

"Why?"

"Last November was ten years since Wesley's accident. And I understand that Richard was—or might have been—somewhat affected by that?"

"You're wanting to know if the man was out of his damn mind."

"Well—not exactly that."

"Yeah, but not *not* that either, right?" said Ebbers, smiling, and Ruben smiled, and then he waited, and Ebbers didn't say anything else. He looked past Ruben, at the studio road, as if waiting for another tour-group convoy to come chugging by.

"So? Mr. Ebbers?"

"Yeah?"

"*Was* he acting oddly recently?"

"Oh man," said Ebbers, and blew air out between his lips. "Word like that. *Oddly.* Who the hell knows, right?"

"Right," said Ruben.

But it was a simple question. Was he acting oddly or not? A simple question, he had asked it twice, and twice Ebbers in his friendly funny way had danced backward, away from actually answering. Ruben studied the man. There was something familiar in all of this, in the play of his sentences, how they skirted just around the edges of having a definite meaning. It reminded Ruben of something, of somebody, and of course it was Shenk—it was always Shenk. Jay Shenk and his ways and means, hiding in everyone and everywhere he went.

"Mr. Ebbers." A thought had arrived in Ruben's mind, tiny and fragile, like a drifting snowflake. "Mr. Ebbers, had you *seen* Rich since November of last year?"

Ebbers cocked his head and thought about this for a second, although Ruben could not help but feel he was pretending; not thinking but making a show of thinking. Then he said, "No, no, I guess not. Not until that night, the night it happened. I went right up to the precinct house, when he called me."

"But why?"

"Why what?"

The big people-pleasing smile was gone from Ebbers's face. He looked at Ruben with a crisp coolness that reminded him of the gun he'd seen at the man's waist.

But Ruben pressed on. He had an idea, and it was probably stupid, but he had to ask.

"Doesn't seem like you guys are all that close. Why did he call *you?*"

"Well," Ebbers said, eyeing him evenly. "Not sure I can say."

"Rich has got a wife. He's got this daughter he's crazy about, and I think actually they're pretty close. He gets arrested, he's got his one call to make, and he calls his friend Bart Ebbers. But you're telling me you're not even really friends."

"I never said that, did I? I just said we're a certain type of friends."

Ruben nodded, sure, OK, but before he could say more a shrill whistle blew from inside the soundstage, and Ebbers turned to it. "I gotta get back to work," he said. "Good meeting you, Mr. Shenk."

"Yeah, no, for sure, it's just—why? You hadn't seen the guy in a long time, it sounds like. Why did he call you?"

"Oh, you know. You know." Ebbers's big smile made one last appearance. He opened his hands. "Not everybody has a lot of experience with stuff like this. Cops and crime scenes and so on. Most people don't."

It wasn't an answer, not really. But it was all Ruben was going to get. Ebbers patted Ruben firmly on the shoulder and went back inside the giant door.

"You have a great day, now, son."

December 9, 2009

1.

The call caught Shenk in the hallway just outside Cates's court-room, and Shenk should have known better than to answer; not a call from a number he didn't recognize; not with two minutes before gavel.

"Mr. Shenk?"

"Yeah?"

"It's Dr. Pileggi."

"I'm sorry—it's who?" For one confused second, Shenk thought it was a physician he'd gone to see, calling to give him test results. "Am I all right?"

"It's Dr. Theresa Pileggi. The neuroscientist. The expert witness."

"Oh. Oh, right, sure. How are you?" He saw Riggs coming off the elevator. He threw him a cheery and unrequited wave.

"I wonder, Mr. Shenk, if you had thought any further about my potential use to you."

"Uh, yeah. No. I mean, sure."

In point of fact, it had occurred to him a couple of times over the summer that he might need to call her. If this thing went to trial, he would need an expert witness after all, and no one else even halfway credible was even *claiming* to know what was wrong with Wesley.

But lately Shenk's mind had been on Paola Garza and the mystery of the missing radiologist; his mind had been on Paul Newman in *The Verdict*.

"Your trial opens on April fifth, I believe."

Shenk grimaced. He did not need that particular reminder at this moment, and besides, had he told her that? Had Liptack? Was she tracking his case?

"As it happens," he informed her, "there's not going to be a trial. We're moving closer to settlement."

He believed it; he was back to believing it. After today, after he got Dr. Allyn on the record, he would be back on track.

"Are you working with another expert witness?" asked Dr. Pileggi coolly.

"I told you, I don't think I'll need one."

"So, no, then?"

He couldn't help it. He laughed. "Listen. Dr. Pileggi. Your keen interest is noted, and I will let you know if I need you. OK?"

Jackie Benson, Cates's clerk and Shenk's pal, came bustling past, on her way into courtroom 5—she looked at Shenk and then meaningfully at her watch, and he mouthed, *I'm coming, I'm coming.*

"You do, Mr. Shenk," said Pileggi.

"I do what?"

"You need—"

Shenk hung up before she could complete the thought, but he knew what she was going to say, she was going to say, *You need me,* and even though it was now past time to be inside, taking his place at the plaintiff's table, he stood looking at his phone for a good ten seconds before he put it away and headed in.

Even with the sly intercession of Ms. Benson, Shenk had had to wait nearly three weeks after his assignation with Paolo Garza before he could get a slot on Cates's calendar.

Shenk could hardly wait—he was bursting at the seams.

Garza had given in, told him exactly where he could find Dr. Allyn, the radiologist who had abruptly and suspiciously left Valley Village in the wake of the Keener surgery. In a perfect world, Shenk would have gone up there directly, shown up on Dr. Allyn's devious doorstep with no warning to squeeze out her secrets like juice from fruit, but he knew that whatever it was—whatever Riggs and the hospital and the hospital insurer were hiding from him—it was better to get it the right way. Get the judge's stamp of approval. Make sure there was no way the testimony could subsequently be disallowed. Once he'd chased this thing down, it would only be a matter of waiting for the phone to ring; only a question of whether they would return to the classy seafood joint for the second round of settlement talks or try somewhere new. Maybe this time, he would write down the number on a napkin.

Cates gaveled in the motion conference and then held it in suspension as he silently read the briefs, humming the famous overture from *Figaro* and gently tapping his forehead with the eraser end of a pencil. Long minutes of respectful but agonized silence, Shenk going berserk in his seat, casting pugilistic glances at Riggs, who was settled and docile as always at the opposing table. Riggs would have sat there all day admiring Cates's performance of judgeship, Riggs no doubt perfectly satisfied to stare into the middle distance and calculate how much, at his hourly rate, he was earning just sitting here.

At last Cates finished reading, looked carefully at Shenk and then carefully at Riggs, as if putting faces to names, and then tugged at his chin. "OK," he said. "Mr. Shenk."

"We need to be permitted to depose this witness, Your Honor," Shenk said as he jumped up. "It is absolutely imperative to my case."

"Yes, yes." A slow nod. Holding up the brief by its corner. "I gathered that. The question is, Mr. Shenk, why have you not done so already? This witness submitted her interrogatory many moons ago. If you found that insufficient, and wanted her testimony compelled, you've had plenty of time to petition the court."

Riggs was over at his table, nodding along, solemnly confirming the judge in his wisdom.

"There has been a shell game played, Your Honor," said Shenk, striding out from behind the defense table. There was no jury present, no one to be impressed by the Atticus Finch routine, but Shenk wasn't entirely performing—his passion was real. This morning he had run three and a quarter miles at nine miles an hour, the treadmill set to a 5 percent incline, and he still had a sheen of sweat all down his back. "Plaintiffs were told that Dr. Allyn had retired and left Los Angeles County. Given that the CT scan findings were available and not in dispute, I allowed—I *graciously* allowed—for her to respond via interrogatory."

He paused, took a breath. "What we were *not* told, but which we subsequently discovered, was that Dr. Allyn's retirement, first of all, occurred a remarkably coincidental three days after Wesley was brought in to Valley Village. And secondly that she didn't really retire, but rather immediately took a new position, in another part of the state. Have you seen *The Verdict,* sir? With Paul Newman?"

"Relevance?" said Riggs tiredly, while Judge Cates narrowed his eyes.

"Let's proceed from the premise," said the judge acidly, "that I have not."

Shenk counseled himself to pull back, to chill out, but it was hard, it was really hard, especially with Riggs now rising to his feet, puffing out his cheeks and neck like a bullfrog.

"Your Honor," Shenk said. "My job as counsel is to try and find out everything of relevance, including interviewing anyone in possession of critical information, whether or not they have been conveniently removed from the line of sight."

"Dr. Allyn, as has been noted," said Riggs, "is no longer an employee of Valley Village. I have consulted with the hospital, and they do not know where she is."

"Well, I do know," Shenk said. "As a matter of fact. I do."

Riggs turned to him. "And how did you find that information?"

"Oh, it's just this fun method I have, called I'm a better lawyer than you."

Jackie Benson, at her clerk's desk, chortled and then covered her mouth. Judge Cates spared her a quick displeased look before he said, "Easy, Mr. Shenk."

"I'm sorry, Your Honor. I am worked up. I confess I am worked up by what's happened here. What is happening."

"Your Honor, if I may?" said Riggs to Judge Cates, with a mild and forbearing expression, as if appealing to a parent when a sibling is being an asshole. "Dr. Allyn, as opposing counsel acknowledges, now resides outside LA County. And, as has also been acknowledged, she's already submitted a detailed interrogatory. We urge the court not to allow Mr. Shenk to inconvenience this woman any further, and certainly not to delay this trial in order to do so."

"And the plaintiff urges the court," said Shenk, snatching away the thread of Riggs's argument and turning it into his own, "not to let important information go by the wayside in the name of arbitrary urgency."

Cates tilted back his chair. He laced his fingers behind his neck and let his gaze turn to the high ceiling of the court, to think carefully and to allow the court to contemplate his thoughtfulness.

"I'm going to allow it," said Cates finally, letting the chair tip back forward and lightly tapping his gavel. Shenk felt a sluice of good, giddy joy pour from heaven right down into his heart. This was it. He was going to find this lady, and he was going to win this thing.

"The court will issue notice to Dr. Allyn to make herself available, at a location convenient to her, not to us." He leveled his gavel at Jay. "But there will be no delay. The case remains where it is on our calendar, which means you have—" He turned to Ms. Benson, who was ready.

"Twelve days, Your Honor."

"Yes. Twelve days. Discovery closes on December eighteenth."

"December twenty-first, Judge," said Ms. Benson, and Cates gave her the evil eye. "Fine." Cates turned his scowl back to Shenk. "And this is on your dime, sir."

"Obviously," said Shenk, his chest tightening for the moment in dire recollection of how few dimes he had left. Never mind— he would figure that out. He risked a Riggsward glance, beaming, eyebrows dancing. Riggs merely shrugged, and Jay kept smiling, affable and gracious and beaming a silent message at full volume: *Try to* Verdict *me, asshole.*

2.

Wrestling? Jesus, what had he been *thinking*? He hadn't been thinking.

Ruben had been rushing out the front door of the school as usual to make sure he caught his bus. Wednesdays and Fridays he took city transit home after school, the Big Blue Bus from Santa Monica: Olympic to Centinela and then down Palms. He let himself in with the key, did his homework, and waited for his dad. But today he had stopped at the side door of the school, drawn by the squeaks and grunts coming from the small gym by the main entrance, and had wandered over to peer inside. Ruben, whose impressions of wrestling had heretofore come entirely from the World Wrestling Federation, big hair and metal chairs and gouts of blood, was struck by the precision and control on display: place this arm here, this leg there; bend this knee and then the other. Strength made into tension; tension put to purpose. There. Now. *Flip.*

Coach Marsden saw Ruben watching and lumbered over. He was a thick-bellied man with a handlebar mustache, always in a polo shirt with the school logo stretched across his massive chest and stomach. Ruben was surprised by the sweet quality of his voice when it emerged: gentle, slow, so low you almost couldn't hear him.

"So? What do you think?" Coach Marsden said, and then before Ruben could answer he took his arm with his hand, measuring it between two big fingers like they were calipers. "I think you might be a fit, young man. I think you might be a fit."

Now, look, Ruben was no dummy. If ever there was a kid to second-guess his own motivations and torture himself over decisions, it was Ruben Shenk. Of course he knew that Wesley Keener wrestled—Evelyn had told him her brother was a wrestler. Is. Was. Was. Is. But he let himself, in that moment in the doorway of the gym, simply go for it. It felt right, so he did it. He signed up. And that was OK. He was not stealing something from Evelyn's brother, he thought, crossing Sepulveda at Palms, carrying a plastic bag full of wrestling gear. It was a tribute. An *homage.*

The plastic bag bopped happily against his leg, filled with the curious artifacts of the unfamiliar avocation. A singlet. A piece of sturdy polycarbonate headgear. Mouthpiece and elbow guards. A new world.

Ruben whistled slightly as he trudged up the hill toward home, feeling unaccustomed flickers of anticipation and enthusiasm; nervous silverfish feelings darting between his ribs.

At the top of Tabor Street, the night man was waiting.

He was sitting in a chair in the center of their lawn. It was one of the heavy upholstered outdoor chairs they kept in the backyard, which were arranged in a large semicircle around the glass patio table. The night man had dragged the big chair from the backyard around to the front, and now he was sitting in it, legs spread, in long shorts and sunglasses and sandals, casual and cool, just hanging out, killing time in a stranger's front yard.

The night man turned his head slowly at Ruben's approach and smiled. He raised one hand and made two fingers into a V of greeting.

"What are you doing here?" said Ruben. He didn't come any closer to his house. He stayed in the street.

"There he is," said the stranger, peeking out over the top of his sunglasses. "There's our boy. How ya doing, Ruben?" His voice was fake sweet, coddling, like a guidance counselor or a youth-group leader.

"My dad isn't here," said Ruben immediately, and then just as immediately regretted it. He was old enough to recognize the childish foolishness of telling a stranger that you were by yourself. He knew what happened when you confessed your isolation: the arm around your neck, the poisoned candy, the predatory van.

Or this. Just this man, waiting in his yard, alone. This is what people should be scared of. The man, Dennis, or whatever his name was supposed to be, slowly unfolded his legs and rose from the chair. Then he walked forward to stand by the mailbox, at the edge of the property, a few feet from Ruben out in the street. He dug a loose cigarette from his pocket.

"That's all right," he said. He clicked the lighter, lit the cigarette, let the fire dance. "I'm here to see *you,* my man."

Ruben felt tremors in his legs. His hand sweated on the handle of the plastic bag. He had been trying to forget him, but the night man was impossible to forget—this man, this cult leader or hippie or whatever he was, who had come into their life along with all the other flotsam and nonsense of the *Keener* case, and who somehow was also the same man who had been in his mother's room when she died.

A man who Ruben had thought for all of his life was a nightmare but who now stood outside his house, blowing smoke at the sky.

"We've been looking for him," the night man said, his smile mischievous, his eyes twinkling. "My friends and me. We've been looking for the Keener boy. And we keep on getting close, but you know what? They keep on moving him. They're paranoid, these fucking people. Treating this kid like he's the fucking *Pope.* Like he's the crown jewels, you know?"

"I can't talk to you."

"You're talking to me right now, Ruben. Aren't we talking?"

Ruben's name sounded ugly coming from the stranger's lips. Like the word *Ruben* was a slur.

A neighbor from three doors down, whose name was Chuck, Ruben thought, walked by talking into his phone, walking his russet border collie. Dennis waved to him in greeting, and he waved back distractedly. *Help,* thought Ruben. *Help.* Chuck cruised past, the collie straining at her leash.

"So I need your help," the stranger said evenly. "You heard what we were telling your dad, right? The good and golden world, Ruben. It's like this spirit, this beautiful merciful spirit, and it is trapped. It's fucking trapped, man. Pardon my French. But we gotta let it out. Out of the vessel and into the world. Maybe your dad can't understand that, but I think you can. I think you do." He paused. He peered at Ruben. "Will you tell me where he is?"

"I don't know."

And he didn't. He didn't know. But with the night man looking at him, with his tangled blond hair, something lecherous in his gaze, Ruben felt like he had been caught. He felt like he was lying, even though he knew he wasn't.

He took a breath and said it again, looked right at where the man's eyes should be, behind the glasses. "I don't know where he is."

Dennis reached up to take off his sunglasses, and for one crazy second Ruben expected him to have no eyes at all. But when the glasses came off, there they were, dark and blazing, like two smoldering coals. The night man seized Ruben's chin and tilted his head up, and his eyes looked just the way they had in the darkness of his life's worst night, when this person had been there but not there, lurking in the room when Marilyn was disappearing, a shadow in the corner of death. Ruben dared himself to stare right back, but he couldn't do it. He looked past him, at the house. His house. The off-white trim around the blue front door. The two little windows over the kitchen sink. The house would never be the same now, now that this man had been here. Now that the night man knew where it was.

"OK, I believe you," he said finally, letting go of Ruben's face, laughing as Ruben exhaled, relieved. "Can't make you know something you don't know, right? That's crazy. Tell you what, though." He took out a business card and slid it, a smooth and intimate gesture, into Ruben's pocket. "If you find out, you'll tell me, OK? How's that?"

He flicked his cigarette butt into a stand of knobby succulents, bulbous prickly aliens that Marilyn had lovingly planted one summer when Ruben was still a baby.

"One more thing." Dennis said it in the same easy voice, offhand and casual. "You're not going to be a fucking wrestler, Ruben. Nobody gets to be happy. You know that, right? Not in *this* world."

As he walked past, he swatted at the plastic bag full of gear so it bopped against Ruben's leg.

"But there's another world, Rubie-boobie." A toddler's ridiculous nickname. Marilyn's name for him. Just between the two of them. "Just waiting. The future is waiting inside that boy, and you can help. We *need* your help, kiddo."

And then Dennis left, one long step at a time, whistling a Beach Boys song, wandering aimlessly off the lawn and into the street. Ruben exhaled, shuddering, so relieved to be watching him go.

But then he called out after him, shouting, "Hey, hey," until the night man turned, grinning, coy.

"If the—the spirit, the better world. If it's inside him, then what are you going to *do*?"

"Oh, didn't I say?" The night man turned back. He slipped the sunglasses back on. When he grinned, Ruben could see the gap between his bright white teeth.

"We're going to crack him open, kid. Get it *out*."

January 22, 2019

Cosmo's was the second in a row of three squalid, low-slung motels, on a particularly unglamorous block, among the taco stands and car washes and doughnut shops that ran along Sepulveda just south of Venice Boulevard. The motel was a remnant of a period of LA history that had never existed but left its traces everywhere: a mid-century space-age of cheerful roadside glamour, when every scuzzy hot-sheet motel had a sign with big rounded letters, advertising COLOR TV and AIR-CONDITIONING and HEATED POOL. Cosmo's was a semicircle of connected rooms, loosely gathered around a dirty and ill-kempt heated pool—as promised—that you could see in its entirety from the parking lot. No hot tub, no diving board, just a handful of stained vinyl chairs in scraggly clumps.

The on-ramp for the 405 was right across the road, and the parking lot was full of dust and fumes. Ruben found a parking space and sat for a second, looking at his own eyes in the rearview mirror and asking himself what he was doing.

If the working plan was to somehow prove that Richard Keener was sufficiently emotionally disturbed—was, as Ebbers had put it, out of his damn mind—he was hardly going to find evidence of that at the scene of the crime. His mandate was to find reasons to lessen the sentence, not to reinvestigate the case, which anyway seemed pretty clear: Richard shot at Pileggi, then he broke her head with a lamp, and then he called the police and told them he did it.

So what was Ruben doing?

The answer, such as it was, lay in Ebbers's elusive half answer to what had been, after all, a pretty straightforward question: when Rich was under arrest, why did he call you?

Not everybody has a lot of experience with stuff like this. Cops and crime scenes and so on.

Ruben got off work on Tuesdays at 7:00, and he'd come right down here. Still in his neon-yellow shirt, KILLER GREENS across the front.

Cops and crime scenes and so on.

This was, Ruben was fairly sure, a waste of his time.

"Joke's on you," he told himself as he got out of the car. In the next space was a pink van advertising Topless Maids, featuring a voluptuous silhouette that leered at Ruben as he headed for the door. "My time's not that valuable."

"No, no, no, no. No, you fucker. No! Fuck you! *No!*"

The front-desk man at Cosmo's this evening was deeply, angrily invested in a ball game playing on the laptop in his office. He was a husky older guy, with sharp eyes dancing under bushy eyebrows, with twin tufts of woolly white hair puffing out from under a Dodgers cap. "Come the *fuck on!*"

"Excuse me?" Ruben said it quietly, cleared his throat, and said it again. "Excuse me."

The lobby was sparsely decorated and smelled of spilled milk or old garbage. A single goldfish, swimming in a clouded, lopsided bowl, looked like a prisoner, underfed and forlorn.

"How you doing?" said the clerk, eyes locked on the laptop

screen. "You need a room?" And then, before Ruben could answer: "Oh, come *on*. Jesus fuck! *Come on*."

Ruben peered at the man's computer screen, at the ball game, which—based on the 1980s uniforms and the grainy film quality—was archival footage, an old game, which made sense. It wasn't baseball season.

The clerk looked up, yawned with his gnarled fist up to his mouth. "Fucking Garvey, huh? All right—just you?"

"Yes, sir."

"Sir?" He snorted. "How about that?"

The old man's desk was a disorienting jumble of paper: sections of the *LA Times,* yellowing receipts, stacks of unopened mail and catalogs. While he sifted through the chaos for a paper and pen, the fish twitched in his bowl, crying for help.

"How long you need?"

"Just, uh—just one. One night."

"One night, all right. Single? Double? You name it. We're pretty empty."

"Single." Ruben said it quietly, suddenly nervous. "I'd like room 109, please."

The clerk had just found a pen. He flicked it back into the shambles of his desk. "All right," he said, and made a thick noise at the roof of his mouth. "Get outta here."

"What?"

"I said get outta here, dude." He doffed his cap and aimed it at the door. "*Get out.*"

Ruben fumbled his thick wallet from the back of his pants. "But I can pay. I have money."

"Room 109 is not available," the man sneered. "But you knew that, right?"

"No. Why? What?"

From the TV, the crack of a line drive, the tinny ancient roar of the crowd. Statistically, Ruben noted, a lot of the people in that crowd are dead by now. "You *know* why not. Because a lady got killed in there, couple weeks ago. That's why. Right? Come on, asshole. You read it in the fucking paper, or on that, what, Reddit, huh? And here *you* are, no suitcase or nothin', and oh by the way it's one particular room you'd like. Ya fucking weirdo. You think I'm born yesterday?"

"No," said Ruben, stunned by the profane rush. "No, actually, I'm . . ."

Nothing. I'm nothing.

Private. Defective.

"Look, sport, you wanna jack off at a murder scene, try the LaBianca house, OK? I'll draw you a map."

"You're misunderstanding."

"I am?"

"I'm not a pervert."

The clerk scowled. "You think I care if you're a pervert? Perverts are my bread and butter. But that room is *closed*. It's in *turnaround*. OK?"

Ruben surprised himself by persisting. "If I could just glance in there—just for a moment."

"It's fucking *closed,* man. You deaf? Deaf pervert?"

"And when," said Ruben politely, "do you think the room might become available again?"

"A while. OK? Someone gets their head bashed in, it takes a minute to clean." He ticked off tasks on his fingers. "We gotta send out the rugs, get the mattress cleaned, rinse the brains outta the carpet. Plus, you know, bullet holes, too, a pair of 'em in my nice wall. And it ain't like we're getting *reimbursed* by anybody, by the way." He snorted, indignant. "So I tell you what, come back in a

few weeks, be happy to make you a reservation. But you might
have to wait in line behind the rest of the ghostfuckers."

If there was anything to find in this dump, in a few weeks it
would be long gone. Steamed out of the carpets, washed off the
walls. Not to mention, Ruben didn't have a few weeks. He had—
what?—he had thirteen days at this point. In a few weeks, Richard
Keener would be sitting on death row.

But he pressed on.

"Can I just explain?" said Ruben. "I'm seriously not a—a
ghostfucker." He smiled awkwardly. "That's not me."

"So then what are you?"

Million-dollar question, thought Ruben. "I'm working the case,"
he said, and that sounded idiotic, like he was on *CSI* or something.
"I've been hired by the defense team. I'm an investigator."

"Oh yeah?"

The guy scratched between his eyes and squinted at Ruben,
clearly finding this information hard to credit. Ruben as he often
did at such moments saw himself through the stranger's eyes, this
random Asian guy with his glasses and his one crumpled ear. Tall
but trying to make himself small.

"So, you're an investigator," the clerk said finally. "Well, that
changes everything."

"It does?"

"No. It does not."

He laughed without humor, and then unpaused his ball game.

Ruben almost left it there, and maybe he should have.

Maybe what he should have done was go back into the parking
lot, climb into his Altima, and call it a night.

Instead he stood, thinking of Evie, putting her hand to his face.
Backstage at the Echo, the singer and the detective, two strangers
who had been friends their whole lives.

"It's good to see you," she had said. "You look really good."

And when he closed his eyes he could still feel the heat of her palm on his cheek.

So what was he going to do now? Stop?

"Sir? Sorry."

The man looked up again, astonished by this further incursion on his vintage baseball game. Ruben laid his hand down on the desk and lifted it again, and the man looked at the small pile of bills and then up at him.

"For fuck's sake," he said sharply. "You tryna bribe me with—" He counted quickly with his eyes. "Nine dollars?"

"Um—yes. Yes, sir."

"OK." The clerk shrugged. "I'll take it."

The door was old, but the handle was new. It had been switched out from the one Richard Keener had broken to get in.

The Rabbi at the threshold, taking stock. His eyes behind his thick glasses moved slowly from one end of the room to the other, from wall to wall.

"OK," he said to himself. "It's a room."

A motel room, dim and ugly and cramped. One window looking out at the parking lot, where Ruben saw his car, parked next to the tawdry pink van. The colors of the room were shades of brown: beige, ecru, rust. Thin, fraying drapes. An ancient blocky television, a few ugly paintings of nothing: just shapes, colors, desultory gestures toward decoration.

The AC unit was unplugged, the cord curled into itself at the baseboard. A thin striped bedspread, laddered with thin beams of moonlight. The whole place smelled like paint and bleach and the dry, dusty odor of recent vacuuming. A room in a purgatorial state, on its way to being restored to its public function. The bathroom door was open; the toilet seat was up; no toilet paper on the roll; the shower curtain tucked up and hanging from the shower rail like a koala.

The room was dark and stale, but it was charged, too, with a shivering doomy energy. As Ruben stepped inside, he was conscious of a crouching sense of risk, which, as he began to move through the room, drew itself slowly up to full height. His dick, unpredictable bellwether of strong feeling, stiffened slightly in his pants. For God's sake, he thought, but after all there are only so many strong feelings. Lust and darkness, murder and sex. Maybe they blur together in places like this. Murder places, with the power of high emotion still flickering in the corners, murmuring out from under the thin bedspread.

Or maybe he was a ghostfucker after all.

Ruben moved gingerly through the room, thinking what a nightmare it was to have a body. To *be* a body, tricked all the time into wanting whatever the body happened to want.

Most of the room was taken up by the bed. There was only one night table, jammed into a narrow space behind the wall, which separated the single room from the bathroom.

"OK," he said, and shook his head, laughing at himself one last time, granting himself permission finally to do what he was doing. Casing a room. Chasing a phantom. Cops and crime scenes and so on.

If you're going to fucking do it, you fucking do it.

"All right," he said aloud, slipping off his glasses and sliding them into a pocket of his pants. "So, I'm Rich."

He stood up tall and pulled his shoulders back and pushed out his chest. He exhaled, growling, feeling a skeptical gloominess rearrange the shape of his face. Then he backed up and came through the door again, coming in slow and heavy: walking Rich's heavy bear's walk, sniffing the air.

He looked down at the world from height, glowered around the room.

"I break into the room." He glanced back at the door. "She's not here." He paused, remembered. "I knew she wouldn't be here. My plan is, I wait. I sit on the bed."

It creaked under his weight.

"I have this handgun. My old gun. I've had it for years." Ruben recalled the details from the police report. A semiautomatic pistol, 8mm, with a sixteen-round clip. "I never use it, but now I'm gonna use it. I'm ready."

He aimed his invisible weapon at the door. "I'm waiting," said Ruben to the empty room, to the moonlight and the smell of cleaning supplies. "I wait."

Then the door opened, he could fucking see it opening, and he aimed his invisible handgun and fired it—shouted *bang*—and watched the bullet's path, an angle from the bed to the doorway.

Fuck. He'd missed. From so close, he'd missed—nervous, maybe, not a shooter, hadn't practiced—

He shot again, screamed *bang,* missed again, and got up from the bed and hurled his massive body toward Theresa Pileggi. Ruben could see her clearly now, her intense expression, unblinking, unsmiling—he caught her by the door, slammed her against the wall.

And there it was, the lamp—right there on the table—Ruben snatched it and then paused, heaving breaths, bent over, the rounded midsection of the lamp clutched in his hand, the cord dangling like an entrail.

It had to be a different lamp. The murder weapon would be in evidence somewhere. Cosmo's probably had a shelf lined with them, in a storage closet off the lobby, rows of cheap, ugly lamps, all the same: the cord wrapped around the brass base, the thin shade that clipped to the wire of the socket stand. Ruben lifted it. It felt like he was holding something substantial; a paperweight or a small bowling ball. Suddenly he took two steps from the bed back toward the door, back toward where Pileggi had come into the room. He swung the lamp in a slow arc over his head, reenacting the central moment, pausing three-quarters of the way through and shouting *crack* before watching Pileggi topple, broken, to the floor.

He did it again, quicker: grabbed the lamp, swung the lamp, grunting with the effort, feeling the small burn of muscle movement in his shoulder. Stopping abruptly where he imagined the lamp base would have connected with Pileggi's head.

Crack.

Ugly sound, final sound, death at the moment of delivery.

He stood there frozen, the lamp in his hand. How strange it was that this *physical* action—the collision of the cheap metal of a lamp base against the bone of the head, the metal like an asteroid smashing into the skull, plowing deep and deeper into the putty of the brain—could have as its consequence the blipping out of this thing that never was physical in the first place: "Dr. Theresa Pileggi" had after all only been an idea, an *abstraction,* the name that the world gave to the collection of thoughts and emotions and physical actions and reactions that operated in the world as one complete functioning system. All the things that had been Theresa Pileggi— the bones and blood, the muscles and skin, the flesh and the molecules of the flesh—none of that disappeared in the moment of contact. All of it was in a box now, in the ground, and all that had died when the lamp hit the skull were the *ideas;* the *thinking;* the *consciousness;* what was gone had never literally physically existed to begin with. The person was the mind, and the mind was gone, but it had never been here, not like, say, the lamp.

Ruben was on the ground. On his back, laid out, eyes open, seeing nothing. He lay where Theresa had lain, after Rich killed her. He had switched from one part to the other, from killer to killed. Now he pulled himself up, flipped over and held that shape, on all fours, head down, an old wrestler's pose. *You've examined the floors and the bed and the furniture. You've held the weapons in your hands. What have you missed?*

If there is something to miss.

But by now, somehow, Ruben was sure that there was. A crime scene held clues, that's what it was, a place for clues, even now, even after the room has been stripped and scrubbed.

"All right, then," he said softly. "So what's the clue?"

A voice answered this thought, a whisper out of the cleaned carpet. Cool and commanding, logical and precise. It was Pileggi's voice, and it said *the wall.* The cranky old bastard had complained about the bullet holes, right? *A pair of 'em in my nice wall.*

Ruben stood up, put his glasses back on, and laid his palms flat on the wall, beneath the light switch. He moved his hands slowly, in unison, one beside the other, wincing as his bandaged fingertip caught on a rough patch of new paint.

The bullet holes, when he found them, weren't really bullet holes at all anymore. Merely indentations. They'd been roughed over with Spackle and covered with new paint, leaving just a pair of shallow indentations in the white of the wall.

Ruben tugged his phone out of his pocket and turned on the flashlight app. He cast the searching radius of light over the indentations. With the nail of one pinky he scraped and poked at the drywall. It crumbled and caved away, and soon enough he was staring at the holes themselves. He bent his knees, angled in to examine them more closely, rolled his thumb gingerly around the rim of one hole and then the other one.

He watched the bullets smash into the wall, disappear into the plaster. Watched the explosion of paint and dust. Ruben narrowed his eyes, brought the flashlight closer, angled the very bright light into the nearer hole, like a searchlight into the mouth of a cave. Then he looked back at the bed, where he as Rich had only just been sitting, waiting, gun drawn.

It occurred to Ruben at this point that the clever thing would be to draw a picture of the holes and what he had noticed about their angle. He was fumbling in his bag for the little notebook he had brought when he remembered that he was literally holding a camera.

He turned off the flashlight and opened the camera app and just took pictures of the holes and emailed them to himself, one by one.

And he felt halfway good, walking back through the lobby, more than halfway. He walked briskly, sailing a little as he went. He tipped a swift nod to the clerk, who grunted and gave him a sarcastic thumbs-up. Ruben wasn't convinced there was meaning in what he had found, but he liked how it made him feel to wonder. The Rabbi felt wise. For good or ill, he felt like he was *doing* something, and the feeling was unaccustomed and positive and good.

The night man was in the parking lot.

The night man was waiting.

He sat on the back bumper of the pink van, half-illuminated by a streetlight, a cigarette dangling from the corner of his mouth. Looking right at Ruben across twenty yards of empty parking lot, with his lopsided grin and his dirty tank top and his sandals. He raised one hand and slowly unfurled two fingers into a V for peace.

He hadn't aged. He looked like he had looked in the hospital, bent over Ruben's dying mom; like he had in the offices of Shenk & Partners, foretelling the good and golden world; like he had the night, in the middle of the *Keener* trial, when he had smashed into their kitchen on Tabor Street, when he had held a knife to Jay's throat, and——

Ruben sprinted across the parking lot, but the night man was already going, and by the time he got there the man was gone. Had never been there at all.

"Come on," said Ruben. "Come *on*." There was a patch of dirty oil behind the van, right where the guy had been, and Ruben stared at the ground, cast about in helpless circles, because there would be footprints, tracks, *evidence,* and there was none. There was no one following Ruben, tracking his investigation, taunting his fleeting sense of progress.

I am a part of this, too.

He imagined the night man out on Sepulveda, ambling south, chuckling to himself.

You can't cut me out, Rubie-boobie.

I'm a part of everything.

December 18, 2009

1.

"You know what?" said Beth, and Rich said, "What?" but then she hesitated.

Here she was, she was looking out at the fucking Pacific Ocean, for God's sake, looking at it through a wall of tinted blue glass, with one of those window shades you could raise or lower with a remote control. This house was a goddamn palace.

But it wasn't right. It wasn't *right*. She turned from the window and looked at Rich, who was already looking back at her with that face of his, braced for whatever it was that was going to piss him off.

"I think we gotta move."

"You're kidding," said Rich.

"No," she said. "But can I explain?"

Rich threw his hands in the air. "I mean, you have to be fucking kidding."

"Sweetheart," said Beth. "You wanna calm down?"

"Yeah. Sure." And he stalked away from her, to the far side of the room, planted himself at one end of the low, sleek, modernist sofa, and waited. "I'm calm. Let's hear it."

The ocean was an endless field of blue. Pleasure boats way out on the horizon line, a handful of surfers nearer to shore. Seagulls wheeling high overhead.

"I just think it's too exposed," she told Richard. "All the glass. And it's perched up here."

"It's isolated," said Rich. "That's a plus."

"It's *exposed*. There are like seventeen entrances."

"There are five. Ebbers's guys went over all of this with us. Front, side, side, back, garage."

Beth was shaking her head. It didn't matter. She knew how she felt. They weren't going to stay here. She had been crazy to agree to this house in the first place. She peered down one long hallway, and down another, both of them hung with different kinds of froufrou modern art. Slashes of color; shit made out of wires.

They couldn't stay here. It just—it wasn't *right*.

"I'm really sorry, baby," she said, and Richard pursed his lips and exhaled, a long, controlled release of breath. "I'm not trying to be difficult."

"OK," he said, and nothing else, just "OK." Which both of them knew meant *But you are, aren't you? You are being difficult.*

Wes walked between them, and Beth reached out to brush his shoulder with the back of her hand as he passed. In his endless unvarying circle he walked, the same here as anywhere, tracing a wide circumference in the massive unfurnished house, from the front door across the grand length of the living room, to the enormous window and back.

The Malibu house belonged to a television star who was the ex-husband of another, starrier television star. The TV star had been granted the house in the custody deal but then immediately got remarried, to a film executive with a massive house of her own, and left this one standing open. When they'd explained it to them, Beth could hardly believe it. You just couldn't fathom there was so much money in the world: people just buying houses, leaving them empty.

"So what are you saying we do?" Rich asked, implicitly conceding the argument. They were leaving the Malibu house. That part was done. "Go home? Or—what—back to the Redondo place?"

"No."

"The trailer, then? The fucking—"

"No. Rich."

"You wanna put him back in the hospital?"

"Oh no," said Beth. "No way."

Wesley passed. His eyes stared at Beth, unseeing, as he moved by. She reached out to him; she was always reaching out to him, as if one time he would stop and reach back.

"So what, then?" said Rich, impatient. "So what do you want to do?"

"I don't know. We just—I don't *know*. We can ask Ebbers, right? He'll find us somewhere else."

"No." He shook his head. "I don't want to go back to Ebbers."

"Why not?"

"Because we don't need to keep bothering the man."

"Bothering him? Rich, we had a tragedy." She gestured to Wesley, who had reached the rear window and turned back. "We are a tragedy. People *want* to help."

"We're not going back to Ebbers."

"Maybe another place'll be cheaper, anyway."

Ebbers's work came pro bono, but all the rest of it—the guards, the private-duty aides, the rental on the house itself—did not.

"I know you're worried about the money part of it."

"I love the way you say that. The money part of it." He looked at his watch. "Shit. I should be at work right now."

It wasn't just the money, Beth knew. Rich hated asking people for help, hated people making allowances for them. He was a guy who solved problems, who built things. Not a guy who *needed*. Not a guy who *took*. Not a guy who bothered anyone for anything, even in the most minor possible way, even for the best possible reason. His fucking kid was *sick*. Worse than sick. Nobody fucking knew *what* he was.

Beth had quit her job a long time ago. Eddie and everybody had been understanding, told her to take the time she needed, and even asked her to consider coming in two days a week. But even two days a week was too much. Two days out of seven trying to give a shit about anyone or anything else? Answering the phone, dealing with people's plumbing emergencies?

Richard was still working, just short-term on-set gigs, abiding by all the protocols Ebbers had taught him: working under fake names, making sure he wasn't followed. He walked around looking over his shoulder half the time, like a goddamn crazy person.

Nobody could get to Wesley; nobody could try to hurt him again. That was the important thing. That was all that mattered.

"We have to do what's best for him," Beth said, and Rich scowled.

"You said this place would be a good spot. A safe spot. We stood here, and we all agreed: Yes. Great."

Beth shrugged. She turned back to the magnificent window. She wasn't going to explain herself. She couldn't. The world was an infuriating, horrible, always-changing thing. Sometimes you just had to keep up.

"Rich. Baby. I can call him."

"Ebbers?"

"Do you want me to call him?"

"No." He sighed. She saw him softening, as she had known he would. She had known him for such a long time. "I'll do it."

Her big husband opened up his arms. They had met when she was fifteen. It was fucking ridiculous. How many married people fell in love in third-period gym class? She shook her head at her husband, at the fact that after everything, they still loved each other. After his motorcycle accident, after all the stupid jobs they'd suffered through, after the two bad years in New Mexico, after the shit with his mom and after *this,* now, this living nightmare. Their boy.

After all of it. Still in love. He was a goon. Her man. He needed a haircut.

She fell against his body and let his arms close around her, and then she tilted her head up and kissed him hard on the mouth. How long had it been since they'd had sex? Christ — was it possible she had not fucked her husband since before the accident? For over a fucking *year?*

She kissed him harder, held herself against him, and they stood that way for a while, the only two adults in the world who knew what they were suffering, pressing their two bodies in one shape, while their son moved in his slow circle around them.

Beth spoke into Rich's chest.

"Shenk says it's looking good. He found her."

"Who?"

"The radiologist, baby." Richard wasn't keyed in. He wasn't really paying attention. He was waiting for it to be over. "Shenk's got her. It's really good. He says when we win, we'll walk away with like four million bucks."

"And what if we lose?" he said.

"Come on. Honey. We're not going to lose."

2.

"Good morning, Dr. Allyn. My name is Jay Shenk and I'm the counsel for the Keeners in this matter, and let me say, first of all, thank you for making the time to talk with us today."

"Like I had a choice."

"Well, sure." Shenk shrugged. "Still. I appreciate it."

"Can we get this over with, so I can go back to work?"

Jay Shenk smiled appeasingly, tossed a quick glance at Ms. Clarissa, the court reporter, who kept typing. "I didn't mean to get off on the wrong foot, Dr. Allyn."

"I was ordered by a judge to do this, so I'm doing it. Can we start?"

"You bet."

They were in La Rioja, California, a map-speck in California wine country, a gorgeous forty-five-minute drive from Paso Robles, the closest town of any size, which was still not really of any size. Dr. Barbara Allyn, formerly a radiologist at Valley Village Hospital Corporation, was seated across from him at a metal-mesh picnic table outside the screening center where she was now employed; there was a plastic sun umbrella emerging from a round mouth in the table's center, the pole of which partially occluded Shenk's view of his witness. Allyn was a sharp-eyed woman with silver hair and strong features, the kind of lean middle-aged white lady who looked like she ate only salad and did a brisk four-mile power walk every morning.

Sitting beside Jay was Ms. Clarissa, who had been flown up here at his expense—this whole exercise, as the judge had warned him, on his dime—and who sat clacking away on her clever little portable machine. Next to Dr. Allyn was the local counsel Riggs had scrounged up to keep a seat warm for this procedure: a twenty-something clown named Smith or Jones or something, whose modishly long hair fell over his face as he took desultory notes, casting longing glances at the paperback novel half-hidden under the *Keener* file on the table in front of him.

"How long have you lived in La Rioja, Dr. Allyn?"

"You know the answer to that."

"I do, yes. But the way this works is that I ask the questions and you answer them. Your feelings about the questions don't come into it. Isn't that right, Mr. Jones?"

"What? Oh. It's Smith, actually."

"Can you tell your client to answer the question, please?"

"Oh. What was it again?"

"I have lived here about a year and a half."

"Since November 2008, is that right?"

Allyn sighed. "Yes."

"OK." Shenk looked around. "It's nice here."

"Is that a question?"

"Nope. Just an observation."

From where they were sitting Shenk could see the quaint town square, populated with benches and old people walking dogs and a little playground area where squealing toddlers chased one another around a play structure. The grass on the lawn was astonishingly green, and the ocean was visible past Main Street and a neat strip of beach beyond it. The whole town smelled very faintly of flowers.

Shenk smiled broadly at Dr. Allyn, and she scowled back at him.

"You responded promptly, Dr. Allyn, to my interrogatory. I appreciate that. Now, I'd like to know what you left out."

She paused for a half second and then said, "What?"

"I've known a lot of radiologists. Great people, by the way. Nice tribe, your tribe. But under-respected. Right? What my radiologist friends tell me is that they'll sometimes point out something to another doctor—a surgeon, say—and the other doctor just over-rules it or ignores them."

"What is this?" Dr. Allyn turned away from him, turned to the dolt with the hair. "What the hell is this?"

"Sorry—what?" said Smith, looking up.

Allyn jabbed a finger toward Shenk. "Are you tryna make some sort of case here, that I'm at fault? That I did something wrong?"

"No. I'm not. Unless..." He raised his palms, the picture of innocence. "*Should* I be?"

"I'm not an idiot. I went to medical school, remember?"

Shenk chose not to list the medical school graduates he'd known over the years who had definitely been idiots.

"I'm just saying," he said instead, "that sometimes radiologists are a little cowed by the surgeons they're working for. Working with. Sorry. You know the type. The arrogant guys—and they are always *guys,* aren't they? The whole God-complex business. Brain surgeons, often. Big beards."

Dr. Allyn's long nostrils were flaring. "What exactly are you suggesting?"

Shenk nodded sharply. Given the doctor's attitude, given the fact that he had a plane to catch at 5:27 out of SLO, given the fact that he was paying Ms. Clarissa by the hour, it was time to cut to the chase.

"I'm suggesting that you saw something that wasn't right. I'm suggesting you saw our friend Catanzaro behave in a manner that was inappropriate and which jeopardized that kid's outcome. Sealed his fate."

Allyn stared at him, aghast. "Like what?"

"Well," said Shenk. "You tell me."

"I have no idea."

"Um." Mr. Smith raised one hand uncertainly. "Hey. What's happening?"

"The man's a bit of a drunk, Dr. Allyn. Let's be honest here."

"Who is? Dr. Catanzaro?"

"Let's not play make-believe, OK? His ex-wife testified to it in their custody hearings."

"Oh my God," she said.

"There are three previous settlements held under seal—"

"Oh my *God*."

"—and I've got three former colleagues, on the record, testifying that the man likes to have a nip at lunch."

Shenk left it there. Dr. Allyn was on her feet, staring down at him, hands clenching the edge of the table. He had made up that last part, about the on-the-record colleagues, but he could clean that up later. What he had wanted was for her to get worked up, and she was, and he was going to get what he wanted.

"Go on, now, Dr. Allyn. It's OK. Tell me what you saw. You saw him drinking, or maybe he was just drunk, and the hospital hooked you up with this sweetheart deal up here to make sure you kept a lid on it."

"This . . ." The radiologist breathed deeply, controlling some wild waves of emotion. "This sweetheart deal, huh?"

"What else do we call it? Only two or three days after Wesley's surgery, you retire from Valley Village. You move up here. Up to lovely wine country."

Dr. Allyn was shaking her head; her mouth was moving, but no words were coming out. Shenk pressed on.

"How much are you earning here?"

"Why is that any of your business?"

"Because I am a lawyer taking a deposition. Do you know who Edgar Gowan is?"

"Of course I do."

"We object," said local counsel, uncertainly, maybe unsure if he was allowed.

"He's the owner of this clinic up here in Paso, correct?"

"Mr. Shenk, we are objecting for the record."

"And he's a board member at Valley Village. Also rather a striking coincidence, don't you think?"

His switch now officially turned to ON, Smith objected again. "This line of questioning is absolutely inappropriate. I'm—I'm—"

"You're going to tell on me, yes, Mr. Smith, I understand."

Shenk turned back to Dr. Allyn.

"Doctor?"

"I'm sorry," she said. "I'm sorry." And across Shenk's hot mind, a brilliant blaze: I did it. Dr. Allyn was sorry because she had misread the boy's scans, or she was sorry for not reporting Catanzaro's catastrophic medical errors. But then she looked up with utter fury in her eyes, her face a tight mask of control, and he could see that she was only sorry for breaking down—only sorry for letting him get to her.

"My dad is dying," she said.

Shenk blinked. "What?"

"That's why I retired abruptly. That's why I left Valley Village. That's why I gave up a job I absolutely loved and was absolutely great at, to come up here and stare at herniated discs, all day every day. OK?" She shook her head tightly and pursed her lips. "He has Alzheimer's, and he has lung cancer. He is wasting away. OK?"

Oh God, thought Shenk. Oh no.

He closed his file. A pair of birds erupted from a stand of trees in the center of the square.

"My mom passed six years ago, and my sister is in no condition to help. But that's none of your business either." She now looked at him squarely. "None of this is your business. And I am sorry if the timing seems *convenient* to you, but it has nothing to do with your client or with Dr. Catanzaro or with anything else. If you want to subpoena my dad's medical records, be my guest. But I'm done."

Dr. Allyn turned to Smith, her putative lawyer, who looked back at her, wide-eyed, dumbstruck and out of his depth, while Ms. Clarissa's clattering accelerated and then died away into silence.

"I'm done," she said again, and then without another glance at Shenk, she left.

Shenk watched her push open the glass door of the screening clinic and disappear inside, thinking, one more time: *Oh no.*

Ms. Clarissa was swiftly wrapping up, closing and securing her portable typewriter, pulling out her phone to order a Lyft to the airport, which Shenk would be billed for along with the flight. Smith was up on the other side of the picnic tale, shoving his sack lunch, his paperback, and his files back into his briefcase. "Hey, great to meet you," he said nervously, and then clicked the briefcase closed. It looked barely used, a law school graduation present.

"Yeah," said Shenk, smiling absently, mind moving a thousand miles an hour. "For sure."

The professor — that woman — the lecturer from Riverside. He was going to need her after all.

January 25, 2019

The Rabbi took out his phone and checked the time again.

"Excuse me, dude," said a bearded hipster in a vinyl windbreaker, and Ruben muttered "Sorry" and moved out of the way.

Evie was late—very late now—and he was waiting, standing politely, awkwardly, by the front door of this noisy and beloved Chinese restaurant, absorbing the hot, sweet smells of the cooking: soy sauce and fish sauce and garlic simmering in oil.

It was nearly midnight now. They had agreed on eleven, although she had warned him she might be a few minutes late. Ruben checked his phone again, wondering what to a person like Evie constituted a few minutes. He shifted on his feet to let in another smartly dressed group of diners.

"Sorry," he said, leaning against a rack of bussed trays for the nineteenth time, trying to make himself small. "Let me just...sorry."

The place was aggressively hip, dark and wild with noise: shouts and laughter, booming terrible pop music, glasses clinking, all overlaid with the chaotic *zing* and *pop* of the vintage video arcade games that lined the hallway to the bathrooms. While he waited he thought over exactly what he had to say to Evie Keener; and checked his phone; and examined once again the large close-up photographs of food, interspersed with those of an elderly Asian woman — Chinese, one hoped — looking stoically into the camera, holding up great loops of noodle.

"Have you been waiting?" said Evie when she came in, and before he could answer she cuffed him around the neck and kissed him very hard on his right cheek.

She was sweaty and gorgeous, her hair still slicked back against her head from the stage. She wore a sheer tank top, and he could see the black of her bra beneath it, and he could see the red pinched lines on her shoulders where she had worn her wings. She took him by the arm and maneuvered them into the food line, and someone behind them said "Oh shit, that's . . . ," but Evie ignored the excited acknowledgment of her celebrity, grabbed two paper menus and thrust one at Ruben. His heart felt wild and weightless.

"The thing to try here is the dumplings," she told him.

"OK."

"Do you like dumplings?"

"I do."

"Attaboy."

She gave him a big, beaming smile and he tried to return it but probably just made a weird grimace. Ruben always felt that when he smiled widely he looked like a skull.

He had exciting news to share. He was glad to see her. The restaurant smelled so good. Ruben wasn't used to being in this kind of mood, and it was disorienting to feel so positive. He felt like his father.

They put in their order at the counter and jostled their way to a two-top, backed up against the wall. She slid into the booth side, and Ruben took a chair.

"So," he said.

"So," said Evie. "Any luck?"

But before Ruben could answer she said, "Shit—do you want water?" And jumped up, deftly navigating the crowd to the help-yourself steel urn, poured them each a cup, and was intercepted on the way back to the table by a man who either knew her or wanted to, a tall man in parachute pants and a wide-brimmed hat, too cool for school, and Evie and this guy talked animatedly for a minute. Ruben toyed with his napkin. He split apart his wooden chopsticks and rubbed them together as if trying to start a fire. Evie came back and sat down, set them each up with a water.

Ruben cleared his throat and said, "So, listen. Evie."

"Yeah?"

"OK. Well. I went to the crime scene."

"You went—wait, to the . . . the motel? Why?"

"Yeah. Cosmo's. I just . . . I had a hunch, I guess."

And immediately—*immediately*—Ruben knew this had been a mistake. Coming to her with his hunch, his pictures, the paper-thin results of his daffy investigative impulse. She was sitting up straight. She was staring at him. "What do you mean? What kind of *hunch*?"

Ruben waved one hand lamely and mumbled, "Actually . . . forget it."

"You went to the motel?"

He nodded, helpless. Evie furrowed her perfect brow.

"We were talking about mitigating factors. About a change in his mental state."

"Yeah, no, I know."

"Are we talking about something else now?"

Ruben nodded, flushed, miserable. Why would he bring her anything that might raise her hopes, when it was so unlikely that those hopes would be fulfilled? A waiter hustled up with their food, three steaming trays of dumplings and two bowls of seaweed salad, and they both leaned away from the table while she expertly slid it all onto the Formica.

At the next table, a young tattooed couple were sneaking peeks at Evie, obviously recognizing her, obviously trying not to. Evie the Golden—Evie the Known. From the back of the restaurant, the dinging and whirring of the arcade games: people racking up scores, shooting asteroids, rolling barrels. Evie looked at Ruben, waiting. He smiled miserably. He took the bamboo cover off the top tray of dumplings and lifted one out with his crossed chopsticks and placed it in his mouth. Just as Evie said, "Be careful," the soup inside the dumpling burst out, filling his mouth, boiling hot, and he spat the whole thing out, gagging and sputtering, onto the table.

"Oh my God. Ruben."

He gave her a helpless thumbs-up, gulping water. Evie was dying. She was giggling helplessly, trying not to, covering her mouth with both hands, her eyes wide with helpless laughter.

He hoped that the moment had passed, that the subject had been changed, but Evie reached across the table and grabbed his arms. "Dude. Come on. What are we talking about here?"

"The gunshots," he said finally. He brought his voice down a little, even though no one could hear them in the noise of this place, not in a million years. "The angle of the shots," he said. "It's wrong."

"What?" Evie smoothed her white hair with both hands, staring at him. "What does that mean?"

"Well, according to the police report and the charging documents, according to what your dad told the police, he broke into her motel room and waited for her to come in. Then he stood up and shot at her. Twice."

"OK."

"Well, so, look."

He got out his phone. He leaned across the table, trying not to get his elbows in the food. She looked at him, a quick startled smile, *Who is this guy with the crime scene photo?*, and then at the pictures he was showing her. "Your dad is, what, six five?"

"At least. Yeah."

"Right. Theresa Pileggi was five foot four. If he is standing and shooting at her, the shots would go down, right?" He made his finger a bullet, shot it toward Evie, almost pierced her chest before stopping right in time. "But if you look—closely—" He enlarged one of the pictures. "Doesn't it look like the bullet goes in the other way? Like—ascending?"

His voice quavered minutely at the end. He didn't, after all, really know what he was talking about. He had convinced himself he was right, but trying to share it with someone else, his discovery suddenly felt thin, as wispy as cotton candy. But Evie was nodding, Evie was going "Whoa," Evie was taking his phone from him and fidgeting at it with her fingers, enlarging the picture more.

Ruben cursed, shaking his head. It had happened. Her hopes were up, they were way up. But then she set the phone back on the table and looked at him, puzzled.

"Wouldn't the police have noticed the same thing?"

"Well, theoretically they would, right?" said Ruben. "But, like: they get there, and here's this guy holding the gun, telling them he did it. Full, immediate confession. I'm not a cop, obviously, but I wonder if maybe their crime scene investigation was a little . . ."

"Cursory."

"Exactly. Cursory. Maybe?"

Ruben had studied the crime scene photographs, of course, and the various reports from the Culver City Police Department, and made what sense of it he could. A ballistics report confirmed that the two 8mm rounds recovered from the wall had come from the same unusual Austrian-manufactured handgun Richard was holding at the scene. But if any of the police investigators had noticed that the holes were going in the wrong way, they hadn't said so in the report.

Or, Ruben thought with a blurry fearful pang, he was wrong about the whole thing.

Evie reached her chopsticks in, slow and thoughtful, and selected a dumpling. The tattooed team at the next table took the moment to lean over, both of them smiling nervously, almost smirking; the man told Evie he fucking *loved* her record and asked if he could be a total dick and ask for a picture.

"No," she said, very sweetly. "Not right now, if that's OK?" The couple withdrew, and Evie looked right at Ruben.

"So, what? He was sitting down when he shot her? Does that matter? Why does that matter?"

"Well, no. He wasn't—hold on." Ruben took a breath, tried to arrange his thoughts. "Your dad told the cops he shot at her, missed, and then killed her with the lamp. What I'm wondering is, maybe *she* was in the room and *he* came in. She shot at *him,* and *then* he killed her with the lamp." He took a breath, summoned some courage, looked her right in her beautiful eyes. "In self-defense."

"Self-defense." She echoed him very quietly, holding his gaze. "Holy shit."

"Yeah."

"Which would make him innocent?"

"Not innocent, exactly, but..." He had done more reading. He had gone back on the website. "But not guilty. I think—what? Evie—what?"

She cried like her mother cried: all at once, furiously, chin thrust out, pissed at herself for crying.

"Evie?"

"She called, Ruben."

"What?"

"Oh my God. She called, Ruben! I never thought . . . I mean, I didn't think it was *her*. Oh my God, I'm an idiot. I'm such an *idiot*."

"You're not an idiot." He had gotten up, without thinking about it, and moved around to the other side of the table and crouched before her like a marriage proposal.

"Tell me."

Evie took a deep breath and steeled herself. She pulled him up and he sat down next to her. "OK, so, there was this—phone call. I don't remember when, exactly. A couple months ago, maybe. Pretty close to the, the—"

"To the motel."

She nodded, rapid tight nods, and then seemed unable to go on.

"Evie? Tell me."

"I was visiting the house, I was in the bathroom hallway, and I overheard my dad on the phone. I just assumed it was about money, because they're always short, always broke, and lately I'm trying to help and he tells me to fuck off. It's a whole problem. But so I heard him, and I thought it was bill collectors, or the mortgage. He kept saying *leave me alone*."

Ruben stared at her. "Leave me alone."

"Yeah. *You people leave me alone. Leave me alone.*"

"Hey," said Ruben sharply to the man at the next table, who was craning around, very slyly trying to take a picture of Evie Keener. "Fuck off."

Evie ignored this, ignored the photographer. She clutched at Ruben.

"Could this be something?"

"He said those words: leave me alone? He said *you people* leave me alone?"

She nodded.

"You said this was a couple months ago?" Ruben thought furiously, trying to fix dates in a timeline. "Was it before or after November twelfth? The anniversary, when you said your dad freaked out?"

"It was after. Later. Definitely. Because I left town after that. I was doing road dates the rest of November. Vancouver, and then Portland. This was when I was back, so it had to be December, the beginning of December."

The murder had been on December 20. By now, Ruben knew the date by heart.

"Ruben, this is good, right? If she was threatening him? If she was, like, harassing him or something?"

"I mean . . ." Her hopes were way up now. It was too late by far. "Maybe. Yeah. I don't know. I could try to find out. I could go talk to her family, in—" He tried to remember. Illinois? Iowa?

"It's insane, Ruben."

"It's not. Not necessarily. I don't know. Your dad would still have to agree to change his plea."

"Let me work on that," said Evie, and in a heartbeat her steely rock-star presence returned to her: it set her chin and flashed in her eyes. "If it would actually get him *out*? He *better* fucking do it."

Ruben was picturing himself on a plane; conducting interviews; digging up dirt. He would have to work fast; the clock was ticking.

"But what about you, Ruben? Your job? What about your life?"

"My life is—" It was sort of a weird thing to say, so he didn't say it, but what he had been going to say was *My life doesn't matter.* Instead he smiled at Evie—Evie the Wondrous, Evie of Old—and said, "If I can help your family in this way, and I *don't* do it, I guess I'd never forgive myself," and she leaned against his chest and put her arms around his neck and held him tight.

"I'm going," he said. "I'll go."

There was a massive cheer from behind Ruben; someone had done something miraculous at one of the arcade games. Broken a high score or beaten the machine. A crowd of Eastsiders in black boots and sleeveless T-shirts was cheering like it was the moon landing.

PART THREE

RENZER'S PEAK

January 28, 2019

The Rabbi rang the bell, and then he waited and rang it again.

Nobody was in there. No one was home.

Plus it was snowing out here, an eventuality he probably could have anticipated. It was Indiana in the middle of the winter. Of course it was snowing. Big thick flakes that tumbled down out of the twilight, fell on his face, crept into the collar of his shirt.

Goddamn it, thought Ruben. At least I could have brought a coat.

Too late now. He rang the bell one more time and stood there like an idiot, snow gathering on his eyeglasses, snow slowly soaking his shoes.

It was a tidy slate doorstep, flanked by two gigantic bronze urns. A limp American flag jutted out from above the door, the snowfall dampening its stars. The house was on Meridian Street, one in a series of stately homes, each set back from the road, each lawn full of tall, handsome trees. The cabdriver had seemed surprised when Ruben gave him the address, raised his eyebrows and muttered, "No kidding." He'd come out of the airport with no luggage, just carrying an old orange canvas backpack, wearing a long-sleeve T-shirt and the same jeans he'd worn the day before.

"Indiana?" his manager, Sunny, had said. "No. You're not going to Indiana, Rabbi. I forbid it."

"It's just for a few days."

"You say that, but what if you get kidnapped by some lunatic and he chains you to his radiator?"

"Why would that happen in Indiana?"

"Are you kidding? Don't you read? That's exactly where it happens." Sunny in her TRUCK FUMP T-shirt had followed him out of the Killer Greens and blocked his way down Third Street. "Wait. Oh my God. Are you being catfished? Did you meet someone on the internet?"

When Ruben told her that no, he was running a kind of errand for his father, she had been yet more incredulous.

"You have a *father*?"

He did. More or less.

Ruben sighed, shivering, and tried knocking on the door instead of ringing. He stepped back from the front porch and looked at the upstairs windows. All were dark. The sky was gray, flat and toneless as a coffin lid. Ruben removed his glasses, wiped them off on his T-shirt, and put them back on.

He raised his fist to try knocking one more time, and then the porch light came on, as bright and sudden as new understanding.

"Yes?"

A voice through the door, a woman's, thin and high and polite.

People in Indianapolis were very polite. He'd bumped into a woman at the airport line and when he apologized she smiled, red-cheeked, and said, *Oh, you're fine.* In the main terminal was a banner declaring it, humbly, THE FRIENDLIEST AIRPORT IN AMERICA, which seemed about right.

And now the door cracked open and a well-dressed woman peered primly at him from inside the house.

"Hi. Sorry. Are you Eleanor Pileggi?"

The woman nodded.

"My name is Ruben Shenk," he said. "I'm conducting an investigation into the death of your daughter." Ruben met her eyes. He had practiced the short speech, muttering it to himself over and over on the four-hour flight from LAX. "I am very sorry for your loss, and for intruding."

"Oh, you're fine."

"I hope you don't mind, I just had a couple of questions for you."

"Well . . ." Her eyes, he saw now, were hazy. The house behind her was not dark, but dim. He pictured a half-empty glass of wine, a lipstick stain on the rim, in the kitchen, on a coffee table. A television that had been muted. "We understood that all of that has been settled. The man had been apprehended. The guilty party." She said *the guilty party* with no particular emotion or emphasis, as if she were referring to someone who'd stolen her purse or hacked her computer. Not murdered her only child.

"Well, yes." Ruben cleared his throat. "He has." He felt a hot rush of confusion and embarrassment. "However, as to the defendant—the killer, the alleged killer—there are some questions that need to be resolved." He had to tell her, of course. He had to tell her right now. "I'm working for him. For the defendant. The defense."

There was more he could say, of course, and he would if she asked. He was here because his father, the defense attorney who had no business being a defense attorney, had sent him, an investigator who had no business investigating, to find some straw to grasp at, and he had found one. *Your daughter, as it turns out, was the aggressor in the encounter that took her life. Your daughter, alone or with accomplices, had been harassing the guilty party, and then she attacked him, giving him reason to act, and so he's not as guilty as we all thought. This new version of events based on what? Based on my dilettante's inspection of the crime scene, based on the defendant's daughter's tender hopes, based on nothing.*

And for this, Ruben was asking to be accommodated? For this he had flown to Indiana, nosed in on the great tragedy of her life? A total stranger. An Asian, and a Jew. All the world's curious otherness, on her snow-white doorstep.

"You're fine," she said. "Actually, I'm glad you've come."

She said this like she had been waiting, and for some time perhaps, for someone like him to show up. For some Los Angeles weirdo to come trudging bootless to her door, to whom she could offer up a bargain: "You're an investigator, you said?"

"Of a kind." Then, with more certainty, and actually feeling it to be true: "I am. Yes."

"Well." She hesitated a long time. Gazing over his shoulder, nodding softly, consulting with ghosts that only she could see.

"The thing is . . ." she said at last, and then paused again, and sighed. "The thing is, I don't know *anything*. And I . . . I just want to *know*. Do you understand what I mean?"

"Yes, ma'am."

"I just want to know about her. About my daughter. So, yes—" She looked him dead in the eye, her small pale face set and serious. "I will tell you whatever might be helpful. But then—anything you find out—about Theresa. *Anything*." Her voice wavered and then returned, like a picture coming in and out of focus. "I hope that you will tell me."

"Yeah," said Ruben. "Yeah, no. Of course."

But that wasn't enough. "Do you *promise*, young man?" She reached for his ungloved hand, pressed her fingers into his bones. "You *promise* that you will tell me?"

"Yes." She held his hand for a moment, clinging to him. The winter wind keened like a bully through the thin fabric of his shirt.

"OK, then," said Mrs. Pileggi brightly. She stepped aside and gestured him in. "Then I'll make us some tea."

Ruben sat down at the kitchen table in his soggy clothes.

"Is your husband at home also, ma'am? Do you think he might want to join us?"

"He is dead," said Mrs. Pileggi flatly, unwrapping a tea bag from its paper pocket, placing it in a yellow mug. "Some years. He wouldn't know anything about any of this."

She sat delicately across from him and smoothed her skirt in her lap. The table was a perfect circle of light wood. The kitchen had very clean white tiles and gleaming iron fixtures. There was a bowl of fruit, each piece of which seemed to have been chosen for the color it added to the room: shining red apples and rich purple plums. Mrs. Pileggi, in a pressed floral-print dress, her lipstick and blush, and her shining gold earrings, seemed overdressed for her own midday home. The smile was a permanent fixture on her face as she bustled in and out of the walk-in pantry for tea bags, as she set out sugar and milk in little brass containers. Providing, even in her grief, the sort of easy graciousness Ruben associated with earlier decades, or centuries. Or with Marilyn actually, really— Ruben felt it like a pang across his chest. The tea and all, the dress. It made him think of his mother.

"Now," she said. "What is it I can tell you?"

Before he could answer, she stood up. The kettle had begun whistling. She moved to the stove.

Ruben, for all his preparation—the notebook, which was open and ready, his phone on the table with the voice memo app running—remained uncertain about what he was actually going to ask. "Do you know what brought your daughter, Theresa, to Los Angeles at the end of last year?"

"I do not. Whoops—careful." She was pouring hot water. Ruben leaned backward, out of splashing range. "I sure don't. I didn't know she was going there, until she—" Both cups full, she set down the kettle. "Until she came back."

Ruben looked down at his mug, watching the water muddy with tea.

Theresa Pileggi's body had been sent here, to Indianapolis, to her people, when the Los Angeles County medical examiner was done with it. He knew that from the files. He resisted the urge to say "Sorry" again. How sorry could one person be?

He felt too small for this. For the big weather of this lady's grief and need. Too small and too young.

"So she didn't mention planning a trip to Southern California, late last year?"

"No. Not to me."

Mrs. Pileggi rose yet again. She walked briskly across the kitchen, to a desk that was built into an alcove in the kitchen, and pulled a plastic card box from a drawer. "But if we're being honest, she never told me much of anything." She set the card box down on the table; it was a rigid plastic box with a snap lid and a worn Staples sticker across the top.

"You know how it is with children. Once they reach a certain age, they are a universe unto themselves."

She said this as if they were both middle-aged, veterans of the heartaches of parenthood, although surely she could see that Ruben was younger than her, younger even than her own dead child. Ruben had left his shoes by the front door. He moved his toes inside his wet socks. Outside the snow was endless, coming in slantwise, gathering in the corners of the windows.

He eyed the box uneasily. Were those her ashes? Was Theresa Pileggi in that plastic box?

"When exactly did she leave for Los Angeles?"

"Oh, I couldn't tell you."

"She was—I'm sorry—she was killed on December twentieth. You don't know how long she'd been in LA before then?"

"I'm afraid I don't."

"Right, but...wait. I'm sorry. Sorry." Ruben fumbled off his glasses, which were steaming now from the tea. "Maybe I'm confused."

"We all are, dear." She smiled rotely. "We're all trying our best. Our very best."

"But she was living here, wasn't she?"

The coroner's report had listed this as her address. It had been the address on her driver's license, on all the identification in her purse in the motel room. And it was what the head of Human Resources at UC Riverside had told Ruben when he called. According to their records, Theresa Pileggi had resigned her position abruptly in the spring of 2009 and returned home. Left an address in Indianapolis so her mail could be forwarded. *This* address.

"Oh yes. She had been living at home for ten years—or, no— nine, I think? Yes. Nine. Which was, between you and me, just such a treat, when she came home. So nice to have my little girl back. Grown up as she was, she was still my child. I am sure your parents would feel the same way."

Ruben let this particular sentiment slide by unexamined.

"And, can I ask—what was she *doing* here?"

"I'm not sure I know what you mean." Mrs. Pileggi's voice took on a slightly aggrieved quiver. What was he suggesting?

Ruben wondered the same thing. What *was* he suggesting? He set his glasses down on the table, beside his teacup. He stared into the two lenses, as if looking into his own eyes, gathered his thoughts a moment.

"Your daughter had a pretty good job in California. Right? She had a teaching position at Riverside, and grants for her research? She owned a home?"

"An apartment, yes. A condo. Not to my taste, but yes."

"But she gave all that up and came back home."

"Yes," said Eleanor. "I believe that something—well, that something *happened* out there. A disappointment. A breakup or a shock of some kind. Young people's lives can be very complicated, of course."

Ruben was noticing something unsettling about the way she spoke: it was like a series of aphorisms, observations drawn from human experience by someone who has never personally experienced it. "Young people's lives can be very complicated, of course."

"Did she say anything about a case? A lawsuit?"

Mrs. Pileggi furrowed her brow. "No. What—do you mean recently?"

"No, when she came home. In the summer of 2009."

"No." Mrs. Pileggi frowned. "Was she in some sort of legal trouble?"

It wasn't worth getting into. All of Pileggi's wasted work on *Keener*. The case itself, its slow buildup and sudden, devastating collapse. The handful of terrible moments when everything fell apart. The look on Theresa's face. On Jay's. Ruben remembered the day for a blurred sad instant and then he let it go.

The Rabbi could have told the whole story if he wanted. He could have chanted it like Torah.

"No, ma'am," he said quietly. "She wasn't in any trouble."

"Whew." Mrs. Pileggi's face, absurdly, was flooded with relief— as if her daughter wasn't, right now, in the worst possible trouble a person could be in. Dead now and dead forever.

Ruben's tea, untasted, was growing cold. The steam had stopped swirling above it. He was feeling his way toward something here, but he didn't know what. The dishwasher was chugging softly in the corner. The snow continued to fall against the windows, wet trails melting in streaks.

"I guess what I'm asking, Mrs. Pileggi, is what she was *doing* here the last nine years."

"Oh." Eleanor smiled. "She was working on a project. Some new research project, for which she required the solitude and lack of distraction that only her childhood home could provide. My Tess was a scientist, you know." Eleanor's smile widened. Her face was lit with pride. "A brain scientist."

"And how did she *seem,* when she was home? To you and—was your husband still living?"

"No. She wouldn't—" She made a hard stop, adjusted her tone. "She wouldn't have come to this house if that man was still living."

Something in the way her mouth closed at the end of that sentence, buttoned shut like a pocketbook, made Ruben know that this subject, at least, was finished.

Ruben saw Douglas Pileggi. He had been staring at him the whole time. There was a formal photograph visible past Eleanor in the adjacent dining room. In it Mr. Pileggi was staring straight ahead, a jowly man with the slicked-back hairdo of a TV-show detective. He was not smiling; Theresa, who must have been sixteen or seventeen in the picture, looked equally unhappy. Only Mrs. Pileggi looked cheerful, and in the context of Douglas's and Theresa's dour expressions, more than slightly deranged. Like all reasons for happiness were gone, but no one had told her yet.

"So she came home, and she was sort of holed up in her room?"

"That's right."

"Working on this—on a project of some kind?"

"Yes."

"And what was she—did you know what she was working on?"

"Oh, not exactly. But she came home and got to work right away, burrowed away there. Buried herself in her work."

Ruben got a strange chill at the words *burrowed away*. At the words *buried herself*.

Whatever Theresa Pileggi was doing, whatever she was working on, it culminated late last year. Ten years since Wesley hit his head. Ten years since they drilled a hole in his skull and he woke up walking. Ruben knew from Evie that she called Richard in early December, a couple weeks before she was killed.

Leave me alone. Evie standing in the hallway, watching her father on the phone, seeing that he was frightened, her father who was never frightened. *You people leave me alone.*

It sounded like this wasn't the first call. And Theresa of course was just one person. So what had he meant, *you people*?

Even as Ruben asked himself these questions, the answers were here. They were floating in the air around him. Even in Eleanor Pileggi's quiet kitchen, the night man was here.

"So her work. This work she was doing," Ruben said. "She was conducting research on the brain?"

"Oh, well. She's so intelligent. But I've never been able to understand anything about her work. Neurons and dendrites and all of that." Mrs. Pileggi seemed uneasy. Confused, suddenly. "She was not, I must say, terribly communicative about it. You know how kids are."

Ruben didn't know how kids were, but he knew how Theresa Pileggi had been, and it was absolutely clear what this period had been like for her mother, no matter how hard she was working to tell herself otherwise. And she was trying so hard. The strain of it like taut ropes at the corners of the smile. Her hands trembling on her mug. Working to remember this as a good and happy time in her own history, and in her daughter's. She's just doing what everybody does, Ruben realized. Struggling to construct a life in a world she can be happy in. Struggling harder than most people have to.

"She would come out for meals. Usually. Not always. Sometimes I would just set food down in the hall. Knock on the door, just to let Tess know I'd made supper." She demonstrated, miming a hesitant tapping. "She was . . . industrious, you know? Whatever it was, it was quite consuming, I can certainly tell you that. She was in there for hours. Just hours on end."

"Working? Writing?"

"No . . . no, I don't . . ." Her smile was absolutely empty. "I don't quite know what she was doing. But she was moving around a lot, I know that. Pacing and—and sort of speaking quietly to herself. All the time."

"Was she——" Ruben hesitated, a split second, and then just said it. "Was she using drugs?"

"She was not . . ." Mrs. Pileggi's hand, tight on the handle of her mug, tightened further. "She was not the kind of person who did that."

Ruben nodded, OK, noting that she hadn't actually answered his question. On the other hand, Ruben didn't think Theresa Pileggi had been using drugs. She was on something, trapped inside of something, but it wasn't drugs.

"Was she on the phone? Did she make phone calls?"

"Gosh, you know, I'm not sure. I did sometimes hear her . . ." Mrs. Pileggi began.

Ruben waited. "You would sometimes hear her doing what, Mrs. Pileggi?"

"Moaning." She looked up. "Isn't that funny? Not like—" She made a surprisingly frank expression. "Not like *that*. But moaning. A very uncomfortable sound. During this time. I would—" She laughed, nervously. "Sometimes I would put my ear to the door, and I would hear her in there. Walking, as I said, pacing, you know, and muttering, or moaning."

"When did she do this?"

"Always. All the time. Just—all day long. And . . . " She looked away, looked back. "And at night, also."

Ruben stared at her. There is a universe, somewhere, in which everything fits together, and everything makes sense. For a blurry instant Ruben glimpsed it, and then it swam away.

He managed to eke out a few more details. Packages came and went. The light was on in her room, all night, every night. It seemed like she never slept. Whatever she was doing, she was obsessed; she couldn't stop; whatever this idea was, this project, she was its prisoner.

And Ruben knew what it was. Of course he did. The night man had told him what it was.

Theresa Pileggi had been in her room—*burrowed, buried herself*— trying to do what he had been trying to do, trying to get where he had been trying to get.

I've been trying for ten years, Dennis had said. To get to where that kid got by banging his head on a fucking bench.

Ruben was there in his dad's office, scared out of his fucking mind, and he was here in this snowbound Indianapolis kitchen and he could see the night man, that was him there leering from the family portrait, the night man as Douglas Pileggi, the night man staring out from inside the dead man's eyes.

Theresa Pileggi had been holed up in her room, trying to solve the riddle. Trying to get empty. Become a vessel.

Ruben took a steadying breath. He looked down at his tea, then up again.

"But you don't remember when she left to go to Los Angeles?"

"November. Before Thanksgiving. I had hoped to do a nice Thanksgiving." She was trying to smile; Ruben could see the effort in her eyes. "The funny thing is . . ."

"Yes?"

"I know that she was there, that she ended up in California, but . . ." She let the sentence die, shook her head a little, and spoke brightly. "I am so sorry, but I have forgotten your name."

"Ruben."

She nodded. "Ruben. Yes. Well, it's very odd, Ruben. But she didn't *go* to Los Angeles."

"Oh." He sat up straight. "Did she tell you she was going somewhere else?"

"No, no. She didn't say anything, one way or the other. She just—*emerged* one day, fully dressed, she had her shoes on, and I was so happy. I embraced her. We hugged. I was *so* happy. But she had a suitcase. She was going. Just as abruptly as she had come."

"*Where,* Mrs. Pileggi, where did she say she was going?"

"That's what I'm telling you. She didn't say *anything.* The truth is she . . . she . . ." Her face was changing. She was pale. She breathed heavily, in and out, and her eyes became hazy. "I'm sorry. Your name one more time."

"It's Ruben."

"Ruben, Ruben, Ruben." She laughed, high and flutey. "Ruben, she didn't say one word to me the whole time she was here."

"Do you mean, for *ten years?*"

She nodded, hummingbird rapid, and then Ruben jumped up

because Mrs. Pileggi was sliding down out of her chair, her body rubbery and flat, and Ruben caught her by the armpits and eased her back up.

"Are you OK, ma'am?"

"I am, yes. Yes, I'm just fine." She glanced over her shoulder, at the snow coming in constant marching rows against the windows.

Ruben meanwhile imagining Theresa, for a decade, while the world turned and turned, Theresa buried in her bedroom, pacing in tight circles, Theresa not eating, Theresa moaning—Ruben trying and failing to imagine it—Theresa captured in there, pacing the four walls of her childhood life, a captive animal, caught inside of madness, this thing grinding her down and down.

The Rabbi stayed focused. Mrs. Pileggi was talking.

"Oh, but this is what I wanted to show you. As I said, she never told me why she was going, or where. But I did find, on her desk..."

She fiddled with the plastic snap-top lid, and the box creaked open. Ruben looked warily inside.

"The letters were gone," she said. "These are just the envelopes."

Ruben stared at them. A dozen; maybe fifteen.

All of them, he saw at once, had the same canceled postmark.

Ruben stood up. Mrs. Pileggi reached for his arm and took it.

"You promised, now. Anything you find out, you'll let me know?"

"Yes, ma'am."

"Just—anything at all."

"Yes."

She stood up, too. Her chin was raised and her gaze steady and her mouth firm, and her agony was so transparent that Ruben moved to embrace her. Holding Theresa's mother, he could feel how substantial his own body had become: the weight of his upper body, the strength of his arms and back, the solidity of his torso as her frail ribs pressed against his own. She was hollow, he thought; she was virtually weightless.

"Oh," said Ruben finally, as he put his shoes back on, seated on the low bench they had by the front door. The last thing. "Did your daughter, when she left, did she have a weapon?"

"No. What kind of weapon? No."

"Are you sure? You did say your husband was a hunter. I wondered if she had taken one of his guns."

"No," she said flatly, and then again: "No. My husband— Douglas—he did keep guns in the house. But when he died, I disposed of them all."

Ruben opened the door. The winter weather that had seemed so miserable before felt like freedom. He wanted to run through the snow, back to the airport.

"Do you have children, Mr. Shenk?" asked Mrs. Pileggi.

"No, ma'am."

"Oh." She nodded, her hand on the knob. "Well, there's still time. Plenty of time."

Ruben did wonder, sometimes, about his parents.

Not Marilyn and Jay, whose fates he knew very well, but his real parents, what people call birth parents.

He pictured them sometimes, not as living people but as a static image, posing unsmiling in front of their home, Asian smallholders in modest Western dress, staring stoically into the camera.

His was a fanciful image, which Ruben had constructed in his mind, out of nothing. He had never had any communication from his biological parents, nor seen any photographs. He had never written a letter to the adoption agency his parents had employed, nor asked his dad to do so on his behalf.

And yet the biological parents did appear, now and then, in odd moments like this one. He shut the door of the Meridian Street house and walked back out into the snow, stepping carefully in his sneakers across the flagstones slick with ice.

The cabdriver had given him his number. He needed to get back to the airport.

January 5, 2010

1.

Wesley walked the length of the dance hall, very slow. He reached the ornate and enormous doors at the far end, and then he turned and came back toward the bandstand. Arms at his sides, facing forward, eyes fixed.

Dr. Theresa Pileggi walked beside him. She muttered to herself, making tiny notations in a thick spiral-bound notebook. She walked exactly at his pace down the parquet floor, one step for each of his. She seemed to be counting as Wesley walked; counting steps or counting seconds.

"Yes," she said to herself, after some unexplained interval. "Interesting." She added something to the notebook, writing furiously, letting him get slightly ahead of her, and then hastened to catch up.

The rest of them watched from the bandstand: Richard with his arms folded across his chest, Beth clutching him nervously, Jay Shenk with his hands thrust in his pockets, bobbling on his heels, uneasy. Jay was watching them watching Wesley, and he could see that when Beth was looking at her son she was, as always, looking for signs of life: her eyes bored into her boy, crawling over him, desperate still to find something. Some flicker of a person inside the walking doll.

But there was nothing there. Wesley's eyes stared straight ahead. His feet moved mechanically. He reached the bandstand, Pileggi just beside and behind him, and she made a curious birdlike cluck as she watched him pivot and go back.

"Look, lady—" said Rich, and Beth said, "Hush," and Jay sighed, exhaling his anxiety, and the slow parade of Wesley and Pileggi moved back toward the doors.

First Dr. Pileggi had looked the child over for a half an hour: pulse, blood pressure, a scraping from the tongue; eyes and ears. For each ministration Wesley would stop, wait with infinite, automatic patience, submitting without protest to her attention. Then she moved aside and let him go, let him walk, while she followed, taking notes.

This peculiar examination was taking place inside a detail-perfect re-creation of the Hollywood Palladium as it had been in 1954. The famous dance hall had been built from scratch on a half-acre of private land out here in Burbank, intended as the climactic location of a nostalgic romantic comedy that had lost its financing. And now it had become a hideout for Wesley Keener, the fugitive miracle, with three armed guards patrolling the perimeter and a nurse living full-time in the fake barroom behind the stage, where the movie lovers were supposed to have shared a secret kiss.

"Oh my God, this is fucking *perfect,*" Beth had declared when Ebbers walked them through the setup. Then she'd asked "Can we afford it?" and Richard had said "Nope" and here they were anyway. The rest of the family was in a spot nearby, an anonymous townhome on a Burbank side street, close enough to check on Wesley every day.

Wesley walked across the patterned dance floor, against the grain of the check pattern of the floor tile, between the rounded columns and beneath the curving balcony, back and forth from the stage.

Pileggi dropped her pen and crouched to get it, and then awkwardly lurched back to her feet, caught up with Wesley, and kept writing.

"Christ," said Rich, while Jay grimaced.

This was his expert witness?

For *this* Jay was paying not only the medium-high hourly rate that Dr. Pileggi was insisting on, but her gas back and forth to Riverside, for fuck's sake, and compensation for the courses she wasn't teaching this semester because she'd taken a leave to work on the case; plus he had agreed to put her up in LA County if and when they went to trial—and he'd no choice but to agree. He'd made a mistake. He'd been sure this case was going to settle, and it hadn't, and there was no time for anyone else. All his chips were on odd little Dr. Pileggi, on her notebook full of scribblings and the theory she claimed to have.

Pileggi was in a beige pantsuit, and maybe it was the same one she'd been in when he had seen her lecturing at UC Riverside, or maybe she had a closet full of the same number, plus a dozen pairs of the same cheap flats. If it were up to Shenk, she would be doing her inspection of the patient far from the eyes of his parents. Bringing his expert witness, especially this one, into contact with the Keeners—she with her semiautistic professorial intensity and the pair of them like two open pits of grief—felt like a mistake; it felt fraught, somehow, even dangerous. But what choice did he have? If she was going to be his expert she had to examine the patient, and Beth was not about to let Wesley be examined in her absence. So here they were, Beth watching Wesley while Pileggi walked along beside him, scribbling away with the stub of a pencil.

But Richard—Richard was staring at Jay, and Jay could feel what he was thinking. Who the fuck was this lady?

"OK," called Pileggi abruptly from way on the far end of the dance floor, standing there writing one last thing while Wesley walked back toward them. "I was right."

"Right about what?" said Rich.

Her voice echoed back through the vast empty room. "About everything."

"Dr. Pileggi?" called Shenk. "Why don't you come a little closer and we'll talk."

They gathered in the center of the room. They were each sitting in one of the metal folding chairs—jarringly anachronistic in the dance hall—that Shenk had found in a storage space beneath the stage.

"To begin with, my hypothesis was correct, regarding the etiology of his condition." Pileggi spoke intently, but quietly, as if to herself. It was one of several habits, Shenk knew, he would have to train her out of before putting her on the stand.

"What is etiology?" said Beth, looking to Shenk. "I don't know what etiology means."

"It just means cause," murmured Jay. "It means explanation." The word-choice stuff; he'd have to work on that, too. "What Dr. Pileggi is saying is that the hospital has been deceitful about what happened."

"Not deceitful, necessarily," said Pileggi. "More likely they just don't understand."

"And you do?" said Rich.

"Yes, I do."

Rich's tone was thick with skepticism, Pileggi's scornful in return. Beth leaned in close.

"So?" said Beth. "So tell us. What?"

Pileggi furrowed her brow, nodded at her notes. "What this patient has contracted is a prion disease."

Not patient, thought Shenk. Don't call him "this patient." He beamed Pileggi the message with his eyes, but Pileggi wasn't looking at Shenk. She was focused on Wesley. He looked exactly the same as when Shenk had first seen him, in room 906, through a scrum of curious doctors, more than a year ago. He had not grown. No new fuzz had appeared on his cheeks. His hair was the same length, despite not having been cut. He was the same.

"At some point in his life, he ingested or was otherwise infected with a prion protein. The prion was dormant, however, and would have remained so except for the surgical intervention, which triggered a catastrophic neurological event, leading directly to the patient's current state."

Not patient, thought Shenk. Child. Boy. Person. The patient was a boy; the boy had a name.

"The resulting condition is a highly specific form of neurodegenerative disorder. Though exceptionally unusual, it is nevertheless identifiable, to scientists familiar with the symptomatology, as Syndrome K."

"What is that?" said Beth. She looked from Pileggi to Shenk, then back to Pileggi. "What is Syndrome K?"

"You said he got infected?" said Rich. "Like a—like a cold, or what?"

"No," said Pileggi flatly, with a cool hint of irritated sarcasm. "Not like a *cold*."

Her contempt for this question, for Rich's layman ignorance, was plain: she literally rolled her eyes. Rich glared at her with undisguised disgust.

Please, thought Shenk. Please.

While Pileggi continued in her galloping, ungainly matter, Shenk kept his eyes on the Keeners. Now Beth, now Rich. Hoping to conjure by his broad empathy a force field to protect them from Pileggi's bluntness. He saw how they were reacting to words like *catastrophic*. He saw how Beth jumped; how even steadfast Rich shivered within his skin. Take it easy, he thought as loudly as he could, in the direction of oblivious Pileggi. Take it slow.

The Keeners needed to hear all this, but they needed to get each piece of this nightmare individually, so it didn't overwhelm them, swamp their systems with the toxicity of distress. Beth already was at the very edge. You could see it in the red of her eyes. Rich, too, looked exhausted, his hair disheveled, his beard wild and untrimmed.

As for Shenk himself, he was grappling with the fact that soon—mere weeks now, a matter of swift-disappearing days—he would have to put this woman on the stand. He would need her, somehow, to win the hearts of a jury.

"A prion is a transmissible pathogenic agent, and it causes damage to a certain category of brain proteins," Pileggi said. "The pathogen is most often undetected and can then lie dormant for years, or, in many if not most cases, forever."

"And Wes has that? How did he get it?" said Beth, franticness rising in her voice. "When?"

Shenk, watching the roller-coaster rise and fall of Beth's reactions, kept up his steady telepathic urging to his expert witness: Go slow. Be cool.

"We will probably never know when or how," said Pileggi. And then, abruptly: "Do you eat meat?"

Rich growled. "Why does that matter?"

"It may or it may not," said Pileggi. "Unlike with some other prion diseases, Syndrome K's means of transmission has not yet been conclusively identified. This is the first actual case I have encountered."

Jay's mouth dropped open. "Wait," he said. "Are you serious? The first?"

She nodded. "Up till now it has been entirely theoretical."

Rich was staring at Jay; Jay could feel him staring.

"But it shares certain traits with the pathogen that causes something called bovine spongiform encephalopathy."

"Jesus Christ," Rich muttered. Beth had her hands in her hair. "Isn't that — wait — Wesley has mad cow disease?"

"Syndrome K is not mad cow disease. But it is contracted from a prion similar to that which causes BSE. The prion, once activated, ravages the patient's brain, with catastrophic effects on all its functional centers, including the prefrontal cortex."

"So, what?" said Rich. "It's like he's had a lobotomy?"

"Oh no," Pileggi said flatly. "It's worse."

Shenk cringed, held up both hands, let's take a second here, but Pileggi kept going.

"In a lobotomy the prefrontal cortex is substantially or wholly removed in order to stop the progress of a malignancy, with the predictable side effect of dulling or even eliminating aspects of personality. In the case of a rapid aggressive neurodegenerative illness like Syndrome K, it is not only the prefrontal cortex, but also the hippocampus, the amygdala, and various other key functional areas, which have not been removed but gravely damaged, or . . . or *anesthetized,* somehow. Draining him not only of his quote-unquote personality but also the feelings of pain, of emotional attachment, of memory. Everything."

Beth's eyes had shut. Jay could not imagine what she was feeling. He could not imagine. Richard growled.

"So why's he fucking walking around, then?" he said. "If

he's all gone. Huh? If his brain is all zeroed out, like you're saying. Why's he walking around like he's looking for his fucking car keys?"

"There are automatic functions," said Pileggi firmly, following Wesley with her eyes as he circled the room. "In the body. This is what is left."

"Yeah," said Rich, scowling, refusing to accept this high-tower horseshit. "But what about the other automatic functions? Huh? He doesn't sleep. He doesn't eat. He doesn't shit. He isn't *growing,* for fuck's sake. Explain all of *that.*"

"I can't," she said calmly. She stared at Richard, unbowed, unafraid. "Not yet."

"He looked at me," said Beth suddenly.

"Oh, don't——" Rich started, and Beth said "No, I'm going to tell her." She reached across and clutched Pileggi's hand, and Pileggi pulled it away, as if assaulted. "It was about a month ago."

"I am sure you are mistaken," said Pileggi coolly.

"No, no," said Beth. "I was with him, we were at this hotel, in Marina del Rey. And he *looked at me.* He was trying to say something. He——"

"That's not possible," said Pileggi.

"All right," said Shenk. "I mean——"

"Don't tell her it's not possible." Rich, who a second earlier had dismissed Beth in the same way, was now offended on her behalf. "She's not an idiot. She knows what she saw."

Beth's hand was at her mouth; her breath was stopped. Rich's eyes were narrowed and some dark rage was building in his chest; Shenk could see it rising. Wesley's circuit took him past the group, just at that moment, and he passed in silence like a traveling ghost.

Maybe this would be a good moment, Shenk thought, to

mention the glowing. *Oh, and also, Dr. Pileggi, just something else for your notebook: at the time of the accident a friend of his saw him glow like a lightbulb, but only for a second. Does that factor into the diagnosis at all?*

He didn't say that. Instead he played the moment's necessary role, sliding between Pileggi and Beth to defuse the tension.

"Now, listen, this is—I'm sure she didn't mean to imply that anybody was crazy. Right, Dr. Pileggi?"

The doctor shrugged, and Jay stared at her until she allowed it. "Of course I did not."

"OK?" said Shenk. "Great. Oh—sorry—"

His phone was ringing, comically loud. Shenk slipped it out, flicked it to SILENT and risked a glance at the screen.

Ah, great. Of course.

He had been calling Mayorski Litigation Financing for a week, trying to get one of those bloodsuckers on the phone, and of course they would call back now, when he was deep in the muck.

He didn't love turning to litigation financiers, anyway, these shylocks who forwarded money against a settlement, as long as they felt like they had a decent shot at collecting. Creeps and usurers, these people, and who needs 'em?

He needed them, of course. At this point, he needed them pretty badly. As the case hurtled toward opening argument, he was out of options, from a financial perspective. He had put Darla on furlough; he'd stopped making his lease payments for his office above the doughnut shop; he was strategically trading calls with the polite finance folks at Ruben's shmancy school; and he was straight-up *dodging* the calls from Wells Fargo on his mortgage.

The phone buzzed again.

"Hey, sorry, everyone," he began, thinking maybe he could get away for a few minutes. "But uh..."

Richard was standing now, aiming an alarming finger at Pileggi.

"Look, lady," he demanded, and Shenk slipped his phone back in his pocket. He'd have to call back.

"You said he got this thing, this pathogen, whatever it is. You said he's had it a long time—a long time, and all that time he was fine. So what happened?"

"Ah," said Pileggi, and looked at Rich carefully, as if seeing him for the first time. "Good question. The simple answer is that the surgical intervention activated the prion where it had been nestled inside the brain fluid, and it began to replicate."

"Fuck's sake," said Rich, and Shenk said "I think what Dr. Pileggi is suggesting—" and Pileggi said "Not *suggesting*," and Rich said "No, I get it. I fucking get it. The doctors. They—what? They woke it up."

"Yes." Pileggi nodded once, sharply. "During a surgical intervention, the body reacts to the trauma by flooding the brain with cortisol. What appears to have happened in this case is that this cortisol activated the long-dormant prion, with disastrous results."

All three of them, then, Rich and Jay and Pileggi, turned their eyes to Wesley, trailing past, staring his empty stare. Beth got up to walk beside him.

Beth walked with Wesley, who was not Wesley, who would never be Wesley again. They walked through the white columns and past the long, sleek nightclub bar. Beth walked with one hand very gently on the small of Wesley's back.

Wesley saw nothing. His arms fixed in place, his legs moving under their own control.

Richard had been pierced by what Pileggi had said. Shenk could read it on his face. Under the bristle of his beard; in the cast of his eyes; the man was churning with understanding.

"So they did this," he said. "They did it. The doctors."

"Yes," said Shenk. "Correct."

He had been waiting for this moment, he realized, the whole time. From the day the Keeners came into the offices of Shenk & Partners on Palms Boulevard, he had been waiting for Richard Keener to choose a side. To realize that a lawyer was different from a doctor, that a monolithic insurance company was different from a hustling sweetheart shyster with a mortgage and a teenager at home. To understand that not all strangers were conniving outsiders, part of a system engineered for your destruction.

It was simple. It was simple after all. *They did this.*

"You're saying if these people hadn't operated," said Rich, looking past Pileggi to Wesley, pointing at him with his big hand, "then he'd be fine?"

"Not fine. He would have had a concussion," said Pileggi. "He might have had mild brain damage. Maybe. But not this."

Not this.

"What we now understand," Shenk told Richard, and raised his voice so Beth could hear him, too, "is that there was negligence on the part of the doctors who worked on Wesley that day. They were reckless, and their recklessness..." Shenk raised his hands, and let them drop. He looked at Wesley, walking past. "Their recklessness had consequences. We just have to make sure a jury understands that."

Rich lit a cigarette, sent an angry jet of smoke up toward the vaulted dome of the ceiling. In Shenk's pocket, the buzz of the voicemail showing up.

"I have a question," said Beth. She brushed her hand across Wes's back as she came back to the group. "With this Syndrome—sorry, what letter was it?"

"K," said Jay, and Pileggi nodded.

"Is it always permanent? Or—I mean—will he ever come back? At all?"

Pileggi opened her mouth and then closed it. She was going to say no. Shenk could tell—she was going to say no, just like that, and snuff out the candle keeping Beth Keener going, turn off hope like a light.

She was going to say it, but she had seen Shenk, had caught at last his warning look. She looked down, adjusted her expression, and then looked up again and smiled, softly, at Beth Keener.

"We don't know. This condition is very rare, and there may be cases we don't know of. So I can't say yes, and I can't say no." She flicked a look at Shenk, glowing with relief. "And finally can I add that I am so sorry for what you are going through." Pileggi lowered her head, shook it just a little bit. "I am just so sorry."

Whether Pileggi was really feeling sorrow for the suffering Keeners, or whether she was choosing in this moment to present a simulacrum of feeling, didn't matter.

For Judge Andrew Cates, for the twelve good folk and true who would form the *Keener* jury, he only needed her to perform a person, and now he saw that she could do it.

Good, Shenk told Pileggi, mind to mind, *Good going,* and smiled, and she, for a split second, returned the smile, and they held each other's gaze, kindness to kindness.

And then she said, "Should I send my invoices directly to your office, or do you use an outside accounting firm to handle payables?"

"Tell you what," he said, and put a hand on her arm. "Let's talk about that later."

2.

Ruben, outside the doors of the fake Palladium, was holding himself very still.

He was so close.

Their expert witness needed to take a look at the boy, and so the Keeners had told Shenk where to bring her, and now here they were. In this very odd and very secret location.

Wesley was protected, of course. He was under guard. There were three security guys, burly men in polo shirts, posted around the premises. None had said hello or acknowledged Ruben in any way, this teenager standing completely still outside the door, as if he were not a person but a statue adorning the entrance.

Ruben had the card in his pocket. He had been carrying it around since the night man slipped it to him. He had told himself a hundred times to throw it away but he had not done so. Instead he had transferred it, every day, to a pocket of the next day's pants. The card was tattered at its edges, beginning to separate from itself at the corners. Every day he had almost thrown it away, but then didn't.

If you find out, though, you'll tell me, the night man had said, and now he had found out. All Ruben would have to do now was find a second to call. Just dial the number on the card. He could describe the route: the 405 to the 101, get off at Vineland, a service road and then another one.

Of course he wouldn't do that. How could he? The card was in his pocket, flat and hot. Ruben listened to the hummingbird of his heart.

"Hey," said Evelyn, and Ruben gasped, surprised, and she looked at him with a thin, curious smile. "You OK, dude?"

She said the word *dude* with a small spin on it, like it was a new thing she was trying out: calling people *dude*.

"Yes," he said. "I'm fine. Hi. How are you?"

"I'm OK. They're in there," she said, pointing past Ruben at the Palladium's majestic exterior.

"I know." And then, for some reason, he said something simple and true. "I'm really glad to see you again."

"Cool," said Evelyn. "Me too." Her smile broadened and sweetened, acknowledging his awkwardness, acknowledging the unspoken mutual affection that had been its context, forgiving him for his boldness. All of it at once. He could have kissed her. They were framed by the closed brass doors of the ballroom. They were surrounded by incongruous Burbank scrubland, the rutted service road, the colors of grass and tan. He *wanted* to kiss her.

"How are you handling everything?"

"OK, I guess. It's weird. The way we're living and all, all the moving around. And my mom is all—I don't know." Evelyn shrugged. "It's weird."

"Yeah. I'll bet."

"Yeah."

A crow swooped in from some errand, arranged itself on a branch above them. Ruben thought he could hear, from inside the dance hall, the low murmur of the adults talking. The building was fake, after all. It was pressboard and drywall. None of it was real.

"Hey. I got my ears pierced," said Evie. "When I turned thirteen. I was always scared before, I don't know why."

"Oh. Whoa. That's cool."

He stepped into her orbit, admired the tiny gold dots, smelled whatever it was she put in her hair, and then felt his heart unlock and swing open like a gate. He thought again to kiss her, felt his heart rattle violently at the prospect, but what he did instead was tell her his saddest secret.

"I don't know when my birthday is."

"Are you serious?"

"Yeah."

Ruben had never discussed this fact with anyone outside of his family before. It was a closely held Shenk secret, although when he was little and had kiddie birthday parties every year, they would make a fun joke of it: Ruben and his dad had the same birthday! It's Shenk Day! But he had been adopted in infancy, and the Tình Yêu Quý Giá Orphanage in Saigon kept no reliable records. Marilyn had also liked to light a candle on the anniversary of the day their plane had landed and they'd stepped off with baby Ruben in their arms—the day he had been "born a Shenk," as she liked to say—but in truth they would never know. There was knowledge in the world that was simply unavailable, and among that body of knowledge was the true fact of what day Ruben had been born.

"That's actually kind of cool," Evelyn said approvingly. "You could pick it. Maybe Christmas."

"Well," he said, frowning. "We're Jewish."

"Oh yeah," she said. "Totally. Sorry. But you know what Christmas *is,* right?"

He took a second to see if she was kidding, and saw she was, and said, "I think I've heard of it, yeah," and she laughed.

There was actually a girl now Ruben sort of liked, in his driver's ed class, named Stacy Leighton. He had thought she had no interest in him, because historically most girls did not, but two weeks ago she had been waiting in the side-door hallway when he came out of the gym, after wrestling, and he had the impression she'd been waiting to see him. Although when he said "Hi," she just sort of laughed and said "Oh, hi" in a funny voice and rushed away.

The crow, summoned back to the sky by whatever secret language speaks to birds, fluttered and flapped and departed. Evelyn Keener was basically different in all ways from Stacy Leighton. She was different from everybody. She was looking at him carefully now. She was thinking him over, somehow, and Ruben had a sense of being inspected. He liked it. Carefully, cautiously, he allowed himself to be inspected. He stood up straight. He opened himself up to Evelyn's curiosity like turning toward the sun.

"What is that?" she asked him suddenly, and he realized with horror that in his right hand was a tattered scrap of thin cardstock. The business card, sweaty from his palm. Why had he taken it out? What—

Rubie came the hot secret whisper of the night man, *Rubie-boobie*—

"Oh," he said. "Nothing. It's—it's not anything."

Not anything my ass, hissed the voice, buzzing in an insect circle around his heart.

And what if it *was* true? What if there is a good and golden world, hidden, waiting, and he could help to bring it through? Behind Ruben was the dance hall; inside the dance hall was Wesley; inside of Wesley was some cosmic future, some better way of being, and all they had to do was set it free.

Ruben jammed the card back in his pocket, as far as it would go. Here was Evelyn, after all, together with him in this moment, with the distant call of winter birds, and the sunlight filtering through the leafless branches, the Hollywood Palladium pretending to be behind them, and this world right here, the actual lived-in world, was actually pretty great.

"So," said Evie suddenly. "This is going to sound: *insane.*"

She said it quietly, almost to herself, and twisted her face to one side, a small gesture of defiant sincerity.

"OK," said Ruben softly.

He looked at her. She looked at the ground.

"There's this dance. At my school. Later in the semester. Just for the graduating eighth graders, and—and, like, their guests."

"Oh," Ruben said again, and his entire insides dissolved and re-formed and dissolved again, sand castles wasted by the tides and rebuilt, over and again in fast motion. He was so powerfully moved by what she had said that he hadn't said anything in return, which he realized only when Evelyn scowled and said "Forget it."

"No. I—I mean—I...it's..." Ruben was trying to find individual words from the swim of the air. "I would—no, yeah. Yes. I'd be happy to do that. To take you. To go. To the—"

Now she was staring at *him*.

If the crow were watching; if it had circled up to the next branch and taken a position of advantage, it might in that moment have assumed the two of them were statues, mutually agape, frozen in their adolescent inability to complete a sentence.

"I mean: yes. Is what I'm saying. Sure. That sounds fun."

"OK," she said. "Cool."

"Cool."

In a perfect world the adults would have come out of the Palladium just then, rescued Ruben from the emotional and hormonal crosscurrents that were tenderizing him like a fillet. But the moment did not end. Rescue did not emerge. The muttering voices continued from under the door. He knew the way that his dad would drive his voice up in pitch to change the dynamic, to signal that a meeting was at its end—*Well, listen, thanks, everyone, for being here...* —and he heard none of that, not yet.

He would have liked to reach out and hold Evelyn's hand. Not so much for *himself,* but for her, because if she was anything like him this had cost her something; the effort of asking, the pain of reaching out across the divide that separates people from people. It had to have been hard. And she *was* like him. In some way he couldn't quite figure out, she was a lot like him.

"Hey, can I tell you something else?" he said. "I'm doing wrestling."

Ruben was not sure why he was telling her this. It just seemed like what they were doing, exchanging small pieces of information. Evelyn seemed stunned.

"*Wesley* wrestles," she said. Obviously, as both of them knew, he wasn't doing that anymore.

"Yeah, no," said Ruben, "I know. I uh . . ."

He couldn't explain it. It had just been an impulse, on the way out of school that day: Coach Marsden feeling his arm, like a piece of meat, nodding approvingly, ushering him into it. But Ruben was turning out to be surprisingly OK at wrestling; his win-loss record was not terrible, three meets in. He still had a ways to go, Coach told him, but he was genuinely enjoying the struggle. He liked incremental improvement: of agility, of muscle mass, of tactics. He liked the raw rub of the mat on his knees, he liked the bruising and the strain. He liked how you got better and better but never good. Never good enough.

He was worried now that Evelyn would be angry. He decided that if she rescinded the invitation to the dance, he would apologize. He would never wrestle again. But she just murmured "huh," and then "cool" and then there was a quiet moment between them. Both of them turning it over, what it meant. A wrestler taken from the world, and another put in.

Still the adults did not come.

Their moment together outside the Palladium stretched out.

"How is he doing, by the way? Your brother?" Ruben asked, and it seemed like a safe question, but of course it made Evelyn's face go slack and sad, and she shrugged.

"The same," she said.

"Oh," said Ruben. "Right."

"He's always the same."

3.

Beth wasn't fucking crazy. She *had* seen Wesley look at her. She knew what Rich thought, but fuck him, he wasn't there. She had *seen* it.

It was just a few weeks ago, during a brief transition period when they were still securing the lease on the Palladium. Miracle boy Wesley Keener was a top secret priority guest at a boutique hotel in Marina del Rey, a six-story two-star outfit at the end of Admiralty Way. The room had been provided by someone who knew the owners, a short-term solution, a place between places.

The room only had one bed, a king, but of course they only needed one bed, and they didn't even really need that one, because Beth—as always when she shared a room with Wesley—pretty much couldn't sleep at all. She woke up every half hour or hour and would watch him, walking, back and forth across the carpet, in and out of the patch of moonlight that came in from the harbor side.

Finally she slept, and she was dreaming or half dreaming, the same thing she always dreamed of: she was at Wesley's seventh birthday party and watching him play with his little friend Bernie. But in the dream Bernie got trapped underwater in their pool, caught under a slippery tangle of legs and arms, and Rich pulled the kid out of the water and laid him on the lawn, and there were these terrible frantic moments before he sputtered and coughed, before his face returned to a human color—and Beth, dreaming in the chair, was little Bernie, trapped in a bubble of half death, sputtering—

Then she happened to open her eyes—or she opened them because she heard something, or felt something shift in the air of the room—and she saw right away that Wesley was looking at her. He had stopped walking and was standing by her bedside, as if drawn by her suffering, and he was looking at her, not the dead-eyed empty stare of his illness but a real stare. He was *looking at her.* His eyes were open all the way.

"Honey?" Beth said.

Her blood lit up and she sat up and grabbed his upper arm, which felt the same as always under her fingers: his light teenage arm hair and his warm, soft flesh. She pinched the arm, and Wesley winced.

"Wes. *Wesley!*"

She let go of the arm, and he didn't start walking again. He stayed right where he was, still staring at her, and his eyes now held a gentle, knowing expression. He *smiled.*

He was awake. He was seeing her. He loved his mother.

"Oh my God," Beth said, and fumbled for the phone, absolutely awake, more than awake, wild with wakefulness, her blood roaring in her ears. "Wesley? Baby? *Hey.* Do you recognize me? Hey!"

She called Rich's cell, and while it rang she stared into Wesley's eyes—he had *stopped walking* and was holding her gaze, perfect clean eye contact. His mouth was moving, as if trying to find a word.

"Come on, Richard!" she said. "*Answer your goddamn phone!*"

But her husband was the deepest of sleepers, dead to the world from the instant his head hit the pillow. She was going to have to get Wes in the car and drive home, forty minutes from here to the

Burbank rental; she would have to run down the hall to the bedroom, shake him awake, yank on his beard and pour water on his
face. She had to get him, though, so he could see—

He had gone away, abandoned his physical frame, and now he
was back.

She got dressed as fast as she could, where the fuck were her
pants, she was casting about for her keys, and Wesley was looking
at her, was he still looking, and she was calling to him, "Wesley,
please—just—please stay here—stay with me—"

She lived the whole life that would be next: Wesley coming
fully into himself, blinking, turning his head, asking for water, and
then he would see her crying and he would cry too, and press
his confused head to her chest, and then at home they would take
things slow at first, give him time to find his feet, to get used to
being upright, and then God how those kids would flip when he
returned to school.

He would pick up his life, right where he'd put it down. He'd
been teaching himself "Blackbird" on the guitar. The Beatles song.
He had the first four measures pretty good. Now that he wasn't
sick anymore, he'd get right back into it, learn the rest.

Beth had found her keys. She had them in her hand. But it
was too late. Too late. Wesley's face had gone slack. His eyes had
emptied out. He was walking.

"Goddamn it!"

She grabbed at him, and he was pliant as ever, so she held
him in place and slapped him, and then again, hard, and his face
pinkened from the impact and his head rolled with the blow but
he did not flinch or cry out. A mannequin. A doll. A dress-
maker's dummy.

She stuffed Wesley in the car and drove to Burbank and rang
the bell and Richard lumbered down the hall, scratching his nuts,

sighing, skeptical, and his skepticism was confirmed: Wesley was the same.

"Beth, baby—" Richard began, and she said "You know what? Screw you."

Wesley walked in their living room while she sat watching him, refusing her husband's efforts to console her, pushing his arm off her shoulder.

"It fucking happened," she told him. "It did."

Hope had been kindled in Beth's heart, in a way it hadn't before, and some piece of every minute that passed from that point on would be dedicated to the idea that what had happened in those thirty midnight seconds, in the Marina Hotel, would, one day, happen again.

But *had* it happened?

There were no video cameras set up in the hotel, of course. Why would there be?

So no one had captured the scene: Wesley's very brief period of normal behavior, the easy smile he gave to his mother, or else Beth's imagining of it. There is no record one way or another of this event, if this event occurred at all.

So he woke up or he didn't wake up; he saw his mother or he didn't see her; he smiled or he didn't smile. These facts cannot be verified, and so they are neither true nor false. But Beth's fervent belief that her son had for those instants been returned to her became a kind of truth in and of itself. And not in some bullshit symbolic sense, because that's what is conjured up by sidelong phrases like "a kind of truth," but literally so.

The event that she perceived is burned into her memory in the same way that real events are soldered onto the consciousness. A memory of a false event leaves the exact kind of neuronal record as a memory of a "real" event. So in the long run it has the same claim to truth.

Meaning, basically, that if Beth believed it and held to it tightly, from that point on, like a diamond pressed sharp into the flesh of her palm, then why can't that be OK? Why can't you let her?

4.

"Mayorski Financing."

"Stella! How are you?"

"Oh. Mr. Shenk. Hello."

"How're the kiddos?"

"They're just fine. Thank you, Mr. Shenk."

"Six and nine—somewhere in there?"

"Mr. Shenk, if you're calling about the loan application, I'm afraid I do have some bad news."

"Oh, you, uh—wait. What kind of bad news?"

"We have reviewed the file—"

"Don't say it."

"—and I'm afraid we can't help you with this one."

"Any particular reason you can't help me out here, Stella?"

"Uh, numerous."

"What?"

"Numerous reasons, I'm afraid. Bottom line, though, is that our analysis department feels you'll struggle to convince a jury of the hospital's culpability."

"Your analysis department? But that's just Jerry, right?"

"Mr. Shenk, as always we appreciate you reaching out."

"Is Jerry around, by any chance?"

"He's looking at another matter right now."

"Stella."

"Mr. Shenk."

"Stella. I'd like to speak with Jerry, Stella."

"Goodbye, Mr. Shenk."

"Wait, now."

Jay pressed STOP on the treadmill and rolled to a halt.

"Wait!"

February 4, 2019

1.

"Oh my goodness. *Evelyn*. Hi."

"Hey, Mom."

Beth reached for her daughter, stunned. She had come here with Jay Shenk to see Richard, and now they had run into Evelyn, unexpectedly, at the threshold of the sterile visiting room. There was something not right about it, she and her daughter happening upon each other here, by happenstance. They should be here together. They should have come together. Looking at Evelyn, holding her lightly by her arm, Beth felt a bubbling of pleasure and bafflement, like she was looking at a picture of someone she'd loved a long time ago.

There were bored prison guards standing in the corners of the room, carrying weapons and wearing brown uniforms. Nothing else in the room but metal tables and hard benches, nothing on the wall but clocks. Come and visit your prisoner. Sit on your uncomfortable bench and watch the time go by.

Beth might have thought that there would be a silver lining in all this, in Richard's arrest and imprisonment. A knitting together of mother and daughter, whose relationship had always alternated between distanced and strained. But no—no. And it wasn't just that this tragedy had come just as Evelyn's career was exploding. Beth would call and get no answer, and then when Evelyn called back she would just watch the phone ring, somehow unable to summon the emotional energy required to say hello. Having to quietly admit to herself that she had been glad when Evelyn didn't pick up in the first place.

"Sweetheart? What are you doing here?"

"What am I *doing* here? Are you serious?" Evelyn—no, Evie, it was always Evie now—Evie with her slick platinum rock-star hair, rolling her eyes like a teenager. "I'm here to see Dad. I wanted to see him before tomorrow."

Tomorrow he would be sentenced, and once sentenced he would be transferred from the relative proximity of the Pitchess Detention Center off of Highway 5 to the death row at the California Institution for Men, all the way up in Chino. From the gray of waiting to the bleak black permanence of his death sentence.

"I know, but *we* were coming." Beth felt confused. She half turned to Jay, pointed to him for evidence. "We could have all come together."

"Well, I didn't *know* you were coming, OK?" Evie's sour adolescent expression hardened, and she planted one hand on her hip. "Can we move on?"

"I wasn't attacking you, darling."

"I didn't think you were attacking me."

Richard watched all of this from where he was sitting, hands chained together, on one side of the rickety metal table. He said nothing, and his silence for once was not mysterious. Richard might be dumb enough to have murdered someone and confessed, but he wasn't dumb enough to get between his wife and daughter in an argument.

Meanwhile Jay Shenk stood behind Beth, shifting on his heels, examining his hands.

"Well, I'm just...I'm glad you're here, Evelyn," said Beth. "And I'm sure your father was glad to see you."

Richard nodded. Beth blinked, feeling confused, exhausted. The lights were very bright here. No hiding from the light in the visiting area. Evie, at last, kissed her mother and allowed herself to be kissed, and then said she was going.

"Well, wait," said Beth. "Let us give you a ride."

"I got a ride from Bernie."

"Wes's friend?"

"He's *my* friend, Mom. He's in my band, remember?"

"OK, darling. OK."

Beth smiled weakly. She *hadn't* remembered, honestly. Her daughter's face, somewhere along the line, had become an adult's face. So familiar and so alien: the bright white hair, the pursed red lips. The row of gold studs riveted into the folded crest of her ear. All the affectations that would be reconsidered or embraced as time went on. No wonder we are a little frightened of our children, Beth thought. They are strange visitors from the future, emissaries from a world we will never see.

Rich had always paid more attention to his daughter's music career than Beth had. He had, over the years, tried to get her interested in Evie's burgeoning success, but Beth found it hard. She was always so busy, and always so tired. Lately her fingers had become stiff, and she worried that it was some kind of arthritis, coming in early and coming on slow. Her knees hurt all the time, so that she was finding ways to cheat out of certain postures that came with cleaning a house. But she had to work, as much as possible, whenever possible. Saving up for the long stretches she spent out in the desert with Wesley. She and Rich made just enough together to keep the place paid up, keep the caretaker on duty. Once there had been a team of them: the home health aides, the tough security dudes, a whole infrastructure dedicated to Wesley's comfort and safety. That was a long time ago.

So no, sorry, Beth, she didn't think enough about Evie. She didn't go hang out in dark clubs at night and watch her daughter sing; she didn't usually respond to the emails from her friends about having read a magazine interview or seen the NPR Tiny Desk Concert on YouTube. Beth was too busy to feel proud.

Underneath it all, the part that Beth was aware of but didn't like being aware of: it wasn't fucking *fair*. Wesley had been the musician, Wesley her funny little poet, and it was Wesley's life Evie was leading, his place she had taken, while he, still stricken, walked in circles.

I should go after her, she thought suddenly, and had a crystal vision of herself like a figure from myth, racing down the hallway and past the metal detectors, bursting out into the daylight, catching her brilliant daughter and begging her forgiveness.

Instead she took a seat on a bench across from Richard and asked him how he was doing in here.

"I'm fine."

"You are?"

"Yeah. Fine."

Beth gazed blearily at her husband. She knew him so well, and not even a little bit.

Here he was, facing the rest of his life in a cage. Fingers laced on the metal table, staring back at her. He was as still as scattered shrapnel after an explosion; he was like a broken fever. They sat together in silence for a moment, while the guards shifted on their feet. The low, hopeless sound of the room's other conversations murmured around them.

"What does he want?" said Rich, tilting his head toward Shenk, who hovered a few feet away, his hands in his pockets.

"He's your lawyer."

"I don't have anything to talk about with my lawyer," said Rich. "Sentencing is tomorrow, right? So tomorrow we're done."

"He's got a question."

She stood up and Shenk sat down, and Rich's whole face changed. Eyes hardened, and mouth sewed up tight. Drawbridge closed. Beth watched anxiously, gnawing on her thumbnail, as Jay got to work.

"Well, look, Rich, it's pretty simple." Shenk scratched his forehead. "Did you shoot at Theresa Pileggi, or did she shoot at you?"

"What?" he said, and behind him, Beth said, "*What?*"

"What you've said is that first you shot at her, that didn't work, so then you hit her with the lamp. But, uh—" He paused, cleared his throat. "There's some evidence, seems to suggest maybe you hit her with the lamp because she shot at you first?"

The clock ticked off three long seconds before Rich answered.

"Why are you asking me this?"

Shenk smiled wanly. "Why aren't you answering?"

Rich wouldn't be baited. He leaned back, crossed his arms, and scowled.

"Sweetheart?" said Beth, and he spoke to her, not Jay.

"I shot at her, and then I hit her with the lamp. That's what happened. OK?"

"My investigator doesn't think so," said Jay. "He thinks maybe it was self-defense."

"What *investigator* is he talking about?" Rich said to Beth. "Whose money is he spending on all this?"

"Rich," said Jay. "Listen—"

"Wait, wait, wait. Hold the fucking phone." Beth sat down, hard, next to Shenk, and smacked her hands down on the table. All the guards looking up sharply, Jay laying a warning hand on her shoulder.

"Is this true?" she said. "Is it?"

"No. I told you. I've told everyone. I killed her. I did it."

"Right, but was it self-defense, like he's saying?"

"No. I mean—who cares?"

"Who *cares?*"

"Look, baby—" Rich leaned forward until his forehead was nearly touching Beth's. But she pulled back, pulled away. "Baby—"

"Hold on," said Jay, and Rich looked at him with such a cold and brutal expression that Beth felt genuinely afraid. There he was: there was the man who was capable of murder.

Jay plowed on. "The thing is, if you killed her because she was trying to kill you, and we can prove that, that's exculpatory. That's—"

"No," said Rich.

"We can change your plea—"

"*No.*" He ignored Jay. He just looked at Beth. "How many times do I have to say it? We're not doing a long trial. And then the appeals, the whole thing—who needs it?"

Beth stared at her husband, astonished.

"He wants this," she said to Jay, and then she pointed at her husband. "You want this. You want to go to prison for the rest of your life. You want to die."

Rich was shaking his head, muttering into his hands. "No. Come on."

"Richard!"

She was furious, burning inside, her fists forming themselves into balls at her sides.

"Richard!"

Shenk watched them argue. He grimaced. He pushed a lock of gray hair behind his ear. He wondered if it was worth it, this new strategy, half-baked and hasty as it was. Rubie had called from a departure gate at the airport on the way to Indianapolis, of all places. Pileggi had shot Richard, not the other way, he said; Pileggi had started it; Ruben was going to prove it, or try.

Except clearly the client wasn't interested.

Richard was on his feet now, staring down at Beth on her side of the glass.

"It's the last thing you need, or Evie needs, after what we've been through."

"You're tired of it. All of it. You're tired of Wesley, and you're tired of me."

"No."

"You don't get to do this." Beth was shouting at Richard. "You don't get to just escape."

The guard was opening the door as Richard lumbered toward it.

Beth shouted still louder. "No!" She banged on the table. All the crooks and their lovers looked over as she screamed at Richard as he was walking away.

"You pussy," she screamed, and Shenk cringed, and the guard stepped forward, and she kept on yelling. "You fucking coward."

The guard opened the thick door that would return her husband to the underworld, and Beth kept on yelling.

"You *asshole!*"

As he bore witness to this argument that had whirled up like a sandstorm, it occurred to Shenk the old performer that this whole thing felt like a kind of performance. Here was Rich, just being Rich all the way, his face all glower and his body like a big stubborn tree, and here was Beth the tragic woman, toy of time and fate, going full-force gale right here in the Pitchess visiting area, teetering on the hysterical. Both of them playing their part to the goddamn hilt.

Beth turned on her heel, banged through the exit, and stormed down the hallway that would take them outside, and Shenk followed, considering her, all over again, all the way back from the beginning, this distraught wife and mother who all along had been the angry one, the one who seemed to suffer most the monstrousness of loss.

Jay thought of his own wife, about what he might have done for her, in those last and most painful days. How far he might have gone to protect her.

All the various facets of a lifetime of love.

2.

Bernie drove a cherry-red 1972 Chevy Impala that had belonged to his childless uncle Jasper. Bernie wasn't a car guy, but he kept it pretty tuned up, kept the hood nice and shiny.

The Impala was in the parking lot of the Pitchess Men's Detention Center, surrounded by the beaters and pickup trucks the hard-luck stragglers drove to visit their fathers and lovers and cousins. Bernie was leaning against it, phone in hand, idly downscrolling, when Evie came out fuming. Bernie nodded, hey, and then waited. She leaned up against the car next to him. She was prettier without all the fucking makeup on. Bernie had told her that once, backstage: he had been on the sofa, getting his Fender in tune.

"You look better without all that shit on your face, do you know that?"

She had snorted at him over her shoulder. "What are you, a fucking cosmetician now?"

Now he jammed his phone into his pocket, scratched his ear, and broke the silence.

"Your dad all right?"

"He's hanging in," she said. "But my mom's out of her mind."

"Beth's here?"

"Yup."

He waited for her to say more, but that was it.

He waited for her to tell him what she was so mad about, but she never did. Bernie had been making music lately with some different friends, when he wasn't busy with Evie's stuff. Just dicking around with some guys, doing some bass-forward neo–R & B kind of jammy stuff. They called themselves River Fever, and they were starting to think about playing out. Bernie'd been meaning to mention it to Evie, but he was afraid she would be pissed.

Although, actually, what he was really worried about, he knew, was that she wouldn't care.

The anger had slowly melted off of Evie, and she got calm, just looking up at the sky, and then she said they oughta get going.

"Sure," said Bernie. "Let's do it."

Something was on her mind, but Bernie couldn't tell what it was. She was as elusive as her brother sometimes. All the Keeners were a mystery, hidden inside themselves, impossible to see.

"You don't want to wait for your mom?" he asked, and she emerged on cue, Beth Keener bursting out of the main door, walking fast, handbag jostling on her shoulder, the lawyer trailing behind.

"No." Evie opened the car door and got in. "I don't."

3.

The Rabbi peered into the post office, uncertain.

This didn't look right. He had come a long way, an impossibly long way, and he had the right address, but this place did not look like a post office. The burly dude behind the counter, with the baseball cap backward and the flannel shirt and the cigarette behind his ear, definitely didn't look like a mailman.

Ruben hovered at the threshold, letting the fog lift from his glasses, until the burly dude finished the pint glass of beer he was working on and put it down.

"Don't be shy, dude," he called out heartily. "The post office is for everyone."

OK, then. Ruben stepped inside.

He was unsteady on his feet—the journey from Eleanor Pileggi's doorstep to Kusiaat, Alaska, had not been an easy one. The flight from Indy to Seattle was followed by five bewildered, nauseous hours at Sea-Tac, wandering dazed through the shopping concourse to buy boots and a black rain slicker and a waterproof backpack to replace his beat-up orange tote. Then came a connecting flight to Anchorage, leading immediately into a rushed, embarrassing incident in which he tried to buy a flight to Homer that cost more than Jay Shenk's already strained credit limit could withstand. Instead he went to a charmless airport hotel, for an evening of confused browsing on the sluggish computer in the hotel's "business center," booking a ticket on something called the Alaska Marine Highway System—which Ruben thought was an actual highway until he got out of the taxi, looking for the bus stop, and was waved by a uniformed policeman toward the long gangplank that led to the ferry.

Even when he got there, he wasn't there yet. There was just one rental car place in Kusiaat County, run by a man named Ed and called Ed's Cars, and Ed only had two vehicles available for rent. One was out already, so Ruben got the other, a beat-up Range Rover that Ruben had paid for—like everything else, from the rain jacket to the boat ride—with his father's American Express card. What a moment it was going to be, presenting his invoice to Jay Shenk. *Here, Dad—here's what you owe me.*

On none of the legs of this journey had Ruben read a book or a magazine. On none of them did he browse his in-flight entertainment options. Instead he thought about Theresa Pileggi. Instead he tried to piece together what he knew, or thought he knew, or was pretending to himself he knew.

After *Keener,* Pileggi abandons her life. Retreats. Flies home to Indianapolis.

She is half-mad, and soon she is mad all the way; she of all people had fallen under the spell of Dennis, of his people, his movement, his story of the good and golden world. The whole ludicrous mythology that Ruben, all these years later, nevertheless could summon up in all its detail.

Last November, she leaves. Before Thanksgiving, abruptly, without a word to her long-suffering mother. And then, sometime after that, Richard Keener gets a strange and upsetting phone call, the call that Evie had overheard. "Leave me alone," he'd shouted. "You people leave me alone."

You people. More than one person. Pileggi and someone else. But who?

—you know who, Ruben—

And then she goes to Alaska—why Alaska?—to find what?— or who?

—you know who, Rubie-boobie, you know you know—

And from Alaska to Los Angeles, to Cosmo's motel and Richard Keener.

Two bullets in the wall, a lamp to the base of the skull.

The Rabbi stood in the post office. There was slush on the edges of his boots. His glasses were smudged and befogged. The postman licked the beer from his lips and spoke loudly. "You look a mite befuddled, my man. What's up?"

"OK, so—"

Where to start?

"I have a question," said Ruben, and the postman said, "I got an answer. You first."

The low din of conversation and rock music filtered in from under the door. The Kusiaat post office shared a building and parking lot with the American Legion Hall.

"Oh, but so just as a heads-up," the postman said. "The metering scale, for weighing packages, is totally fucked. And anyway we're outta stamps. So if you're wanting to mail something, you've come to the wrong place."

The postman had a second beer queued up behind the one he had finished, and now he took a healthy swallow. Besides the beer, he was eating a plate of chicken wings and mashed potatoes on a paper plate. He had a big head, with the mottled cheeks and dense beard one expects to see on the men of Alaska. Under his flannel shirt he wore a black Metallica T-shirt.

"That's OK, actually. That's not what I'm here for."

"Ooh," said the postman. "The plot thickens. You want postcards?"

He pointed with his chicken wing to a small rack, over by the door, boasting a bedraggled array of what looked like homemade cards. Behind it was a display case, indifferently stacked with Priority Mail envelopes and boxes, the only actual physical evidence that this was a functioning postal facility.

"I'm looking for a person."

"Oh yeah?" A wary expression came over the postman's face.

An Alaskan mistrust of people who were too interested in other people.

"Here."

Ruben dug his phone out of his pocket and set it down on the narrow counter. He had kept the phone all juiced up, although he'd had no service since he got north of Anchorage. Leaning in close, he smelled the sauce of the chicken wings, the wheat of the beer. The tinge of sweat and stink coming off the postman's collar.

"A woman." Ruben opened his photos and found the old picture of Theresa Pileggi, from her faculty page at UC Riverside. "Her."

The picture was a decade old, probably older, but the postman recognized it right away. He looked at Pileggi, then up at Ruben, then back at Pileggi.

"Oh," he said. "Sure. Yeah. I know her."

Before Ruben could allow himself the thrill of victory attendant on this information—he had *done it,* he had developed a hunch and followed a feeling and hauled his ass outside of the continental United States and he had been *right,* it was real—the guy pushed his cap back on his balding forehead and squinted at Ruben skeptically.

"This gal? Is a friend of *yours?*"

"Yes."

"Like—a *friendly* friend?"

For some reason, Ruben found the implication distressing. "Uh, no. Yeah. Not like . . ." And then, inexplicably: "She's my sister."

This, apparently, was even harder to accept.

"You don't look like her brother."

"Well—yeah. I'm adopted."

Which was true, of course, but not strictly relevant.

"Huh," said the postman, nodding sagely.

"Have you seen her, or not?"

"Yeah," said the postman. "I have."

"Recently?"

"Yeah."

Ruben drew a breath, ready for the next question, and the door separating them from the American Legion Hall kicked open, and a man came in bearing a beer can in each fist. A burst of laughter and the chorus of Pearl Jam's "Jeremy" rolling through behind him.

"Whaddup, bitch," said the postman to the new arrival, who said, "Whaddup, dickface," and then stopped short at the sight of Ruben, looked him over disapprovingly. "Who's this?"

"This, my dear Langstrom, is a man on a mission."

"Oh yeah?"

Langstrom set his beers down on the postal counter and wiped his hands on his jeans, as if to shake hands, but then he just kept right on staring. He was a narrow scrap of a guy, brightly red-faced and squinting, with greasy long hair drawn back in a snake of a ponytail. Like the postman, the postman's friend wore a sleeveless T-shirt, but his arms were ropy and thin as two wires.

"You're never gonna guess who my man here is hunting for."

Langstrom squinted, which didn't do anything for his face.

"Who?"

"Hey." He pointed to Ruben. "Show Langstrom the picture."

The three of them huddled over the phone, and when Langstrom saw Pileggi he just whistled, through his front teeth, a long and loud whistle like he was calling an animal.

"You *know* her?"

"Yeah."

"She's his sister," said the postman.

Langstrom squinted. "Really?"

"He's adopted. Fucking racist."

Langstrom grunted "Fuck you," and then: "We have seen her, yeah. Did you tell him?"

"Didn't get a chance," said the postman. "You came in pretty hot."

Langstrom gave the postman the finger, and the postman gave it back, Ruben waiting. His heart thumped. Once, twice.

"Tell me what?"

Theresa Pileggi had arrived at the post office on the first day of December, last year. Both men remembered her vividly. For one thing they didn't get a hell of a lot of strangers up here—"There was her, and then...let's see...you, I guess..."—and for another she was notably, *woefully* underdressed.

"No coat, no hat. She was wearing like, *office* shoes or something. Wasn't she?"

"Yup. Fucking crazy."

Ruben did not move while he listened. He barely breathed. He stood absolutely still, like he used to, when he was a boy, when he was so concerned about appearing excited that he'd order himself to stand frozen in place.

"Is there anything else you can tell me?"

"About what?"

"This woman. My sister. How did she seem?"

"Well..."

The men looked at each other for a moment; a hesitant look. *Shit, it's the guy's sister.* Then the postman shrugged.

"A little *wild,* man. A little off, you know? She was wanting to know how to get to the ranger station, OK? And I was like, you mean the visitors' center? 'Cuz, you know, there's the state park maybe six miles from here, and they just built this new visitors' center—"

"Didn't *just* build it, dumbass. We were in elementary school."

"Kinda beside the point. But she was like—your sis, man, she

297

was like, no, the *ranger's* station, till I realized she was talking about Renzer Station, which was, like—what? No one goes out there."

"Why?" said Ruben. "What is Renzer Station?"

"It's a ranger station, like she said. From, like, 1930 or something. Up on Renzer's Peak. But it's decommissioned. Out of service or whatever."

"Way out of fucking service," Langstrom put in.

"Renzer is not like a super-frequently visited area up here. I don't know if you noticed, we're pretty remote. There isn't any money for a working ranger station. Even the visitors' center is only open, like, four hours a week. My uncle Jimmy's father used to work up there, back in the day."

"That guy was a fucking loser."

"Who? Jimmy?"

"Yeah."

"He was a little retarded, is what he was."

"Yeah, and a child molester."

"Hey, so—" Ruben tapped his fingers on the counter to gather the dudes' attention back in. "You said she seemed wild. By that, do you mean . . ." Ruben tried to think of another word but couldn't. "Crazy?"

The postman brayed laughter, while Langstrom just shook his head.

"Bro," he said. "I run the post office in Frozen Tits, Alaska, know what I'm saying? Everybody I meet's at least a *little* crazy. That's the baseline. But having said that, yeah, she was fucking crazy. You ever see a person's eyes, and you're like, whoa. It was like, wherever she's going, she wants to get there *bad*. She needs to get there. I told her she was talking about a full-day hike, and she was gonna need to get a jacket. Maybe get ahold of some boots."

"And did she? Get the right clothes and things?"

It's funny. Ruben felt scared for her. A rush of fear, like he was actually her brother, and he was racing to save her. But she was already dead. Whatever had happened, it was already done.

"No, man. She just left. Right away. I swear to God, she saw what direction I was pointing and she just started walking."

Ruben had a coat. He had solid boots. He was ready.

"Oh," he said. "One more thing. Was she carrying a weapon?"

"Your sister? No. Not that I saw. You talking about a gun?"

"Yeah." Ruben struggled a moment to remember. "A handgun? Eight millimeter—"

But the postman was shaking his head. "Man, she didn't even have a purse. If she was carrying *any* kind of gun, I'd of seen it."

"Right. Of course. Well, listen. Thank you." He zipped up his coat and turned to the door. "Thanks for all the information."

"Hey, though, wait," said Langstrom. "My cousin Terry sells knives and shit outta his house over by the diner, if you're looking?"

"He doesn't want Terry's bullshit knives, man."

Ruben had stopped listening. His mind had turned to what he now understood was coming next.

He opened the door, pushed out into the cold.

The Rabbi was on his way.

April 5, 2010

What Shenk needed was a good jury.

You always needed a good jury, of course; you prayed for it, you strategized toward it. Sometimes, if you could afford it, which Shenk absolutely could not on this occasion, you paid a smug focus-group hustler to help you secure one.

Shenk used to have a golfing buddy named Mickey Trevaney, a Glendale-based slip-and-fall guy who said that jury selection was like the first song of a Broadway show: it doesn't matter how amazing the rest of your production is, if you whiffed the opening number your ass was toast.

But today Shenk *really* needed a good jury. Not just good—what he needed was the best of all possible juries. He needed the most liberal-minded, victim-loving, anticorporate SoCal jury that the trial gods could conjure. And why? Because now, today, as Shenk in his blue suit with the silver inlay pushed into the civil courthouse, as he nodded with forced good cheer to John Riggs, as Judge Andrew Cates at long last sat down solemnly to gavel in *Keener v. Valley Village Hospital Corporation,* Shenk knew in the heart of his litigious heart that a bullseye jury was his only remaining hope.

Nothing had changed in the last few months; nothing had

improved. Not Shenk's financial situation, now rapidly approaching dire, and certainly not his case. Shenk's last desperate maneuver had been to commission a survey, hastily conducted by a pay-for-play medical research consultancy out of Bakersfield, of two hundred seventy-five subdural hematoma surgeries conducted in the last five years—a Hail Mary effort to discover a pattern of appropriate conduct that Catanzaro and his team had failed to observe. The preliminary results of the study had not been encouraging, and the final results Shenk would never see, because his second payment had been by check, and the check had not cleared.

His chances thus lay entirely on the slender shoulders of Dr. Theresa Pileggi, who would take the stand to talk in her robotic voice about Syndrome K, presuming he could scrounge the cash together to pay *her* invoices through the day of her testimony, early next week.

All of which meant, bottom line, he needed to pick himself a hell of a jury.

Shenk summoned his spirits. He smoothed his hair. He sashayed up to the thirty-six Angelenos who had been led in like cattle from the holding pen downstairs, and beamed a welcoming grin across the bow of the box. The prospective jurors were of all kinds, drawn from the astonishing vastness of LA County, as varied in their ethnicity and gender and age as the city itself: Black, Asian, Caucasian, and Latin, young and old. Thick-bellied workingmen and reedy office types, nurses in scrubs, Hollywood agents in suits that shined like new-minted currency.

"Good morning, Mr. Janes," said Shenk, sidling toward the first of the candidates, a portly African American gentleman with a union T-shirt and a combative glower. "And how are you today?"

"I've been better," said Mr. Janes, folding his arms over his belly, signaling furious restrained distaste for jury duty, for sitting around, for sacrificing a day's wages on this shit.

"I gotcha, sir," said Shenk. "I hear ya."

They were all watching him, all these could-be jurors, taking his measure just as he was taking theirs, in their turn: their outfits and their eyes, their haircuts and their skin color, the relative slump of their shoulders. Each was broadcasting a particular attitude, knowingly or unknowingly: they were anxious or they were irritated or they were bored, or—in some rare cases—eager. Mr. Janes was not eager.

"Mr. Janes, have you ever served on a jury before?"

"Yes," he said, gruffly alluding in one syllable to what an enormous pain in his ass that previous service had been.

Unfortunately for Mr. Janes, everything else about his answers Shenk liked very much. Working-class background, high school education, a slipped disc that no doctor had ever been able to heal.

"Oh dear," said Shenk, "I am so sorry," thinking what a gift he was going to give this man: a doctor he could punish.

"We'll be happy to seat Mr. Janes," said Shenk, turning back to his table so as not to see the man's reaction, winking at Beth Keener, who sat in the front row, clutching the wooden railing so hard it might snap.

Mr. Riggs rose slowly, in his brown suit and bad haircut, like a large but unfrightening monster surfacing from the deep. No doubt saving his objections for the truly objectionable, he allowed for Mr. Janes, and the judge banged his gavel and asked Jackie Benson who was next.

Next was a Ms. Rodway, and after her a Mr. Bissell, and after him was someone else, and one by one Shenk the thermometer took everybody's temperature. Shenk knew how to do it. Shenk knew all the rules. Young people were better than old, and women were better than men, and working people better than professional. He knew that racial minorities were in the aggregate more sympathetic, more likely to have been screwed by places like hospitals and people like insurance-company hacks.

But neither could you just go by the rules of thumb; each prospective juror had to be taken on his or her own merits. You might have thought Shenk would jump at the chance to seat Samuel Ricks, whose wife, Patty, had lately died in a hospital. But under further questioning he recalled, voice trembling, how Patty's doctors had worked "tirelessly" to save her; Shenk patted him with kindness on the hand and sent him on his way.

Riggs, for his part, jettisoned Ms. Elisha Jackson, a phone-company worker so skeptical of corporate power that she let out an audible puff of air between her lips as Riggs approached her in his Company Man suit. But Shenk *did* get Nancy Koechner, a recent college graduate in social work (social work! God bless her bleeding heart!); *and* he got Darlene Stephens, not only a retired elementary-school teacher but an octogenarian at least; and he even, after Riggs wasted the last of his preemptory challenges, was blessed with Marvin Leighton, who was not only an African American male but twenty-seven years old and radiant with pursed-lipped antiauthoritarian distrust.

As Cates tapped his gavel, officially impaneling Mr. Leighton, Shenk fidgeted with the knot of his tie. He was doing well, actually—he thought he was doing pretty damn well here.

It was madness, when you thought about it, that this was how justice worked. No one who has tried a case before a jury can possibly imagine that justice is some permanent thing, fixed and stable over time. How can it be, when there are so many elusive factors introduced with the addition of each new human person—each with her own prejudices and inclinations, her own preconceptions and distractions. Somehow the cross-pollination of all these disparate influences is not only supposed to magically divine the correct verdict but also the dollar amount that correlates precisely to the injury that has been sustained? The very notion of it was preposterous.

Shenk's most daring selection came toward the end of the day, when they considered one Celia Gonzalez, who though only forty-seven years old had retired two years earlier from the Los Angeles Police Department and now worked in private security.

Riggs eyed Shenk suspiciously as Shenk stood back from the box, hands clasped behind him, and said, "The plaintiffs will be glad to seat Officer Gonzalez." It was dogma, of course, that cops were bad jurors for the plaintiffs. Cops were institutionalists; cops were wary of nuisance suits; cops were traditionally indisposed to blame professionals for acts taken in the course of professional duty. But Officer Celia Gonzalez had stolen Shenk's heart.

She was a *female* officer, for one thing, and she was a *young* female officer, for a second, and lastly—oh, Celia!—she was blond-haired and blue-eyed despite bearing the surname Gonzalez; she was, in other words, a white woman who was married to a man named Gonzalez.

And then there were twelve, and Shenk loved them, every one.

Cates took one of his ruminative pauses, inspecting the *Keener* jury and humming "Goodnight, My Someone," from *The Music Man*. Finally he asked Ms. Benson what time it was, and when she said 4:30 he pointed his chin upward, turned this fact over for a few moments, like Oliver Wendell Holmes weighing a tricky question of Fourth Amendment jurisprudence, and pronounced that they would begin with jury instructions tomorrow.

Cates brought the gavel down, and everybody got up, and Shenk felt a touch at his elbow.

"How do you think it's going?"

"Good, good. It's going just fine, Beth."

"Are you sure?"

Beth Keener had her fingers sunk into his elbow, like an owl gripping at a branch.

"Very much so, Beth. And you don't need to come every day. I will tell you when I need you here. OK?"

Beth looked wiped out, her eyes red at the rims, her fingers slightly trembling from the sheer effort of watching every instant of what was, really, just the beginning of this. Reacting to everything, weighing the meaning of everything. She won't make it, Shenk thought with alarm — she'll die.

She was in all black — dress and pocketbook and shoes — as if it was a funeral and not a trial.

"We are doing great," Shenk told her, keeping his expression neutral, his voice low. Still in court; still on display. He shifted position slightly and angled Beth slightly away from himself, so his nice new jury had a clear sightline on the suffering mother. As long as she's here, let them see her. Let them look upon her drawn, angry face, the need for justice that burns in her eyes. Let them see what these people have done to her.

Maybe this was it, he thought, rising on a fresh gust of optimism. Maybe this excellent jury, this good and kind and victim-loving SoCal jury, would be inclined to buy what Dr. Pileggi was selling them, and keep his ass out of the fire.

And indeed, he noticed one of the jurors, on the way from the box, lingering, her hand on the rail, eyes resting with obvious sympathy on Beth Keener.

It was Officer Gonzalez, and Shenk thought, I like you, Officer. You, I like.

Shenk whistled on the way out of Cates's courtroom, even

winked mischievously at poor dumb Riggs, and at home he made Ruben breakfast for dinner before getting started on prep for the morning.

And all the rest of it was coming, just over the line of the near horizon — a ghost ship, invisible, steaming closer.

February 5, 2019

Renzer's Peak was not a peak at all. It was less of a mountain and more of a hill, and really less of a hill and more of a long rise, angling upward out of the landscape toward its hazy white top. The trailhead was at one end of an oblong patch, unmarked and muddy, just off the state road.

Ruben left Ed's car and started up the narrow path. He switchbacked unevenly up the ascent. He walked until the car was out of view behind him, and then he kept on walking.

A quarter mile in, ducking under the overstretched branch of a spruce, he brushed against it with the top of his head and brought down a cascade of slush, filling the narrow space between his shirt collar and his coat.

"Fuck," said Ruben, and then the sky opened up and it began to rain. "Fuck," he said again.

It hadn't been raining at all when he left the post office, and it had stayed dry while he was finding his way out of town, looking for the trailhead, but now it had started, a steady ugly drizzle. He ducked his head and said "fuck" a third time, and then it came hard, as if summoned.

Ruben kept on going. Set his feet down carefully, kept the hood of his slicker tight around his head.

The path was narrow. It cut back sharply, again and again, crossing and then recrossing the face of the hill. Ruben stumbled, righted himself, stumbled again. He gritted his teeth. He tugged tight the hood of the rain slicker, pulled it taut around his hair, his neck, so just his face was exposed to the bitter air.

The rain came straight down at times and slantwise other times. It didn't bother him at first, and then it did—it was awful.

"This sucks," the Rabbi grunted to the empty woods, but he kept on going.

A crop of blisters began to form on his toes. He adjusted his stride, taking big, long steps to try to lessen the pressure.

He walked a long time. His socks, supposedly high quality and weatherproof, grew damp and then soggy. After stopping three times to hike them up, he quit trying and marched on with the socks puddled around his ankles.

Still walking, one step at a time, eyes looking straight ahead, motion locked in. He felt a faraway ache in his right thigh, a distant memory of a wrestling injury that twinged sometimes when he ran.

A thick fallen tree lay diagonally, like a passed-out drunk across the path, so Ruben took a giant's step onto it, then slid down the other side, splinters biting into his ass.

After he'd been walking for what? For an hour? When he was starting to tire, when he was thoroughly soaked, when he was maybe starting to think he'd made a mistake, maybe thinking about slowing down, he instead decided to run.

No. He didn't decide. It burst up out of him, and he ran. He just started running.

He took his glasses off and slid them into the top pocket of the rain jacket, and made his hands into fists and rushed up the rutted path, through rough churns of mud. He put his head down and breathed like runners know how to breathe, evenly and deep, and felt the muscles tighten in his neck. His feet navigated the rocks and roots. His hamstrings began to burn and his lungs burned with each breath of cold air.

He went fast, then faster.

It was colder the higher he got, but the cold was good and right. The cold was electric on his skin. *Faster.*

The rain became sleet, stinging at him, biting at his cheeks and the exposed backs of his hands, and it felt good. Every drop was a knifepoint, slicing him at the corners, opening him up, peeling him away. He ran faster, up the incline, breathing something in, breathing something out. The hard weather stripped his skin and revealed what was underneath, exposing him to the air, raw and red, and the sleet kept biting him, burning him, and he still rose, bending into the wind, closer to whatever was waiting.

He crested the hill, and the ground evened out, and the path opened up slightly, a wide track with muddy ruts on either side. He ran beneath overhanging branches, fattened by snow and shrouded in fog. A little ways farther and the trail separated, a smaller path diverging from the main, and there was no way to know which was better. Neither route was right.

But the Rabbi was on it now—he was in it. By gut he picked a route and when it branched again he picked again, not thinking, just going, and whatever truer, stronger, smarter self had been exposed by the elements, it was telling him where to go.

Here.

Here.

Here.

The path ended all at once, splintered into a tangle of small paths, all of which petered out around the rim of a clearing. Ruben stopped running.

A building stood in the clearing. Four brick walls and a faded green door and a slanted slate roof.

Ruben's body thrummed inside his skin, wanting to keep running. Pulse and breath and blood all roaring in protest.

A sturdy little chimney poked up like a snout from the corner of the roof of the building, giving off no smoke.

The Rabbi stood staring. He stood with his boots sunk in the mud and stared at the old bricks and the green door. He found his glasses in his pocket. He licked his chapped lips. Then he cupped his hands and called out.

"Hello?"

His voice echoed and then died, swallowed by hundreds of empty acres of Alaskan silence.

"Hello?"

He heard a small distant noise, the *skritch* of an animal moving through bushes or leaping through branches, and all of a sudden all the fear he'd been suppressing or ignoring came clamoring up in him. His stomach went to water. He felt like he might piss, or shit, or both.

Bad idea.

Go back.

Who do you think—

At least Theresa Pileggi had a reason to come. Maybe she was out of her fucking mind, maybe she had fallen into this crazy idea, slipped underneath it, slipped below its surface like drowning. Maybe she had entered into some sort of murderous conspiracy with these monsters, and had come up here to find them, but what about him?

What was Ruben doing here?

He had followed this bloody story like a red thread, pulling at it as if it were pulling at him, drawing him forward like a reverse unspooling. But now all of it—Rich, the lamp, the motel room— none of it had valence anymore. Not out here, under an endless gray. Looking up the slight remaining rise that separated him from this brick cabin in the woods, standing squat against the wideness of the sky.

We're all always trying to remain just one thing, but sometimes you feel incohered. You can't help it. You stand there looking at the object of your search, this ancient red-brick house, with peeling paint and a cracked roof and the drainpipe hanging off of it, and you have this disintegrating feeling, like it's not yourself looking at this house, because there is no such thing as yourself. There are molecules in shapes, there are ideas that contradict each other, there are memories and dreams and visions and emotions. You are a thing that is made of other, interlocking, intermingling, overlapping things.

Ruben could only hope that sometimes the reasons for things reveal themselves in the aftermath.

His phone shivered in his pocket and he jumped and then laughed at himself for jumping. He had *service*. Suddenly, somehow, three days into his Alaskan sojourn, the mysterious gods of cell service had smiled on him.

He pulled out the phone and laughed again, out loud this time. He'd gotten a notification: Postmates was gifting him fifteen dollars off his next delivery. Ruben, deep in the Alaskan forest, a stone's throw from the slanting brick cabin where Theresa Pileggi had come, two weeks before she came to Los Angeles to die, said "Thanks, Postmates." He started to put his phone back in his pocket.

Wait, though. He had *service*.

He called his dad, and his dad answered right away.

"Oh God, Rubie," he said. "Rubie! I been calling."

"Listen——"

"I thought you were dead."

"No," he said. He took a step toward the ranger station. "Listen."

"Are you OK?"

"I'm fine. I'm in Alaska."

"You're——what?"

"I'm trying to figure it out, Dad. I'm following her trail."

"Ruben, baby——"

"Pileggi came here, to Alaska, before she came to LA. And she came to LA to kill Rich. I was right. He shot her in self-defense."

Another step closer. There were two windows on the wall of the ranger station, small and square and laced with frost. Something was in one of the windows——a smudge of black, a shadow, a——

"Can you prove it?"

"What?"

"Ruben?"

Ruben stopped talking. There was a man in the window. Looking out.

"Ruben?"

Ruben didn't answer. The man was looking at him. Long hair, tangled and matted, a mouth full of straight white teeth. A twisted scar, ugly and waxy on his cheek. Looking straight ahead through the grimy window of the cabin, looking right at Ruben, eyes flat as glass.

Ruben stared, he was staring, the man was turning slowly from the window, walking away, back straight, arms hanging at his sides.

A distant tinny sound from the air somewhere. His father's voice, from his hand, from the phone, down at the level of his waist: "Ruben? Sweetheart? Are you there?"

It's him—

Ruben stepped closer to the window, blinking, watching the night man walk, into the interior of the cabin, walking in a long, slow circle. He reached the rear of the cabin and turned back, and Ruben saw it again, the face, framed in the smeared window glass, blank and expressionless. For all of his life this person, this *thing* had stalked Ruben's nightmares, all cool ease, a golden striding jackal, and now he moved stiff and automatic, arms hanging as if weighted at his sides.

Hollow. Hollow like Wesley—

"What are you?" said Ruben, his words visible in the cold, and he heard his dad say his name one more time, but he wasn't listening to him anymore. He was talking to the man in the window. To the night man. *"What the fuck are you?"*

And then something hit him brutally hard on the back of his head and his consciousness lit up with stars and pain, and he screamed and fell down.

The way it worked in movies, the way Samir had probably intended it to work, was that he'd smack Ruben on the back of the head with the flat face of the shovel, and that single clean collision would put Ruben out of commission. And then, while Ruben was unconscious, maybe he would have, who knows, tied him to a tree or something.

What actually happened was that the shovel's face glanced off one side of Ruben's head, and either Samir was too weak or Ruben was too hardheaded for it to do anything near the kind of blunt-force damage that would have been necessary to disconnect him from consciousness.

God, it fucking *hurt,* though, like Ruben's head had been smashed in the door of a car, bounced off of concrete. He looked up, clutching his head, and saw a skinny dark-skinned man in a T-shirt and jeans, gaping down at him with the shovel clutched in his fists like a baseball bat.

"Hey," he said, and Samir brought the shovel down again, swung it like a mallet, and Ruben rolled away just in time, and heard the ugly *chunk* of the shovel's sharp edge burying itself in the frozen mud. Samir let out a high-pitched animal shriek, leaping onto Ruben's back, clawing and clutching, while Ruben struggled up onto his forearms.

Samir stayed on top of him, riding his back, digging his fingers into Ruben's neck, and Ruben could feel his bone-thin body, curled along the length of his spine.

Ruben growled as all his old wrestler's instincts snapped to life: his shoulders squaring off like two soldiers, his thigh muscles straining like dogs on leashes. He flipped both of them over, putting Samir on his back, pinned. Ruben punched him, once, a clean cut across the jaw, and rolled off, thinking that this was done—but then Samir hissed and scraped the side of his face with long, ragged nails, cutting into him, drawing blood.

Ruben punched again, viciously hard, and then once again, with the other hand, and he felt the hot sting in his knuckles and watched Samir's head roll on his wiry neck, saw ropes of blood shoot out of the side of his mouth. A third hit and Ruben felt teeth go loose. A splatter of blood painted itself on the muddy snow. But Samir was like a demon; Samir wouldn't quit. He brought a skinny pointed knee into Ruben's gut and knocked the wind from him, got on top of him again, choking him, a line of bloody drool dripping from the corner of his mouth until it dangled, disgusting, just above Ruben's own mouth. God, did he *stink,* an eye-watering stench of decay coming off him like a cloud.

The man is gone, Ruben thought. He is all gone.

He had seen Samir twice, ten years ago, once in the office and once in his house. He had been thin and healthy and well-scrubbed, a keen and earnest young man, and now he was fucking *gone*. He looked like a refugee: eyes like marbles, cheeks hollowed out by time and hunger. He had the wild beard and desperate savage strength of a shipwreck victim, fighting to stay alive. A lost man from a storybook, abandoned by fate, long since having traded away the last human instincts in exchange for one more day's survival.

"Jesus Christ, man," said Ruben. "Stop." But Samir kept going, digging, clawing, jamming the sharp angles of his elbows into Ruben's stomach, striking at his eyes. He sank his teeth into Ruben's wrist, and Ruben yelped in pain and frustration. They grappled, rolling around in the slushy mud of the forest floor, off the trail and then back onto it, in and out of the small piles of animal shit that dotted the muddy path.

Finally Ruben caught the man's arms behind his back and jerked them until Samir made a guttural, deflating sound, half sob and half scream, and went limp.

Holding him this way, Ruben could feel just how threadbare his body had become; every individual bone fragile as a pencil under the fabric of his skin.

Ruben released his grip very slowly, and just slightly, but Samir didn't move again. He lay panting, eyes closed, shuddering like a spent child. Ruben was quicker in catching his own breath. His freshly wounded wrist throbbed, and he stared at it, hoping he hadn't just gotten rabies or something.

He turned his attention from his assailant. Long enough to point to the window.

The figure was still there. Appearing and disappearing at the window. Visible, then invisible. Walking in circles.

"What is going on up here, man? Is that your friend? Dennis? Is that him?"

"No, that's—" said Samir, and then the effort to speak caught up with him, and his voice collapsed into a spate of dusty coughs. The gift of speech returning haltingly, as if he hadn't spoken in years.

"That's not a person."

The face again at the window, then gone again. Back and forth, back and forth, back and forth forever.

"It's a *vessel*."

"Hey," Ruben said softly, and kneeled beside Samir in the snow. There was so much to understand.

He helped Samir up until he was kneeling alongside him. The two of them on their knees, like two penitents in the muddy field, their eyes angled up toward the house.

He took Samir's hands in his. Like a brother; like a father; gathered up the other man's two hands and clasped them between his own.

"Listen, dude."

He used the familiar, goofy little word. It felt right somehow. Like: look, all this crazy shit aside, we're just two guys, right? Just a couple of dudes out here in the woods.

"Why don't you tell me the whole story?"

Samir nodded. He started to crawl toward the lodge. Ruben followed him up.

In April of 2010, after their final, violent, failed attempt to seize the Keener boy, Dennis and his followers fled Southern California. First, Samir recalled, they went to Tempe. Then they spent some time in Texas, he thought, but it might have been Oklahoma. New people drifted in and out of Dennis's circle of charismatic influence. Lost souls. Schizophrenics. Perpetual outsiders. For a long time, Dennis was fixated on returning to Los Angeles, on having another go at Wesley Keener. The trial was over, the publicity had died down. The boy would be less protected.

They could get him now. Crack him open.

But then one night—Samir thought it was six months later, or a year—and he thought they were somewhere in Montana, Big Sky Country or something—their leader, whose extraordinary revelation was at the heart of their beliefs, had another one.

Ruben listened patiently through the story. He let Samir talk, and he listened.

There had been a lightning storm. They were staying in a campground, in a circle of ragged tents. Dennis woke up panting and shivering, seized by this fresh vision, and got the rest of them up. It was the middle of the night, and they stood together beneath the elements, as the lightning exploded over and over, and the rain came in sheets. They were a dozen, more or less, at that time: his acolytes, his stalwarts, his true believers. Katy was there, of course, rapt, her tears mingling with the rain, ecstatic to hear a fresh round of truth. And Samir, bent over the small notebook he carried to write down everything Dennis said.

Another chance was coming, Dennis told them. This was the substance of the revelation; this was the heart of it. If they had missed their chance to open the vessel the Keener boy had become, there would be another chance, and they had to be ready. The future was always coming. The good and golden world would try again to pour itself into this one, to strip us of our pain and grief, and we had to be *ready*.

Dennis was determined, this time, to be the vessel himself. This was his pronouncement. He touched each of them in turn; he looked them in the eye, while thunder roared in the dark sky. They had ten years—not ten years from right then, from the night of the Montana lightning storm, but ten years from the last time, from the Keener boy.

They shivered in the rain. They cried out in ecstasy. The mission was clear. The future was coming.

Samir was shivering now. He clutched at his skinny arms. Ruben sat beside him on the dusty floor of the ranger station, their backs against the wall, like kids in the middle-school cafeteria, talking quietly at lunchtime.

And while Samir told his story, Dennis was walking. From the window to the door, from the door to the window, and each time he passed within feet of them, within inches of the soles of Ruben's boots. Dennis was in heavy work pants and a tattered collarless gray shirt. He did not move his head. His arms were straight beside him. He just walked, back and forth, tight circles in a small room, and every time he passed, Ruben felt the same small shudder of horror.

This ranger station when it was active had been a true working outpost, not any kind of visitors' center. A cot, a desk, a trunk for supplies. But whatever it had been, it wasn't anymore. The cot was a rusty metal frame, the lid of the trunk was thrown open, loose from its hinges, the edge of a blanket hanging out. There were food wrappers everywhere, broken bits of wood and flakes of paint.

And it was full of blood. While Samir talked, Ruben looked around the room and saw blood in every corner. Blood in splatters on two walls; an archipelago of blood on the floor.

Ruben tried to tell if the blood was new. Tried to summon whatever investigative instinct he had found at Cosmo's. Was the blood tacky? How red was it? It didn't seem new, but not old either.

Samir meanwhile was in the past, out on the road. With Dennis, when he was still Dennis, cool and charismatic at the core of a ragged band, hustlers and madmen and thieves on their secret and glorious mission to summon the other side. Stealing drugs, stealing money. Working shit jobs, robbing strangers, undertaking other activities that even now, in his dead-voiced wilderness confessional, Samir could not bring himself to confess.

Dennis was working to empty himself out. Letting the others handle the material things, while he disappeared into the maze of his mind, focused on that riddle, on getting himself all stripped down so the good and golden world could find him and fill him up.

Eventually they drifted up here, to the great wilderness. The cold and undiscovered country. Mid–last year, Samir thought? Maybe September. The time had blurred together, the seasons collapsing.

"Why?" Ruben asked. "Why Alaska?"

"Cheap. And we had to leave Tacoma. Quickly." Samir looked fleetingly distressed, remembering whatever had happened in Tacoma. "Someone's brother knew about this place."

He was still having trouble speaking. He was taking greedy sips of water from the canteen Ruben had brought from the store in town. Ruben had put out a small pile of granola in front of him, and Samir picked at it like a bird, taking fingerfuls and pushing them into his cracked lips, chewing them drily, having small sips of water.

"And we didn't have much time. Dennis was close. He thought he was close."

By now most of the others had drifted away, and it was back to the three of them, the same core group who had visited Shenk & Partners a decade ago. Katy and Samir and Dennis, Dennis crouched on the ground most of the time, bent over, palms pressed together, muttering and murmuring.

It was going to happen, he told them, when he was lucid. When he was present in the room. Time was ticking. It was fucking *imminent*.

"He wanted to be somewhere safe when it happened. Somewhere we could be alone." Samir paused, licked his cracked lips.

And meanwhile, thought Ruben, Theresa was at home in Indianapolis, in the birdcage of her childhood, in the grips of her parallel madness. Pacing and muttering. Tunneling in. Wandering in circles, moaning behind the locked door.

Until, in November of last year, she had her own revelation.

She understood it all, including the part of the secret that Dennis had chosen not to tell.

It was on the strength of this understanding that she flew forth. Emerged at last from her room, suitcase in hand, and left her bewildered mother and got herself all the way to Alaska and found Dennis and his acolytes, trying to work the same miracle she was.

Dennis walked past again, and Ruben watched him, his lank blond hair and his pale cheeks.

Ruben felt a surreal wash of pity for his old nemesis. Laid low. Hollowed out.

It had happened on November twelfth, Samir reported. Exactly ten years since it happened to Wesley. Ruben would have bet it was the same day Theresa Pileggi experienced her revelation, back in Indiana.

The day Dennis finally did it.

The day he became a vessel.

"So then, you know . . . " Samir coughed, spat on the ground. "Then we were just waiting."

"You were waiting for what?"

The sky had opened up again, and now, as Ruben eased Samir

toward the end of the story, rain hissed and muttered on the roof of the station.

"Waiting till it was time to do it. The future was inside of him now." Dennis walked past, slowly, eyes empty, reached the door, and turned around. "Now it was our job to bring it out."

Ruben knew exactly what Samir meant. He would never forget it: the night man smiling on his lawn, a thousand years ago, when Ruben asked what they would do to Wesley Keener, if they got him.

Get it out, the man had said. *Crack him open.*

"Katy wanted to be the one to do it," Samir said. "She had become—I don't know." Samir shivered, recalling whatever Katy had become. "She was very keen. But so yeah. We had a gun. There was one here, in the station. This guy, Jonathan, he was with us for a while, but then he took off. Him and a girl, Elsie. He left it behind."

"What kind of gun?"

"It was a handgun," Samir said. "Some kind of semiautomatic."

Ruben knew the rest, of course. A Donner P-90. Very unusual gun. He was there—he was almost there—he almost understood everything. He could almost tell Samir the rest.

"The thing is, we had to wait. It was supposed to be that once he became like"—he paused, pointed at Dennis as he walked past, empty and staring—"like *that,* then after some time, he would *glow.* Like the boy did, your boy. Wesley. Light up, like, like, from the inside. But Dennis didn't . . . he never did that. So we didn't know if we were supposed to. I kept saying I wasn't sure, you know? What if he's just—just sick, or—I don't know. I mean can you imagine, if we—you know, if we—we killed him and . . . and nothing happened? I just thought we oughta wait, and I told Katy that. So we waited. Katy was so ready, and I said let's just give it a week. A month. Let's just wait."

Samir trembled. He coughed. Ruben waited, and then he prompted him. He didn't ask. He told Samir what happened next. "Then Theresa Pileggi came."

"Theresa," said Samir, softly, almost fondly, like he had just learned a pleasing secret. "Was that her name?"

Ruben nodded. Streaks of rain clawing at the window like fingers.

"She did, yeah. That's right. She came. She was here."

Ruben could picture it. There was something about Theresa Pileggi that was always so locked in, so *certain*. It made sense. Once she had understood the truth—the real truth—what she thought was the truth—she had come not hesitantly, but like a locomotive. Like a bullet from a gun.

She found Dennis walking and she found these two emaciated wild-eyed misfits trying to steel themselves to murder him—to crack him open—and she told them to stop. She told them they had to stop.

Don't do it, she said. *You can't do it.*

She explained what was really going on. The revelation she had received in her Indianapolis bedroom. She explained the part that Dennis had left out. What would happen if they went through with it.

Katy wouldn't accept it. She told this new arrival she was wrong; they had to do what Dennis had told them to do—they had to release the good and golden world.

And now Samir told all of this to Ruben. Rain battering at the roof. Dennis walking and watching.

"And you believed what she told you? It made sense?"

Samir laughed, a dry, terrible, cracking sound, and then he couldn't *stop* laughing. He bent forward, shaking, clutching himself and laughing.

"Did it *make sense?*" he managed at last, flecks of spit and blood on his lips, his eyes wide with the hilariousness of it all. "Did it make sense? Does any of it make *fucking sense?*"

Poor Samir had given his life to this. To all of it. His was the dilemma of the zealot, the cult victim, the fundamentalist with blood on his hands. He had believed it all. How does he stop believing it now? And then Theresa came in, carrying this last piece of truth. The final piece of the puzzle.

The answer to Ruben's question, finally, was yes. Samir had believed her. He had wanted to believe her, maybe, because he didn't want to go through with what they'd started. He didn't want to crack open Dennis, even though that's what Dennis had told them to do, because in the end it would just be murder, after all. So he was looking for a reason not to go through with it. He was ready to receive the warning that Theresa had brought. Ready to believe her.

"I believed her, yeah. But, um—but—"

Ruben looked past him. At all the blood. "Katy didn't believe her?"

Blood on the walls. Blood on the floor. A world of bright red blood.

"Yeah, she, um—she said no. She said we had come this far. We have come so far. We have to go through with it. But—what did you say her name was?"

"Theresa."

Samir nodded, his eyes watering. *Theresa.*

"Yeah. Theresa was pretty insistent."

Samir described the struggle for the gun, Theresa smashing into Katy, battering her with her fists, her arms, and Katy firing wildly into the walls of the cabin—a bullet hole there, see, and there— trying and failing to get a shot into this insane stranger. Samir screaming the whole time, trying to pry them apart, wedging his slender body between them, and meanwhile Dennis walking slowly back and forth between them, correcting course automatically whenever he almost came in contact with the melee. A madhouse, a nightmare.

And then Theresa—"I never knew that," murmured Samir again, "I never knew her name"—she had the gun but Katy would not stop, could not stop, so she shot her. One shot, very close range. Blood on the walls and on the floor.

"Blood just everywhere," Samir concluded. "Fucking everywhere."

Ruben realized, as Samir approached the end of this woeful tale, that the sound of the rain had ceased on the roof, and looking outside he saw that it was snowing now. Not hard. Thick clots of snow, coming in against the window as they had at Theresa's house in Indy. All part of the same world, the same water.

A sentence reached up to him from some ancient distance. From the Classical Poetry Confab he had briefly attended in middle school.

This is the poem of the air. Slowly in silent syllables recorded.

Was it Wordsworth? Longfellow? One of those guys.

This is the secret of despair. Long in its cloudy bosom hoarded.

He had never paid attention. All he remembered was Ms. Hutchins's ruddy cheeks as she declaimed; all he remembered was blushing at the word *bosom*.

Now the words clutched and shuddered in his chest.

Now whispered and revealed to wood and field.

Theresa killed Katy and left Dennis here. Samir in place to guard him. To make sure that what they had wanted for a decade—for the vessel to be cracked open, for the world inside of Dennis to be released—would not happen. Must never happen.

And then she left. Back down the hill, clutching the gun. On her way to California, eyes sparking with madness, to spread her words of warning.

"Is she coming back?" Samir looked pleadingly at Ruben, who was getting up. It was over. He had what he needed here. Samir's hands were in his hair, and his eyes were wild with need. "Is she coming back?"

"No," said Ruben. Then he took the poor man into his arms and held him tight. "But I am."

Shenk, he would tell you with all due modesty, did a pretty solid John Riggs.

Having installed Theresa Pileggi in the rolling office chair he was using as a witness box, having sworn her in on the ancient Yellow Pages that still banged around in his office, having agreed to pay her time and a half for this Saturday afternoon trial-prep session now extending into evening, Shenk dropped into character. He hunched his shoulders and puffed out his cheeks to fatten his face. He jammed his hands deep in his pockets and loped across the room. He gave a mild groan before each question, as if even condescending to examine a plaintiff's expert caused him some gastric distress.

"Could you tell us one more time . . ." A pause. An exhale. "The name of this . . . condition?"

"Syndrome K."

" 'Syndrome K.' " Shenk's Riggs put skeptical quote marks around the phrase like a pair of handcuffs. Pileggi looked back at him unfazed from behind her thick drugstore eyeglasses.

"And, sorry, but what exactly does the K stand for?"

"It is not an initial K. It denotes that this syndrome is the eleventh named variant in a related but distinct family of syndromes, some as-yet entirely hypothetical."

This diction was a smidge too technical, but Shenk let it ride. Bigger fish to fry. He made a glum, dissatisfied Riggs face as he considered Pileggi's appearance. Her black hair was uncombed, pinned up on her forehead with two girlish barrettes. She wore no makeup. She had on some kind of terrible pale-yellow top and a blockish blue blazer. She looked like the captain of the high school debate team.

There was going to have to be some shopping, thought Shenk from within his Riggs cocoon, suppressing an alarming flutter of anxiety about how little credit was left to him across his various cards.

He was trying to remain calm. Steady as she goes, through the opening days of trial. He had put up his witnesses, one by one, and one by one Riggs had neutralized whatever small advantage they might have provided. So it had been with Wes's pal Bernie in his ill-fitting suit, too short at the legs and arms, recalling the traumatizing moment of Wes's injury. Same with the EMTs, who had kept him stable in the ambulance ride, and the triage nurses, who rushed him to the ER and summoned a neuro consult, precisely according to protocol.

With each witness, Shenk tried to paint the picture he wanted the jury to see: a child who should not have been operated on, a paramedic team that didn't take a full history, a surgery undertaken in haste. He had even tried to introduce Dr. Catanzaro's custody dispute to the record, as a way of backdooring in his history of lunchtime tippling, only to have Judge Cates call him into chambers and thunder at him for twenty minutes. He had hoped to make some progress by slicing away at the diagnostic certainty of Dr. Amandpour, the ER physician, sidling up to the crucial decision: "The boy was stable when he was brought in?...The scans showed a hematoma, yes, but not one growing at an alarming rate?...And in your experience, Dr. Amandpour, wouldn't the prudent course be to implant an EVD, to monitor progress—"

"My experience was not relevant," Amandpour had said, cutting this line off clean. "It was Dr. Catanzaro's decision."

After each of these witnesses he would glance at Gonzalez, his beloved former police officer in the second row of the jury box, and note her expression, which remained determinedly neutral.

But it didn't matter. All the things he had presented thus far were red herrings; they were side doors, leading away from the only real question left. If Theresa Pileggi could make the jury understand that the operation had led directly to Wes's condition—and that Catanzaro should have known better—they'd win. Otherwise, they would not.

Shenk & Partners after midnight was a quiet place, even with the window cracked to let in the cool night air. They got the occasional snatch of conversation from a late-night dog walker below, murmuring into a phone; they had the low, inconsistent hum of traffic from the I-10 a quarter mile north. The streetlight at Palms and Overland peeked in, flickery and yellow, and it made a quiet occasional crackle.

Shenk made another of Riggs's distressed exhales before delivering the next question with a flat smack, like putting a slab of paper-wrapped fish down on a counter.

"And you are the inventor of this syndrome?"

"Respectfully, sir, one does not invent a syndrome."

"Good," murmured Shenk, from inside his mask of Riggs, "'sir' is good."

"If you are asking how my colleagues and I identified the existence of the disease, it was the result of a latitudinal metastudy, synthesizing data from seven hundred and twelve studies of PVS patients."

"Easy, Theresa," said Shenk, snapping back into himself, shaking his head and grinning. "Don't get too Spocky on me."

She scowled. He wondered if it was because he had called her Theresa. She had a sip of the tea she drank endlessly from a steel thermos. "Spocky?"

"Yeah. Like Spock? Oh my God, are you too young for *Star Trek?*"

"I know who Spock is."

"Good. Great. I will have already gotten all the details out of you on direct, so by the time he gets to cross we don't need 'em again. Don't let him draw you out into a whole complicated back-and-forth. Short and simple. OK?" Then, instantly, Shenk was back into Riggs, the voice and the hunched affect, backing up the tape: "You identified this syndrome how?"

"By studying other studies. Looking for patterns. Narrowing it down. Thinking, as I believe the expression is, outside the box."

"Good! Yes!" Shenk popped back out from the disguise, clapping his hands. "Just be careful with your face."

"My *face?*"

Pileggi's indignation, unfortunately, made the face problem even worse.

"Yes. I mean, not—there's nothing *wrong* with your face. Your face is fine."

Pileggi narrowed her eyes. "Is that a compliment?"

"You just don't want to look like you think you're smarter than him."

"You said he was an idiot. You said he was a block of wood."

"Oh, he is. Believe me. Block of wood is a *generous* comparison, with this guy."

Theresa smiled. Just barely, but she did.

"But your job here is to *be* smart, without letting on that you *know* you're smart. You need to be likable up there."

"Likable?" Pileggi crossed her arms, leaned back in the office chair so it let out a slight squeak. "Would you say that to a man, Mr. Shenk?"

"Actually, I might. I really might. But, listen—we don't have time to solve the great issues of the day. Let's just focus on winning this case, OK? Do you need anything?"

"No."

"More tea?"

"No."

"A bathroom break?"

"Let's keep working."

"Spoken," he said lightly, "like someone getting paid by the hour."

She smiled tightly, and Shenk slipped back into character, hands back in his pockets, weight shifted forward, jowls puffed out, ready to rock.

But he had spoiled his own good humor, joking about the billable hours of his expert witness. He had been trying very hard not to think about it tonight, about his catastrophic financial situation. After the polite but firm no from Stella at Mayorski, he had tried other litigation financing companies and gotten the same result. Nobody thought he had a case, so nobody would stake him. By now Shenk had scraped his savings clean, turned out his pockets, written a note to Darla apologizing for the late back pay, joking pathetically that if she wanted to sue him he knew a good lawyer. He was making do with his own ad hoc courtroom exhibits, but that hadn't stopped Earmark Litigation Services from dunning him relentlessly over the ones they'd already produced.

And then there was the house. The house, and the car.

And then—Shenk's chest got tight when he thought about it,

which is why he tried not to think about it—and then there was Ruben's school. Two days ago the financial official from Morningstar had at last caught Shenk on the phone, regretfully given him a firm deadline, three weeks hence, to provide for this semester's tuition, and last semester's, still outstanding.

Which is why, late last night, he'd called Joey Boston, his financial adviser, whose office was in New Jersey, even though his name was Joey Boston.

Jay's wife, Marilyn, God rest her soul, had come into his life along with a pot of money. Her father, born in a Belarusian shtetl, had made his American fortune in the diamond business—a *small* fortune, to be sure, no kind of Rothschild fortune—and that diamond money had sat sacrosanct since Marilyn brought it into the marriage. Shenk always having wanted to be the one to provide what they needed. When she would mention the money, when she would suggest they tap into it for, say, furniture or adoption fees, Shenk would wag a finger at her. "What money? That money does not exist!"

It was only when Marilyn had insisted, over Shenk's mild, vaguely principled objections, on sending Ruben to private school for K–12 that Shenk had been forced to remember the existence of the money and begun to chip away at it on a quarterly basis. But still he had trained himself not to think of it. Certainly not for the operation of the business that he had sworn would support him and his family—certainly not for anything so petty as trial costs. The money belonged to Marilyn, and in the tragic aftermath of her death, it was the boy's. For the future. For Ruben's future, for the remaining years of private school, for college, for law school.

So imagine how Jay had felt, coming home after trial yesterday to find darkness at Shenk & Partners. The lights had been shut off by the city.

So he sat there in the darkness and called Joey Boston.

"Hey, man, listen" is what Joey Boston had said, annoyingly cheerful considering the enormity of the moment. "It's your money."

Shenk thinking, well, it is and it isn't, and then reminding himself that he'd put it all back. As soon as the verdict came in, there would be a returning tide of hospital money, of hospital-insurance-company money. It was coming right back in.

"Now," said Shenk as Riggs, peering at Theresa, forcing himself to focus. "According to your testimony yesterday"—referring to testimony that had not yet actually occurred but which Shenk as Shenk would carefully solicit when the time came, probably mid–next week—"if there is such thing as this Syndrome K—"

"There is."

"Don't."

"What?"

"Don't interrupt him."

"*Ever?*"

"Never. Be easy. Let it ride." And then, as Riggs once again: "If there is such a thing as this Syndrome K, then, if I understand your testimony correctly, there is no way Dr. Catanzaro could have known that Wesley Keener had it. Because the—I'm sorry, what was it again?"

"The prion."

"Ah yes, the 'prion'—face, Theresa, careful of your *face*—the 'prion.'" Shenk, as Riggs, said the word *prion* like someone else might have said *unicorn* or *Bigfoot*. "The prion is invisible, and does no damage, until it suddenly does. Yes?"

"Yes."

"So is it correct to say there is *no way* Dr. Catanzaro could have anticipated this potential complication of surgery?"

"Well," said Pileggi. "*Actually.*"

"Ugh."

"What?"

"Let's not say *actually*. Let's never say *actually*. And your *tone*." Shenk was waving his hands above his head, like a brakeman signaling a train. "You gotta watch your tone. Especially going into this part, about how he should have known. We're rounding third here, this is the big moment. I don't want the jury to think you're being..."

"Being *what?*"

"Being..." Shenk sighed. "Haughty."

Admittedly, this was an impossible task he was giving her. To present herself as the authority on the boy's ailment—without being arrogant, without being obnoxious.

"Fine," she said, and Shenk said "Fine" and then immediately dropped back into Riggs. "Just so we're clear, Ms. Pileggi—"

"Excuse me?" said Pileggi, indignant.

"Whoa!" said Shenk. "Take it easy, sister."

Pileggi said "Is that him, or you? Telling me to take it easy?"

It was he: it was Shenk, peering out from inside dull Riggs's eyes. "It is very likely he will get casual with your title, every once in a while, just to be a prick. It's needling. Don't be affronted. Don't react. Gently correct him."

Pileggi was shaking her head, lips pursed tightly.

"You can't get upset," Shenk told her. "Not in there."

"I'm not upset. I'm impatient. Do you want to work on the testimony or not?"

"Theresa, all of this stuff: this *is* working on the testimony."

Shenk himself was getting upset. He was sorry this was hard for Dr. Pileggi, but she had lobbied for this job and she needed to do what he told her. He was *paying* her to do what he told her.

"Shall we get back into it?"

"Fine." She exhaled, sharply.

"Don't do that, either."

"Don't what?"

"Breathe."

"Don't *breathe?*"

There was a stern moment of quiet, and then, as if by mutual acknowledgment that they had come to the end of some sort of comedy routine, both of them laughed.

"OK," said Jay. "Now *I* need to pee."

When he returned from the bathroom, Theresa Pileggi had disappeared from the office.

He found her on the steel catwalk outside Shenk & Partners, looking out at the parking lot, smoking a cigarette.

"No!" he said.

"No, what?"

"You *smoke?*" cried Shenk, genuinely aghast.

"I do," she said. "Sometimes. When I am—" She looked at him carefully. "When I am feeling bombarded."

"I cannot believe you smoke." Shenk felt betrayed, somehow. "Maybe you're not as smart as you think you are."

Pileggi rolled her eyes. "I've done the math, Mr. Shenk, and my odds of getting cancer, factoring in my demographic category, my genetic history, and the fact that at most I go through a pack every six weeks, are relatively low."

"Oh. Excuse me. Pardon me, folks. The young lady is protected by a force field made of science."

He smiled wryly, shaking his head, and joined her at the rail. It was the middle of the night, and there were only the two cars in the lot down there: his tan Subaru and Pileggi's pokey little Nissan. She was staying at a hotel for the duration of the trial, the Courtyard by Marriott on Twentieth Street, in Santa Monica. On his dime, of course. Down the street, parallel parked, was a silver sedan, a Corolla. The engine was on, and someone was sitting in shadow in the driver's seat. The only other sign of life in the universe.

Jay watched Pileggi smoke for a second, remembering an old silver Corolla he used to drive, maybe twenty years ago, as a law school bachelor. It was like he had come from his own past, parked on Palms to peer in on himself, see how he was doing.

"My wife died of it."

"Of cancer?"

"Never smoked, but she got it anyway."

"Oh. Oh shit."

"So I'm a little crazy on the subject."

Looking at her sideways, Shenk could see appropriate words and phrases tumbling around in Pileggi's head, trying to find purchase. She was really very young. Accomplished and composed, but young.

"It's OK," he told her. "Everybody goes sometime. How's that for science?"

She let the half-smoked cigarette go. It tumbled end over end and disappeared into the black of the asphalt below. Shenk smiled faintly, watching it fall.

"And what about you?" he said.

"Sorry?"

"A family, Dr. Pileggi? Do you have parents, or did you emerge fully formed, like Athena from the head of Zeus?"

"No, no," she said, as if the question had been serious. "I have a mother. In Indiana. That's where I'm from."

"Indiana?"

"Have you been?"

"No. Do they have Jews there? It might be awkward."

When Pileggi smiled her face was a thousand times less severe; there was a charmingly dorky high school nerd in there still, sharing space with the abrasive adult genius.

He turned half toward her, leaned one elbow on the flimsy steel railing.

"OK. So we were born in Indiana. Is this Bloomington?"

"Indianapolis."

"Do we have siblings?"

"No."

"And no husband? No children?" She looked alarmed. Shenk laughed. "OK, just the parents, then." A beat of silence, Shenk waiting for more, finally giving her a little push—"Let's do school now," he said. "Public? Private? Oh wait—Catholic? I bet Catholic."

But Shenk had misread the moment. He had pushed it too far, and Pileggi had become suspicious.

"What are we doing?" she said. "How is all of this relevant?"

"To tell you the truth, Theresa? Is that OK, I call you Theresa?"

She shrugged, allowing it, and Shenk couldn't help but feel he had won an enormous concession.

"I need you to be a full human person up there. If you're on the witness stand just doing a dry recitation, from your article, then I might as well just *bring* the article. Save myself whatever I'm paying you." *Stop talking about money, Jay. Stop it. For Christ's sake.* "For this to work, they need to trust you, and for them to trust you, they need to *like* you. With my apologies to Gloria Steinem, you need to be likable. So I am searching out your soul, my friend, so I can see it and make sure the jury sees it, too."

Pileggi turned this over. Ugly yellow lamplight bouncing off her glasses, protecting her eyes from being seen. The silver Corolla

Shenk had seen idling suddenly lurched out into the lane, disappeared down Palms.

Finally: "Well, one thing about my mom. She loves this kind of stuff."

Shenk felt a trill of happiness, deep in his heart. He leaned closer. "What kind of stuff?"

"Legal stuff. The law. She watches all those shows, you know?"

"Like what? Like *Law and Order?*"

"Oh yeah. *Law and Order, JAG,* all of those. She used to love *LA Law.*"

"Oh, sure. Marilyn loved that one. My wife. We never missed it. Corbin Bernsen. I was never a jealous husband, but my goodness the way Marilyn looked at Corbin Bernsen."

"I don't know who that is," said Pileggi. Shenk moved on.

"She'd dig this, I bet. Right? You being an expert witness and all?"

"Oh, yeah. Yes."

"You tell her about it?"

"Not yet," said Pileggi, frowning a little.

"You got to."

"I will."

Shenk nodded, smiling softly. *There it is,* he thought. One thing Shenk knew, one thing he had learned, was that people do things for reasons: They don't always know them, and they're not always clear, but the reasons are always down there somewhere. *I'm paying her all this damn money, and she's doing it so her mother can see something in her she can understand. Something to feel proud of.*

"And what about your father?"

A long pause. Pileggi studied the darkness of the parking lot, her lips drawn tight. "He's dead."

"I'm so sorry," said Shenk. "Was that when you were young?"

Pileggi paused, and then she said, very quietly, "Not young enough."

She made this small joke without a smile. And Shenk under-stood that her air of steadiness, her near-robotic calm, required near-constant maintenance. There was a whole system in there, fortifications and battlements.

He looked at her now and she looked back and held his gaze, and a savage nighttime history was clear in her eyes. A girl who was trapped, a monster seething inside a man. Shenk could see it and he could feel it, and he could see and feel his imperfect witness in a way he had not seen her before, not really seen *anyone* in a damn long time. Jay was well aware that his specialty was not in seeing people as people, per se, because he tended to see them and slot them into roles, useful or not useful, smart or not smart, client or civilian, friend or foe. But here before his eyes, in the street-light silence, he was seeing Theresa Pileggi in three dimensions—or even in four, actually, her past trailing luminescent in the air around her. The darkness from which she had emerged made into visible light.

Just being totally honest here, he was still pretty sure she was going to be a terrible witness. But he knew he would never meet another person like her.

"Let's get back to work," she said.

"Yes. Yeah. This is good, though."

"What is?"

"Me learning about you. As I said—now I can put you up there and show the jury you're an actual human being. With a soul and all."

As if leery of the accusation, Pileggi pivoted from the topic. "Surely it's more important that I'm right," she said. "About this patient. And in that I am a hundred percent confident."

"Oh, I know," said Shenk. "Listen, your confidence is great. Your confidence I do not worry about."

That whole sentence he would turn over, later. Among a few other key moments, decisions, stray phrases, which he would carry with him forever like rocks picked up off a path. Clacking together in his pockets and making holes in the fabric.

"Actually, you know what?" said Jay. "It's late. I'm gonna let you go, and we can pick this up tomorrow. Is that OK?"

"You're paying me by the hour," said Pileggi. "So it's up to you."

Affection, like everything else, has complicated chemical origins. It is not an intangible force; it rises from neuronal pathways and chemical combinations and recombinations, forming itself from itself, molecules reaching out to other molecules. Dopamine in the hypothalamus, epinephrine flooding the circuits.

That does not make affection less real, by the way, but *more*.

Poet's love is a kind of bullshit, nothing made out of nothing, a figure drawn on the empty air by a tracing finger. But the scientist's love can be broken down into its component parts, calculated and corrected, expressed in formulae.

Give me the love that can be written on a chalkboard, if you've got a chalkboard big enough.

"Oh God, Rubie," Shenk cried out. "Rubie! I been calling."

"Listen—"

"I thought you were dead."

"No. Listen."

Shenk was in the chaos and noise of the hallway, trying to hear, outside Judge Scanlon's courtroom. A finger jammed in the opposite ear. The line was crackling. "Are you OK?"

"I'm fine. I'm in Alaska."

"You're—what?"

Shenk circled in search of a quiet corner. He crouched by a bench, ignoring the sullen look of a teenager in baggy jeans, down here also, plugging in his phone.

"I'm trying to figure it out, Dad. I'm following her trail."

"Ruben, baby—"

"Pileggi was here, here in Alaska, before she came to LA. She came to LA to kill Rich. I was right. He shot her in self-defense."

Against this baffling tide of information, Shenk stood up and braced himself against the wall. He was the one who was supposed to be in charge. He was supposed to be the lawyer. "Can you prove it?"

"What?"

If Ruben was talking, Jay couldn't hear him. He couldn't hear anything. Shenk cursed, walked to the other side of the corridor, searching for a clear signal. He passed a row of people, standing against the wall as if in a police lineup, a snaggletoothed old lady with her arms crossed and her middle-aged daughter, bent over and weeping into her forearms, and here's the granddaughter, with tattoos up both arms, clutching the handle of a stroller, little baby in there wailing and waving her fists.

Shenk jammed the finger back in his ear to block it out, to block all of it out.

"Ruben?

"Ruben?

"Ruben? Sweetheart? Are you there?"

It all felt like a dream.

The sun had come up that day like every other day in her life, like every other day of her marriage. Beth Keener had been up. She'd watched it rise. Coffee, clothes, the car, all of it vivid and real.

But now, downtown, in the courtroom of the Honorable Judge Scanlon, nothing was clear. The fog that had come over her, off and on for a decade, had swallowed her today almost completely, and whether this was confusion or mercy, she felt on this day like she did not entirely exist. She was beamed in, watching a hologram, or maybe she *was* the hologram. Inside the dream, watching not people but flickering weird visions from another world.

Like Jay Shenk, staggering in from the hallway, haggard and uncertain, clutching a file against his chest as if it were some thin plate of armor. The file said KEENER on it, in crooked black

Sharpie-marker letters, and Beth blinked at it, groping for the meaning of the word.

Then the sheriff's deputies brought in the man of the hour, all in orange, manacled at hands and feet. All the fury Beth had felt yesterday toward her husband had flared down and was now just an ember, a pilot light in her gut. She looked at him as if from a distance. A thousand miles, a hundred years. It was what it was. What it was always going to be.

Judge Scanlon came in and the world was asked to rise, and Beth rose.

Why had all of it happened, and what would she do? There were all these answers that Beth Keener would never get.

"OK. Good morning." Judge Scanlon licked her lips, once, and looked quickly around the courtroom, rapid and lizardly, just a quick scan to make sure everybody who was supposed to be there was there. "Everybody ready?"

"I'm actually, uh—no, I'm not. Sorry."

"That was rhetorical, Mr. Shenk."

"Yeah, no, I know. Listen, though—"

"Ready, Mr. Thomas?"

Mr. Thomas, the handsome Black prosecutor, was born ready. He rose, nodded, pronounced the State of California ready indeed, and sat again.

"Good. The State is here, the defendant is here."

Richard was just behind and beside Shenk, staring straight ahead, a statue of a man.

Shenk stood up and cleared his throat and raised one hand, cringing somewhat, as if apologizing in advance for what he was about to say. He was distracted. He didn't know what had happened to Ruben. Ruben was in *Alaska*?

"Your Honor."

"What, Mr. Shenk?" Scanlon's sour face got sourer still. "What do you need?"

"Well, can I come talk to you for just one sec, before we get going?"

Shenk came out from behind the little table where he had been planted, and the bailiff stepped toward him, alarmed.

"Hey. Whoa. Slow." Judge Scanlon held up her hands. "You say, 'Permission to approach the bench.'"

"Permission to approach the bench."

"Denied."

Shenk flinched, and Thomas for the State, over at his table, made a low clucking noise that may or may not have been a laugh. They had to know each other well, the judge and the State: Shenk had parachuted into this world they lived in together, and they must think of him as a dilettante, if not an ignoramus, and he wasn't exactly proving them wrong. Shenk felt utterly lost in this unfamiliar universe of the criminal courts. He couldn't bend reality to his will in here, couldn't shape the air around him. He felt like a cursed wizard, stripped of the source of his powers.

Richard Keener stood staring straight ahead, saying nothing, though Jay was sure that behind his silence, his client was enjoying the hell out of his discomfort and disorientation. Could he have killed someone simply for the dark pleasure of seeing Jay Shenk make an ass of himself?

Beth was somewhere in the courtroom, a tattered and spectral figure.

"Judge. Please." He raised his hand again, and then raised the other one, so he had both in the air, a surrendering bandit. If she wouldn't let him approach the bench, he'd just have to lob his appeal over the wall. "I've had some new information. Or—well, it's hard to explain." He cleared his throat. He tried to smile and failed and stopped trying. "I am hoping there's some mechanism I might exercise, which could postpone today's sentencing."

Scanlon scowled. "We've been over this."

"Right, except I've got some new information."

"You said."

"Your Honor?" Mr. Thomas at the State's table shot up, already talking. "If the defense has evidence it has not shared——"

"Yes, yes," said the judge, talking over and around Thomas, who finished his sentence, "——we have the right to examine it," even as she finished it for him, "you'll get to see it," the two of them overlapping, as if the docket was so stuffed in here that everybody had to talk at the same time, in the name of efficiency.

Shenk watched the two of them, helpless, like he was watching a tennis match, until Scanlon pointed at him——"So? What is it?"—— and he had to concede that there was no new evidence, not really. "It's just that there *may* be something on the way."

"What sort of something?"

"I have an investigator in the field, Your Honor, and you see I've lost contact with him." He held up his phone to the judge, as if the fact that Ruben wasn't on it, right now talking to him, proved his point.

"Your *Honor*." Thomas, his indignation pulling him up out of his chair again, even as Judge Scanlon waved him impatiently back down: *sit, sit, it's not necessary.*

"Mr. Shenk. Your job today is to provide the court with any mitigating factors we might consider in sentencing Mr. Keener. *Not* to present new evidence. And definitely not to raise the possibility of evidence that you haven't seen, and which may or may not exist."

"Yeah, no, I know. But, see, my son——"

"Your *son?*"

"Yeah, he's . . . my son is also my investigator. And vice versa. And, see, he, uh—he was going to—I think he said Alaska— but I haven't been able to reach him . . . but his, uh, what he was thinking was . . ." Shenk had wandered into a bramble. It would be useless to say anything about Ruben's theory, about self-defense, until he could make the whole presentation, all together, when Ruben came back.

In the corner of his eye, Mr. Thomas for the State of California was looking down, studying his hands.

"Honestly, Your Honor." Shenk blinked helplessly up at Judge Scanlon. "I would only ask for a brief delay."

Scanlon hissed. "Does your client want this delay?"

Shenk shot a quick look at Richard Keener. The prisoner waited a moment, and then without looking at Shenk he shook his head.

"For the record, please," said Scanlon.

"Let's go," said Rich. "Let's fucking get to it."

Mr. Thomas smiled at his hands. Judge Scanlon made a low, frosty chuckle.

"Let the record reflect that the defendant would like to fucking get to it."

Twenty minutes later, it was over.

Shenk came out of the courtroom and headed for the elevator bank. All he wanted was to get out onto Hill Street so he could try calling Ruben again. What the hell had happened to the kid? If anything had happened to him—

Someone took his arm.

"Jay?"

Beth's hair was a wild mess. She looked colorless and

confused. She looked like a drawing of herself, faint pencil lines, half-erased.

"What now?" she said.

"What do you mean?" said Shenk. He didn't feel like having this conversation. He couldn't bear it. "He was sentenced to death. He goes to prison. Eventually, he'll be executed." He rubbed his forehead with his palm. "I don't know when. A long time from now. I don't know. Who knows?"

He looked up, and Beth was blinking back at him.

"But . . ."

"But what?"

"Can we appeal?"

"Beth? *He pled guilty.* I told you there was nothing I could do, and guess what, I was *right*. OK? Now are you satisfied?"

"No," said Beth. Very quietly. Almost inaudible in the chaotic noise of the hallway. "No."

"Well, look," said Shenk, and jammed his hands in his pockets, and turned to go. "You wanna explore more options, knock yourself out. But you're gonna need to get another lawyer."

Ruben had presumed all along that he'd get to attend every day of the trial, but Shenk at the last minute had changed his mind. No doubt he'd heard Marilyn in his ear reminding him that this was April, for heaven's sake, and you're not gonna yank the kid out of school in the middle of the semester. Finally Ruben and Jay and the memory of Marilyn had come to an accommodation, and Ruben had been permitted to choose three days, over the course of the trial, as long as it wouldn't mean missing any tests or anything.

As a minor child he was not permitted to sit at the plaintiff's table, but he set up right behind it, attached to but not officially *of* the Shenk & Partners delegation, in his white dress shirt and navy blazer with gold buttons, a notepad balanced on his lap. In the morning Jay would be presenting a man named Dr. Douglas Cudley, a pudgy workhorse of a hired gun, whom he had contracted at a bargain-basement price to give the jury an Idiot's Guide to CT scans. The afternoon would be given over to the main event: the appearance of Dr. Catanzaro.

Ruben's job was to keep an eye upon Officer Gonzalez, Juror Number 7, to chart the warmth of her sympathy and the keenness of her attention.

The problem was, from the minute the judge brought the gavel down, Ruben's attention kept drifting to Evelyn Keener, with whom he had merely exchanged a shy "Hey" on coming in, both of them probably a little cowed by the solemnity of the room and the occasion, or maybe the enormity of having contracted to go to the dance together, now coming up. He had thought maybe she wouldn't be here and then was surprised that her parents let her come, and he figured maybe she'd also asked for permission to come on certain days, too, and they'd both ended up choosing today, and wasn't that cool?

Like him, Evelyn was wearing fancy clothes for court. She had on a sheer off-white blouse with eyelet cutouts along the collar. He noticed a slender strap beneath the thin fabric of her court dress, and he wondered if she was wearing a tank top under the shirt, or an actual bra, and then he told himself he was a pervert and turned his attention furiously back to Juror Number 7. He watched her watching Dr. Cudley as he described the differences between the various kinds of scans, how on a CT a brain bleed turns up as bright white, against the mass of gray brain around it. He saw that she was sort of listening, and he wrote "sort of listening" in his notebook.

The day of the dance was April 24. Three Saturdays from now. He had circled it in the wall calendar on his desk and put a notification on his phone.

Shenk, for all his protestations and hand-wringing, would have liked nothing better than to have Ruben, junior partner and great love of his heart, at his side for every minute of this thing: sitting beside him biting his lower lip and furrowing that little brow of his and showing in every way the intensity of his interest and affection.

The only problem was every time he caught Ruben's eye, every time he gave him a deep, knowing wink—*We got this, my lad, we are in this together*—his heart seized and squeezed because of that call he'd made over the weekend to his money man in New Jersey.

"It's your money," Joey Boston had said, and now even *that* money, the money he had sworn he'd never spend, was all but spent.

Relax, Marilyn told him from the other side, *it's going to be fine.*

And Shenk did relax. It was going to be fine. Although of course a lot of times those voices that comfort us, the ones belonging to our wisest counselors, our beloved ancestors or dear departed lovers, that's just us, right? That's just your brain talking to itself, that's just people telling themselves what they need or want to hear.

Dr. Catanzaro was being sworn in, with his placid eyes and his monastery beard. He swore to tell the whole truth, one plump hand raised like a statue.

"Good afternoon, Doctor," said Shenk. "Thank you for finding the time to testify today."

"You're welcome," he said softly. "I'm happy to do it."

No you're not, thought Shenk. He thought it as hard as he could without saying it aloud. Go fuck yourself.

Dr. Thomas Angelo Catanzaro proved as unflappable on the witness stand as in the deposition room, cool as a marble Buddha. He suffered all of Shenk's needling with the same heroic forbearance he had displayed in the Telemacher, Goldenstein conference room. He described how Wesley had presented, described how in his judgment the surgery had been not only necessary, but urgent. Again and again he parried any suggestion that the decision was made in haste, that he had been somehow overeager to operate; as he had in deposition, Catanzaro turned his undue haste into a badge of decisiveness. Catanzaro with his deep voice, his wise eyes, his thick white beard.

As to Wes's *condition,* post-surgery, Catanzaro concluded sadly that it remained a medical mystery.

"A mystery?" wondered Shenk.

"Yes, sir."

"And it could not have been prevented?"

"Tragically, yes, Mr. Shenk. There is nothing that could have been done."

This was a trap. Shenk could see into the future, he knew what Pileggi was going to say tomorrow, and he knew that with his own certainty Catanzaro was digging the hole he would fall into.

Still, Shenk didn't like it. He didn't like the way the doctor's pronouncement seemed to settle across the jury like truth itself. He looked to Ruben, and Ruben was looking at Celia Gonzalez, who was looking at the witness with something approaching awe.

"May I say one more thing?" said Catanzaro. He turned to the judge. "Would that be all right?"

"Counselor?" said Cates, properly deferring the answer to the lawyer who had the floor, but Jay's eye had been caught by someone in the crowd. A stranger sitting in the court, in a back row, among the crowd of the curious and fascinated who had come to watch *Keener.* Shenk could not make out the man's face, only the shape of him, the stiffness of his shoulders.

Shenk was tugged by a dim but urgent sense of remembrance: I *know* that guy. For some reason he thought of the silver Corolla that had been outside his office, the other night, when he was prepping Pileggi for trial. His old self, remember? His old self, sitting in his old car—Shenk from a previous life, come to visit.

"Mr. Shenk?" said Judge Cates again, and Shenk nodded, distracted, trying to catch a clean glimpse of the stranger.

"What I wanted to add," Catanzaro continued, great wet tears appearing in his solemn eyes, "is how much I wish there was something we could have done for this boy."

Shenk snapped to attention, realizing too late what the sneaky bastard was doing, as Dr. Catanzaro produced a giant handkerchief from some recess of his tent of a doctor's coat, and blew his nose elaborately.

"We are doctors, but we are people, too. I'm a father myself."

Shenk stood with his hands on his hips, flustered, frustrated, his eyes still seeking the stranger in the back. "OK, thanks for that, Doctor," said Shenk. "I'm sure that's appreciated."

Beth, God bless her, in her seat at the plaintiff's table, glared at Catanzaro, showing no sign of accepting his empty sentiment. But Celia Gonzalez, the key to the jury box, was looking at the doctor with open sympathy: this poor man who had experienced the tragedy of failing to keep Wesley Keener from turning into a golem.

"Dr. Catanzaro..." said Shenk, rummaging in his mind for one more thing, some needle to deflate this great Macy's Thanksgiving Day balloon of a witness, before he would have to turn him over to Riggs, who would only exalt him further.

The man in the back row stood up. Shenk watched him rise, but before he could see his face he turned away.

"Mr. Shenk?" said Judge Cates.

"Yeah?"

The man was gone. The courtroom door closed behind him.

Oh God. Holy shit.

"Mr. *Shenk?*"

Holy *shit.*

"Your Honor, could I have a brief recess?"

"What?"

"Just a—I just need a second, Judge."

"Mr. Shenk, you have a witness on the stand."

Of course Cates was going to reject this insane request, and that was fine, it was OK, he had help. He rushed over to the defense table and scrawled a note and balled it up and tossed it to Ruben in the front row.

Ruben read it, brow furrowed, and got up.

Silver Corolla, it said. *Get him!*

"My client will not be pressured into putting himself in the path of legal action. My client has a clean conscience."

"Your client was sitting outside my office in the middle of the night, trying to work up the courage to come and talk." Shenk pointed at the young man in the white shirt and thin tie and blue jeans, whom he had last seen poolside at the swim and tennis club, dripping with spa water and indignation.

Now he looked at Paolo Garza while Paolo Garza, in Judge Cates's chambers, surrounded by lawyers, looked at the floor. "Right, son?"

Garza mumbled "Right."

He was miserable. His lawyer, a red-cheeked blowsy woman named Donna Rourke, wasn't too happy either. Apparently what had happened was, this handsome young radiology tech had shown up in her third-floor office on Wilshire a few weeks ago, having gotten her name from a friend of a friend. He had information relating to a pending litigation, and she had accepted a retainer and then ordered him in no uncertain terms to do *nothing,* to let her *handle it.* She was going to *monitor events* and let him know if and when it made sense to bring what he knew to the attention of the court.

But Garza, sensitive soul, had found himself unable to heed that instruction.

"It was—it has been eating away at me," he said softly, one hand clutched in the other, avoiding not only Shenk's gaze but that of the judge, that of John Riggs, and that of his own counsel, this infuriated woman Rourke. "Eating away. I have tried to ignore it, but I—I can't."

"Of course you can ignore it," said Rourke. She was right behind him, chomping at a piece of Nicorette. Shenk could smell it, minty and stale, from across the room. "That's what ya do, son. You *ignore* it."

It, of course, meaning the twinge of conscience; meaning the small inner voice saying what the right and wrong things are to do. Shenk smiled graciously at Rourke, who was shaking her head with sadness at this naive young fellow, at the frailty of humans in general and of clients in particular.

"It would be marvelous," said Judge Cates, stern and consternated, "if someone would tell me what is going on here."

"Yes, sir," said Garza, and Rourke said "Hang on," and the judge turned to glare at her.

"Respectfully, Your Honor," she said, except with the gum it sounded like *ya ahnah.* "Respectfully, my client won't be saying anything until we have some reassurances."

Cates's glare intensified. Riggs made a muted hippopotamus grunt. They were crammed together in the judge's inner sanctum, far from the ears of the jury, using up all the chairs plus one ottoman, on which Shenk was awkwardly but happily perched. Judge Cates's chambers, unsurprisingly, were a monument to Judge Cates, the walls covered with plaques and commendations; one towering shelf was lined with law books and collated law review articles; another displayed his esoteric reading interests—*Europe Between the Wars,* a collected Keats, a biography of Tallulah Bankhead.

"What kind of reassurances are you referring to, Ms. Rourke?"

"Mr. Garza wants to do the right thing here," she said. "He's a good kid. Of course his impulse is to get the truth out there, say what he knows."

"Whether he wants to or not," said Judge Cates sternly, "it is his responsibility to do so."

"I must say," ventured Riggs, "that I do not like new information being entered at this late date."

"Yeah, me neither," said Shenk. "I certainly would have entered it, had I known about it." He looked at Garza scoldingly. "Whatever it is."

"I didn't know about it either, Mr. Shenk," said Riggs, offended.

"You sure about that?"

Riggs narrowed his eyes at Shenk, who winked at him, greatly enjoying his discomfort. Shenk was slightly tipped back on the ottoman, trying to forecast what hidden secret we were talking about here: Was Catanzaro a drunkard after all? Had his ex-wife poured her heart out to young Garza, her unlikely bosom buddy? Had Shenk been right the first time, and Dr. Allyn had witnessed some surgical hijinks and been paid off to leave town?

Shenk's only regret was that Ruben—no doubt pacing in the hallway beyond—couldn't be here to witness the denouement. It was his heroic intercession, after all, that had saved the day. Ruben, racing down six flights of stairs to beat Paolo Garza to the short-term parking lot on Olive Street; Ruben, looking younger than he was, playing the helpless child, separated from his dad and missing his phone and worried about getting in trouble; Ruben who had gratefully accepted Garza's phone to make a call and then handed it back, said "It's for you, actually," leaving Garza, confused, to say "Hello?" and hear the voice of Shenk like a strict God: "Young man, I believe you have something to tell me."

"Look, the thing is," said Rourke now, laying one hand on each of Garza's shoulders, "is that I can't let this kid spill his guts until I can be assured that he won't face retribution down the road. Him, personally."

"No one here can offer you immunity before we know what you're going to tell us, son," said the judge.

"He hasn't committed a crime," said Rourke quickly.

Garza looked like he was going to say something, and Rourke squeezed the shoulders hard, in warning.

"He's just got information, and he doesn't want to end up in the crosshairs for giving it over."

Cates stroked his beard slowly for a moment, and then a moment more. As these moments passed, Rourke kept her pose, hovering above Garza, looking first to Shenk and then to Riggs, clearly not accustomed to the judge's slow, deliberative style. She probably thought he was having a stroke.

"It seems to me," said Cates at last, "that the only person who can offer the reassurance you're seeking . . . is Mr. Shenk."

All eyes turned to Jay, who nodded and let the ottoman tip back forward, so all its little square feet were on the carpet.

"Well, Ms. Rourke," he said, though he was looking right at Garza. "You have my word."

Garza looked at him fleetingly and then tilted his head back and looked up at Ms. Rourke, pleadingly, this random woman in whom he had put all his trust. He wanted to talk; he was dying to. His conscience was a sad animal, locked in a box, scuffling against the lid and waiting to be freed.

"Oh, all right," said Rourke, and Shenk exhaled, and *Keener*, like a battleship, changed its course.

It had been a simple mistake.

People made mistakes all the time, but Paolo Garza had been a radiology tech for five years and had never made such a mistake before.

Three days before Wesley Keener, another patient with a traumatic head injury had been seen in the ER at Valley Village. A boy of sixteen years old named Martin Smithson, from Sherman Oaks; an accident at hockey practice; nonresponsive; swelling on the brain.

So when Wesley was brought in, Dr. Catanzaro requested the scans and Dr. Allyn ordered them and Garza took them and processed them, and then—and here Garza let Ms. Rourke take his hand in hers, and looked to Shenk, a thousand times more vulnerable than he had been, dripping wet and virtually naked, when first they met at the country club pool—he said he'd presented the doctors with the incorrect scans. He had miskeyed the date on the computer, summoned up the wrong CT for display.

Dr. Catanzaro, in hurried consultation with Dr. Allyn and Dr. Amandpour, had operated on Wesley Keener based on Martin Smithson's CT scan.

"Holy smoke," whispered Shenk, and Cates, white-lipped, told him to keep quiet. He was asking the questions now.

"When did you discover this error, young man?"

Garza shut his eyes again. "About—maybe—a half hour later."

Meaning, when Catanzaro had already begun. When Wesley Keener's scalp had already been peeled back, when his skull had already been drilled with holes.

Riggs was processing his surprise and grief by writing furiously, the pencil gripped like a kidnap victim in his thick hand, his heavy cheeks and jowls quivering in a way Shenk found quietly delightful.

"My God," thundered Judge Cates, gaping at this trembling soul. "Why didn't you say something?"

"Because it didn't matter," he blurted, and then, before Cates could react, he went on: "I mean of course it *mattered,* I don't mean it didn't *matter,* but it was the exact same kind of injury, the same problem. The doctors would have done the same thing. The scans were virtually the same."

He stopped. He took a deep breath. But he had gotten it all out. He had said it.

Cates was struck dumb with shock, and Rourke was shaking her head, chewing her gum, while Riggs just wrote and wrote, wearing his poor pencil down to the nub. Shenk risked being the one to ask. "What do you mean, *virtually* the same?"

"Well . . ."

Garza looked up at Rourke, who gave him a why-not shrug. He'd come this far.

"The CT. The new one."

"Wesley's."

"Yes. It had a——I don't know. Like a *shine* on it."

A pause. The room waited, breathing softly.

"I didn't even think it was anything. But, yeah, like a, a bright patch, kind of. Blood is white. On a CT scan, blood shows up white. Brain matter is gray. The spaces between are black. The ventricles, the subarachnoid space, that's all black. But this . . ."

He looked helpless. He shrugged.

"It was *bright.* Some sort of brightness."

Cates had stood up and walked to the window of his chambers. Riggs had finally stopped writing, struck at last by what was happening to his case. Not Shenk, though; Shenk had more questions.

"Where?"

"Back here." Garza pointed to his own head. "Near the brain stem. Just a . . . a brightness. But like I said, it was nothing. It was probably nothing. I don't think it would have affected the surgical decision-making."

"Oh, you don't think so," said Shenk, and then—unable to resist—"Mr. Riggs? Did you hear that? Mr. Garza, in his judgment—as—no offense, kid—in his judgment as a five-year veteran of the radiology tech department—he doesn't *think* so."

Riggs exhaled slowly, turned toward him, but Shenk didn't press it further, because he didn't have to—Riggs knew, the judge knew, any juror in the world would know, that Garza was unqualified to have made that determination.

And that Catanzaro, for all his acumen, had been operating without all the facts.

"I am sorry," said Garza, his face crumpled in his hands, while Judge Cates stood at the window, shaking his head at the woeful incompetence of the world.

As for Shenk, he reached out and put his arm around Garza's neck and held him, as the man kept going: "I am so, so sorry."

What happened in light of this new information was entirely predictable, although it happened even faster than Shenk might have thought. It was all of two minutes, after Cates said he would need until tomorrow to rule on how to proceed, and sent them all out of his chambers.

"Mr. Shenk? Jay?" said Riggs, hands jammed in his pockets, hunched forward, contriving to maintain a neutral expression. "I wonder if we might chat for a moment?"

They took the elevator together, and Riggs got right down to brass tacks, right there in the vaulted front lobby of the courthouse, illuminated by rows and rows of skylights, surrounded by a copse of potted trees.

Riggs got right to it, and Shenk played dumb, one of his least accustomed ways to play.

"I'm so sorry, John. I don't understand."

"Oh. Well. I think it would be appropriate, at this moment, to think about bringing this matter to a mutually agreeable compromise."

Of course Shenk knew what this was—given the grenade that had just exploded inside his tent, Riggs was ready to surrender.

But watching Riggs's plump little mouth form into the shape of the initial overture—it somehow repulsed him, and he recoiled.

"You want to settle?" he said, too loud for the lobby, drawing glances from a crowd of junior associates moving in a clump of navy blue from the elevator to the door. "*Now?*"

"Come on," said Riggs. "Let's not pretend this is a surprise. The facts have evolved."

Oh, they had evolved all right. They had certainly evolved. Shenk waited for the flood of mingled emotions that was surely on the way. Righteous triumph; giddy joy; the good green feeling of financial relief. Instead he felt like wood. He felt like a totem that someone had wheeled into this sunlit lobby on a cart and propped up against the wall.

"Well," Riggs began again. "For my part, I have always wanted to see this matter concluded swiftly and amicably."

"Oh, that's funny," said Shenk. "'Cuz there was this guy I had lunch with in Beverly Hills, and he looked an awful lot like you, and when I threw some numbers out he had a very different perspective. Very different."

Shenk could taste the acid tone in his own voice. Riggs smiled carefully.

"I'm not sure that's a fair characterization, Mr. Shenk. I believe what I said is that my clients were insistent on coming to trial, contrary to my own advice."

"And now I've got you people by the balls, and it's time to sing a different tune," said Shenk.

Riggs raised his hands. No point in denying it.

So this was it, then. Break out the bubbly. Right? A year and a half of banging his head against the wall on *Keener v. Valley Village Hospital Corporation,* and it was time to make space in the garage because the money truck was backing up.

But Shenk didn't want to settle. He didn't *want* to.

A rush of civilians came past, everyone clutching a paper cup of coffee, all of them smiling like idiots, chatting about bullshit. Don't they get it? thought Jay. Don't they know what's on the fucking line here in the lobby?

"We have both been involved in complex litigation before, Mr. Shenk," said Riggs. "Surely you can respect my recalibration."

"Well? So what is it?"

"What is what?"

Jay had a dark smile frozen on his face. "What's the *number,* John?"

"Four point nine."

Shenk raised his eyebrows. Four point nine million dollars was a lot of dollars.

"Gee, John," Shenk said, "I don't know what to say."

"Really? I don't think I'm giving you a hard decision here."

Riggs leaned back slightly as another rush of people made their way from the glass fronts toward the elevator bay. Shenk did the same.

"I'm just not sure. Given what has emerged today, I don't think this offer represents a fair settlement for my client."

"Despite the fact that we are only several hundred thousand off from your initial settlement offer? Several hundred *higher.* Or have I misremembered?"

"You turned that offer down." Shenk brought his Riggs impression briefly out of retirement, hangdog and jowly. "Or have I misremembered?"

Riggs raised his eyebrows. "I would only add that, although this new information is rather damning——"

"Yeah," said Shenk. "I'd say so."

"——it is not sufficient, in a malpractice suit, to show fault. You must also show that the fault was the cause of the injury."

"Wow. Hey. Thanks for the refresher, Mr. Riggs."

"You are being sarcastic. That's fine. I merely wished to remind you that this matter may not be as open-and-shut as you now think, but I am nevertheless making a very generous offer. I would think that at the very least, you might make a counteroffer."

Name your price, is what he was saying. *Just name it, and I'll give it to you. Name your price and get my clients out of this.* The Keeners could get a settlement of five million—northwards of that, Riggs was saying—an enormous settlement for a med-mal with no economic damages, and though they would owe Shenk forty percent of the first fifty thousand, thirty-three and a third of the next fifty, and so on from there, the Keeners would end up with more than enough to move on with their lives—not healed, never healed, but the next best thing: provided for.

Which was not nothing. Which was a lot. And yet.

"I have no counter, Mr. Riggs."

Riggs looked at him, puzzled, even slightly sad. "OK . . . so . . ." He opened his hands. "When can we expect one?"

"Frankly, John, my strong inclination, given today's turn of events, is to put this one in the hands of the jury."

"And you think you'll do better?"

"I do."

"Better than four point nine?"

"Much better."

"Better than..." Riggs palmed his mouth a moment, waggled his head back and forth. "Five point two?"

Jay closed his eyes. Five point two was really a lot.

"No," he said. He opened his eyes. "I'm not negotiating."

"Really?"

"Yeah. Really." He stared defiantly at Riggs. "You've been telling me for eighteen months how your clients were playing it fair and square, how Dr. C and his team of angels were doing God's work over there, and, hey, gee, now it turns out they flat-out fucked it up. They turned this kid into a wooden soldier."

Riggs seemed genuinely perplexed, so adamantly angry had his rival become, in the face of being offered $5.2 million. After all, this was how it was done. This was the game as it was played, and Riggs had merely played it—was merely playing it—exactly as Shenk himself had done.

"So, no, I am not inclined to accept your offer. What I am inclined to do is put Paolo Garza on a spit and slowly rotate him. See if we can't get your five point two up to fifteen. Maybe twenty."

Shenk had become red-faced, jabbing the point of his finger in Riggs's formidable slab of a chest. Riggs merely stared at him, chewing on his cheek, eyes scrunched up like a zookeeper puzzling over some strange form of animal behavior.

The elevator door made its sly shooshing noise, and more people came off, and more people got on. More stories, more traumas, more injustices to be set right.

"Understood, Mr. Shenk. But I trust you will present my offer to your clients?"

"Of course. Yeah. Of course I will." Shenk nodded up and down, up and down. "I'll ask them, and I'll let you know."

And he almost did, too.

He got back to his office and loosened his tie and took out his cherry-red flip and found Beth's number.

She had left court the moment it was gaveled out of session, as she did every day—back to Wesley, back to her vigilant sleepless watch. Walking with him in his circles, studying his eyes for the flicker of life that never came.

Shenk didn't press SEND. He flipped the phone shut and put it down on his cluttered desk and stared at it for a second, as if it was the phone's job to decide whether to make the call or not.

Then Jay decided to go for a quick run on the treadmill, just to shake out the day. Process the craziness, distract his brain.

He didn't have any running clothes with him so he stripped down to his T-shirt and his work slacks and started slow and easy, at a very comfortable four and a half miles an hour. Warm-up pace.

The problem of course was that he *knew* what Beth and Richard would say.

He would tell them, *Look, this is a good offer, but we can do better at trial. This new information about the CT, this is gold. It's pure gold. There was a clear medical error, and it was subsequently covered up. This will set the jury on fire. These people have lost every leg they had to stand on.*

But Rich—Rich would be skeptical. Shenk ran a little faster, playing out the conversation in his mind as his blood began to rush. Richard, furrowing his brow, puzzling it out: *You're saying the offer is higher than we even started with. How is that not a win?*

Beth, who had never been in it for the money, not exactly, Beth would rally, shake her head, insist that they stay the course. But Rich would scowl, say *Hold on,* do the numbers, and Beth's rally would collapse. The trial, no matter the justness of the cause, was a strain, and it was getting worse every day.

What a mercy it would be, for it to end.

Shenk turned up the machine from five to six and then to seven, and then he punched in an incline. Faster now, faster and uphill, and he could feel his heart pulsing in his neck.

What Rich would do is, he would ask whose decision this is, ours or yours, and Shenk would concede the point, and then Rich would nod.

All right, then. A single nod: Obviously. Of course.

He thought, ludicrously, that he should go home and ask Ruben what he thought. Then he laughed out loud at himself, clicking the speed on the console up to eight. *Ruben's just a kid. This decision is way above his pay grade.* It was an attorney's responsibility, ethically and legally, to present his clients with a good-faith offer of settlement. How the hell was Ruben, at fifteen years old, to help him decide whether it was an appropriate time to abdicate that responsibility?

Of course the real problem was that Ruben would tell him the answer and would be confused as to whether it was even a question. The real problem was, Ruben wouldn't hesitate.

But he had meant what he shouted at Riggs in the hallway: Settling would be crazy. It would be crazy! When the jury heard about all this, they'd be as incensed as Shenk himself. They were going to want to punish Dr. Catanzaro for his error, and doubly punish Valley Village for their complicity in covering it up. Five point two million was a lot, but he could get more. He *knew* he could.

Enough to keep Wesley Keener cared for forever by professionals, enough for all the armed security and private nurses they would ever need to keep him safe and comfortable; enough for him, Shenk, to pay back all the money he had scraped out of the bank, to fill back up the account that was earmarked for Ruben, and all the other ones besides.

So no, he did not present Riggs's offer to Beth and Richard Keener. He made the decision on their behalf, entrusting their future to his superior wisdom, while he ran faster and faster on his treadmill, its glowing panel the only light in his empty office.

And if there was some hidden part of Jay Shenk's mind—a large part or a small part, a lawyer's part or a part belonging to the human person, the person of flesh and feeling, if there was some tender place in Jay's mind that was thinking also of Dr. Theresa Pileggi, and of how settling at this point, before her testimony, would rob her of the opportunity to stride to the stand and put her hard-won expertise to use, after they had practiced so hard—well, he did not allow that part to impinge on his conscious deliberations.

He just ran and ran, Jay Shenk in furious motion, running to leave his body behind, until he felt like his heart was going to roar and leap from his chest, and then he went home and turned his phone off and showered and went to sleep.

PART FOUR

THE NIGHT MAN

April 14, 2010

It was root beer floats with three scoops of ice cream that night, and you better goddamn believe it.

It was Shenk in his brightest humor, god of lovingkindness, dancing across the kitchen to the freezer door and singing his way down to the lowest shelf, where they kept the dented cardboard cartons of ice cream. Shenk rummaging for two tall glasses, for two long straws and two long spoons, lining everything up neat like he was running a parlor.

"Mr. Shenk," said Shenk in a flutey, funny voice to Shenk the Younger, and Ruben, catching the fire of his dad's good humor, playing his role: "Yes, Mr. Shenk?"

"Would you care for chocolate or vanilla?"

And Ruben, bowing his head in the little half bow that was expected of him, selected vanilla because root beer floats were the custom, and chocolate in soda was not a root beer float, it was a Brown Cow, which was obviously delicious but not traditional.

Tonight was a night for tradition. For celebration. Tonight was the Shenks in their glory.

"Are we seriously having floats now?" Ruben said uncertainly, brow furrowing, unable even in the face of his father's joyousness to fully silence the voice of worry. "We haven't eaten dinner."

"There *are* some nights," explained his father with heavy gravitas, dropping generous glomps of ice cream into frosted glasses, watching them slowly roll and effervesce, "when dessert must come first."

Ruben laughed, and accepted the glass that Shenk slid toward him, and saw himself in his father's eyes.

Shenk at the last minute had decided to let him miss another day of school, even though it meant skipping out on the social studies final, so he could be present in court for today's climactic testimony. An exam could be made up, after all, and at the prices Shenk was paying, Morningstar wasn't going to just let the kid fail social studies, right? He should be there—he should be there to see his father deliver the killing blow to fat John Riggs and all the starchy Riggses of the unjust universe.

And Lord God had the day delivered.

Thinking back over all his years of practice, Shenk was hard-pressed to think of another day that had been so satisfying, that had so thoroughly met his expectations for success.

First, in the morning, it had been Paolo Garza, shaved and shorn and abashed up on the stand. In careful sentences he repeated the confession he'd made in Cates's office, of his careless error and what it meant, while Rourke sat in a front-row bench, snapping her gum, and Riggs watched helplessly, the color on his cheeks darkening slowly, like a setting sun. Shenk for his part had kept his gleeful eyes on the jury, watching with enormous pleasure as it all sank in.

The wrong chart. They had mauled this kid, they had monkeyed with his brain, based on the wrong chart...

And then, after lunch, came Dr. Theresa Pileggi.

"You saw her?" he said now, to Ruben, his eyes swimming with pleasure. "You saw?"

"I saw her, Dad. I was there."

"God, she was fucking amazing. Oh. Shit. Sorry." They tried not to curse in the house. Shenk looked up at the ceiling and past that to heaven, blew Marilyn an apologetic smooch. "But the gal fucking *nailed* it."

Pileggi's testimony had been a thing of beauty, precise and on point from *would you state your name for the record* onward. She was concise and she was clear and she was *likable,* chauvinist double standard be damned. What had seemed heretofore like her diffidence had played as politeness; her smugness as restrained humility; her arrogance as well-deserved confidence.

She rattled off her credentials crisply and with due modesty— the honors at Caltech and then the PhD from, ahem, *Duke,* and her current gig at Riverside; a humble lectureship, yes, but in a prestigious department, and tenure-track despite her tender age. Dr. Pileggi had detailed the extraordinary facts about Syndrome K: its origins in a molecular pathogen, its invisible dormancy and long period of gestation, its catastrophic effects on the brain once awakened—not on one or two discrete sections of the brain, but on whole systems, whole clusters of systems. Shenk made a show of prodding Pileggi, prying open her modest reluctance, until she conceded that it was she herself who had discovered it.

"So basically," she said, asked in the end to summarize, "Syndrome K is an exceedingly rare form of a larger category of abnormal protein deposition neurodegenerative disorders."

"Can I ask you to put that in layman's terms for us, Doctor?"

"Oh yes." A smile. A smile! "You betcha." Shenk, dying inside, melting with pride and pleasure: *you betcha!* "A lot of folks have heard of mad cow disease, right? It's different than that, but that's the general category we're talking about."

"OK. But Wesley Keener didn't get this illness from a diseased cow, did he?"

"Well, that's the tricky bit. We may never know *how* he became infected with the prion. We only know what caused it to emerge."

"Emerge?"

"Brain surgery is a traumatic event. What the body does, to cope with a traumatic event, is release certain chemicals. These sudden changes in chemistry activated the dormant prion."

"So—just to be totally clear. No surgery, no syndrome. Would that be fair to say?"

"Yes, it would."

Shenk's only job through all of this testimony was to nod at the right places, furrow his brow at others, interject occasional questions, not because Theresa didn't know what to say next, but to highlight the passages where he wanted dear Celia Gonzalez paying extra attention.

Shenk now, reliving it all, reveling in it all, still holding the ice-cream scoop and waving it like a barbarian's triumphant club. Recalling the big finish. "Now, Dr. Pileggi. You were present for the testimony from Dr. Catanzaro, yes?"

"Yes."

"In which he said that Wesley's condition has not been seen before, and therefore could not have been detected or predicted?"

"Yes. I was present for that testimony."

"And what did you make of it?"

"Well. The thing is, I hate to be..." She inhaled; she twisted her lips; a little show of hesitance. They had practiced this, late at night in his office, the stutter step of humility. The little ol' twentysomething gal not wanting to show up her superiors in open court. They had practiced it and practiced it.

"It's OK, Dr. Pileggi. Go ahead. Were they correct or not, when they testified that this outcome could never have been predicted?"

"No, Mr. Shenk, they were not," she said. "My colleagues and I published an article about Syndrome K in the Spring 2006 issue of *Proceedings in Neuropathology.*"

"Oh." Shenk turned to Riggs, pulled his face into a shocked pantomime. "Maybe Dr. Catanzaro let his subscription lapse."

"Objection," said Riggs flatly, and Cates sustained it, but it didn't matter. The point had been made. Catanzaro hadn't known about the danger, but he could have. He *should* have.

Shenk risked a direct glance at Officer Gonzalez, who not only nodded but looked at him directly, making eye contact, like an old friend. To Pileggi he said "I thank you," but what he might have equally said was "I'm very proud of you."

Riggs was already standing for cross-examination, but Judge Cates, after an extended examination of his watch, after a long, thoughtful exhale, called them into recess for the day.

It was because the judge's son was due back from college that day; it was spring break at Oberlin and he was coming home for a visit.

That's all it was, a trick of the calendar, pure randomness.

Shenk would find this all out later, years later actually, at a bar, when he ran into Jackie Benson, whom he hadn't seen in a good long time and who, at first, didn't recognize him. Normally Judge Cates would not have been concerned about pushing the day's testimony for another hour, but young Ellis Cates was at that moment on a plane home from Ohio, and the judge's wife had planned a small special dinner at the family's favorite seafood place, in Playa.

And as we know, the universe turns on such inconsequentialities.

"We'll proceed tomorrow," Cates announced, and lifted his gavel and smacked the future into place. "Ten a.m."

"Dad?"

"Yeah, honey?" Shenk looked up from his reverie with a broad grin on his face, scooper in one hand.

"Dad, I think there's someone in the house."

"What, bud?" said Jay, and as sometimes happened on Tabor Street the parent-child roles were flipped: while Shenk was lost in his happy memory, Ruben had been paying attention, nervous and responsible, but at the same time he was right, someone was in the house, and he knew who it was, too, but before he could say more the light behind Jay went out, and Jay's glass fell from his hand and exploded on the linoleum, because Dennis had yanked him by the ponytail, pulled back his head, and pressed a knife to his throat.

Ruben screamed, and Dennis grinned, revealing the pearl-white line of his teeth. "This is great," he said casually. "I'm so glad you guys are home."

Someone grabbed Ruben now, and held him tightly from behind: the bar of a forearm pressed across his chest, individual fingertips jammed into his upper arm, just below the shoulder. It was Samir who was holding him, the thin Indian man who had been with Dennis in the office that day, wearing a white dress shirt like he'd worn then. Ruben fought against his grip, struggling so hard he lifted himself off the ground. He was a kid, though, he was only a kid, and Samir was a full-grown man, holding him tightly, squeezing while Ruben kicked and howled.

"Take it easy, Ruben," said Dennis sweetly, and angled the knife so it dug slightly farther into Jay's neck. The blade winked back at Ruben in the moonlight. "Be a good boy, now."

It was a serrated knife, the bread knife from the knife block on the counter. Marilyn had replaced all the knives in the kitchen the year before she died, knowing that soon she'd be gone. She had wanted that Jay in his widowerhood would have a kitchen he would use.

The big knife with its sawtooth blade was for bagels, for baguettes, all things resistant to cutting. Now Dennis had it drawn tightly against Shenk's throat. His hair was blond and stringy, streaked with moonlight, falling lank around his pale grinning face. His hands were dirty and callused, but—Ruben noticed it now, why was he noticing it now?—the fingernails were perfect, clean and pink as seashells.

"It's OK, sweetheart," said Jay to Ruben. "I'm all right."

"It's OK," murmured Dennis, a sickly-sweet echo, his eyebrows dancing, humor twinkling in his pale blue eyes. "He's all right." He raised his voice, called into the other room. "Katy, honey? You find anything?"

"Not yet. I'm looking."

"Take your time, sweetheart. Take as much time as you need."

"OK."

Katy's voice from the living room was thin and wavering, on the brink of panic. What had she been before she fell in with all of this? An accountant, Ruben thought. Maybe a medical student. Ruben could hear her rummaging through papers, opening boxes. Fumbling open the rolltop desk.

Samir's fingers trembled where they were pushed into Ruben's shoulder. He was just as scared as Katy. They were doing what they had to do, what they had been commanded. They were in thrall.

Ruben wondered if he could maybe get free. Pull his arms away from Samir, kick him in the nuts, punch him in the gut. But then the night man would kill his father. Slit his throat, release his grip, watch Jay slip to the ground while the life pulsed out of him. He would *slaughter* him.

"OK, so, look, man," sighed Dennis into Shenk's ear. "I know this sucks. Violence, the threat of violence. But you gotta understand, I have been chasing this thing for years. I'm, like—maybe a little crazy on this. I need to know where these people are, and we have run out of options."

"We don't know where he is. I told you that."

"Yeah, no, I know, that's your line, man. The lawyer's line. Nobody told me nothing. I'm in the dark." He adjusted his hand on the knife handle. The blade kissed Jay's Adam's apple. "So OK, so we'll see. We checked your office, now we're checking here. Katy's looking." Then, sharply, "Katy?"

"Not—not—no, nothing yet."

"Nothing yet." He grinned. "So maybe you just cough it up, Katy stops looking, you save us some time. But." He licked his lips, gave his head a little shake. "But. But if you tell me you *don't* know, and then it's here all along, that's when things go red, man."

Dennis's voice was calm and even, but his eyes were wild. They twitched in their sockets. Ruben looked helplessly at Jay, who looked right at him and mouthed the words *I love you,* which made Ruben more scared.

"You understand, right, that I'm not doing any of this for *me,*" Dennis went on. "None of this is for my own personal benefit. It's for *you.* It's for everybody that lives and breathes, in this brutal and terrible world. It's for fucking mankind, OK? It's"—his voice rose slightly and Ruben could see a strange heat in his eyes—"it's *here.*

The future, the good and golden future, it's *here*. It wants in. But it is still trapped inside that boy."

They heard a thump, Katy maybe knocking a file box off the desk, and then they heard her say "Shit," and Dennis hissed.

Ruben shut his eyes. He could smell Samir's skin.

He had seen the Keeners at the Palladium that day; he had talked quietly with Evelyn while Wesley was walking endlessly inside. He could have called Dennis right then—*I have him! I got him! He's here*—but he didn't do it, because how *could* he do it, and now he was sorry, he was so sorry and he was so scared. Now the Keeners were somewhere else, they were in some other secret location until the trial was over, and he didn't know where. He would tell if he knew. It was awful but if it would make these people leave, he would have told. Ruben was about to pee in his pants.

He heard a dog barking as it walked down the street. "Hey," a man said to the dog, his chiding tone clearly audible from the street. "Hush up."

It was that collie, Ruben thought desperately. That ugly little brown border collie. Surely the owner would wonder why it was barking—surely he'd call for help. Surely the Shenks' terror was a tangible thing, billowing out from this troubled smashed-glass kitchen like smoke.

"Just tell me, Mr. Shenk," said Dennis at last. "*Where the fuck is he?*"

"I've told you," said Jay in a low whimper. "I don't know."

"Hey, should I—" Samir started, and Dennis looked at him fiercely. "Maybe I oughta take the boy somewhere else?"

"To the contrary!" Dennis said, and then, loudly, "Katy? Nothing?"

"No." She sounded frantic. "It's not here."

"Nothing in writing. Is that it, Jay?" He pulled away a little bit, to make eye contact with his captive, never letting the knife leave his throat. They were like a two-headed person, examining himself. "Once more. Where is he?"

Jay swallowed hard, and his Adam's apple rolled under the line of the knife. "I don't know."

"We should go," Samir said. "I think we should go."

Dennis considered for a moment. He adjusted his knife hand, flexed the fingers of the other. And then made a low hissing noise, a tiny growl in the back of his throat, as his eyes lit on Ruben.

He handed the knife to Samir.

"Cut the kid's finger off."

"What?" said Samir, and Jay shouted "No!"

Ruben felt heat on his leg. He had done it. He'd peed. He started to cry.

"Index finger. Left hand." Dennis smiled. "For starters."

Shenk shouted "No" again, and then "Please," and Dennis punched him, hard, a quick thump to the side of his head, and Jay's head rolled and when it came back up his eyes were clouded. He blinked and smiled at Ruben, as if from miles away and years ago.

"Rubie," he said softly, "oh, Rubie . . ."

Dennis said "Now" to Samir, "the finger," but Samir was shaking his head, lips quivering, mewling, "I can't, I can't." Ruben lurched out of his light grip and was free, but Dennis booted him in the stomach and he fell backward and the small of his back slammed into the kitchen cabinet and jolted him forward onto the floor. He landed in the pool of spilled root beer, spiked with broken glass, and he screamed as the shards bit into his kneecaps.

And now Dennis had the knife back, pressed again into Jay's throat, the edge of it sunk into the pale flesh of his neck. A bright red line of drops appeared, as if by carnival magic. Ruben's father whimpered; he moaned.

Ruben would never forget the sound. He knew right away that he would never forget it, and he never did.

"I mean, Jesus, kid." Dennis looked down at Ruben carefully. An intimate whisper, just between them. "How many parents can one person lose?"

Ruben lunged out of his crouch holding a thick piece of glass in his hand, a convex shard from the fat base of the glass, sticky with sugar and blood. Not thinking, no time to think. He stabbed the night man in the cheek, dug in the glass and turned it, and Dennis's hideous smiling face exploded into red. Then he grunted and pushed Ruben hard, with two hands, knocked him over and climbed on top of him.

And then there was a siren, screaming and screaming in the night.

Dennis jerked his head up, showering blood down across Ruben's face. For an instant, he looked scared, and then the next instant he did not. It came and went from his eyes, jumping back and forth, in and out: he was the night man, a beast from the dark place in Ruben's own heart, and at the same time he was just some dirtbag, a con man and a cultist—he was *both,* he was a criminal *and* he was a monster who lived only to loom over Ruben, to fuck with him and follow him and drip blood in his eyes.

"Your blood is all over this room," said Jay Shenk quietly, from where he was curled up against the wall, as the sirens cried out. Shenk the lawyer, the expert, working the lever he knew. "Your fingerprints. That's all evidence."

Dennis stood. The sirens were getting closer.

"If I were you," Jay said, "I'd go."

"Yeah," said Dennis, thinking it over. "Maybe."

Katy rushed into the kitchen, her eyes popping with fear. Samir grabbed her and she grabbed him. The sirens were very close. "What's happening?" she said. "Let's go. Are we going?"

"Yeah," said Dennis. "Going. Now."

Jay exhaled. It turned into a cough.

"We're going," Dennis said, and he crouched one more time and touched Ruben's face. He arranged the boy's hair, tucked a stray lock behind his ear. "We're gone."

For a very long time, the Shenks, father and son, sat trembling on the kitchen floor. Slowly they moved, but didn't speak—not for real, not for a long time. Ruben got the first-aid stuff out, and gingerly they cleaned each other, dabbed Neosporin on their wounds. Applied bandages.

At some point, much later, they gave their report to the detectives: two women, both with severe buns and solemn, skeptical expressions. Evidence was taken—fingerprints from the wall, fingerprints from the back door, fingerprints from the bloody hilt of the knife.

A case was opened. Technically it's probably still open now. Dennis and the others became fugitives. They disappeared, leaving behind the trembling Shenks, trailing blood and shards of what was broken. They went dark, they lost themselves in the darkness. In the months and years to come they would spend time in Arizona, in New Mexico, in Texas, and in Montana; their numbers would grow and fall away; and Ruben would see none of them again— not for years and years.

As for Jay, his concerns were immediate. He was aghast at the possibility of what would happen next. What if these violent lunatics did, somehow, find their way to the Keeners, and to Wesley, wherever they had hidden him away?

But that's not what happened.

———————

Dr. Theresa Pileggi was in her room at the Courtyard by Marriott, drinking tea and reviewing her notes from today's testimony, preparing herself for tomorrow, when she would be cross-examined by defense counsel.

She looked up at the sound of the elevator, rising in the hallway.

"There's no rest for the wicked——"

Evie the Soulful——Evie the Wise——in the studio, hard at work, her bright white hair pulled back and covered by giant head-phones——

"——but we fools all sleep like babies every night——"

She stopped and scowled. "Once more. Go again."

The engineer rolled his eyes and puffed out his lips, as if he thought she couldn't see his irritation through the soundproof glass. The engineer's assistant, Bobby or Robby, was chewing on a piece of licorice, writing something on a notepad, keeping track of takes, counting wasted hours. Evie Keener was too young to be a diva but too good to be told. What they were making in this storied studio in Hollywood proper was theoretically the first single on the second album, everybody participating in the recording industry's mass delusion that albums and singles were still meaningful commercial objects and not mere marketing devices, space-time events around which tours could be booked and interviews given, from which some tart quote or controversial interaction might pierce the skin of Instagram and draw attention, but Evie——Evie the Naive, Evie the Willful——believed in her art, like some old-fashioned idiot, and she had a particular melody in her head, a little rise and fall on *babies*. And no matter how many times Fat Face and Red Vine said it was time to move on, she would not move on until she got it clean and clear on the master, and meanwhile in the corner of her eye her brother was laughing, leaned against the foam-padded wall, egging her on, since this was one of those days where Evie was so conscious of the past that it was like a living thing inside her. Like one of those jungle trees that splits down the center but keeps growing, in two parts, standing on the forest floor with smaller trees growing up between its legs, with vines spiraling up inside the core.

So, for example, right now, here she is, at Sunset and Gower, the enormous headphones making her cheeks sweat, trying not to fuck up these lyrics she doesn't even necessarily love, and also here she is at twelve, out by the lap pool in the immaculate backyard of a B-list movie star's guesthouse, in pink corduroys with rolled cuffs, her toes tickling the water line, leaning her head back against a lounge chair while her brother walks a slow circle in the gated yard, since the star was shooting in Vancouver and had generously made her home available to the Keeners during this, the time of their literal trial.

All the things are at once. Evie was in the studio, thinking about herself as an audacious twelve-year-old, and Evelyn was twelve, remembering herself at twenty-two, and we are rolling again, and she is bent to the microphone, singing words she wrote but doesn't entirely understand, throwing open her arms to expand her voice, climbing the melody toward the end of the song—and by the stranger's pool she works her way up to her question, glancing over her shoulder to watch Wesley walking even as she draws out the final note.

Hey, dude.

Her brother had started calling her dude of late, in the months before the accident, a signal that he now included his little sister in his circle of recognizable humans, and so she called him that now, rising from the waterside and padding across the grass to stand in his way, so he stopped walking. She leaned her head on his chest.

Hey, dude.

Nothing. Sometimes she would make these jokes, when nobody could hear.

"Why are you giving me the silent treatment, Wesley?"

"Is there something on your mind?"

"Speak up, dude. Can't hear you."

Or she'd open her notebook and tell him she was going to read him a poem, and when he didn't answer, when he just walked away, she'd tell him, "Well, you gotta listen. You're my prisoner."

It was hilarious, after all, the whole thing, the whole idea that this was her brother: a creature made of flesh and in the shape of a person. He didn't answer, no matter what. He never spoke. He didn't know where he was. This whole great preoccupation of their family, their big lawsuit against the hospital, he didn't even know about. But his heart was beating because she could hear it through his T-shirt and his skin, metronomic, and when she finished the vocal she listened to the playback with her head tilted back, and then she gazed at the engineer and his boy on the other side of the glass, knowing they were waiting for her to say something, to say *let's go again* or *we nailed it* or *can we take a break,* something, but she wasn't looking at them; she was looking at her own face reflected in the soundproof glass, wondering in what sense she was the same person who had loved her brother so much in the movie star's backyard.

She kept forgetting how she got here. She'd grown up, drifted out of high school and into a first band and then another one, lived on and off with her parents, fucked the boys she had fucked and gone to the parties she had gone to, and all of these points of experience somehow connected in a backward arc to the girl poolside and forward to the girl in the studio with the bulky black pro-grade headphones on and the sound of her own voice a disappointing echo in her ears. It's like there are all of these individual stars, specific small points of light, dozens of them or millions, and it is possible to look at them a certain way, if you want to, not as lots of small things but as one big thing, one complete thing: a human being, an experience of existence, stable over time. And the stars become constellations, if you choose to let your eyes see them that way. Otherwise they are only stars. Or even less: balls of gas. Flicking mirages. Each a distant illuminary nothing.

Evie started singing again, not asking if they were rolling or telling them she was going to, just started singing like a boulder tipped down a hill. She sang a moony waltz that was about a monster in the woods but which was really about her brother because they were all about her brother, and as she heard herself sing she was listening, too, to the small sound of the pool lapping against its tiles, and then she got to the chorus and stepped away from Wesley and looked him in the eyes that did not see her back, and asked Wesley if, as long as he wasn't using it, maybe she could borrow his guitar?, and then she asked him again, and when she asked him the third time and he stayed silent, she took it for a yes. She stepped out of his way and let him keep on walking.

Her phone was supposed to be off, but it rang loudly in her pocket and ruined the take, and she took off her headphones and rushed outside to answer, the recording engineer muttering "fuck's sake" as she blew past.

"Evie? Hey. It's Ruben. Um — Ruben Shenk?"

"Yeah, hey." Evie, in the stairwell of the studio, noticed immediately that the acoustics in here were at least as good as in the booth. "I don't know any other Rubens."

"Oh right. Sure."

There was static on the line on his side, the faint hiss of distance. Ruben's voice made Evie warm and glad.

"Where are you calling from?"

"Alaska. I'm—"

"Alaska?"

"Yeah, but—" His voice was swallowed by a blast of noise behind him—the distinct crack of pool balls colliding. A blast of classic rock, the bulletproof opening measures of "Don't Stop Believin'."

"Hold on," he said. "I might lose you. Service is weird up here."

"Are you at a bar?"

"Yeah. Kinda. It's kind of the post office."

"OK."

"We can get him acquitted. Your dad."

"Ruben." No. Evie closed her eyes. No, no. She leaned against the wall of the stairwell.

"That gun was not his gun. Pileggi brought it with her. She stole it from a ranger station in Alaska and brought it to Los Angeles to kill him."

"Ruben."

"They said he was waiting for her, but *she* was waiting for *him*. He hit her with the lamp because she was *shooting* at him."

"Ruben. Dude."

He stopped talking at last, and she heard all around him the chatter of conversation, the bellow of laughter and the ordering of drinks, the dumbass bar-rock song reaching its climax.

"It's too late."

"No," he said.

"It's over."

"Wait——" he said. "What day is it?"

She could picture him up there, handsome, quiet Ruben, fretful and young and sweet, surrounded by Alaskan strangers. A fish forever out of water. "My father's been sentenced already, Ruben. He's on his way to Chino. It's over."

A long devastated silence on the other end, and she tried to imagine just what the hell Ruben had been up to——what he had gone through, trying to figure this thing out. She leaned forward over the stair rail, the stairs going down and down and down.

"Hey," she said. "Call me when you get home, OK?"

"OK."

"Will you?"

"Yeah," he said softly. "I will." And then, out of absolute nowhere, he said, "I'm sorry we didn't get to go to that dance."

Evie laughed. Oh, Ruben. Ruben forever. "Me, too. I was pretty pissed at you, actually, about it."

"Were you?"

"I was."

"Did you end up going? Like, by yourself, or with a group of friends?"

"Nope. Stayed home. Hung out with my brother, as I recall. You should have taken me. You said you were going to."

"I guess I just figured you would be mad at me because we let you down."

"You didn't let me down, Ruben. You were *fifteen*. Remember?" Evie felt adamant. She stood up straight, alone in the stairwell, and said it loud to make sure he was hearing her. "You were just a kid."

"Thank you," said Ruben.

"Anyway," said Evie. "You know, they have it every year."

"Have—what?"

"That dance. At my school."

Ruben gave a mournful laugh, barely audible, but Evie wasn't laughing. "We would be outliers, for sure. But they do have it."

The Rabbi, with his phone smashed against his ear in the Legion Hall adjoining the post office in Kusiaat, watched a middle-aged lady in a long hippie skirt spin alone on the center dance floor with her hands outstretched. Tears formed behind the thick windows of his glasses.

"Are you serious?" he asked Evie Keener. "About going to the dance?" But then the next song started, the opening riff of "Werewolves of London" eliciting clamorous applause that swallowed up whatever she said after that.

Midway through the first leg of the long journey back to Los Angeles, Ruben went into the bathroom of the plane and slowly unwound the mummy gauze around the index finger of his left hand. Gingerly he touched the swollen raw end, and then he pursed his lips and blew gently across it, feeling his breath on his exposed nerves.

It was not healed, but it was healing.

Back in his seat he used the wounded finger to press the call button and asked politely for a cup of coffee, black. Then he simply sat with the coffee, feeling the soreness of his joints, the bruising on his back, the tenderness at his wrist where Samir had bitten him. Feeling the fog of the last week begin to lift, feeling himself come back to himself. He didn't make small talk with the grizzled Alaskan fisherman in the seat beside him. He didn't look at the *New York Times* he'd bought from a departure lounge newsstand; he didn't turn on the tiny, grimy screen on the seat back in front of him. At the layover in Sea-Tac the grizzled fisherman got off and was replaced by an old lady with spiderweb wrinkles and tightly curled white hair.

The Rabbi stayed still. He had a secret, impossible and invisible, nestled inside himself.

It was not his secret, but Theresa Pileggi's.

The revelation that she'd had, at home, at last, the revelation that she had brought with her all the way to Alaska.

The bad truth about the good and golden world.

Don't do it. Bursting into the cabin, burning with understanding, shouting at them to stop. *You can't do it.*

Don't let it through.

Don't let it in.

The Rabbi sat in silence, for thousands of southbound miles. It stirred inside him, the fledgling feeling of new knowledge. It fluttered as it came to life. It pulsed delicately as if perched on the end of his finger.

At some point over northern Oregon, after he had risen to let the old woman go to the restroom, after he had sat down again and maybe begun to drift off, head lolling slightly sidewise, the Rabbi found that he had returned to the ranger station.

Not as he had found it, but as Theresa had found it, when she arrived in Alaska. As it had been when she smashed into the cabin, wheeling wildly up from the lower forty-eight, determined to make them stop. To make them see.

He gazed out the window, watched the changing shape of the sky.

It was playing in his head as a short loop, the dance steps of violence—Pileggi coming into that isolated cabin in a fury of intent, grabbing the gun, the uncertain weight of it in her hands. The weight of its purpose: To make them stop.

Ruben lived the final moments as Samir had described them— Katy grabbing for the gun, Theresa firing—Samir trying to pry them apart—the three of them whirling—

The three of them.

The final understanding starting now to grow and glow inside of him, like the dense blue gathered light at the heart of a candle's flame.

Ruben was on the plane and Ruben was at the ranger station and Ruben was back at Cosmo's, too, examining the crime scene.

Three people in the room. Three.

"Oh no," the Rabbi said out loud. "Oh God."

"It's OK," murmured the old woman. "Don't you worry."

"Oh. Thank you," Ruben said. She put her hand, small and sandpaper dry, on top of his. She was talking about the juddering motion of the plane as it began its descent. Small, lurching, turbulent jumps that Ruben hadn't noticed.

"My husband was always very steady, on airplanes," she said. "He would encourage me to breathe through it. Just *breathe*. His name was Edward. He was a doll. Just a doll."

"He sounds like it." Ruben put out his hand and laid it over hers. "I'm not frightened," he told her. "I'm OK."

"Oh," she said. "Then why were you crying?"

In his Koreatown apartment, Ruben hung up the black North Face rain slicker and put away the thick-soled winter boots.

He drank some water, and used the bathroom, and opened the manila folder his father had handed him twenty-six days ago in the courthouse cafeteria. He settled cross-legged on the floor and spread the few scant pages out once more before him.

He read for a while, made a few new small underlines, and then went to his window and watched cars stop and start at the red light on Wilshire.

The previous tenant owned a cat, and Ruben noticed for the first time that there were light scratch marks in the windowsill. Maybe *he* should get a cat. Would this be how it turned out, in the end: that he was just the same person, except with a cat?

The investigation was over; there was one more part of the investigation. He had to go now; he didn't want to. He wanted to sit down on one of his two chairs and sleep. Then when he woke up he would go for a run. Then he would take a shower and go to work.

That's all he wanted, for things to go back.

The Rabbi wanted to go back in time.

April 15, 2010

"Good morning, Ms. Pileggi. My name is John Riggs and I'm representing the Valley Village Hospital Corporation in this matter."

"OK. Hi."

Shenk looked up sharply. Riggs had called her *Ms.,* and they had *known* that he would do that, accidentally-but-not-accidentally putting her in her place, and she knew what to do: don't get upset, but gently correct him. Don't let him talk down or bully you. Shenk caught her eye, and Theresa nodded, corrected the error.

"It's, uh—it's Doctor, actually," she said to Riggs, and Riggs said, "Pardon me, of course. Doctor."

Shenk began to sweat. He had worn a black turtleneck under his blazer, covering the gauze at his throat, covering the shallow knife cuts that ringed his neck. An unorthodox outfit, but he was an unorthodox lawyer, and he would be goddamned if he was going to let a little scratch keep him out of court. Not today.

"Now, this brings up an important point, Dr. Pileggi," said Riggs. "You are not a *medical* doctor, is that correct?"

"Yeah. Right. I'm just a . . . I do some research. I teach."

No, thought Shenk. No, no, no. You don't "do some research"; you are an expert in neurobiology. You hold degrees from Caltech and Duke University. You're fucking preeminent in your field.

His expert witness said none of that. The sweat crept down Shenk's back. Theresa was *ready*. She had been *prepared*. Shenk had prepared her.

Except this morning, she didn't look prepared. Her hair was combed, neatly pinned up with barrettes, and she had worn just a little makeup, as Shenk had humbly, apologetically requested, but her eyes flitted, disconnected. She looked tired. Confused. She sat slightly hunched, as if ready to collapse in upon herself. Shenk had never seen her this way—not even close.

What was going on?

The elevator creaked and groaned. Dr. Pileggi heard its protesting noises through the thin walls of her hotel room. He was coming. He was almost here.

She sat up straight.

Who? Who was coming?

A mechanical sigh and then a muted ding *as the elevator settled at the third floor. She heard the doors wheeze open.*

He's in the hallway.

Who?

Shallow footfalls on the carpet of the hallway of the Courtyard by Marriott. He was coming to see her. It was obscure to her how she knew that, but she did know. Whoever was coming was coming for her.

She set down her papers on the coffee table. Jay had told her not to spend the evening prepping for Riggs's cross-examination. He said just relax; get some rest; watch whatever's on cable; get a drink downstairs. But she had been preparing, describing Syndrome K to herself over and over in careful layman's language. Now at the sound of the man in the hallway, coming closer, she put down the file and waited, holding her breath.

The door of the room was so thin that when the man knocked, it shivered on its hinges.

Theresa stood up.

————

"So you are *not* a medical doctor," said Riggs, enunciating carefully, finding his own bulky rhythm, "and have never performed a surgery, let alone one to relieve a subdural hematoma."

He paused, letting the statement become a question.

"Yes," said Pileggi softly.

"Ever worked in a hospital?"

"No."

"Have any medical experience of any kind?"

"No."

"With all due respect, then, Ms. Pileggi . . ." Riggs sighed, as if the question pained him. "What are you doing here?"

Theresa blinked. "I don't know."

Shenk's mouth dropped open. Riggs, who had been slowly pacing, stopped and turned back. He glanced at Shenk, suspicious of some trick, then back to the witness.

"You don't know?"

"Yeah. No. I mean—" she said. "I really don't know."

Shenk was stunned. She didn't know? Yes, she did. Of course she did. He sent a desperate telepathic message to his witness: *Clean it up. Walk it back. What are you doing?*

But it was too late. Riggs, astonished by his good fortune, was moving on. "OK," he said. "You don't know."

Panic rose in Shenk. He thought about calling a recess. Jumping to his feet. Pulling a fire alarm.

He looked at Beth, seated in the gallery, and she looked back at him. He was the one who was supposed to know what was going on.

————

Theresa Pileggi stood at the door with her palm on the handle and waited. There had been two knocks, and then no more. Maybe he was gone.

He knocked again.

There was no room service. She was expecting no visitors.

"Jay?" she said softly. "Is that you?"

"No," said a voice from the other side. "It's not Jay." And then, very quietly, "Open the door."

She hesitated, and the voice said, simply, "Theresa? Theresa, I'm coming in anyway."

There was a cheap lock at eye level. Softly, slowly, she drew back the chain. Stepped back from the door and pulled it open. It shushed on the thin carpet. Her visitor was in a tank top and jean shorts, tan and handsome and young. His skin was golden. He had wavy blond hair. When he smiled his teeth were bright white, with a slight gap between the front two. He was bleeding out of his face. A thick, curving gouge in the center of his cheek, bandaged haphazardly and oozing at the edges.

Pileggi had never seen him before, but he smiled like they were old friends. There was something electric in the smile, in the way he stood. In the shape of him in the doorway. "You're here," he said with fondness. "I found you."

He didn't ask if he could come in. He just sort of wandered past her into the little hotel room, looked around approvingly at the sofa, the TV, the kitchenette.

"These Marriotts," he said, nodding approvingly. "They're actually pretty nice."

To Theresa Pileggi's hotel room the night man brought no knives. He didn't even bring his comrades. Katy and Samir were waiting in the car, maybe, or maybe they were in the lobby, trembling, fearful, trying to be cool. The night man came alone.

"Who are you?" asked Pileggi, curt and stern, although already the flinty voice was an effort, something she had to summon up. "What do you want?"

"Honestly?" the stranger said, touching her once, softly, on the arm. The wound on his face didn't seem to bother him. He seemed to be in no pain. He sat where she had been sitting, put his feet in their brown sandals up on her pile of papers. "You're my last hope."

"I don't know what you're talking about."

He sighed. "Sure you do. Of course you do." He patted the sofa, and she came and sat beside him.

Riggs smelled blood. Shenk knew the look because he had smelled blood, how many times had he smelled it, and though Riggs was very dignified and very restrained, still his nostrils quivered and Shenk could see them quiver at the smell of blood—Pileggi's blood—his own.

Riggs went right for the jugular.

"You told us yesterday, Dr. Pileggi, that Wesley is suffering from a heretofore unknown illness called, quote-unquote, Syndrome K. Something you, personally, claim to have discovered, and which is caused by—sorry, what was it?"

"A, uh . . ." She seemed embarrassed, as if caught in a lie. "By a—a prion."

"Right. Which lay dormant in Wesley's brain for some indeterminate amount of time, until it was—activated? Yes? By the surgery. My question is, how is it possible for you to be so sure that this is the only explanation for Wesley Keener's condition?"

Pileggi looked off into the distance. Her eyes seemed to go out of focus. Riggs waited placidly for his answer.

Shenk waited too, not breathing. They had practiced this. This exact question, and she knew exactly how to answer.

"I'm not."

Shenk closed his eyes.

"I'm sorry, Dr. Pileggi, can you talk just a teeny bit louder?

Thank you. So—just so I'm clear. You're *not* sure what caused Wesley Keener's condition?"

"No," she said. "I—I'm not."

She slumped back in the chair. She looked like she wasn't sure of *anything*.

Theresa Pileggi did not know where to find the Keener boy.

She had studied his scans and his charts many times. She had spent hours within the folds of his cerebral cortex, confirming her suspicion about the precise etiology of the rare syndrome he was suffering from. But she had only been in his actual physical presence once, when she examined him three months ago, and she had no idea where he was hidden now.

She told all this to Dennis, who had asked her to call him Dennis, and he turned it over, humming to himself. He studied her face. He searched her eyes for deceit, considering them carefully, like a jeweler studying a diamond for flaws. He did not torture her, nor imply that he might. He did not insist, or threaten, or cajole. He gazed at her for a long time, toying with a lock of his blond hair, and then decided that she was telling him the truth.

That should have been it, right? Didn't he have to go?

The shiftless dirtbag drifter who had smashed into the Shenks' kitchen and left blood evidence all over their tiny house, the man who had to run and knew he had to run, who soon would be living a step ahead of the law, moving around the country hungry and homeless for the next decade—he had to go, man, he had to fucking go now.

But that wasn't all that he was. He did not go. He considered her, lazily, discerningly, wondering with slow pleasure if there was not something here that he could use.

Theresa Pileggi was watching him, too. She watched him from the back as he went to the sink and slowly poured himself a glass of water. He turned, sipping the water, and smiled.

"You're the one that made the diagnosis, huh?" he said finally, wiping his chin with his wrist, like a kid. The packed gauze on his face flapped loose, and he pushed it back into place, fixed the tape.

She nodded. Her papers were scattered all over the table, having been rearranged by his feet. Some had been pushed onto the floor.

"Okeydoke," said the night man. "So—let's hear it."

"I want to make sure I understand what you're saying," said Riggs. "And I want to make sure the men and women of the jury understand. You are here as the expert on 'Syndrome K,' and now you're no longer certain that what we're seeing in this case is an example of it."

A pause. Pileggi, looking not out at the courtroom like she was supposed to, but down at her hands, which were twisting in her lap. "That's right."

Riggs moved his head on his doughy neck, one way and then the other. "Can you assure us that there even *is* such a thing as Syndrome K?"

"Well . . . no."

Someone in the jury gasped. Shenk closed his eyes again. There was a pain, a twisting pain, somewhere inside his chest.

"What it sounds like, Ms. Pileggi, is that you have no *idea* what is wrong with Wesley Keener."

"The brain, you know . . ." Theresa Pileggi raised her hands in the air, helplessly, then let them fall into her lap. "It's a mystery."

Shenk jumped up to object. But to what? What objection did he have?

"Yeah, no, but what I'm saying is: how do you know?"

This was the stranger's question. Again and again, to whatever she said. They had fallen into a long and detailed discussion about the etiology and presentation of Syndrome K. She told him about her paper in the Spring

2006 issue of Proceedings in Neuropathology, *and Dennis nodded and asked questions, smart questions about blood flow in the nervous system and the typical course of a prion virus. Theresa carefully explained that the prion causing Syndrome K differed in its molecular structure from the one that caused BSE, presumably resulting in their radically different symptomatology.*

And he said it again: "But how do you know?"

She told him that she didn't, not really, and he smiled slyly, challengingly, rising to pour himself more water while she explained to him that in the absence of facts we hypothesize, and that only when more cases were discovered, when more patients were studied, would it be possible to arrive at a fixed and permanent definition of Syndrome K. Her visitor listened respectfully, but he made low, skeptical noises in the back of his throat.

Dennis had not touched her, not since the brief brush of connection when she let him in. If his intentions were lustful he kept them hidden.

His manner was cool and cosmic. The thrust of his argument was epistemological, or rather anti-epistemological. She explained Wesley's baffling MRI results, she theorized on his body's refusal to metabolize, and he said "But you don't know — but how do you know," until she began to smile each time and say it with him, say it before him — how do you know? — a little inside joke between the two new friends: How do you know? How can you know?

It was late. It had grown very late. Her eyes were bleary and the paperwork of her preparation was all over the floor.

"I am going to tell you how you know," said the stranger at last, answering his own insistent question. "Because you are a person who needs to know." He leaned closer. "Right? You've always needed to know."

Pileggi held her breath.

"Right?"

She nodded. Right.

She was there and she was somewhere else. This man was here, he was Dennis, and he was someone else.

"*So you built your knowledge like a fortress,*" he said softly. "*And you crawled inside. To escape. To escape from him.*"

Theresa's breath caught in her throat. Him.

The great horrible Him of her childhood. The shadow across her door-way. The weight of love and fear.

But how did this man know about any of that? This stranger in her hotel room, how could he possibly know? And she almost asked him, his own famous question, how do you know?

"*You built all of it into a fortress,*" he said again, pointing at the scattered papers, the charts and scans, and by "*all of it*" he meant science, he meant truth. "*But can I tell you another word for a fortress, Theresa? A prison.*"

She looked at the scattered mess. All her work on Wesley Keener, on the disorder that had destroyed him. It was just paper. A pile of paper, words crawling like insects.

"*What are you?*" she asked the visitor. The room in the air breathed strangely. His face was sinister and kind. "*Why are you here?*"

The night man settled happily back on the sofa and began to tell her about the good and golden world.

"Let us posit as a hypothetical that Dr. Catanzaro acted in error. He would demur, and say he made no errors, and I happen to believe him, but let us pretend that he did."

Riggs, hands behind his back, head bent slightly forward.

"Let us say he should not have operated for the subdural hema-toma, that he should have implanted an EVD, as the plaintiff's other experts have suggested, and adopted a *wait and see* attitude.

"Yesterday you told this court that because of the surgery—now, in my hypothetical, an unnecessary one—Wesley has Syndrome K. Today you tell us you're not even sure there is such a thing as Syndrome K."

He waited. Pileggi said nothing.

"Dr. Pileggi," he said, and now the word *doctor* sounded like a little joke, a taunt. "Dr. Pileggi, I have to ask: How certain are you that if Dr. Catanzaro had followed a different course of action, the result would be any different?"

"Certain?" She looked at him, her eyes wet and wide. "I mean— who can be certain of *anything*?"

And then Riggs said it, decisive as a coffin nail:

"No further questions."

The other world has always been with us. Above and around us, unseen and ever present. Trying to get in.

He told it to her the same as he had told it to Samir and Katy and all the rest of them that had come and gone over the years. Same as he had told it to Ruben on his doorstep on Tabor Street. There are books about it, going back centuries, if one knows where to find them, and how to read them. There are different routes that the curious and the believers have taken over the centuries, trying and trying to make it happen.

What is the history of human life but a long attempt to make that life bearable? To build peace, to live without fear and grief. All the drugs and all the potions, from mandrake root to methamphetamines. All the meditation and stargazing and seeking. Everybody trying to get to this other place, and here it is. It's been here all along, Theresa, trying to get in.

"You of all people should want that, right? To live free of suffering."

When she didn't answer, he leaned a little closer. He clasped her hands between his. His hands were soft, giving, slightly warm.

"You of all people, right, Tess?"

He held her as she trembled.

And then, after a time, he whispered the words. He cooed them. "Can I tell you a riddle?"

February 11, 2019

"The two pieces don't add up," Ruben said, stroking his chin contemplatively, as he and Sunny drove west on the 10, from his Koreatown apartment to Cosmo's motel. "That's the problem."

"Wait, what now?"

Sunny wasn't really listening. She was driving with one hand, working Spotify on her phone with the other, scrolling through a playlist. Ruben was talking to himself. That was OK.

"If I'm right, and it was Theresa who was the aggressor that night, and Richard shot her in self-defense . . ."

"Wait—what? Hold on, Rabbi."

She had found the song she wanted, and now she was fumbling to plug the phone back in.

"Then it no longer makes sense for him to insist on pleading guilty. It's one thing to save yourself and your family the time and trauma of a trial, if you did it. If you're innocent, though? Not even Richard would make that kind of sacrifice."

"Literally nothing that you're saying makes sense," said Sunny. "But you're cute when you talk."

She had agreed, no problem, to scoop him up at his apartment—

when he called, she said, she had just locked up Killer Greens and hung up a sign that said CLOSED FOR NO REASON.

"But, Rabbi, this whole deal you're rocking? The whole brooding detective thing is very Marlowe. Very McNulty. *Very* sexy. I'm serious."

He kept turning it all over, giving her the occasional direction: left turn on Centinela, cut across Washington Place to Culver.

The only explanation left was that Richard had insisted so firmly on his guilt because he *wasn't* guilty. Not because he had killed Theresa Pileggi in self-defense, but because he hadn't killed her at all.

Somebody had killed her, because she was dead, and the Rabbi knew who it was, and didn't want to know, and had to prove it, and didn't dare.

"Here," he said to Sunny, pointing into the parking lot, and she turned in and found a spot. Either the pink van advertising the topless maids had never left, or it had this space reserved.

"Damn," said Sunny, eyeing the dilapidated parking lot, the peeling paint of the decades-old motel. "The fuck is this place?"

"Murder scene," murmured Ruben, eyeing the door to 109, and Sunny shuddered, pulled a face, uncharacteristically serious. "I'm out, then. No fucking thank you on the murder scene."

"We're not going in," he said. "We're fleeing the scene."

"What?" she said, but he had already taken off, and Sunny trotted after him.

"If I am running away," said Ruben. "If I am dying to put space between myself and what I've done, I do not go north. I go south."

Directly to the north of Cosmo's was the highway off-ramp, where the westbound 10 disgorged itself into Culver City, the endless spill of cars coming in hot off the highway.

"Wait — who are you, at this point?" said Sunny.

"I don't know."

He knew and didn't want to know. It was like a children's game. Richard is in the motel room, waiting for the police. Pileggi is dead on the floor. So who am I?

Ruben walked south, head slightly bowed, hands in his pockets, mouth screwed up. He put urgency in his stride, felt the heat of panic in his cheeks as if he had really done it, as if he was fleeing the scene. Sunny rushed along beside him, playing along.

"So you killed someone back there."

"Yeah. I think. Let's say I did."

"You bad, Rabbi. How'd you do it? Gunshot?"

"Lamp."

"No shit? Blunt object."

"And I'm bloody. I am covered in the blood."

"Hate when that happens."

Ruben swerved to miss a dog walker with a clutch of leashes, being tugged chariot-like by his unevenly sized pack. Sunny hurdled a Pomeranian and kept pace.

A few blocks south of Venice, Sepulveda for a quarter block became a bridge, a short span over the ugly brown run of the Ballona Creek.

Ruben stopped at the crossing, and Sunny stopped beside him.

"So I've got these bloody clothes——" Except not clothes, thought Ruben, because by now he knew exactly, didn't he? He knew exactly what he was looking for.

"And you gotta ditch 'em. Is that it?"

"It is."

"Right. So let's do it." Sunny stepped off the sidewalk onto the gravelly garbage-strewn path that ran roughly parallel with the river, sloping down to its banks. Ruben tripped carefully, just behind Sunny, goat-stepping down the shallow embankment. The uneven path led all the way down to the waterline, and Ruben's heels slipped uncomfortably on the patchy concrete. The ruts in the slope were filled with clots of mud-thick river water. It smelled like decay.

"Oh man," said Sunny. She had gotten to the bottom and discovered a homeless encampment. The creek ran as a trickle here, leaving plenty of space on the damp banks on either side for a small village of people, living rough in a collection of mud-flap tents, the Sepulveda overpass for a roof.

One of Ruben's favorite memories of his mother was the time she took him to a food pantry run by their temple. They had stood side by side, handing individually wrapped sandwiches with great care to the poor souls shuffling down the line. Tiny Ruben had experienced this outing with a mixture of pride and sadness, confused about how the world could have arranged itself in such a way: that a little kid was providing food and comfort to these adults, who seemed to him so childlike in their need.

"Remember the feeling," his mother had said to him gently— without him having to say anything, she was always one step ahead, reading his emotions right off his tender heart like it was a TV screen.

And he *had* remembered it. He thought of it now, scrabbling on his heels down the paved embankment, toward where the ugly water sucked and drained out of the pipe hole.

"Hey," said Ruben. "Will you hand me that?"

Sunny, who for now had run out of jokes to make, gave him the long, bent stick he'd spotted bobbing half in and half out of the water. He gripped it with one hand, crouched as low as he could, and jammed it up the narrow opening, against the trickling current.

The water rose and fell, swelling into and then easing out of the storm drain, again and again. The homeless people stayed in their tents and ignored the interlopers—sleeping or smoking inside their individual universes.

Ruben looked as far up the narrow tunnel mouth as he could but couldn't see much.

Probably this was a waste of time, anyway. A wild guess, a goose chase. Anything up here would have been washed away, or taken and repurposed by one of the drifters on the banks.

Ruben steeled himself against the self-criticism. He was tired of it, and he was even tired of the crabbed chiding voice telling himself to stop criticizing himself. He was sick of being sick of being sick of himself. It was exhausting.

Ruben flattened himself into the mud and jammed his stick all the way up.

What if? thought Ruben.

"Well?" said Sunny. She was huddled up next to him, peering over his shoulder into the darkness.

Let me be wrong, he thought, and Let it not be there, even at the very instant when it was. The tip of the stick brushed against a clot of fabric, and he snagged it and coaxed it out, very slowly, so it didn't come loose off the end of the stick.

He brought it out and held it up, and then reached out and gingerly unpeeled the fabric, squishy with river water, from itself. A crushed tangle of lace and wire.

"The fuck is that?" said Sunny, behind him. "Is that somebody's bra?"

"No," said Ruben, finishing the unfurling, feeling the water seep into his palms. "It's wings."

He had no evidence bag, of course, nothing like that, so he just smushed the wet wings into his backpack, and as they walked back it dripped out, getting sludgy water onto the backs of his legs.

Back in the Cosmo's parking lot, before they got back in the car, he and Sunny stood together for a moment, looking at the murder-scene motel, both of them lost in thought.

He felt jet-lagged. He felt insane. The last month had been a dream. The last ten years.

Then Sunny, for once not smiling or pretending to scowl, took his glasses off, folded them up, and slid them into his breast pocket for him, a gentle and intimate gesture, and for one second he thought she might be about to kiss him.

"Can I tell you something?" she said, clutching his chin and looking into his eyes. "You always think I'm kidding, about wanting to fuck you, right? And I *am,* definitely, but that's just because I am a hundred percent gay. But you *are* hot, Ruben. No joke, straight up. You should fucking own that. OK?"

"OK," he said.

"OK?"

"Yeah."

She patted him on the cheek. "OK. Now, go and solve your fucking murder."

April 16, 2009

All that came after was in shards and fragments, the remaining days of *Keener v. Valley Village Hospital Corporation* raining down like the pieces of a smashed glass dome.

Shenk did his haphazard best to undo what had happened, to staunch the bleeding. Let the record reflect that he did try. He summoned the last reserves of his fighting spirit and came out relentless with Pileggi on redirect, treating his own star witness like a hostile, reminding her of the confident assertions she had made, becoming adamant with her about her own research, her own impeccable credentials. The clear fit between Wesley's condition and the hypothetical syndrome she had identified.

But these efforts were doomed to failure, and they did fail: the more he pushed, the more Pileggi receded, her voice growing fainter and fainter, her words smaller and smaller, her presence deflating like a balloon.

His closing argument was a desperate stem-winder, a pointillist re-creation of the entire trial, of every piece of evidence. He raged about Garza's error, about the surgery having been performed on the basis of someone else's scans, but—as Riggs reminded the jury in his own closing argument—this error would only matter if it had caused Wesley's condition, and this crucial link the plaintiff had not established. The world's great expert in Syndrome K had admitted that Wes might not have it; that Dr. Catanzaro hadn't given it to him; and that, oh yes, it might not even exist.

It was useless—Shenk had lost the jury. Darlene Stephens, the retired elementary-school teacher, made a show of not buying a word of it, crossing her arms firmly across her chest and pursing her thin lips. Mr. Janes stared angrily at Shenk, shaking his head slowly, clearly getting ready to blame him for the lost hours.

Celia Gonzalez would not meet his eyes at all.

When the verdict came in, Shenk stood up immediately, stuffing papers in his briefcase.

Beth said "*Wait*" and clutched at his arm, and he could see that she was having trouble breathing, having trouble standing. It was the belated suddenness of the verdict, the hammer falling after months and months of hope. She was baffled by shock, by this redoubling of tragedy, by the years—the *lifetime*—of financial uncertainty that would now be added to the burden of grief—but her lawyer would offer her no comfort or counsel. Shenk rushed past her and headed for the door.

Riggs offered a handshake and Shenk ignored it, pushing through the massive oaken doors of courtroom 5 and into the hallway, down the stairwell to the lobby.

"We'll appeal, right?"

Who was this? Ruben. His son, tugging at his arm.

Ruben had followed him out of the courtroom and down the stairs and was tugging on his coat, as he had when he was a toddler. He grabbed his father's shoulders, trying to steady him.

"Dad? We can appeal?"

But Shenk shook his head. He clenched his teeth. There were no grounds. There was no money. There was nothing.

He stopped and grabbed Ruben's face, too firm, too fierce, and Ruben saw in his raw red eyes not the details of what his father had done—all of that would come in time—but he knew. Fifteen years old now, and he *knew*. The depth of the hole they were falling into together but would crawl out of apart.

February 13, 2019

Ruben knocked and got no answer and knocked again, like a persistent suitor. Evie lived in a bungalow in Echo Park, on Montrose, just across from the park itself.

The bungalow was small and old, with stone walls and a terra cotta roof. Evie had no doorbell. He knocked again and waited.

It was a Wednesday, in the middle of the afternoon. Evie worked at night. She was home.

Evie was sitting just inside, actually, on the floor of her living room with her back to the front door, so that every time Ruben knocked she felt the vibration in her spine. It felt good, but she wanted him to leave.

But he kept knocking.

He would never give up.

She was home, she was here, and he was not leaving until she came out.

So she opened the door. He stood there twisting his mouth to the side like he did sometimes, and his eyes were full of pity and accusation, so she just said "Fuck," and he opened up his arms and she fell into them, and she kissed him and they kissed for a long time before anybody said anything. Everything coming out into the open together, all the truth and all the feeling.

They pulled apart and she looked him up and down.

He had grown up nice and tall, her Ruben. Her face fit nicely into the curve of his neck, and she breathed on him, feeling her warm breath against his body.

"All right," he said, after they held that shape awhile. "You ready?"

They went out to the yard, where she had a pair of plastic Adirondack chairs facing the boulevard and the park. They sat not on the chairs but on the grass, a pair of outsiders surveilling normal human activity. People getting tacos from a taco cart. Families making circles in the pedal boats, past the shallow fen full of ducks.

Evie of course had grown up in the Valley, and Ruben wondered if this was why she lived over here now—not because this was where the young and interesting people lived, but because this place bore no relation to the places that had formed her life.

"I want to start with what's real," Ruben said quietly.

Evie nodded. She looked at the pedal boats. She didn't look at him.

"You went to the desert with your parents, on the anniversary of Wesley's accident?"

She nodded. Yes.

"And your father had a breakdown. He fell apart."

Another nod. So that much was true, what she had told him backstage at the Echo, when they first talked. Ruben had stumbled onto this notion, that Richard's sentence could be mitigated by arguing he was in an altered state at the time of the murder, and Evie had leaped at that possibility. All that was real.

Ruben wished he could stop here. In this world, where they had been working together, all along, allies united by cause. He wished he could live in this world forever.

But—instead—

"Later on, at the Chinese restaurant, you told me that you had overheard a phone call. Richard saying *you people leave me alone*. And when you told me that, that encouraged me to believe this new theory I had. That it was self-defense. And then we got excited together about me going to Indiana to track it down." He turned, a quarter way toward her, and looked at the side of her face. "Was that part true?"

She didn't say anything. She shook her head.

"Evie?" he said. He felt like a judge, in a courtroom. "I need it for the record."

There really had been a phone call. Theresa had called Rich, and it was even right around when Evie had said it was.

"I didn't overhear it, though," Evie said. "It wasn't some mysterious thing. My dad called me and told me about it. He calls me all the time. We talk a lot. I was just back in town from playing a bunch of dates in the Northwest, and he goes, 'That girl Pileggi just called me, remember her?' And I was like, you know—*yeah*. Who could forget her? He said he hung up on her, but she called back ten times in fifteen minutes."

Theresa had been calling Richard from the road, from what sounded like a pay phone at a gas station. The crackle of the old line, the rush of highway noise. She called Richard at the house, and God knows how she got the number, although all the old security and secrecy is long gone by now. Nobody cares anymore. Pileggi said she had to talk to them about Wesley. She was coming to town, she was on the way, she would be there soon. She had important information. Crucial. She was coming. She was on the way.

She had to see Wesley.

"My dad sounded, like, horrified," said Evie. Still looking out at the lake. "And furious."

"I'll bet," said Ruben. His own emotions were subdued. He was curious and kind.

"He said I can't believe it's happening again. Like in a horror movie: It's happening again. You know?"

Ruben nodded. Yes. He knew.

Ruben, by now, knew more than Evie did. Theresa had called on her way down from Alaska, having already stopped Katy and Samir from cracking open Dennis.

But he didn't say anything. Evie was telling the story now. Ruben let her talk.

"You have to let me see Wesley."

This was Evie now, telling Ruben what Theresa said to Richard, when finally he answered the phone again: *I have to see him I have to see Wesley I have to—*

It was necessary. It was *imperative.*

"And my dad was like—well, you know my dad. He was like: 'You go fuck yourself.' Right?"

Ruben smiled. "Sure."

"But he knew that nothing was going to stop her. She would come to LA, she would come to our house, she would never stop. My dad was like, we can't do this. We have been through this before, and we can't go through it again. Which you know just meant I can't put *her* through this."

"Your mom."

"Yeah. He really loves her so much." Evie shook her head, half admiringly and half bewildered. "He loves her so fucking much, and he knew what would happen. Beth would get all worked up about it, whatever new idea Pileggi had about Wes. Some crazy new hope. It was the last thing she needed. No thanks. And I agreed with him, by the way. No fucking thanks."

Evie apparently had not redyed her bright white hair, and it was growing back in brown. Streaks of the natural color intermingled with the rock-star blond, layers of Evies. All the versions.

Ruben put his arm around her without thinking about it. She had tricked him. Thrown dust in his eyes. Sent him on a chase.

On the other hand, he'd been wanting to put his arm around her for a number of years. Possibly his entire life.

"So we made a plan."

"We? Meaning the two of you?"

"Yeah. My dad and me, you know . . . in all of this. In all of it, since Wesley, we've kind of been. I don't know." She smiled up at the dim February sun. "Buds."

Ruben felt a clutch at his chest. Right at that moment, as if sent by the symbols department, a father came into view along the banks of the lake, holding the hands of his kids, one with each hand. Ruben watching them pass, thinking of all the different forms a relationship can take, between a parent and a child.

Evie and Richard had made a plan together to deal with this looming disaster of Theresa Pileggi roaring back into their lives. A plan to protect Wesley. To protect Beth. To fucking *handle* it.

"So my dad basically goes, to Theresa, next time she calls— she's closer now, it's like a week later, she's calling every day, ten times a day. He says look, OK, I'll see you. Sure. She wanted him to bring Wesley, she *had to* see Wesley, and my dad goes OK. Fine. But he tells her don't come here. Get a motel room, I'll meet you there. The plan was he would show up and warn her off. That was it. Come to her hotel, motel, whatever, make it absolutely clear that we as a family wanted nothing more to do with her, and that if she showed her face anywhere near us again . . ." She shrugged. "I don't know. He'd do something."

Ruben nodded, waited. Evie sighed. "I wasn't supposed to go. We made this plan together, but Rich told me absolutely not. I had a gig that night, and he said you go and play your show. You do your thing. But I, uh . . ." A hitch in her voice. A pang of distress tightening her face. "I wanted to know. I wanted to hear what she had to say. Isn't that stupid? Some part of me, I guess . . . what if she had something? What if she could fix him?"

God, Ruben thought: she played me perfectly. Played on their old affection, on his lifetime of sympathy for her. How clever she'd been, how instinctual. When he got as far as Richard's altered mental state, Evie saw a way to have it both ways—escape her own culpability, while helping her father escape the worst sentence. But then when she realized how close Ruben was to seeing the whole picture, she'd found a way to send him out of town. Suddenly she'd remembered these mysterious threatening phone calls Richard had been receiving, *you people leave me alone,* which seemed to buttress the self-defense theory, and Ruben volunteered to go and investigate, and Evie . . .

She'd deceived him at every step. It was all for good reasons, all perfectly understandable, but she really had played him for a fool. He was not, really, a great private investigator.

Still he kept his arm around her, still he let her cry quietly for a moment, not interrupting.

"So I got all ready to play my show, you know, but I drove to the motel instead."

All ready, thought Ruben. Wings and all. Standing outside in the parking lot, ear to the motel door. Listening to Theresa Pileggi in the grips of madness, shouting at her father.

"You can't imagine what she was like, Ruben."

Except he could, of course. He had been to Alaska. He had seen the ranger station. He knew exactly what she was like.

Richard in the motel room found Theresa Pileggi waiting with the handgun, screaming. She *needed* that boy. She had to *take* him. Where was he?

Ruben shuddered to think of it, a night so like the night that Dennis and his motley crew had burst into the kitchen on Tabor Street, needing the boy, demanding him. Their vessel. Their gate to be opened.

But this time was different. What Theresa kept saying, Evie said, was that she needed the boy because she had to *protect* him. To keep him safe. If anything happened to him, then what was inside him would be unleashed.

"That was the word she used," said Evie. "*Unleashed.*"

Ruben just nodded.

It was the same word she had used in Alaska, when she told Katy and Samir they absolutely could not go through with it, crack open Dennis and let loose the future trapped inside.

Because the future was doom.

The promise that was bottled up inside Wesley, the spirit that would strip away fear and grief and anxiety, would do so by stripping away *everything*. A merciful spirit, oh yes, but the mercy of chloroform, the mercy of ether. This was the secret of the good and golden world, this was the part the night man kept to himself as he drove his followers toward its unleashing.

With knowledge comes suffering, so let there be no knowledge. With love comes the agony of loss, so let there be no love. With consciousness comes pain, so let us be washed clean of consciousness, and let ours become a hollow world, a world of wandering Wesleys.

That had been Pileggi's final revelation, in her madwoman's bedroom in Indianapolis, and it's what had taken her to Alaska, and what she had come to Los Angeles to tell the Keeners. The other world was trying to come in, and we could not let it. It had to be contained, forever.

If anything happened to Wesley Keener, the consequences would be dire beyond imagining. So she had come to take him away. She would take him to Alaska; she would take him to the North Pole; she would take him somewhere, and spend her life protecting him, keeping the vessel sealed; keeping the good and golden world contained.

None of this made any sense to Richard Keener, so she just pointed her gun at him, demanded he bring her to his son, and he lunged at her and she started shooting. Evie screamed and rushed into the room. Richard had grabbed Theresa to take the gun, and he was holding her, but she wouldn't drop it, and—

"It was out of control," said Evie, rubbing her nose. "It was beyond. I didn't know what to do. All I knew was, she was going to kill him. This fucking lady was going to kill my father." Evie looked at Ruben, right in his eyes, needing him to believe her, needing him to understand, to acknowledge, to *know*. "She would have killed my father."

Ruben nodded. He did not doubt it. She was talking about Theresa's urgency, her mania about Wesley, and he was thinking of Dennis, of Samir and Katy. A serrated kitchen knife against his father's throat. He didn't doubt it at all.

But he had to hear the rest. "So?"

"So I hit her with the lamp," said Evie. "As hard as I could."

And there it was. Ruben waited. She went on.

"She went right down. Like—collapsed. I didn't mean to kill her."

"I know," said Ruben. "I know."

"You know that, right?" She turned to him, needing to know. "You believe me?"

"Of course. Evie. Of course."

Pileggi's brain inside the fragile ceramic of the skull, rattled into uselessness by the single hammer blow of the lamp. She is there, Theresa Pileggi of Indianapolis, Indiana, this human person all full of motives and lusts and misunderstandings and memories and just like that she blinks out, because after all there is no such thing as a human being, just clusters of memories, connected by wires.

Richard, she said, did not miss a beat. Evie was paralyzed with terror, clutching the lamp that had become a bludgeon, and he grabbed it from her and said "*Go.*"

"What?" Evie said. "No." But he kept saying it: "Go. Honey. Evelyn. Baby. Go."

Telling Ruben this last piece of the story, Evie—Evie the Guilty, Evie the Damned—was all full of tears. She blinked them away and they kept coming. She was so tough, steely and beautiful and self-assured, and yet she was still a child as Ruben was still a child, as we all are, all the time. Not so far below the surface. All caught like Wesley is caught, in the thrall of the past, walking in circles forever.

"I shouldn't have let him do it. But he did—he insisted."

All that Richard wanted, in the aftermath, was for her to go.

All that he said was "I will not lose you also."

His daughter was all he had left. Wesley was gone, and Beth was in Wesley's shadow world half the time.

How could he lose her, too? How could he?

So Evie left. Stripped off her wings and tossed them in the sewer, went to her gig and played it. She went on exactly at 9:15, and so was onstage at 9:25, when the murder was committed. The thing was, though, and this is what Ruben had double-checked, reviewing the police file in his apartment, the time of the killing only came from one source, from the killer's confession, and the killer had waited fifteen minutes or half an hour even to call the police.

Given his daughter time to go, to get there, to change, to get onstage. Given her the time to get free.

Evie the Free even debuted a brand-new number that night, that alternate-universe Bob Dylan thing. She wrote it on the fly, eyes closed, her band scrambling to follow the changes, the audience wising up and finding it with her, running alongside her, a thousand voices into her one.

Nobody.

Feels.

Any pain . . .

Meanwhile, Richard waits to be arrested. Richard calls Ebbers from the police station, asks his sort-of friend how to convincingly explain how he ended up in possession of an unregistered handgun. Richard confesses, and he knows the police will never investigate this too deeply—not when they've got the killer, who they found on the scene, sitting with the murder weapon, covered in blood.

And who pleaded guilty. Who wanted to get this thing over with "as soon as possible," get himself sent away and the fucking case closed.

The Rabbi stood up. He had gotten it all right. Solved the mystery. But he felt no relief or satisfaction. What a world it is. How confusing and frustrating and crowded with pain.

He looked at Evie, and she looked at her feet.

"I don't know if I can do it, Ruben. I don't know if I can live with it, him sitting in prison. How can I do it?"

"I don't think you have to."

And then the two of them were kids again. The first day they met. Ruben quoted himself, maybe remembering or maybe not remembering. Maybe it was just the past punching through in that moment to the present.

"Listen, Evelyn. Hey. My dad is the best," he said. "He'll find a way to fix it."

CODA

SUMMER 2019

The Rabbi returned, just like he promised, and when he got up the hill, Samir was waiting.

Ruben had gotten lucky once again at Ed's Cars in Kusiaat. He drove the same beige Range Rover back to the post office, where he was greeted like an old friend.

As Ruben had expected, the postman and his scrawny friend Langstrom were up for anything. A long walk up the hill, pulling a laden sledge; a day's labor at the old station. Ruben and the two dudes, laughing and heaving wood and hammering plywood up over the windows. Drinking their way through the case of Labatt's the postman had packed onto the sledge.

Samir sat on a tree stump, watching warily, his eyes jumping. Every once in a while he would get up and pace a minute, back and forth, just like the man they were walling inside.

Ruben's first idea had been to lead Dennis into the forest on a rope, hike until they found a ravine or a gully, or maybe just dig a hole wide enough to push him into.

But this was better. This made sense. They shut off the old ranger station; they bricked in the windows and welded shut the doors. There had only been two exits, and now there were none.

Langstrom spray-painted the words RADIOACTIVE: CAUTION over and over, in bright neon letters, on all the walls.

"Nice work, dingleberry," said the postman, but Langstrom

ignored him. He stepped back, surveying their handiwork, wearing a surprisingly wise little smile.

Ruben rubbed at the cartilage of his right ear, nodded at the men, then said, "Let's go."

They left the night man inside, walking.

He couldn't think of the last time he prayed.

But Ruben prayed now, walking back down Renzer's Peak. They trudged back all together, this strange parade, Samir shivering in Ruben's North Face jacket, the pair of jovial Alaskans weaving a little, howling like wolves. A cool rain stung Ruben's cheeks.

He prayed to his mother. To Marilyn, up there in heaven or wherever she was.

"Keep him safe," he told her. "For as long as you can."

And then he got to the bottom of the hill, and all the way home to Evie.

"It will be helpful, this time around," Jay Shenk told Richard Keener, "if, during our conversations, you were to actually talk."

There was long enough of an empty moment, of Rich just staring back like he always did, that Shenk worried his client was once again opting not to cooperate. That he hadn't understood the plan, which Shenk had communicated via Beth. That he had rejected it, or agreed but now changed his mind.

"Yeah, I know," said Rich finally. "I hear you."

He was not sullen. He was not cool. He looked scared. He had fucked up, and he was running out of chances.

Jay saw it all, and if he could have hugged the guy he would have, but they were on opposite sides of thick meshed glass. Richard was at Chino now, in the California Institution for Men. Death row had its own rules, and flesh-to-flesh visiting was not allowed.

So Shenk leaned forward and put his head on the barrier and said, "It's gonna be OK."

Our bodies are constantly generating new cells to replace the ones that die and slough away; the flesh of our bodies like the flesh of our brains is forever expanding, degrading, rewiring, being made new. So the figurative idea is also literally true: Neither Jay Shenk nor Richard Keener was the man he used to be.

"Jay," said Rich. "I'm sorry. About all of this."

"Rich," said Jay. "I was gonna say the same thing to you."

It's hard to really smile in a deep and true way, on a death-row tier of a state prison. But they both smiled at least a little, and then Shenk said, "But listen. It's time to tell the truth. OK? Now we're going to tell the *truth.*"

And then Jay Shenk told him what the truth was going to be, doing what he had always done for all the days of his life, picking the right details of the story, shifting the outlines, pouring the facts into new shapes.

It was one visitor at a time up here. When Shenk was gone, Beth came in.

"Hey, baby," she said, and he couldn't even answer. God: all his big, dumb fucking ideas, trying to control an out-of-control situation. It was all like some game he'd been playing. Look at her, looking at him through the glass. Beth with her thick black hair. This was it, man. Those eyes. This girl.

He must have been crying, he must have looked down at the counter to hide himself from her, because she was tapping on the glass, knuckling it hard, and she was saying, "Hey, dummy. Hey, asshole. *Hey.*"

He blinked, rubbed the tears out of his eyes.

"Years," she said, and he said, "What?" Dragging his thick fore-arm across his nose, which was bubbling with snot.

"We're gonna get years."

He put his big hand up on the glass, and she put hers up on her side, and they touched, separated by nothing, because what was it, just glass and wire?

"Years and years and years."

"No," sang Evie—Evie the Wild, Evie the Free—and the crowd sang it back to her: *"No!"*

". . . body!"

"Body!"

Nobody feels any pain.

She was hitting her fucking stride today. She was on fire. The air up by the stage smelled richly and pleasantly of weed. There was a bit of wind; the late-summer sunlight was a kind of miracle.

Her thin legs were planted on the stage, and she sawed at her guitar with big jagged strokes, pick hand diving back down, over and over, her new and bigger band behind her giving it the business as the melody took its time to grow. She'd added a second drum-mer, a guy named Big Nicholas who rumbled his rattletrap kit like a fucking truck. She'd always wanted to have two drummers.

"So, look," said Evie Keener, when the song was over, and then paused, smiling, to acknowledge a couple of wild hoots from the crowd, a couple of boisterous *Love you, Evie*s.

"Most of you know what we're doing here, right?"

Light cheering, scattered claps. The crowd was sprawled out on the lawn of the old zoo, spread out on picnic blankets, climbing on the railings of the empty enclosures, which would once have held giraffes and lions.

"Well, if you *don't* know," she said. "We're here for my dad."

The concert was a fundraiser for the legal defense fund that had been established to subsidize Richard Keener's appeal. It was a great story—it was a fucking saga. The story of Evie Keener, the indie darling, whose life had already been hard enough, and now her father had been falsely charged with murder, and then been screwed over by his own lawyer. One of these ambulance-chasing shysters. The guy had decided to make an easy thousand by taking on Keener's case, take ten minutes to show up in court, file a guilty plea. But then evidence starts coming out that Keener was innocent, that he'd acted in self-defense. The lawyer realizes how much time it's gonna cost to actually follow the leads, how many months and dollars it'll take to vigorously represent this client, and he's like thanks but no thanks. Buries the evidence. Watches Evie Keener's father go to death row to save himself the time and trouble.

But now—a few weeks ago—the lawyer confessed everything. His own private investigator ratted him out, and then the lawyer— Shenk his name was, Shank or Shenk or Shink—provided a hand-wringing mea culpa in the pages of the *LA Times,* sitting down with the A1 columnist to express the intensity of his remorse. The whole tale—of the singer-songwriter, her tragic brother, their unjustly incarcerated father, and now the father's lawyer—was the kind of messy interfamily drama, with the overlay of legal peril, that made for good copy and great publicity. It was the sort of story that pricked up people's ears, especially now, with Newsom's moratorium, with everybody talking about how fucked up the death penalty was anyway.

Before she started the next song, Evie brought to the stage the magnetic Erskine Buxley, the renowned litigator who would be arguing the ineffective-assistance-of-counsel case on appeal. The man's face was familiar, from CNN, from the steps of the Supreme

Court. Buxley, a tall and striking man with a short graying afro, took the mic to say some inspiring words.

The point was, they would #FreeRichKeener. And this so-called lawyer, this asshole Shenk, he'd get disbarred, for sure. Disbarred, at *least*.

Buxley stood beside Evie, their respective charismas each burnishing the other, and they clasped their hands together and held them high, like prizefighters. The crowd whooped. They'd paid top dollar to be here, to see Evie Keener and to raise money for her dad, and there were buckets going around, too. The appeal would take time. It would take money, a lot more money than indie darlings still recording their sophomore efforts had on hand.

Evie was happiest when the talking was over and she could start playing again. They launched back in with a new song called "Dare Me to Forget," a melancholy midtempo thing with a back-and-forth verse that Evie and the bass player sang together. The truth is that Bernie had written this particular song, but he had asked her not to introduce it that way, so she didn't; he did smile singing it, though. He smiled the whole way through.

Evie saw Ruben out there. It was a good turnout, a big crowd, and she had on sunglasses, but she could just make him out: his quiet private energy like a buoy, steady and calm in the rollicking sea of strangers. They had a plan to spend time together this weekend, now that he was back from his trip. He'd been back to Alaska, back to Indiana. He'd had a couple of loose ends to tie up, he'd told her, from his investigation. She had asked if he wanted to tell her more, and he just shook his head. "It's over" is what he said. "It's all good."

Ruben the mysterious. Ruben the kind.

Between chords she waved, and decided he was waving back.

He was. He was waving.

"All right," said Beth, tilting the mouth of her beer bottle toward Shenk to say thanks for the round. "So? What about you?"

"Me? Who cares about me?"

They sat side by side like old soldiers, belly up to the bar at some harmless touristy roadhouse in the High Desert, fifteen or twenty miles outside of Palm Springs. Beth took a swallow of her beer.

"What's your plan?"

"Come on," he said. "I'll scrape by a couple years, till the kid can support me. I could paralegal. Maybe get myself a job over at Telemacher, Goldenstein."

Beth couldn't tell if Jay was kidding or not, but she could tell that he was happy. His hair was tugged back in that ridiculous little ponytail; his face was open, full of laughter. There was Bob Seger playing on the sound system in the bar. Shenk looked relaxed, and younger, somehow, than when she'd first met him.

After she finished her beer, Beth left Shenk in the roadhouse and went across the road to spend some time with Wesley.

This was where he had ended up, after the years of being shuttled, place to place, under expensive guard. When the money ran out, when the publicity died down, they'd found this spot out here, just off Highway 74: the Desert Star, a motel that was really just a clutch of cabins, laid out haphazardly, the dusty paths between the cabins crowded with night bloomers and Joshua trees. Since each room was its own small building, you didn't have to see the other guests if you didn't want to, and nobody had to know that Wes was in here. Tourists came and went, throughout the year. Coachella people, stargazers, solitary seekers. Nobody ever saw him. He made no sound.

Beth walked past the stand of scraggly desert foliage that stood outside cabin 4 and knocked gently on the door. Wesley's boon companion these days was Moshe, a burly Israeli, supposedly ex-Mossad, who worked for nothing. He liked the peace, he said. He found the boy to be inspiring, although all he was inspired to do was set up multiple chessboards on multiple upturned shoeboxes, which Wesley automatically navigated around in his unending circuit of the room.

Moshe was castling his queenside king at one of those boards when Beth knocked. He rose, putting one hand on the holster at his hip as he lumbered to the door. As he brushed past Wesley he murmured, "Excuse me, son," with grave politeness, as he always did.

"Hey, Mo," said Beth, and he said, "Good evening, ma'am, how are you?" in his husky sabra accent.

"I told you to knock it off with the *ma'am* shit, asshole."

He raised his arms in mock surrender. Besides the gun on his belt, he had—or said he had—a dagger in his boot.

"I'll fucking strangle you where you stand," Beth told him.

"Yes, ma'am," he said, dry as the desert sand, and Beth punched him on the arm. She liked Moshe—he reminded her of Rich, in his broad-chestedness and in his habitual silence.

The thought of her husband, of the future they might yet seize hold of together, fluttered her heart, and she smiled.

"Give us the room for a minute, will you, Moshe?"

The big guard ducked his head and slipped past her, out into the night. For a man of his size, he moved in absolute silence: a born spy.

"Oh my love," said Beth to Wesley, and planted herself before him, so he stopped. Then she took his shoulders in her palms and went up on her toes to kiss his forehead.

"I gotta tell you something," she said. "OK?"

She stepped out of his way, and immediately he began again to walk. Beth tossed her big pocketbook on the bed and sat down next to it. The bed was pushed up against the wall, unmade. Moshe slept on a chair, and Wesley didn't sleep.

"Are you listening?"

He wasn't, of course. He was just walking: there to here, here to there.

In talking to Wes, Beth was talking to herself, telling herself a story.

There was one small window in this room, and through it she could see right across the road, where she had left Shenk in the roadhouse, jawboning with the bartender about the baseball season.

"You're a hero," she told Wes, standing before him and holding him still. "You're my hero."

Beth had never totally believed in Syndrome K.

She had needed to believe it, when it was going to bring justice to her family. But it had always felt slightly far-fetched. The dormant pathogen, the trauma of surgery, the cortisone flaring through the brain, shutting it down like a circuit. Even Dr. Theresa Pileggi's precise articulation of the medical science, presented in all its granular detail, which Shenk had been certain would sway the jury . . . it had never gripped her and demanded she believe it was true.

But then she had heard this *other* story: how there was a dark and dangerous spirit trapped inside her boy. How if released this spirit would swell out across humanity, relieving every person of their feelings, their emotions, their intentions, their *selves*. Stripping away not only the pain of consciousness but consciousness itself.

She looked at her darling Wesley now, at his eyes looking at nothing, at his body just moving and moving, and there was no doubt in her mind. This had not *happened* to him, by terrible chance, because of a bad fall and some fluke of neural chemistry. No. Something had been *done* to him. A force had invaded. He had been filled up with this darkness, which if it escaped would do irreversible harm to every human being on earth. Make them better. Make them worse.

The scale of it was breathtaking.

What it meant was that her son was not a block of wood, not a vegetable, but a rock at the mouth of a cave, protecting the whole of humanity. And it all sounded insane, but it was, after all, no more insane than what a brain actually *is,* this clod of dirt, this seat of wonders.

The nice thing about something that can never be known is that you, yourself, get to decide. There is no such thing as what we know for sure—there are only manifestations, impressions, and the meanings we choose to assign to them.

And so it was with Beth Keener, gathering meaning, zipping it up like a sleeping bag, weaving it around her body, like a cocoon.

Either Wesley had been stricken for nothing, by the brutal arbitrariness of life, or he had been stricken for a reason, and the fate of mankind depended on him remaining in this state forever.

Beth knew the answer. Her answer. She held it against her heart. It had to be, and so it was.

Beth Keener slung her pocketbook back over her shoulder, and for just a little while, before she went back out into the darkness to put Moshe back on duty and pick up Jay to drive back to the city, she did what parents are supposed to do, in the end the only thing they can do: she walked behind her kid, a step or two behind, not getting in his way, and just saying

"Thank you.

"Thank you.

"Thank you."

ACKNOWLEDGMENTS

I am deeply grateful to all the professionals who gave to me so freely of their time and knowledge as I wrestled with this book. Having an excuse to talk to smart people about what they know is always my favorite part of writing anything.

First, the lawyers: I had meaningful and very useful conversations with Alex Ficker, Sarah Christian, Diana Pugh, Randy Reis, and Kimberly Kirkland, and especially, repeatedly, with Laurice Cheung of the Los Angeles Public Defender's office.

As always, my favorite legal analyst is the one who has to talk to me: my brother, Andrew Winters of the Concord, New Hampshire, firm of Cohen & Winters.

In August of 2018 I sat for an unforgettable hour with plaintiff's lawyer Jim O'Callahan, of the storied LA firm Girardi and Keese. We talked about our families, about the law, and about legal thrillers. He generously and expansively answered every tiny question I had about medical malpractice suits. I was saddened to hear of Mr. O'Callahan's sudden passing, on January 29 of 2019. My heart goes out to his family and colleagues.

I spoke to a lot of doctors and scientists, including William Truitt at the Indiana University School of Medicine; the Los Angeles neurosurgeon Alexander Tuchman; and the UCLA radiologist (and my pal) Whitney Pope.

And if one is going to write a novel involving the human brain, I highly recommend having a first cousin who is not only *literally* a brain scientist but also a brilliant, effusive, and enthusiastic observer of its many weirdnesses—a thousand thank-yous, therefore, to Dr. Stephanie Simon-Dack of the Ball State University Department of Psychological Science.

Thank you to Rob Kirsch on adoption, and thank you to the private investigator Frank Knight. Thank you to the musicians Gabe Witcher (of the legendary Punch Brothers) and Madison Cunningham.

Thank you to the novelist Chris Farnsworth, whose early read provided crucial insights.

Thank you to my editor, Josh Kendall, whose many, *many* reads—early, late, and in between—led me gently but firmly to what mattered. Josh and the team at Mulholland Books— Pam Brown, Sabrina Callahan, Michelle Aielli, Lena Little, Helen O'Hare, Sareena Kamath . . . oh, who am I forgetting?—are always such a joy to work with. Thanks especially to Ben Allen and copyeditor Eileen Chetti for the final and crucial passes.

Thank you to my marvelous literary agent, Joëlle Delbourgo; to my overseas agent, Jenny Meyer; to my sometime Hollywood agent and forever friend, Joel Begleiter; and, in a book about lawyers, to my very own, the dapper and unflappable Bruce Gellman.

Most of all I am grateful to my family.

To my parents, Sherman and Adele Winters.

To my wife, Diana, and to our kids, Milly, Ike, and Rosalie.

(Rosalie who, in the week before starting sixth grade, accompanied me on a research trip to Culver City to figure out where to hide the bloody evidence of a crime. As this book comes out she is finishing eighth grade, and therefore maybe old enough to read it.)

This book is about a lot of things, I guess, but mostly it's about family. I am so, so lucky in the one I got.

—*Ben H. Winters*
Los Angeles, November 2020

ABOUT THE AUTHOR

Ben H. Winters is the *New York Times* bestselling author of *Underground Airlines* and the Last Policeman trilogy. He is also the author of the novel *Golden State,* the horror novel *Bedbugs,* and several works for young readers. Winters has won, among other prizes, the Edgar Award for mystery writing, the Philip K. Dick Award in science fiction, the Sidewise Award for alternate history, and France's Grand Prix de l'Imaginaire. His writing has appeared in *Slate* and in the *New York Times Book Review.* He also writes for film and television and was a producer on the FX show *Legion.* He lives in Los Angeles with his family.